OUR VICIOUS DESCENT

ALSO BY HAYLEY DENNINGS

This Ravenous Fate

OUR VICIOUS DESCENT

HAYLEY DENNINGS

HODDERSCAPE

First published in the United States in 2025 by Published by Sourcebooks Fire,
an imprint of Sourcebooks
First published in Great Britain in 2025 by Hodderscape
An imprint of Hodder & Stoughton Limited
An Hachette UK company

The authorised representative in the EEA is Hachette Ireland, 8 Castlecourt Centre,
Dublin 15, D15 XTP3, Ireland (email: info@hbgi.ie)

1

Copyright © Hayley Dennings 2025

The right of Hayley Dennings to be identified as the Author of the Work has been
asserted by them in accordance with the Copyright, Designs and Patents Act 1988.

Internal design by Tara Jaggers/Sourcebooks

All rights reserved. No part of this publication may be reproduced, stored
in a retrieval system, or transmitted, in any form or by any means without
the prior written permission of the publisher, nor be otherwise circulated in
any form of binding or cover other than that in which it is published and
without a similar condition being imposed on the subsequent purchaser.

All characters in this publication are fictitious and any resemblance to real persons,
living or dead, is purely coincidental.

A CIP catalogue record for this title is available from the British Library

Hardback ISBN 9781399727174
Trade Paperback ISBN 9781399727211
ebook ISBN 9781399727181

Typeset in Minion Pro

Printed and bound in Great Britain by Clays Ltd, Elcograf S.p.A.

Hodder & Stoughton policy is to use papers that are natural, renewable
and recyclable products and made from wood grown in sustainable forests.
The logging and manufacturing processes are expected to conform
to the environmental regulations of the country of origin.

Hodder & Stoughton Limited
Carmelite House
50 Victoria Embankment
London EC4Y 0DZ

www.hodderscape.co.uk

> *To anyone who has ever been afraid*
> *of the dark parts of themselves.*

Black history is Black horror.
—Tananarive Due

If we must die, O let us nobly die,
So that our precious blood may not be shed
In vain; then even the monsters we defy
Shall be constrained to honor us though dead!
—Claude McKay, 'If We Must Die'

PROLOGUE

ALL SHE CRAVED NOWADAYS WAS BLOOD. WHEN empty, she felt a cruel longing that turned her stomach inside out, drove pain through her limbs, made her teeth beg to meet flesh. Where the tenderness gave way to blood was where she felt the most at home.

An immortal savior had taught her that. From the gentle hands that pried apart her doubts and turned the most ruined parts of her into something that could be loved, she learned to accept her changed fate. Poison spilled between her lips with a bittersweet taste. Her pristine white bow unraveled from her hair and wrapped around her throat like a satin noose. It collected the blood and venom from her wounds, its soft edges seeping with rot.

From darkness she emerged, bringing light in her wake. Mortality left her, though she would never forget the haunted spirits of mortals and knew their fates to be crueler and more lasting than divine punishments. The poison in her writhed, promising a slow descent into ruin, where her skeleton would rub away into dust and all that would be left were the memories of her.

Memories that would be met with apathy.

Now she crushed her white ribbon in her hand. The bow still dripped; it deigned to turn away from the hollowing of her and face the heat of her rage. She let blood spill where her flesh had become a grave and welcomed the monstrous urges claiming her mind. For she did not only need blood; she *wanted* it.

She would be a warning—a catastrophe in the dark that couldn't be ignored.

She would turn her ruination into blessings. *A nasty, vicious little creature* was what they called her. But she would be worse.

1

THE FIRST SNOWFALL OF THE WINTER WAS ACCOMpanied by spilled blood and a broken promise. Blood seeped into the white powder, its warmth melting the watery flakes. The scent was fresh enough to make Layla's nose sharpen, and she wiped at the fallen snow on her cheeks. As she turned away from the dock toward the street and the oblivious person nearby, she began to fully register the urges rising in her. Hunger twisted in her like a snake, poisonous and vicious. Her stomach rolled, and she dug her nails into the wood of a dock piling to keep from succumbing to the powerful desires.

Even after two months of doing this, Layla still felt strange acting alone. Working in packs had always been the Harlem lair's way, but things were different now.

The scent of blood drew her attention back to the man hurrying down the street in her direction. His footsteps tracked the stuff as he ran, leaving behind an inadvertent trail of carnage. The blood did not belong to him, Layla knew that much. She had left the blood house before she could become a witness to the massacre. These days, no reaper needed more reasons to be watched closely by authorities. Tonight, she would need to be extra careful, lest she bring more attention to her dwindling clan.

So, when the man reached the shadows where she lurked, Layla stepped out, her presence quiet and calm.

He skidded to a halt in front of her. Snow kicked up around his legs and settled on Layla's boots. Panic drained the blood from his already pale face, chest heaving with his quick breaths. "Why are you here? I paid for your venom back at the blood house—"

Layla shook her head. "I don't want your money." She nodded to the bulge in his coat pocket, where glass clinked with his trembling. It was hard to ignore his fear, knowing she was exactly what he was afraid of. The hunger gnawing in her chest only compounded her impatience. "I want my venom back."

The man's mouth fell open. "You sold it to me. It's *mine*." All his fear seemed to vanish at the notion of losing his investment.

"Do you really want to see how well you'd fare against a reaper in the middle of the night with no Saint to hear you scream?" Layla's voice went hard as irritation pricked at her nerves. The man backed toward the water, the gentle current lapping at the edge of the rotting dock. She stepped closer to him, but he pulled a gun from his coat.

His hand shook as he pointed it at her. The silver revolver looked ordinary, like the weapons most gangsters and Saints used around

Harlem, but Layla had no way to know how deadly it would be unless she could see the bullets for herself. "I have Saint bullets. Come any closer and I'll shoot you."

Layla couldn't help but wonder if the man was lying. Bullets made with Saint steel were humans' only true protection against reapers. A cautious reaper would heed such a warning from a scared human, but Layla had faced enough mortals to know it was often an empty threat. She narrowed her eyes and raised her hands in a placating gesture. "There's no need for violence. I don't want to kill you, or even hurt you. I just need that vial back."

The man began to say something, but a ripple in the water behind him stole his attention. In an instant, a darkness arced up from the glossy surface and took hold of him, dragging him down. His arms and legs flailed, but he remained caught in the beast's grip. Moonlight glinted off the silver revolver, a bullet exploding from its chamber. Layla lurched forward, but a sharp pinch of pain spread across her side as the bullet grazed her and spun into the darkness beyond.

Through the burning pain, Layla could only focus on one thing: the glass vial of her venom bobbing as the man thrashed and shouted. She reached forward and plucked it from the frothing water before backing away. There was no worse place for her to be than in the presence of a dead body at night. Reapers would pay for it come morning. This time it would not be her.

Layla turned and fled, leaving the man behind, gurgling and bleeding in the merciless water.

Blood still seeped from her wound as she returned to the Hotel Clarice. Any other affliction would have healed within moments, but her skin remained split open and raw. Reaching up to place the vial in the back of her dresser almost had her doubling over in pain. *Damn Saints.* The dozens of glass vials clinked together as she slammed her drawer shut. It was enough to kill at least a hundred humans. Her first sale at the blood house months ago had taught her that.

Layla grumbled out a curse beneath her breath while she pulled her shirt back to bandage her midsection. Another Saint scar to heal and resent. She tried not to think about the implications of an attack involving a man who was high-profile enough to have Saint bullets. Whatever beast was hiding out in the water would have to deal with the consequences. Layla had far more important things to worry about.

The building seemed to groan in response around her. With Valeriya gone, the hotel had to be older than most reapers it contained now.

Layla watched the dust floating in a slant of moonlight from the cracked window. The Clarice had housed countless reapers over the years. How many atrocities, she wondered, had these walls borne witness to before Layla's arrival? How many more would they stand through?

She fell back onto her bed and pressed her face into the pillows. But even as she tried to sleep, Layla still felt blood and poison pooling in her veins. They widened and bulged, black and brutal beneath her brown skin like snakes wrestling their prey. She dug her fingers into the pillow hard enough to tear through the case and free some feathers. Her hunger seemed to starve what was left from the Alhambra attack. Months had passed since she had been infected with Stephen's poison and turned into a worse monster that tore everything in her path to shreds—including the one scientist who had created this strain of monstrosity. Despite the Saint heiress having given her the antidote to turn her back, the poison remained, idle and waiting in her system. In quiet nights like these, it spoke to her, begging her for a release.

But Layla refused to feed it. Tonight it would get only nightmares and exhaustion, just as she had for the past two months.

2

Elise Saint dreamed of death. Where death had once worn a pretty face in her nightmares, now it haunted her like a blood-soaked ghost and refused to let up even during the day. She saw death in the letters she wrote, the guns she polished, the newspapers she read—everywhere. The truth was, Elise spent most of her time thinking about it and believing she was as good as dead.

It had begun as mere thoughts. But weeks of her cyclical thinking turned the thoughts to full-on beliefs that could only be relieved, temporarily, with repetitive compulsions to regain control over her mind.

Yesterday, it had been the spin of Jamie's pistol on her finger. She kept the gun in orbit, going around and around by her head, her finger rotating with the trigger. The sound of the metal had become her personal orchestra while she stared down at countless newspaper clippings before her.

Today it was the familiar smoothness of the rifle trigger beneath her finger. She brushed over it again and again with each new thought. For a moment, the rising tide of anxiety was quelled, but then it would return moments later, and she could only reset her hand and start the rhythmic compulsion again.

It did not help that last night's snowfall had stuck, rendering the view outside Jamie's living room window a mess of white flurries and hazy streets. Snowflakes catching on the edge of her lashes and melting on her upper lip prevented her from sinking into the fantasy she had been conjuring for the past two months. Through the snow, she could hardly see the people bustling around outside, much less pretend she was among them, instead of rotting inside. Her knees ached from crouching by the window, waiting for an ounce of excitement.

"You should be resting," Jamie called. He rested on the couch with his feet propped up on the coffee table, the newspaper open on his lap. The angry gray cat he called his son purred on the couch arm.

In her hyperfixated state, she hadn't noticed the gangster had returned from his morning errands. Elise carefully pulled the gun off the windowsill, and after setting it on the floor by her carefully annotated map of Harlem, she crossed the room to Jamie. "No need to rest. Mail?"

"Nothing for you." The gangster snapped the newspaper once and looked at her with tired blue eyes. Melting snow darkened his blond hair, and the outside cold still had his cheeks tinged pink. "And not that you'll listen, but I did already check this and there's nothing noteworthy."

"Sometimes you miss things," Elise muttered as she took the paper from him, almost missing his eye roll.

"I can read, Saint."

"I didn't say you couldn't."

"You implied it." He fell silent for a while, the only sound filling the apartment being the hushed whistling of wind outside. Then: "You haven't slept in three days, and your muttering and pacing is keeping me up as well. It's starting to feel insane. *You* are starting to *look* insane."

Elise settled back down by her board, ignoring his concerned tone as she read. "That is not important in the grand scheme of things."

"Grand scheme—you know, I could turn you over to your father at any second," Jamie said roughly.

As much as the words bit into her heart, all Elise could do was shrug and clutch the papers harder. "I promise you, he does not care about me. Not while my sister is still missing." Though Elise replayed her final moment with Valeriya in her mind every day, she could never find something new in the memory that would lead her to her sister. The ancient reaper might as well have taken all traces of Josi with her in death.

Elise scanned the news stories, looking for any mentions of a little Black girl. Relief slumped her shoulders when her search came up empty. The only mention of children came from a brief article about their disappointment at the plans for a *Negro Coney Island* being shut down on Hart Island.

Jamie grumbled. "Maybe not, but he would take you back for a great deal of money." He sighed. "I could use a great deal of money."

"I take it your crime is not going well?" Elise asked, finally setting the papers down to look at him.

The gangster now had the cat in his lap as he stared intently at Elise. He smiled while Hendricks purred. "I will have you know my crime is keeping the lights on here. It's thanks to my *crime* that you now know how to shoot and protect yourself. That being said, business is slow. Word is there's another gang that's moved in and is taking over major enterprises."

Elise frowned. "What happened to your speakeasies?"

"Layla says it's—" Jamie cut himself off as Elise's expression turned cold. He held his hands up, apologetic. "*I have heard* it is unwise to sell liquor right now because of the risk of the product being tainted. We would not want a repeat of the happenings at the Cotton Club. I certainly would not want to be responsible. The police have been unbearable lately. Just sticking their noses in everything. Here's something for your little map." Jamie pointed at Elise's map of Harlem covered with a web of notes. "There were two more bodies found in Jungle Alley. Presumed to be patrons of—"

"One of the blood houses?" Elise nodded. "I already have that down. It was reported in the news yesterday." She raised her eyebrows at him. "You missed it."

"I just don't care. Not my men, not my problem."

She scowled. "But somehow I am? Since you won't let me leave the apartment."

Jamie lifted his hands in defense. He gestured to the room, forcing a smile. "You do enough now. You polish my guns, you guard the apartment, you feed Hen, you clean—somewhat obsessively, but you get it done."

The apartment had come a long way since Elise's arrival. Gray walls had gone from plain to picturesque with elegant art in golden frames, and couches had gone from lumpy seat options to comfortable velvet lounges. The angry cat had even straightened out. Though he still hissed at Elise whenever she came too close to him, he no longer yowled with displeasure just at the sight of her. With all that done, however, Elise craved more purpose. She didn't like being kept a secret, and she hated doing nothing even more.

"None of that matters. You can teach me to shoot all you want, but what's more important? Knowing how to shoot? Or finding perhaps the only scientist who can finish Thalia's research for a reaperhood cure?" Elise turned back to pick up her map. She'd drawn a line that went out of Harlem and stopped at the edge of the page with a large question mark—indicative of the unknown whereabouts of Dr. Gray, Thalia's mother. She looked at Jamie. "I sent that letter to Dr. Gray's address in Switzerland weeks ago. I am certain if I could leave this place, I could find her much faster."

Jamie pinched the bridge of his nose. "*I* am certain if you practiced shooting as much as you complained or cried, you would be the best sharpshooter in New York. Maybe even the country." He leaned against the couch and crossed his arms. "Why not find other scientists who would be more than happy to take advantage of Harlem's decomposing state?"

Wind swept over the roof of the apartment building, sending

snow swirling over the windows. Even the moonlight, half hidden by the thick clouds above, was not enough to illuminate the night outside. Elise huffed out a breath. "It's been too cold to go on the roof for practice. And Dr. Gray is the only one I trust. After Dr. Harding and Stephen Wayne, and the scientists who plagued the world with reapers to begin with, we cannot hand the valuable research to just anyone."

"Well, Stephen Wayne is long gone. From here at least," Jamie muttered.

At this, Elise blinked with surprise. "Last I'd heard, he still had a plan to use reapers as weapons. What's happened since then?"

"He's spreading his wealth in the South. Georgia, I think. He got to influence Mayor Arendale here; now he's off to poison other areas." Jamie pursed his lips. "You have not heard much at all, have you?"

"Whose fault is that? You don't let me go anywhere. And I am almost certain your mail is being intercepted because why have I not received anything?" Elise reached for one of the chess pieces scattered across the board on the coffee table and placed it far beyond her map of Harlem. Then she marked it with *allegedly, Stephen*.

"My mail would not be intercepted because much of it is written in code to protect against exactly that. You should know better. Half of Harlem likely wants you dead."

"*Likely*. You don't even know for certain." Elise swallowed hard. "She promised she would not tell them I killed Valeriya. There is a chance no one knows it was me."

Jamie took the newspaper and folded it neatly on top of the chessboard. "No, they definitely want you dead. Many reapers are not great at keeping promises. When you kill the most famous reaper in the world, you have to take precautions. I actually find it funny. So many reapers want to kill you, you have become almost *valuable*. I am quite positive reapers would pay to torment you. And you being unable to say her name only proves my theory."

He was not wrong. The bad blood with Layla had forced Elise to flee to France for five years, and that had been just one newly turned reaper with a deadly grudge. Now, with an ancient reaper who'd had over three hundred years of history to her name dead at Elise's hands, she might as well have granted herself a death sentence. Layla, on the other hand…she was more an enigma than a danger, but any mentions of her wounded Elise in a way she had not experienced since she had first arrived in Paris all those years ago.

Elise knew her refusal to say Layla's name was only a matter of superstition and obsessive paranoia. As if speaking her name out loud would further solidify the distance that had grown between them. But Jamie already suspected something was terribly wrong with Elise—she refused to continue to prove him right.

"Me dying would probably be for the best," Elise murmured. Her eyes grew damp. Three nights of no sleep for fear of giving in to the voices that plagued her nightmares and forced her to walk in the darkness, and yet all she could think about was getting to her sister. Anything to make sure Josi was safe. But she couldn't do that while she was trapped here, spiraling deeper into her own head.

The gangster spoke with a softer voice. "You can't help anyone if you're dead."

A low sigh slipped past Elise's lips as she faced the map again. "I am useless with no one to protect." She'd had a legacy once, but that was now squandered in the name of believing in something that had turned out to be false. All the damage she had done to her family's empire could not have been for some reaper who refused to acknowledge her now. It could not have been for nothing.

"Just think about it. With these new shooting skills, you can easily protect your sister," Jamie said softly.

Elise's heart stumbled in its rhythm at the mention of Josi. She closed her fingers around the chess piece so hard, it dug into her palm. "If I ever find her."

3

Layla dreamed of blood again. It spilled over her like rivers, a brutal display of her own violent nature. The flesh she tore into felt real in her hands and beneath her nails. Each scream she pulled from her dying victim sent chills down her spine that only fed into the ravenous beast spurring her forward. It begged her with sharp teeth and venomous claws: *More, more, more, more—*

She lurched upward out of her sleep and vomited. Or tried to. Layla dry heaved over the side of her bed until her throat ached and a thin stream of blood trickled from her nose. A bitter copper taste filled her mouth, souring every breath she gulped down to settle her system. Already, a winter chill had taken hold of the air blanketing the room, but sweat beaded on her brow and her chest, where a feverish burning had sparked.

Layla pressed her hands to her face and wiped at the dampness.

When she pulled them back, she found blood beneath her nails and flaking on her hands. Panic seized her, and a violent tremor passed through her body as she tried to recall the events of last night. But all she could see was the nightmare from minutes ago that still chased her thoughts.

A sharp knock on her bedroom door tore her focus to pieces. "Layla? I'm sorry to bother you, but the old blood you've been getting from the butcher is starting to get…old. Honestly, I don't mind it that much, but the others are refusing to drink it." Celie's soft voice floated into her room. She sounded so unsure compared to the older members of the clan, despite being just a few years younger than Layla—only fourteen years old.

"It's disgusting!" Laure chimed in. A soft struggle sounded against the door, and Layla imagined Celie trying to cover her friend's mouth with her hand. The thought almost made her smile, as it reminded her of how she and her late friend, Mei, would act when they were younger.

"I know it's been two months since I joined the clan, but Julius reminded me that it's tradition to have a first hunt to become fully welcomed. We're really, really hungry, Layla. I can hunt for us," Celie said.

The mention of a hunt had Layla's stomach twisting. Pain descended upon her body like a wild flame, rushing and burning her from the inside out. Her veins pulsed until her hands shook, and with the blood still coating her skin like incriminating gloves, all she could think about was the last person she had seen and threatened. Layla flew from her bed and threw the door open.

Celie and Laure looked at her with wide eyes, both girls going ashen with alarm at the sight of Layla. Ignoring their shock, she brushed past them and left the lair.

"I didn't kill him," Layla insisted. She hid a sigh of relief when she saw the body.

Jamie kneeled before her, examining the dead man beneath the dock. "At least there's a body this time. I'll give you that, Quinn. This is, however, the fourth time you've called me out for your little lapses in judgment."

Layla hissed, "This is not a lapse in judgment." The lie slipped away from her as swiftly as her confidence in her actions from the previous night. Starvation made her dreams mingle too vividly with her memories nowadays. Seeing the body helped solidify her reality. "Something came out of the water and attacked him."

"You can't distinguish between your dreams and reality. You can't remember whether you killed someone. What else would you call that?" Jamie demanded. After shoving the dead man's gun into his own belt, Jamie straightened, his gloved hands clenching into fists by his sides. He watched the twitch of Layla's lips and the muscle feathering in her jaw. "Thirsting after a dead man, are you?"

Layla scowled. Wind coming in from the nearby port brought a new flurry of snow, and she lowered her head to prevent it from getting in her eyes. Sure, it might have been her fault that she was hungry, but it was not her fault that blood tempted her. No matter the case, no matter the cause, she would always crave it. Layla hated herself enough for it already—hearing Jamie's lackluster complaints did not solve anything.

Before Layla could open her mouth to speak, another voice cut in. "I would call it *irresponsible*."

Layla turned to see one of her clan mates approaching the scene. Snow dusted the top of his cropped curls and deepened the rush of blood in his dark skin. Even through the long coat he wore, there was visible tension in his muscles, bunched and taut against the thick fabric. Her skin prickled with unease at the sight of his primed stance. "Julius—"

"I hear this isn't the first time you've called on a gangster for your reaper troubles. Remind me what happened last time you found yourself indebted to this man?" Julius inquired.

The reference to her past involvement with Jamie ending with her in a jail cell made her glare deepen. She had to bite down on the inside of her lower lip to keep from snapping at Julius as bitter anger tightened her muscles. "What are you doing here?" Layla demanded.

Julius gave her a sideways look. "I do find it interesting that you are allowed to hunt, but the rest of the clan isn't. If this is truly a matter of self-confidence and trust, then there's no need for drama. I can relieve you of your duties and take over as acting clan head for you."

"*Acting—*"

"Until you produce our old leader's killer, you are no official replacement. And this…" He gestured to the dead body and wrinkled his nose. "This is only further proof of your incompetence."

A sharpness dug into Layla's heart at the mention of her old mentor. It had been two months since she had taken that fatal taste of Elise's blood and died unexpectedly. Valeriya's death might as well have sent every reaper in Harlem into a state of hysteria. Rogues like Julius felt like they had some kind of claim over the lair now, even though the title of lair leader had gone to Layla, who had taken on more responsibilities for her clan.

The truth about Valeriya's death was the most important lie Layla had ever kept.

Layla ground her teeth. "Once again, not only is it uncouth to show up at someone's clan and demand a role, but it's also ridiculous of you to infringe upon a partnership you have nothing to do with. *Leave.*"

"I don't think I will. As a member of the Harlem reaper clan, I would like to be involved in such partner transactions to ensure you are not throwing any of us to the wolves. It wouldn't be the first time," Julius said.

The deceased man lay in a heap on a thin layer of snow, half his body hidden beneath the walkway leading to the dock. With her hunger clouding most of her cognitive resources and her body working to fight the poison still plaguing it, Layla had almost no energy left for her recent memories. No matter how hard she tried to convince herself this murder had nothing to do with her, all she could see were her nightmares that told her otherwise.

"You were a rogue reaper just two months ago. I doubt you have shed the hostility so quickly," Layla mumbled as she moved closer to the body. Though Jamie had already inspected it, she would not put it past him to hide things if only to make her look worse. Just one look at the body gave Layla a new perspective. She yanked the dead man from beneath the dock, and the sight of his body made Jamie curse. The lower half of him was nowhere to be found—his body cut off at his middle, where his intestines and other vital organs seeped from the brutal separation of his flesh. Parallel markings ran deep into the earth beneath the body—Layla could describe it only as damage made by large claws. Even blackened dust akin to soot spread beneath the man. Nothing any normal reaper would have. She dropped the man's arms and looked back at Jamie. "There's blood everywhere. No reaper would leave this much waste."

Julius nodded solemnly. "Even a rogue would rather gorge themselves than waste anything."

"So you're saying there's a new monster terrorizing Harlem. Like we don't already have enough death following us around," Jamie said.

"In Harlem, nothing stays dead. Not really. Especially not with a poison turning everyone mad," Layla countered. She wiped the blood from her hands. "Can you take care of this for us?"

Jamie tilted his head to the side. "It will cost you."

Layla blinked. She considered how the little money she made selling her venom at blood houses was already going to this man to protect a girl she had not seen in months. "How much more?"

"Honestly, our first agreement is getting a little…prickly.

Insufferable, if you will. I might have to inflate your fee if you want me to keep my protection up to its usual standards," Jamie said.

"*Jamie,*" Layla warned. She felt Julius's suspicious eyes on her nearby, but she ignored his self-important stare and glared at the gangster in front of her. His words should not have fazed her so much. But as long as she was paying him to keep his mouth shut about Elise, the Saint heiress would remain her problem.

Jamie shrugged. "Up to you if you want to keep things civil. I'll send my guys over to collect later." He stalked off then, leaving no room for further argument.

With her new position as her clan leader, Layla should have found it in herself to defend reapers. But the bone-deep exhaustion that had been weighing her down for the past few months kept her from getting into it with Jamie, trying to convince others of reapers' innocence again. She had done enough of that with Elise.

Julius reached for his wallet. "Just say the word, Quinn. I can handle this."

"No," Layla spat. The thought of being in debt to this man made her skin crawl.

Her clan mate shifted, removing his hands from his pockets as he faced her. "I know you can't afford that. Most reapers don't have that kind of money because this city does not allow us to work among humans. I know for a fact that you are jobless—which is why you cannot provide for your clan—and that you betraying your old leader is why your entire clan lives in chaos now. I'm surprised you haven't just asked your Saint girl for some—"

"She's not my girl," Layla seethed. Her blood heated at the mention of Elise, and the sound of her name in his mouth nearly had her fangs springing out. She bit back another snapping remark, forcing her nerves to settle before she spilled more blood around them.

A tiny smirk curled Julius's lips. "If the Saint heiress is so invaluable, why don't you turn her over? It could be a way for you to win back your clan's favor. She's caused nothing but grief for you anyway. I'm sure she has some extra cash lying around too. You could end this now."

This time Layla didn't stop her fingers from curling into fists and her fangs from slipping free. Layla turned to Julius, leveling at him a glare so cold, she saw her own ire reflected back at her in his black eyes. "Shut the fuck up, or I swear to God, I'll rip your heart from your chest. I don't answer to you. You answer to *me. I'm* the one hunting Valeriya's killer. If you really cared about the lair, you would respect traditional clan rules and listen to the new leader."

Julius clenched his jaw. "The clan awaits the results of your hunt. They're angry, they're impatient, and they want vengeance on her killer. You know how feral a beast can get when it has been starved for too long. You would have brought them a head a long time ago if you really deserved the role of clan leader. You're hiding something, and I think it has everything to do with the Saints. I'll figure it out sooner or later."

Layla didn't have a proper response to that. All she could do was watch as he left, unflinching while snow settled on her.

4

SPILLING BLOOD HAD BECOME A REGULAR OCCURrence after sundown in Harlem. Lights from the theater marquees illuminated the crowded path lined with those desperate for a taste of debauched ventures. Open windows from above let out smoke from wilting cigars, while the various jazz notes floated through the doors below with each person who stepped beyond the entryways. Layla stuck to the shadows, weaving between late-night club goers and through shadows as she navigated Jungle Alley. Eventually she stopped by the back entrance of a particularly seedy-looking club. The sight of it never failed to make her skin crawl, no matter how many times she visited. Just the scent of the old blood and grime that coated the outside of the building made goose bumps rise across her skin. Memories of the last time she had come and the screams that had followed her home that night resurfaced in her mind.

With her fist raised over the door, she hesitated. Perhaps it would have been better to take Julius up on his deal. Let him pay for the mess at the dock and settle the debt with Jamie. Anything would have been better than this.

But the thought of owing that man made her knock immediately.

The door swung open after a few moments, revealing a young Black woman with a curious smile. Maria. One of her fangs glinted up at Layla in the low light. "Back so soon already? You're normally in only on the weekends."

Layla swallowed the rise of bile in her throat. "Something came up. I need money tonight." She glanced behind the reaper in an attempt to scope out the movement inside, but the older woman shifted, blocking her view. Layla sighed. "Is there any way I can—"

"No. You know the rules. You give, you receive. If you need money, you must give yourself up." Maria nodded toward her. "So, what will it be tonight?"

For what felt like the hundredth time that month, Layla found herself trapped between four suffocating walls. Though the blood had been cleaned thoroughly—as it always was after each use of the room—she still smelled it buried in the divots and cracks in the dark paint. If the walls were white, there would have been stains and clearer proof of the depraved pursuits that occurred.

The roaring in Layla's ears muffled the sounds of the club bumping overhead.

Only curtains closed her off in this room, separating her from the other illicit deeds taking place throughout the blood house. The reaper at the door had been kind enough to leave her a bottle of wine should she need it to soothe her nerves. But Layla knew the night would haunt her long after she left, no matter how much wine she poisoned herself with.

Just as she was beginning to settle back against the plush leather seating, the curtains shifted, and in stepped a masked young woman. She walked on long pale legs that her fringed dress struggled to contain. The wide gray eyes behind the mask dampened her confident stance. Layla could practically pick out every ounce of fear in just her expression, despite it being half hidden by her extravagant accessory.

Layla tilted her head to the side, eyeing the young woman. "The mask is not necessary, you know. I won't hunt you down. And even if I wanted to, I wouldn't need to know your face." Just the implication of blood had Layla's fangs emerging. It had been a long stretch without feeding—the longest she had gone in ages. Being here was more dangerous than it was smart, but Layla trusted her self-control. She had to. It was either that or succumb to her urges and end up just like she had at the Alhambra two months ago—violent, vicious, and merciless.

Her hands tightened into fists, and she ground her teeth so hard, her jaw ached. Layla was glad when the woman spoke again, since she had something else to focus on before the visions of her past horrors could resurface.

"I know never to trust a reaper. I will not take any chances." The woman rolled her shoulders and took a step closer.

"Yet you are here, presumably for some of my venom," Layla said, her voice level. She could have been colder. She could have promised this woman violence and scared her half to death just to make herself feel bigger. Night after night, Layla had heard other reapers doing just that to their human patrons, for no reason other than their own wicked desires.

The adrenaline from their fear makes their blood taste better. Sweeter and more delectable, one had told her in passing after witnessing a particularly brutal bite. This was how some rogue reapers got their fill of human blood without causing a scene. Reaper venom was as persuasive as it was addictive, and every human here was infected with it.

Still refusing to remove her mask, the young woman stood in front of Layla with her hands folded behind her back. "And you want my blood."

Layla shook her head. "I do not."

"No?" The woman took a seat beside Layla and drew closer to her. The intoxicating scent of her human blood coaxed Layla's fangs out. She turned on instinct, her eyes finding the rapid pulse in her throat. The woman laughed softly and pulled her hair over her shoulder, baring the slope of her neck. "You look like you do."

Everything in Layla wanted to lean in and sink her fangs into the soft flesh before her. She could tell herself it would mean nothing. That it would taste like every other human's blood she'd had before.

Maybe it would even be better. But she knew that would be a lie. No matter how much she yearned for the warmth and purity of human blood, her stomach twisted at the thought of consuming it from anyone besides *her*—

"Saint," Layla cursed under her breath.

The woman startled a bit, her eyes going wide. "I am not a Saint."

"I know," Layla snapped. "And I don't bite, so put your neck away."

"Really? A reaper who doesn't bite? Strange. How will we exchange our arsenal if you do not bite?" the woman asked. "I specifically requested you because I enjoy a challenge. They say you're worse than karma."

At this, Layla almost flinched. "What does that even mean?"

"People who come to see you never return. Your venom works instantly. Karma…doesn't hit until much later," the woman said breathily.

It took a moment for Layla to realize she was speaking about another type of venom. Layla had never considered whether her venom was as satisfying or functional as other reapers'. Not while it was too lethal to be used. She only hoped the rumors about it were good enough to get her paid.

Layla pulled a knife from her belt. The same knife she had used against Elise's throat just a few months ago when she had broken into the Saint estate during their tenth-anniversary celebration. Saint steel made up the blade while the handle remained a heavy sterling silver with intricate designs—the most damning of them all being the Saint lotus flower and north star.

The woman gasped at the sight of the weapon. "Are you the one who caused all that havoc with the Saints?"

Truthfully, Layla had not been by the Saint estate since Tobias's oldest daughter had denounced herself as heir months ago. What had become of the place was none of her concern, though part of her wondered if Elise had ever returned and what she thought of it now that the place had crumbled more than thrived. "Is that what you've heard? It was reaper instigated?"

"It always is. Whenever reapers and humans come together—"

"Are you here for a debate, or do you want my venom?" Layla cut her off. She reached for the glass by the wine bottle, already feeling the points of her fangs digging into her gums. Blood welled in her mouth, but more importantly, her own venom surfaced like mist after an unforgiving rainstorm.

The woman shifted beside her and nodded. "Many believe you are a blight on mankind. I would think you would be more worried about the Saints' future plans for reapers. But then again, other reapers seem ready for revenge. You, however…I've never seen a reaper as…sad as you."

As much as Layla wanted to ask what this woman meant about the Saints' plans, she had to remind herself that she was no longer involved with that family and she never wanted to be again. All Saint business was bad business. She was here to forget and move on. Layla squeezed the knife in her hand, hissing through her teeth. "If you are trying to provoke me into biting you, it will not work. All I will do is kick you out. Understand?"

The woman shook her head, laughing. "Understood."

Maria pressed a wad of bills into Layla's hand just outside the curtain. The patron was long gone by now, though Layla had been waiting by her room for ages to get her payment. Judging by the quieter sounds from above, it had to be nearing three or four o'clock in the morning. People had tired themselves out from dancing and drinking in the club and were finally going home, but the wicked below continued their often-fruitless hunts for satisfaction. Layla was no exception.

She glared at the bills, then up at Maria. "That's it?"

"According to the patron, you did not bite her. You receive less for that." Maria tried to shrug her off, but Layla stepped closer.

"My venom will work the same—"

"People pay for the experience in addition to the venom. If you so badly need the money, then you should consider loosening your morals. Many reapers here have returning patrons. It would be better for you to not scare yours off, or worse. We already have fewer numbers this quarter because of other blood houses leeching our customers and a strange sickness going around."

"We don't get sick—"

"Tainted blood. Be careful who you let in, and if you do start feeling sick, tell me immediately. And before you say anything, I know that's not why you refuse to bite. Your 'no biting' rule feels more like a shtick than anything else," Maria hissed.

Layla scoffed. "Is that what you think I do? I scare the patrons off?"

Maria's easy smile faded. "I think you do worse. Some have reported finding your past patrons dead. I understand being hungry, but perhaps think of the business before hunting its customers down." She began to walk off as Layla bristled, but they both tensed at the scent of fresh human blood filling the air. A bright red pool of it seeped beneath one of the curtains lining the hallway they stood in. Layla did not have to look into the room to know how much blood had been spilled. If the sounds of flesh tearing and the slowing struggle of a human were any indication, there was more blood outside their body than there was inside it. Maria turned back to Layla, a sly smile turning her lips up. "If you wish to make more tonight, I have a cleaning job that just became available for you."

While Layla had no problem pretending for the night and damning her morals, that amount of blood was currently too much to face. Her fangs had yet to retract from the smell alone, and already, the adrenaline pooling in her veins made her body heat and her heart pound.

"Not tonight," Layla said through gritted teeth. She pushed past the reaper and nearly stumbled into the fresh air outside, gulping it down until her fangs slid back into place.

The unwanted presence of men nearby helped distract her from the approaching blood fury. Even just their grating voices had her spine straightening and her focus turning from pure hunger to anger.

Three men—gangsters, as determined by the guns in their

holsters and their matching tattoos—crowded around one man almost huddled against the building. Shadows hid their faces, but Layla caught the glint of a Saint badge and the handle of his own gun on him. Any other time, she might have run. A Saint and a reaper had no business together—especially not outside an illegal blood house. But watching this man get cornered by people the Saints had considered to be beneath them for years made her hesitate. The man looked like he had just walked out of the ocean. Water soaked his clothes and plastered his hair to his head. Even in the low light, Layla noticed the disturbing gauntness to his pale cheeks and brilliant red vessels in his bloodshot eyes. He looked as close to death as a starved reaper, and Layla might have assumed he was one if it weren't for the human warmth of his blood beneath his cool skin.

"I just need help. I need…to see…" Each word emerged with a gurgle, as if water choked him from the inside out.

The gangsters looked unimpressed. One turned his nose up at the man, his eyes narrowing with suspicion. "Maybe go to a hospital. We've had enough rats recently to know any human suffering an ailment only means to do us and our workers harm." He plucked the Saint badge from the man's jacket and tossed it onto the ground. The silver honor hit the pavement with the dull sound of metal scraping against cement. "This means nothing here. You cannot walk into reaper and gangster business and demand our services. We all saw how quickly you people fell at the Alhambra. Your empire is crumbling just as fast now."

Layla tensed at the threat in his voice. It might have been two months of the Saint empire's decline, but their power remained abundant in the streets. She still remembered how swiftly they had locked her away for a vague suspicion—things would only be worse at the blood house if Saints had another reason to survey it. She stepped closer to the group of men and shook her head. "Leave him alone. Or else you'll have the rest of them after us soon."

"How long are you going to defend the Saints?" one of the gangsters demanded. He straightened, his jaw going tight as he brandished the gun at his belt. "As far as I'm concerned, one less Saint is a blessing for us all."

No part of Layla wanted a fight, and she hardly had the energy to defend her decision anyway. She was almost grateful when a new voice snuck between them and drew their attention away from each other.

"I need a refund," snapped a young Black woman, no older than Layla. She stood with her arms crossed, one foot tapping while her eyes darted around everyone in the alleyway. She was outfitted in a nice dress, various pearl strands draped around her throat and dangling from her ears. Her shining aura did not belong in a dingy place like this, yet she stood like she owned even the air. It took Layla a moment to notice the rapid and intense beat of her pulse. Despite standing several feet away, she sensed the overwhelming heat of the woman's blood thrumming beneath her delicate brown skin.

"For what?" a gangster asked.

The woman let out a sharp breath. Her golden-brown eyes

seemed to glow. With anger or pain, Layla could not tell. "It didn't work. I paid for good venom, and it did nothing for me."

The mention of venom made Layla think of the patron she had just served and how each moment passing meant she moved farther away with a lethal dose of venom. Layla glanced out of the alleyway, impatience building as the conversation carried on around her.

"Buy more," the gangster said.

But the woman's chest heaved with a frustrated sigh. She groaned and walked forward, her shoulders tense and trembling. Her scent overcame Layla suddenly. Bitter and putrid, it washed over the alleyway, burning Layla's nose. It took every ounce of strength in her not to gag. Her fangs emerged, and she backed away, hissing.

The woman snapped her gaze to Layla. "You. I'll take yours."

Layla opened her mouth to refuse, but the cornered Saint member fell into a fit of coughing so bad, blood sprayed from his lips. The smell alone was enough to make Layla's skin heat. It overrode the woman's odor, and she found herself gazing at the fresh blood dripping down his chin. Layla didn't realize quite how vulnerable she had made herself until the woman's hand came swiping up to touch her fangs. The moment her fingers made contact with her teeth, Layla reared back and slammed her hand into the woman's throat. She flew into the wall, her head snapping against the brick hard enough to leave a smear of blood behind. Any other day, Layla might have worried about fresh human blood being spilled so close to her while she was on the brink of a blood fury, but the substance that came from this woman could only be described as rotten.

The woman's face had changed. Red covered the whites of her eyes like crimson curtains, and black veins spiraled out beneath her lips and across her cheeks. It was as if her face, a bronzed picture of beauty, had begun to crack and splinter. Her jaw unhinged in a guttural scream that ended in choking as she collapsed. Black and red fluids fountained from her mouth and eyes. Her skin seemed to melt with the substance as her body sloughed into a puddle of blood and guts. At once the woman had become nothing more than rotten, necrotized flesh. Layla had seen many horrific things in her life, but never had she seen something as disturbing as this. No reaper, no matter how cruel, could have justified feeding on such a poisoned corpse.

Layla still felt the woman's touch on her mouth. Her hand drifted to her lips, where her fangs had dug in and drawn blood. She thought back to her patron that night—the woman with the mask who now carried a vial of her venom—and how Layla should have been tracking her by now to get it back.

"What did you do?" one of the gangsters demanded. His partner stood behind him with wide eyes and a dropped jaw. Even the Saint member, who had only just recovered from his coughing fit, looked dumbfounded.

Panic clutched Layla's chest like a fist made of flames. She backed away from the carnage, her hands shaking as she traced the steps her patron must have taken out of the alley. There was no point in trying to answer the gangster's question. Not while someone still existed with her venom—the very thing that could have caused such a macabre end.

Layla sprinted, grateful for the rush of fresh air against her face. She gulped in breath after breath, occasionally catching whiffs of her patron, albeit faint. With adrenaline spurring her on, Layla caught up to the young woman's fresh tracks in the ice-slicked streets. She found her hurrying across the way, mask and vial in hand. Layla almost slumped with relief. Her pace quickened, and she barreled right for the young woman. Before they could make contact, however, something heavy slammed into her. She fell backward, the snow cushioning her fall as her head hit the ground. Layla tried to roll onto her feet, but a man pressed her into the ice, his body—nearly twice her size—pinning her arms and legs to the spot. Blinking with surprise, Layla's eyes met angry amber ones that she had once known to show her tender love.

"Sterling—" she gasped.

"You don't know how much trouble you're in, Quinn," the Saint member snarled.

At her full strength, Layla would have been able to overpower him with the perks of her reaper affliction. But now, with her body starved going on a month now, she could only fight the urge to bite into the flutter of blood rushing through his jugular. The cold touch of metal from the gun he pressed against her chin didn't help either.

A light giggle sounded nearby, and Layla cursed as the young woman ran off with her venom. Had Layla been fully fed, she would not have fallen into this trap; her mind would have been able to focus on her surroundings, rather than just on the hunt before her. Now Layla was no better than prey trapped by a worse predator. She glared up at Sterling, whose own frown had not let up. "Kill me then. Fucking kill me," she snapped. Venom seared over her words, and even Sterling looked taken aback by her conviction.

His gun hand faltered a bit, but he did not let her go.

All Layla could think about was what Valeriya had said to her when she had found Layla standing on the roof of the Clarice five years ago, Saint bullets in one hand and a gun in the other. *When a reaper has had enough—when her grief has grown longer than her days and immortality has become more a curse than a blessing—she wants nothing more than to drive the blade into her own heart. But now is not your time, Layla. Ma chère. Give me the gun.*

Even unspoken, the words tasted bitter on her tongue. Layla wasn't sure she could believe them anymore.

"This is what you've always wanted, isn't it, Sterling?" she hissed. "Because you've always been so fucking jealous that Elise liked me more than you. She loved me. You tried so hard, but you were never enough. Not for her, not for Josi, and never for Tobias. You'll never have another family, no matter how hard you try—" Her breath caught as Sterling shoved the gun deeper into her throat. She felt her own pulse beating against the barrel, saw the fear mixing with anger in his eyes. How similar they once had been, the two of them— orphans shrouded in darkness and begging for something light. Perhaps in another life, they would have grown together rather than apart. Maybe Layla would have been able to convince him that the Saints caused him more hurt than healing. Looking into his eyes, she saw herself amid the hate. How long could she belittle him before it came back to hurt her just as deeply?

Her fangs, bloody and slick with her venom, dug into her lower lip. The pain nearly matched the anguish in Sterling's gaze, but Layla ignored it and allowed her own blood to spill over her chin. When it hit the ground beneath them, all she could see was Elise bleeding out and dying on the floor of the Alhambra with Sterling's bullet in her chest. Layla hissed and forced as much ice as she could behind her next words. "If you don't kill me now, I'll kill you."

Much to her surprise, Sterling shook his head and loosened his grip on her arm. The pressure of his body on hers lessened, but she still felt the heat of his ire. "I won't give you that satisfaction. You owe me an explanation for whatever the hell is going on, and you owe me the location of Elise and Josephine."

"I don't know what you're talking about," Layla gritted out.

"A drug is spreading and it's killing people. It's coming from this club."

As if on cue, a commotion sounded at the blood house Layla had just escaped from. Sterling looked up, and the moment his gun slipped away from her throat, Layla took her chance. She shoved him onto his back, her hands going around his neck.

Sterling gasped for air as her fingers dug in. Blood burst from the vessels in his eyes, and Layla tightened her grip, feeling the rush of satisfaction and pleasure coursing through her veins. It wasn't until he began to writhe beneath her that she felt her senses return. The bloodred mist over her vision receded, and she released him, her hands stiff and trembling as she took in her actions. Once again, the poison Layla had tried so long to nurse into dormancy shifted in her system. Memories of the Alhambra and the heads she had torn from bodies under the wrath of Dr. Harding and Stephen Wayne's poison emerged. Her rage then had nearly consumed her. Now Layla almost let it happen again.

She released Sterling and bolted before he could finish catching his breath. The pull of the beast lurking within her only grew stronger with each step she took back to her lair.

5

THE FOLLOWING MORNING, ELISE WAS STILL STARING at her map. All night she had sat and stared and thought. Even with more information on Stephen's whereabouts, she could not find anything that connected to the new poison seemingly hitting blood houses in Harlem. If a scientist was involved, they were acting far outside the area.

There was an ache in her bones that went so deep, even slight movements became agony. So, when Jamie emerged from his bedroom with the cat trotting after him, all she could do was slide her gaze over to watch his expression go from tired to alarmed.

"Fine." Jamie shoved the map with the edge of his slipper, sending it out of Elise's line of sight. Shaking with anger and pain, she tried to rise to her feet, but Jamie held his hand out, stopping her. "What do you need to hear to make you sleep at night?"

Elise lowered her hands. Already, relief loosened her muscles and the tension in her head faded as she watched Jamie. "That my sister is okay."

Jamie hesitated. His brows bunched together as he pursed his lips, thinking. "I should not be telling you this, but your sister is just fine. She's safe with your parents. You do not need to worry about her. Layla made sure of that," he said. His voice had gone quiet, but the sentiment echoed loudly in Elise's head.

It was all she had been wanting to hear for months. But some part of it still felt wrong. Despite Layla keeping her distance, she continued to look out for Elise's sister? That tiny thread between them—the small hope Elise held on to the past two months—went taut. Layla's presence reached out to her just through his words. "Josi is okay?"

Jamie nodded, though he looked away.

More devastating thoughts threatened to crowd Elise's mind—specifically the possibility of Josi still being infected from Valeriya's venom, but she forced them out by turning to the next most important subject. "And…what about *her*?"

Jamie settled on the couch and ran his hands through his hair. Blond strands twisted around his fingers as he contemplated, his pale eyes roaming over her rigid form. "You know, Saint, I'm not sure I want to be involved in this. I already have to tiptoe around her when she thinks I'm going to bring you up—"

Elise closed her hands so hard, her nails cut into her palms. "That's exactly the problem! Did you know I told her I loved her and she ran away? She *ran away from me*, Jamie. Who does that?"

"Probably someone with commitment issues. I once got shot

when I told someone I loved them. It could have been worse." Jamie pulled his collar back to reveal a silvery scar on the side of his neck. "The bullet grazed me and I healed, but the pain still lingers. You're lucky Layla didn't do something worse. She seems very out of touch with her emotions."

Elise blinked. "She *has* done worse."

Jamie let his shirt fall closed and stared down at the map again. "Maybe letting go of Layla is for the best. What good came of you two being together anyway?"

Despair tightened Elise's throat. She looked over Jamie's shoulder to the window and watched the snow fall against the brightening morning sky outside. All this cold blanketing the city and Layla preferred to be out there, protecting beings that craved death all because of Elise. Sometimes she regretted her hand in the events that had occurred two months ago. Elise had been so close to Layla's affections then and managed to squander it in the name of revenge and protection for someone who was no longer the person she remembered.

Josi, Elise told herself, was worth the coldness. She would kill the immortal darkness that was Valeriya a thousand times over if it meant her younger sister was safe.

In the span of a few days, Elise had nearly died for one beloved and killed for another. Yet there was nothing to show for it besides more violence and bloodshed. Perhaps she was not destined for blood. Not like Layla was. And maybe that would be their downfall.

Elise flinched. *Death, death, death.* Each thought of it made her heart race until her eyes pulsed with the hot, hammering pressure of her blood. She pressed her fingertips to her lips and kneeled by the map, silently begging for a solution to her endless ruminations. Until she saw her sister, fully human and well, Elise would never stop. "I should be there for Josi," she whispered. *Alone in that house with our father—Josi will suffer. And it will be all my fault if I do not do something—*

"You're going to make yourself sick, Elise," Jamie muttered as he retreated to the kitchen.

Embarrassed heat bloomed in her cheeks. Elise rubbed a shaky hand over her hair, the torn and scabbing flesh tormenting her fingers catching on her wild curls. She knew better than anyone else that she was already sick.

The Clarice welcomed Layla as it usually did, with ice and promises of darkness. Bone fragments, still stained with blood, littered the floor before the double entry doors. A quick assessment told Layla they were animal bones, but their very presence still made her eye twitch. It was a sign as clear as any; their hunt had resumed, but with spoils that might get worse as time passed without change. Layla had always known her clan mates to be decent and orderly. It was unlike Harlem reapers to leave a mess behind. If she didn't know any better, she would assume they were learning to be worse from rogue reapers.

Shadows cloaked the interior of the hotel lobby despite the many lit candelabra. Some reapers tucked themselves away in the dark as she walked in, while others stood and approached her right away. Celie caught Layla's eye.

"You're back," she said it almost cheerfully, but the moment the words left her mouth, Celie looked around with wide eyes, as if searching for a lingering threat.

The place hummed with an unusual energy the longer Layla stood in the lobby. "I've only been gone for a day," Layla said. "And I see you've all made a mess." Her voice grew louder as she looked about the foyer. Several reapers bristled at her tone.

Celie flinched, facing her again. She fidgeted with the curls that escaped the ends of her two braids. "Some of us are gone. I'm not sure where they went. Laure thinks they just…went to find another clan or join the rogues, but I think something worse happened—"

"You're only fourteen, Celie. Leave the catastrophic thinking to me," Layla muttered.

The younger reaper visibly relaxed. She let out a soft sigh and nodded. "I'm just nervous. I guess I'm still not used to having a proper roof over my head and clan mates to watch my back."

Her words pierced Layla's heart. Having been a reaper for the better part of a year now, Celie had initially gone the hard route of lawlessness and joined rogues. She reminded Layla of her younger self, albeit more wounded and bruised, with a resulting hardness in her eyes that never seemed to go away, no matter how gentle Layla was with her.

A tall figure stepped down from the landing above, and Layla resisted the urge to roll her eyes. "You let them hunt," she said flatly.

Julius nodded. "They're hungry. We all are. We must feed. Unless you want everyone to lose control and kill half of Harlem, or die trying?" He leaned against the stairway, his golden eyes glimmering with the faint flicker of candlelight around them.

Layla glared. "There's something spreading. You can't know what's infected and what will poison you. I've seen what this stuff does to reapers and humans—"

"So what? We sit here and starve for an eternity? I thought you were smarter than that, Layla. Or has self-imposed starvation made you clueless?" Julius snapped. "We're losing reapers every day because of your stupid rules."

"She's trying to protect us, Julius!" Laure called from the upstairs balcony. She frowned down at the older reaper. Despite her being several feet above him, when he swung his piercing gaze up to her, Laure shrank, her confidence waning.

"You defend a traitor, little girl."

Celie's lips parted in shock. "Hey!"

But Julius ignored her, turning his attention back to Layla. "Should I tell them what you do at night? What you wrestle with? Or rather, who? How you are not really hunting Valeriya's killer, but rather spending time in the darkness, feeding on human blood while you deprive them of a proper meal? How you lust after a Saint while they continue to hunt and kill us? Your loyalty is dead. Soon your clan will be too if you do not pick a side."

The room seemed to go still with his words. Even Celie and Laure looked astounded, and much of the warmth they'd once regarded Layla with vanished from their eyes. Layla could only take in deep breaths to steady her racing heart and impulse to grab Julius by his throat so he could no longer speak back to her. She was glad when another presence entered the room, halting the rising tension before it could get too hot.

In a flurry of expensive fur and perfume, the ancient reaper took a seat on the other end of the couch opposite from Layla. Her black dress dragged along the floor as she crossed her legs, her fur shrug snaking down her arm. The entrance had been so grand, Layla almost did not notice the mud caking her boots and the hem of her skirt. For a moment Karine didn't speak; she just pulled a cigarette from her diamond-studded purse and lit it. After a long drag, during which she let smoke spill from between her lips and envelop her face in a wispy cloud, Karine finally turned to Layla. "He's not wrong. You must choose."

A few clan mates tried to eavesdrop from the stairs above, but they stopped abruptly when they saw Julius. He shot them a fiery glare, and they scrambled off, disappearing back into the dark hallway.

Karine continued. The diamonds around her wrists glinted as she lifted her cigarette to her mouth again. "And it would be a shame to pick the weaker side. We are mighty beings, stronger than any human. There is no reason for us to be on the bottom. You might be too meek for this job."

Layla's lip curled. "You do it then. You've been around for long enough by now. It's been months since you arrived, yet all you've done is criticize my every move."

Julius laughed roughly. He leaned against the mantel across the room. No fire sat in the fireplace, but the old wood creaked beneath his weight, sending ash from the soot-caked stones within onto the charred log pieces below.

"Oh no. I had enough responsibilities in France. I do not need to position myself into exhaustion from taking on too much again." Karine waved Layla off. Her French accent rode her words so swiftly, Layla half expected her to switch into her native language.

"Is that why you introduced more blood houses to New York? It's just enough of a job to make a profit without taking too much from you? I'm sure you've noticed how they're actively ruining the neighborhood, yet you do not seem to care," Layla said.

Karine pursed her lips. "Blood houses have been around for ages, Layla. I've only encouraged their upkeep here. I am bringing wealth to the neighborhood. Harlem seems to like the taste of blood and poison. It runs through the veins of this place. The whole country, really. Sena knew that better than anyone, and that is why she offered me a fresh start here. A chance to rebuild what has been broken. I did not realize that start would involve her death. Perhaps I should have paid better attention to her letters. Let that be a lesson to you: Pay close attention when someone tells you who they are. And even closer attention when someone tells you who you are. If you do not wish to run this clan, then don't. But do not make things worse for reapers because of your own personal weaknesses." Karine reached into her pocket and pulled out a handful of the glass vials that contained Layla's venom. The clear substance had grown murky with time, its cloudiness holding bubbles and a foul smell.

Layla's eyes went wide while Julius lifted a brow. "Where did you—"

"I've seen every reaper's attempt to control their affliction over time. I've lived with reaperhood for centuries now. You cannot stop monstrosity. It's what we are. But it's what makes us powerful. The moment you understand that, you might actually do some good for this clan," Karine said.

A breath shuddered out of Layla. She watched the bubbles in her venom pop, hearing the screams of the woman who'd rotted before her eyes outside the blood house. "My inherent ability to instill fear in others does not make me powerful. I am a monster and nothing else."

They wanted her violence and her carnage—they wanted her to be like Valeriya. Her presence alone had been enough to keep most of their enemies away. Chills covered Layla's arms at the thought of having to take on Valeriya's actions, from keeping human hearts as warnings to delivering the heads of enemies to their territories. Layla wasn't sure she could handle so much extra bloodshed. Not while she was barely keeping herself fed.

Julius snorted. "That would be an understatement. Layla is too lost in her own head to keep the lair afloat, and rogues are constantly threatening our power. They're poaching our clan mates by encouraging them to join their plan to eradicate the rest of the Saints. And who knows; we might be next on their list if we don't get our act together. With the Saint empire dissolving, everyone is jumping at the chance to claim something greater than what they have. We're sitting ducks here."

Karine cleared her throat. "Gangsters, reapers—whether rogue or straight—we all have something in common. In a place that values humanity, we are minorities. Together, we would be much stronger, but I know that is not possible. In times like this, we should be selfish and prioritize protecting our own. At least until we have a handle on what's going on. The only beings we can fully trust right now are Harlem reapers. And judging by the state of affairs, you need to ensure no one in this lair is attacking humans."

Julius glanced out the window, his focus waning. "I can absolutely make sure of that." He left the room without another word.

Layla was glad for it. Being around him worked her up almost as much as her state of near starvation did. She faced Karine, sighing. "I regret letting in certain rogues after Val—Sena's death." Her late clan leader's true name still felt foreign on her tongue. Layla had known her as Valeriya, while Karine had known her by her given name, Sena.

Karine sat back against the couch, drawing Layla's attention back to the dramatic layers of clothes that covered her thoroughly. All to protect against something as natural as the sun. "You did what you needed to do to grow your clan again. There's no need for this animosity," Karine drawled, taking another long drag of smoke. "You need to give them a name. Put a face to Sena's murderer and allow them to have some catharsis. Make a decision before they make one for you and force the truth out."

Layla's lips parted. It was easy to gravitate toward Karine. She had shown up hours after Layla's mentor died with a connection to her and her ancient history. In a world where most had turned their backs on Layla, she had no one else to look to besides Karine. "My clan would never turn on me."

Shrugging, Karine sighed and knocked the ash from the end of her cigarette. "Reapers live to feed, and your clan is ravenous. I have been alive for a long, long time. I've learned to recognize patterns in the living and the damned. Reapers love to hold grudges. For many, they continue beyond the grave."

"You know so much about running a lair for someone who says reaper communities are not nearly as thriving in France," Layla said.

Karine didn't wait a moment to answer. "Why are you so afraid?" She pointed her cigarette at Layla, and a small ember fell onto the couch between them. It burned for a less than a second before fading into a lump of meaningless ash.

The question should not have startled Layla as much as it did. She bit her lip, turning away. Every night her dreams consisted of destruction wrought by her own hands, bringing her back to the time she had come close to losing the one sweet thing she had left in this life. "I cannot help anyone or anything." Though fisted, her hands shook. The tremors traveled up her arms and carried through her body until she became one vibrating husk of a creature.

"That survival instinct of yours is not something to suppress,

Layla. In this world, it's the only thing we are guaranteed," Karine said slowly.

Layla frowned. "What about you? You came for our help, and though we have not delivered, you are still here. Why?"

Karine studied Layla's sudden break in patience. Her red lips curled up at the ends and she broke into a knowing smile. "Many countries in Europe enjoy pretending we do not exist. They keep us in the darkness and point an accusing, mocking finger at the U.S. despite many of them dealing with much worse reaper policies. Frankly, I am tired of the hypocrisy. The first time I visited here, years ago, I saw how vicious the Saints could be even with an agreement established with Sena. It disturbed me. But now I wish to change things. It's too bad Sena will not be around to see it."

Layla bristled, but Karine waved her off and continued. "I have taken care of her body and shipped her off to the biggest reaper research lab in Europe. Switzerland, specifically. I promised you I would return the favor of welcoming me into your lives. Her death will not be for nothing."

The older reaper stood and placed her hat back on her head. With winter quickly approaching, the sun set much earlier, but even the faintest rays made her turn into something ghastly, a being that belonged in the shadows. Darkness covered most of her face now, but Layla could still see the red of her lips when she stood and followed her out of the room.

A whiff of her scent met Layla's nose, and she paused, her mind struggling to place its familiar notes. "What is that?"

Karine drew a hand along her jaw, stretching her face up so her throat was more visible and the scent more discernible. Still, Layla couldn't figure it out. "Do you like it? My new fragrance. It's youthful, isn't it?" She gave Layla one last strange smile, then left, leaving behind the haunting scent of stolen innocence.

6

For the first time in weeks, Elise put her map away and attempted to release herself from the prison of her thoughts. Living had become easier once she knew her sister was safe and in good hands. Knowing there were fewer responsibilities tethering her to the misery that had become her life after being pent up in this apartment for so long, Elise could finally breathe.

She turned the radio on, hoping the music would help keep her intrusive thoughts at bay while she ran a hot bath. The jazz reminded her of homes in Harlem and in France. Her heart ached at the soft piano notes that took a background role beneath the trumpet and saxophone melody. It had been ages since she had put her fingers to the smooth keys of any piano. All coping she had found in music had turned to crushing internal torment only relieved by repetitive physical motions. Muscle tension and cramps used to be her only worries. Now, as she dipped a hand into the bath to test the temperature, she jerked back with a hiss of pain. The wounds on her fingers from picking and biting until she bled had not yet healed. Even the scars on her palms seemed to glimmer beneath the water droplets, as if mocking her for her poor attempts at self-soothing. Perhaps tonight would be the night she slept without nightmares. Perhaps, Elise wondered, tonight would be the night she slept at all.

The jazz music faded out, but instead of another song continuing, a broadcast began. Elise had half a mind to ignore the presenter's words until a familiar voice stilled her body with cold apprehension.

"It has been two months since I lost both of my daughters. All I want is for them to return home. My youngest, Josephine, is only ten years old. She needs her mother, and this city is not safe for someone as young and defenseless as her to be alone. Elise, my lovely Elise. I know you are out there as well. Please, please come home."

The pain in her mother's voice nearly brought tears to Elise's eyes. She abandoned the bathtub and crumpled by the radio, her knees sinking into the rug as her hands cradled the wooden box. It barely registered to her then, that Jamie had spoken not one word of truth the other day. All that mattered was the warmth of something familiar.

"Thank you, my love." Tobias Saint's voice hit Elise like molten steel. She dropped the radio, her hands shaking as it crashed to the floor. Still, he continued. Static nearly covered his voice, but Elise could make out the most important words, carried by his tone of unwavering confidence. "The city has grown more dangerous with each passing day. It is imperative that we stay vigilant and prepared. I assure you that the Saint empire is ready to take on more responsibilities to ensure the safety of Harlem. It is with great devastation that I announce the end of our search for my youngest, Josephine. She is presumed to be dead, and we cannot risk facing the increasing violence any longer. We invite you all to join my wife and me tonight at Charlotte's Sanctuary—our private park near our home—to honor my daughters and put forth blessings for a new, better future. We welcome anyone who might have information on the whereabouts of my daughters and anyone who is willing to serve the Saint organization to protect this city. Peace be with you all…"

The roaring in Elise's ears covered the final few words of his address. She was not sure how long she remained crouched and catatonic on the floor before Jamie's voice cut through her frozen state.

"Elise? What happened?"

She stood and faced him. All her rage reflected back at her in just the panic in his eyes. They flitted between her and the broken radio, each time growing more and more aware. "You lied."

Jamie swallowed, his hand coming up to rub his face. A muscle ticked in his jaw as he contemplated, choosing his words carefully before he spoke again, "You were going crazy. You cannot live between these two worlds, waiting for Layla and hoping your sister is okay. You need to move on. Your obsessive thinking is tainting everything. You cannot trust yourself right now—"

"I cannot trust *you*!" Elise screamed. "I cannot trust anyone!" She did not wait to see his reaction. Elise stepped into her shoes and pulled on her coat while he groaned.

"Do not leave, Elise. There are reapers just waiting for a chance to tear you apart the moment they catch your scent—"

But Elise had already snatched one of his guns from his belt. She gave him one final look that simmered with a promise of violence before storming out of the apartment.

"Do you think they are still alive, the Saint sisters?" Celie asked.

Layla's jaw remained tight from hearing the radio broadcast. She had tried to keep a neutral face while her clan mates watched her, but eventually her eye had started twitching, and even Celie had begun to look at her with a perplexed expression. Layla turned the radio off and faced the rest of her clan. They had all gathered in the foyer the moment the broadcast started, all thanks to Julius, who had claimed the news would be important.

"Why would I know?" Layla almost snapped.

Celie swallowed. "You were close with them in the past, right?"

Layla studied each clan mate's face, searching for any change in expression. Whether it be animosity, fear, or anger—she could not lose track of their feelings toward her. Day after day, she wondered how Valeriya had managed to keep up with everyone and everything so well.

"She sure was. We know you have a complicated history with the Saints, Layla, but it is unclear where your loyalties lie now. Especially after everything that happened with Elise Saint just a couple of months ago," Julius interrupted.

Layla met his gaze with ire. "You want to discuss loyalty now?"

"I have been nothing but loyal to this clan. As a member for only two months, I have done more for them than you have in the five years you have been a reaper. How does it feel knowing just how useless you are in the face of tragedy?" Julius glanced out over the audience, as if expecting pushback, but no one intervened. All the reapers watched with bated breath. "We want change. Tonight is a good time to make some. The Saints are trying to rise again, but we can stop them before it's too late. Rogues are already planning on attacking—"

"No," Layla said strongly. "You strike them now, there will be hell to pay. We are not strong enough yet after all that we lost the last time we faced the Saints and Stephen. They will crush us."

Julius let out a rough laugh. "Is there a reason you continue to defend the Saints?" Murmurs from the clan rumbled through the foyer. "Beyond the mask of righteousness you wear, I mean. We are not a righteous group. We demand blood and vengeance. If you try too hard to be faithful to Valeriya's old rule, you will end up just like her."

Layla shot to her feet. She started toward Julius, stopping only when her fangs slipped out and pierced her own lips. Blood welled in her mouth, and she hesitated, her rage settling with her impulse control. The battle Layla had tried so hard to avoid for the past two months was nearing too suddenly. Just as she had lost her grip on the one thing she had promised herself not to, she would lose this too. Her clan's loyalty to her had already begun to slip, much to her own surprise. Layla had always known reapers to be faithless when it came to humans, but she'd proved to them that she was not worth believing in either.

Laure cleared her throat. She presented a neat white envelope with the Saint family crest on the seal to Layla. "This just came in."

In all her rage, Layla had failed to notice any Saint presence in the area. She took the letter from Laure and ripped it open. "*The Saint empire wants retribution. We are giving you a choice—turn in the reapers who are causing chaos in Harlem, or we will move forward with our plan to eliminate your entire clan. You have until the end of the day to turn someone in.*"

A buzz of anticipation passed through her clan mates. Layla pursed her lips as she lowered the letter and her stomach twisted hard enough to make her throat go dry with pain. "The Saints want names to put to the recent murders. If we don't give them some reapers, they will kill us."

Rage erupted throughout the hotel lobby. Her clan mates bickered back and forth for a few moments as Layla gathered her thoughts. She met Julius's eye across the room briefly as she held her hand up and waited for everyone to settle down. "You all have nothing to worry about."

"How can you guarantee that?" Julius demanded.

Layla swallowed hard. She gazed out at the hopeful yet scared faces looking back at her. "So long as you do not strike the Saints tonight and stay far away from the estate, I can make sure you are all safe. I'm going to turn myself in to the Saints."

7

DESPITE HAVING ONLY A SCARF TO COVER HER head and a thin coat to protect her from the frigid air, Elise felt no cold as she walked through Harlem. Months ago, she might have allowed fear to chase her through the streets, but now rage drove her forward, unrelenting and vicious even as she slipped through the gates to the Saint estate.

Returning to her old home felt like crossing into a graveyard. She had expected it to be empty with everyone gathering at the private Saint gardens a few blocks away, but the estate appeared to be abandoned. Elise stepped through the front door and shuddered. Where there used to be family portraits and collected paintings beside ornate golden wall sconces, there was only dust and gloom lurking in every corner between the now-bare walls. With the gathering cobwebs and abandoned furniture, no part of the place felt remotely like her home. Leaving it had been an impulsive decision, and over time she'd wondered whether it had been the right one. There was no telling what her father or Sterling might have done had she chosen to stay and work with them to help rebuild. Every night when she remembered her sister's disappearance and what had become of the empire, Elise had to remind herself that it was better than what could have been. She could still feel the cold of the raindrops as they slithered down across her skin the night she'd left for good, still feel the aching pain of her racing heart, which wouldn't calm down even when Layla assured her that Tobias would have no idea to search for her at Jamie's apartment.

It wasn't the idea of being hunted that had terrified her that night. Elise had been hunted since Layla's violent descent into reaperhood, and she had survived that. One could argue that she had been hunted ever since she was born into a world that refused otherness in its tapestry of white excellence. But Elise could only think about the fact that despite all her efforts to protect Josi and keep her father happy, she had failed. And now, where Layla had once been to assure her, there was an empty space.

Elise turned away from the massive family portrait still hanging over the grand staircase and continued on through the rest of the house. Wrinkled envelopes and pamphlets from the mailbox outside covered the floor, reminding her that some people expected things of her father and assumed he still resided there. Inspecting the letters took only a few minutes. Most of them were from business partners and past buyers who demanded more Saint steel or reimbursements for delayed shipments. Elise was sure her parents were living elsewhere now; she'd overhead Jamie's associates talking about rogue reapers trespassing into the Saint estate.

As she stepped into the sitting room, her heart fluttered at the sight of the grand piano. It sat in a patch of dusty sunlight, its surface still glossy despite its abandoned state. Her body flushed with a warm familiarity. After months away from the instrument, returning felt like reuniting with a lost love—a bittersweet moment among devastation. Sheet music littered the floor around the piano, pages clinging to the ruined patterns in the ornate rug. Elise noticed faint bloodstains spotting the fabric. She wondered if the reapers who'd come here claimed this place as their own now that her family had moved out. Elise might as well have entered a rogue's lair.

She could not find it in herself to care. Elise took a seat on the piano bench, trailing her fingers over the edge of the fallboard. Dust coated the sleek curves, but through it all, she could still see the faint smudge of fingerprints against the gloss. Elise lifted the fallboard and startled at the blood splattered along the keys. Her breath left her in sharp huffs, the metallic scent mingling with her perfume. For this beauty to be drenched in the carnage of others—

Elise slammed the fallboard down.

Groaning, Elise stood up and made her way to her father's study. Just as it did the rest of the house, darkness and dust covered most surfaces inside. She brushed the crumpled-up papers from his desk and searched for any more important documents that might have indicated contact with Dr. Gray.

In the end all she found was a letter mentioning the new Saint address—still in Harlem, on a street she knew was filled with modest brownstones. Elise muttered the address beneath her breath as she jotted it down on a scrap of paper. A stack of barely used stationery caught her eye just as she prepared to leave. If mail was still coming to this address, then surely the mail collectors would also take mail to send.

Elise grabbed a sheet and began writing.

Dear Dr. Gray,

I do hope you're well, as I've been trying to reach you for ages now and the lack of response is filling me with concern.

Harlem is in trouble. Everything and everyone I have ever loved and cared about are in trouble. I am sure you know this already, as I remember you always followed the news when I was younger. You used to bring up topics about the state of the world whenever our families shared a meal and I remember thinking it was boring—because what small child truly cares about anything beyond what they are going to have for dessert? But now I understand. I've been forced into a position of caring too much and I desperately need your help. Even when I was little, I understood your desire to help the world. Whether it was through medicine or science, you had plans and hopes. You passed that desire on to Thalia, and if her untimely passing told me anything beyond just how unfair it was, it's that the world needs people like you.

I no longer consider myself part of the Saint empire and I only hope to reverse their contributions to this neighborhood's demise.

So, please, I'm begging you, return to Harlem. Or send me a letter and tell me of your whereabouts. We need you.

Best,
Elise Saint

She lowered her pen and sealed the letter before she could change her mind. This letter was more honest and forward than the others she'd written to Dr. Gray. If it went ignored, that would be a clear response.

A faint noise sounded in a distant part of the house. Elise's hand clenched around the letter in her pocket, and she stilled, listening for more movements. Sure enough, footsteps neared the door. She reached for Jamie's gun, lifting it in preparation to aim, and pressed herself against the wall by the door. Standing on Saint ground now, devastated as it was, would offer her no protection. Elise desperately hoped the past two months of gun training with Jamie would amount to something if she came face-to-face with a rogue.

"Looking for trouble?"

The unrecognizable voice sent Elise stumbling back. She twisted around, halfway to squeezing the trigger as she pointed it in the face of a young Black man. "Who the hell are you?"

The man offered her a cruel smile. "Should I say I am a friend of your father's or a friend of Layla Quinn's? Which one would make you less hostile?"

Elise's gun arm shook, but she kept her finger steady on the trigger even as the man walked forward. The closer he got, the more nonhuman features Elise detected. His eyes held a distinct reaper shine, making the brown more brilliant than any human's could ever be. He moved with a grace only immortals possessed, with years of practiced stealth and certainty. "Nothing. You should say nothing. I do not know you, and you should not be here."

"You should not be alone, Ms. Saint," he murmured.

One more step back and she was back against the wall. Elise swallowed a gasp of surprise. "This is my house."

The reaper tilted his head to the side, "*Was* your house. You no longer live here. You also no longer have a reaper's protection. That partnership with Layla did not work out. Why is that?"

Elise willed herself not to react to his words, but her blood vessels constricted and her heart raced. Every part of her felt alight while this reaper dragged his gaze over her frame, watching and waiting for her next move. "I could kill you."

"You could, but if you were going to, you would have pulled the trigger already." The reaper pressed a hand to his jaw, his expression softening while he studied her. "You smell different. Human, but not quite right. I, personally, would love to kill you. I think my clan would love to see you dead. Layla, on the other hand, would hate it. She still subscribes to old Harlem reaper rules that your family is off-limits. Saints were untouchable once. But times are changing. I think we need just one small thing to tip the scales and move power in the right direction for once." He lifted a finger and smiled. "This might be that thing."

Elise's brows furrowed. She lowered the gun as he walked off. "What are you talking about?"

But the reaper gave her no answer. He left her, lost, in the middle of her old home.

Night had taken over Harlem by the time Layla made it to Sugar Hill. The thick rush of people scrambling to get to the Saint garden in time kept her mostly hidden from the various guards posted around the property. Layla wondered how many people were truly there for the Saints rather than just attending to gain their protection. It was a bold move on Tobias's part to see how many people remained loyal to his empire's cause.

Tracking Elise down had proven to be more difficult than she'd anticipated. Layla had first gone to Jamie's place, planning to warn both of them about a rumored rogue attack on the Saint property and to tell them to stay away. All she got when the apartment door opened was a peeved Jamie and a smug cat.

She's gone home.

Those three words sent Layla into a bigger panic than she wanted to admit. Caring about Elise was no longer an option—not when their crossed paths had led them to more pain and destruction than resolution. For the past two months, Layla had tried hard to not think about the Saint heiress. Every thought sent her heart racing and her blood into a heated frenzy. It woke in her a beast she had hoped was permanently put to rest at the Alhambra. But now Layla wanted more than anything to find her and make sure she was still breathing. To do so, she let hunger guide her thoughts for once.

For the past few months, Layla had tried to convince herself to forget everything about Elise, from her scent to her laugh to the sound of her voice. But even now, steps away from the Saint estate, Layla easily caught her scent in the cold air. It felt almost natural following the essence of Elise. The closer she got, the more apparent her starvation became. Blood pounded in her ears. Each breath from her heaving chest was agony from having gone so long without tasting the sweetness of Elise. By the time Layla made it to the edge of the Saint gardens, Elise surrounded her. Or at least it felt like it. The heiress was within reach—the closest they had been in months.

Something shifted in the shadows dancing just beyond the garden gates. People mingled within, waiting in the pale light cast by the streetlamps for Tobias and Analia Saint to take the small stage among the perfectly manicured hedges. No matter how hard Layla tried to block out the memory of the last time she had visited this place, it resurfaced in full force with the aroma of the countless flowers. The gardenias, the roses, even the bubbling fountain—everything sweet reminded her of Elise. Even now, with the flowers dead under the winter freeze and the fountain still, the instinct to devour consumed Layla. Her fangs refused to retract, and every movement sent shocks of lightning down her skin.

A primal danger stood along the edges of her awareness. Between the overwhelming Saint guard presence, the sensation of something unfamiliar lurking nearby, and her own waning self-control, Layla could not determine the biggest threat. To her or any of the mortals in the area. The longer she stood around searching for Elise, the more Layla's own purpose faded from her hunger-stricken mind. Memories melted into urges, and she forgot every reason that had brought her to this garden. Crimson covered her vision, her pupils widening until her eyes looked nearly black.

The moment she laid eyes on the object of her desires, all Layla could do was freeze. Layla sensed the spike in Elise's blood pressure. She felt the heat of her blood like it was her own, the soft beating of her heart swelling to a thunderous peak. Layla's lips moved to form her name, but a familiar scent dragged her attention away from Elise. A young woman with pale skin and blond hair stood just a few yards away. The delicate sound of her laughter grated on Layla's fragile memories, taking her back to the previous night at the blood house. Her heart skipped a beat. Sure enough, when Layla recognized the young woman as the masked patron that had paid for her venom, she noticed her lifting the vial to dump the remainder of Layla's venom into her mouth.

Breaking her close contact with Elise tore something open in her, but Layla charged past her anyway, not stopping until she was close enough to slap the glass vial of her venom from the young woman's hand.

Startled, the woman flinched away from Layla. Fear lit her eyes, and she scrambled to pick the vial up. Most of it had spilled into the snow, but she only dusted ice off the top, scowling. "How dare you."

"I'm trying to save your life. Have you taken any of that?" Layla asked quickly.

The young woman scoffed. "What I do with my purchase is none of your business. And you shouldn't be here. Should I call Sterling to come catch you again? He rewarded me quite well for giving out your location last time."

Layla narrowed her eyes. "How do you know…?" She glanced around, noticing the growing crowd by the stage. One man stood out to her from afar—none other than Mayor Arendale. Layla looked back at the woman. "You're working for them," she breathed.

"Not yet. But I want them to see me. I'm not a nobody. I wanted to know just how valuable your venom is. And why everyone is going so crazy over it." Without another word, the woman dumped the rest of the venom into her mouth.

Layla didn't think. She just lunged for her, tackling her to the ground. The vial flew from her hand, but the venom was already in her mouth. Some of it trickled past her lips, but most of it had gone down her throat. As much as Layla wanted to help her, there was not much she could do unless—

"Layla?"

Elise's voice made her go still. Layla barely noticed as the young woman scrambled away from her. She turned, and for the briefest moment, her eyes locked with Elise's. Layla saw the whole world in Elise's gaze. The small second stretched on for an eternity between them. Time might have stopped. Though they stood less than a foot apart, an icy ravine might as well have opened up in that distance, with Layla's burning hunger trespassing the bounds.

But the fear in Elise's eyes sent a shiver down Layla's spine. It had been a compromising position to be found in—her on top of an innocent human while trying to wrestle something from her. Layla might have been able to bear disgust and fear from anyone else, but from Elise…her heart cracked at the sight of it.

People around the garden began to sense the commotion. Layla didn't care. She stood and stepped toward Elise, hoping to explain herself and promise that she had come to make peace, not add more fuel to the burning embers of hatred between their alliances.

They never made contact. In her shameless pursuit of satisfaction, Layla had failed to notice Julius's presence behind her. He pulled his arm around her waist and hauled her away into the darkness. She tried to fight, but he clamped his hand over her mouth. Layla sank her teeth into his fingers. As he gave a choked-back howl of pain, she expected him to release her, but Julius's grip only tightened on her waist, and much to her own surprise, the world grew hazy as his blood dripped from her lips. Before she could register herself losing consciousness, the darkness already had a hold of her.

"Elise, my love?"

For once, when Elise turned, she was met with someone she wanted to see. "Mother." She threw herself into her mother's arms and buried her face in her shoulder. Analia's body tensed against Elise at first, and she wondered if her mother would throw her off just to scold her for wrinkling her fine dress. But to Elise's relief, Analia embraced her back, her arms soft yet secure around her.

Elise wanted to cry, but the tears would not come. All she could do was press her smile into the crook of her mother's neck. In this moment, she felt like a little girl who needed her mother more than anything in the world. Elise wondered, if she asked, would her mother kiss her wounds like she used to when she was younger and hold her until she fell asleep? Would she see her as the girl she'd once been and remain gentle until Elise was ready to stand on her own again?

After a long moment, Analia pulled back. One hand cupped Elise's cheek, and she smiled, tears in her soft brown eyes. "My darling, you look like you've seen a ghost. But it's just me." Analia rubbed her thumb over Elise's skin.

Elise placed her hand over her mother's, nodding solemnly. "I am sorry to have been gone for so long. I missed you more than you will ever know. But with Father upset and the reapers—"

"Elise." Analia silenced her with her own name, gently spoken like an oath. "None of that matters now. What matters is that you are here and that you are home."

"But Josi…" Elise swallowed past her tears and the painful lump in her throat. "I'm sorry, Mama."

Analia shook her head. Her hand, still warm against Elise's cheek, felt like the relief of rain on a hot day. "I do not seek forgiveness from my children. I love you, and I know you love me. Everything else is nonsense."

Elise tried to listen to her mother's words, but just a slight look behind her led her to her father's gaze trained right on them from several feet away. Time and stress had sprouted new gray in his hair and lines in his face, but the visceral resentment in his eyes had not aged a day. Acid pooled in Elise's throat, and her stomach lurched. Analia took one glance back before she pulled Elise into her.

"I will call our driver and take you back to the house. Let's get you home and away from this…" Analia continued to tug Elise through the gardens, further from the crowds. Just steps away from the entrance, Elise's shoe snagged on something. She reached down, expecting a root, but instead, her hand came back up with a white ribbon. Blood stained nearly half of it.

Elise bit back a gasp. The ribbon could have been anyone's, but the blood made her chest tighten with panic. She looked up at her mother, whose face had gone ashen.

"Josephine…" Analia whispered. Her breath hitched, and Elise reached for her arm, hoping to steady her, but Analia was already taking off. "Josi!" she screamed. "Josephine!"

All Elise could do was try to catch up to her mother. But even with her own adrenaline, fueled by the thought of finally finding her younger sister, she remained one step behind. The sounds of the crowd faded behind them the farther they drifted into the gardens.

Shadows moved around her, and Elise suddenly remembered the real threat of reapers. She called out for her mother, but it was no use.

Suddenly Analia stopped, and it wasn't until Elise looked down that she realized why. That girl Layla had attacked sat crumpled on the ground. She rocked forward on her hands and knees, a low moan leaving her as she sat up to face Analia. Even from several feet away, Elise saw the blood pouring from her eyes. Black veins spider-webbed across her face like cracks spreading through delicate china.

"I'll get help—" The moment Elise took one step toward her mother, a massive form shifted in the darkness ahead of them. Heavy footsteps shook the ground, and before Elise could register the danger, blood flew from the young woman's mouth, splattering over Elise's face. She blinked past it, gasping at the sight of talons poking through the woman's chest. Just above her lolling head, Elise found red eyes boring into her through the darkness.

As Elise pulled her gun from her belt, the beast drew nearer. She opened her mouth to scream while her hand closed around the gun. Before the words even left her throat, her mother threw her body into her. Elise hit the ground so hard, her teeth rattled. She looked up just in time to see the beast shove its other taloned hand through her mother's chest. Bones snapped and muscle fibers tore as it ripped Analia in two. The creature flung her so hard, parts of Analia's body flew into the crowd yards away. Blood sprayed, coating Elise with a blanket of wet warmth. It continued to rain down for what felt like an eternity, even as the beast retreated, seemingly spooked by the sudden commotion of the guests. Screams started in the distance, but they lowered to a faint buzz against the roar of her pulse in her ears. She walked slowly toward her mother's remains. The ground beneath her boots was so slick with blood, her knees suddenly buckled, sending her sprawling in the grass.

Wrapped around her mother's leg, like a snare holding prey, was another white ribbon, soaked through with blood.

8

LAYLA DREAMED OF HER AND BLOOD AGAIN. Everywhere she looked in the darkness, she saw Elise's face and heard her song. The melody, once sweet and pure, had turned haunting in a matter of weeks. Even the keys she played seemed to bleed, her fingers dripping scarlet and smearing blood along the porcelain pieces. It wasn't until Elise finished the song and turned around that Layla saw the disgust on her face.

Oh, Layla. You have turned into something worse than death itself, the Saint murmured. Disgust melted into pure fear as her eyes trailed back to the piano. Beneath the lid, several body parts stuck out, from severed arms to rotting rib cages and heads full of hair. *Layla…look what you've done…*

Distance, Layla found, did not make the heart grow fonder, but instead more voracious. Layla still sensed Elise all around her. It was more than just her scent; this time she felt a bone-deep gnawing, like

Elise herself had made a home in her. All the prickly, angry parts of the Saint heiress seemed bound to Layla. She began to fear what she might do to rid herself of any thoughts of her. Layla was beginning to hate how destructive Elise's presence made her feel. The past few weeks had told her enough about their compatibility. Hunger consumed her and left her empty, but Layla craved more than just Elise's blood. She feared nothing would stop the yearning that built in her every day.

The piano started again, this time more monotonous and juvenile. It was no sound that could have ever been produced by Elise Saint. That alone tore Layla from the remnants of her dream state. Her eyes fluttered open, and Julius's blurry form came into view above her. She was lying on the floor in the Clarice foyer. Julius stood at the decrepit old grand piano, pinning Celie against the instrument so hard, the notes crashed into one another like the sounds of shattering glass.

The younger reaper screamed, blood and tears streaming down her cheeks as Julius held her down and carved into her chest with a blade. A quick glance at the burns accompanying the slices in Celie's flesh told Layla it was a Saint blade. The torture he inflicted on Celie was meant to be lasting. Layla tried to get up, wanting to push past their watching clan mates, but sitting up had her head swimming and the room spinning around her. Layla collapsed back to the floor and cursed. "*Are you out of your mind?*" she snarled.

Julius merely cracked a cruel smile down at her. "Nice of you to finally wake up." He let go of Celie, who straightened up with Laure's help. The young reaper pressed trembling fingers to her chest, where *traitor* had been carved into her flesh. Blood still dripped from the wound, and Celie whimpered as she regarded the new markings done to her. "You should be grateful it's been done to her and not you. She had the nerve to defend your treasonous actions. It makes me wonder what truly transpires while I am not around to keep things running properly."

Layla tried to ignore the agreeing whispers around her from their clan mates, but she felt their accusations like hot needles being dragged across her skin. Julius continued, gesturing to Celie. "This one has one more chance to abandon her rogue ways before I kick her out."

Celie flinched, turning into Laure's arms for comfort. Laure glared at Julius but made no move to counter his arguments.

Julius lifted himself from the piano and crossed his arms while he stared down at Layla.

Though still groggy, Layla could begin to make out the rest of the Hotel Clarice foyer around them and many of their clan mates gathered nearby to watch. She forced herself into a better sitting position, and her head throbbed. While the room swayed, Julius appeared before her twice. She planted her hand firmly on the floor to keep herself from toppling over. "What did you do to me?" Layla demanded through gritted teeth.

"Don't worry, it will pass. When I was first turned, I could not help but continue my practices as a physician. I found myself to be the perfect specimen—an immortal creature that can endure and survive but still undergo changes necessary for observation... It appears your bite is worse than I anticipated, but my tainted blood did what it needed to do to keep you down." Julius's expression hardened as he lifted his hand, examining the teeth marks Layla had left in his flesh. He grimaced and fisted his fingers, then snapped at one of their watching clan mates. The reaper scurried off but was back rather quickly, carrying a small syringe. Julius snatched it from him and sank the needle into his bicep. He exhaled as his muscles loosened, his fist unclenching.

Layla's breath shuddered out. "You poison yourself so much, you're no longer able to heal as a reaper should."

Julius tossed the syringe back at the waiting reaper. "Now, Layla, this is something you could have known had you chosen to pay attention to me when you let me into your clan. A true leader knows everything that occurs in their lair, with all their clan mates. I know you. How predictable you have become just by the things you avoid. Talking about the Saints is a sore subject for us all, but for you, it's like a knife in a healing wound. It made me wonder, so I had to follow you out last night. And imagine my concern when I found you sneaking around the Saint property after your dramatic warnings against doing so. I think we would all like to know..." The older reaper paused, his eyes sweeping over the crowd of reapers before them. "Why."

Layla let out another rough breath. "I told you I was turning myself in. You should have let me go. If you want the lair so badly—"

"I cannot help but feel like something is missing from your explanation," Julius said.

All their clan mates shifted and whispered among one another. Layla felt their eyes on her like pins prodding her flesh. She could not bring herself to look back at them and find betrayal in their gazes. Not when all she had done the past two months had been to keep them safe. All her efforts—the starvation and the forced distance from the only things she cared about—could not have been for nothing.

Julius pressed on, ignoring her flinches. His nostrils flared, and his lip curled with disgust. "You reek of the Saint girl."

She reeled back as several clan mates hissed their disapproval. Even Celie's and Laure's expressions darkened with disappointment. Layla pursed her lips but said nothing as Julius continued to stalk toward her.

"Is this how it will be now? You choosing them over us? Need I remind you what happened last time you brought your Saint into our home? Unless you have plans to hurt us again. With another false promise at retribution and being cured." He gestured to a painting of Valeriya that had been hung on the wall over the Hotel Clarice's grand staircase landing just weeks ago. Oil paint strokes done by Celie depicted their late leader as a severe woman with dark skin and eyes changed by immortal years and cruel poison. *A gift*, Celie had said when she presented the painting to the clan. *To remind us of how far we've come and how far we still have to go.*

Layla met Julius's eyes with a cold stare of her own. "I already told you—"

Fire lit Julius's eyes and his voice lifted, conviction seeping into his words. "Saint sympathizer."

Ignoring the rise of angry shouts from her clan mates calling for her banishment, Layla pressed on. She faced Julius with her teeth gritted against the commotion. "It's better to have Saints with us rather than against us. If I find Josephine Saint and return her to the Saints—return her to Elise—we will have allies in the Saint empire—"

"They have had too many chances. If you find that girl, you will kill her. We do not need any more Saints running around Harlem, no matter how small they are. You better hope you're the first one to find her. If it's me, her death won't be so pretty, and I will start a war against the Saints in your name." He backed away and turned to face the crowd, though his words still addressed her. "The next time you come here reeking of a Saint, it better be their blood, or I will turn this entire clan on you," he hissed.

At this, several reapers cried out in anger. The room seemed to swell with their heated emotions and shouted curses. Layla rose to her feet, still shaky from the effects of Julius's tainted blood. She gave him a lethal scowl and allowed her hands to close into fists. "You fight dirty, Julius. Poisoning me just before you intend to challenge me before our clan. Did you not think you could win a fight against me at my full strength?"

Julius scoffed. "*Please.* I will, however, accept your agreement to fight for the role of leader if that's what you're insinuating here. Is it?" He held his hand out, as if to shake hers.

Layla stared down at his backward offering. She knew if she shook his hand, it would be an agreement to bare their worst selves, and once blood had been spilled, there would be no coming back from that. There would be no winner, no matter who was left standing over the other's dead body at the end. Such displays of violence claimed everyone involved. Or so Layla thought.

Whatever choice she made, it would haunt the Harlem reapers for an eternity.

It was barely dawn, but enough light spilled into the Saint garden to expose the truly horrific circumstances Elise and her father stood in. Blood stained Tobias's suit and fine white shirt; dried blood flaked away by his collarbone and jaw, where he had cradled his wife to his chest and cried into her hair just hours earlier.

It had been another sleepless night for Elise, who had yet to change out of her bloodied clothes as well. Part of her felt an instinctual urge to keep them on if it meant holding a piece of her mother close to her for a little while longer.

The more she tried to convince herself that her actions were not cursed, the more she believed they were. Every step of the previous night played in her head over and over and over again. Had she not picked up the ribbon, her mother would have never run into danger. Had Elise not cowered under her father's gaze, they never would have walked into the ribbon. Had she not shown up back home at all, her mother would probably still be alive. The whole incident had been a blur, but more than anything, it was perplexing in a way that not even Elise's tortured mind could rationalize. A reaper—the biggest and most damning one she had ever seen—had entered Saint property and killed her mother.

Everything that went wrong, as simply put by Elise's overactive brain, was her fault. She had not done enough to prevent the harm that occurred.

"You don't really believe that, do you?" Her father's voice pulled her from her endless reflection.

She glanced up from her hands, where her nails had picked so many previously healing wounds into bloody oblivion. "Excuse me?"

Tobias gestured to the giant bloody lotus flower that had been hastily drawn on the far wall of the garden post-attack. What had once been a symbol of prosperity and protection now turned into a macabre display of violence. "You do not believe that the Saints can be mocked, do you?"

"No," Elise said firmly, surprising herself with her own strength. She could hardly focus on him over the chants of protesters in the distance outside the Saint estate. Cries of "Make Harlem safe again" rang out through the air over and over.

Her father turned to one of the Saint associates, who stood by a police officer. "So why have you suggested such a thing? We are not a business that can be ridiculed, so surely this lotus flower means something else."

"Sir, while I understand your sentiment, we have reason to believe this was a planned attack specifically against your family. The symbol only supports that claim, whether you want to believe it or not," the officer chimed in. Several of his comrades circled the scene, some with cameras flashing every few minutes to document various angles of the evidence left behind. What happened to be left was her mother, in two parts, and the blood that spilled from her body. "We are to assume this was another reaper attack. It is fair to assume rogue reapers in this area would have animosities toward your family. We will have to take your wife in for a full autopsy. As soon as the coroner arrives—"

"No," Tobias said sharply. Red lined his eyes, which had gone dark with a despair Elise had not seen since her own attack five years prior. He stepped closer to the officer and lifted a shaking hand.

"Sir?" the officer asked, frowning.

Tobias closed his shaking hand into a fist, then stretched his fingers out, his thumb twisting his wedding band. "You will not take my wife away from me. If you have to do the examination here, then so be it," he snapped.

"Mr. Saint," one of his associates said in a low voice. As Tobias fought to settle down, his shoulders heaving with his heavy breaths, the associate spoke quietly to the officer.

Elise stared at the white sheets dotted with crimson stains that covered her mother. Her hand slid into her pocket, feeling for the bloody ribbon she had yet to let go of since nearly tripping on it. All she could think about was just how much blood there had been when the attack happened and how much remained on the ground now.

Before she could consider her father's reaction, Elise was opening her mouth to speak. "If it was a reaper, why is there still so much blood?"

The officer in conversation with the Saint associate blinked down at her. "Plenty of reaper attacks can be quite violent without the need to feed. This one appears to have been more of a demonstration to make a statement."

"My mother was a Saint. Her blood would be considered valuable among reapers; this is too much waste, even for a cruel mastermind," Elise said. Her fingers twisted around the ribbon as she watched the man's expression go from doubtful to agitated.

The officer's brows knitted together, and he sighed. "Do you believe we should risk lengthening this investigation because you want to believe reapers are smart and, God forbid, capable of making sound business decisions?"

The condescension in his tone only made Elise's quietly simmering anger burn hotter in her chest. It had been four long hours of waiting and pretending to be okay while everyone else did their jobs. Now she had no more energy to maintain a mask for his comfort. Especially knowing how little he truly cared. "I believe you should consider every angle to ensure you build the best case and find what killed my mother," Elise said sharply. To speak to an officer like this would have been a death sentence if her father were not the one responsible for the weapon that kept him safe every day of his job. His hand brushed over it now, despite Elise not having moved an inch in his direction. Her words, she'd found, were enough to make the right people uncomfortable.

A cold hand closed around her arm, and Tobias pressed into her side. "You will have to excuse her, Officer. I am afraid she has been taught to think like a reaper as of late."

The officer nodded slowly. His eyes found Elise once more, contemplating and curious this time. "We plan to interrogate the Harlem reapers. You mentioned Layla Quinn being at the gathering last night, but we have been unsuccessful in seizing her at this time."

"Shocker," Elise said flatly. Anger heated her skin, and she pressed her fingertips together to keep from shaking too hard. "She's the one who matters the most."

Another voice spoke up. "I believe it." Mayor Arendale had arrived at the scene. The man took up ample space, commanding his surroundings with his broad shoulders and accusing eyes. Elise hated looking at him almost as much as she hated being in the vicinity of her father.

The mayor gave her a steady nod. "You and Layla Quinn were the last to see an innocent young woman before she died last night. According to our experts, her death was consistent with the effects we've seen from karma. I think we should reopen the investigation on the new drug. If our youth are not safe, then no one is." He nodded to a nearly empty vial on the evidence table that had been set up nearby. "This reaper venom was found at the scene, assumed to have been consumed by that woman. It is believed to be the main ingredient in the karma drug that is spreading rapidly through Harlem now. I know you know these reapers and how far they are willing to go to keep Saints and their allies down. Your mother and that young woman will certainly not be their last victims. Harlem will not be safe until we can neutralize this deadly agent."

Much to her surprise, he did not ask any questions. The man instead turned to her father, who then gave him one final nod before they watched him walk off with the police officers. Elise felt Tobias's fingers tighten on her arm before he turned to face her. "I want to tell you how I need you back in this empire, but you've shown not a single ounce of self-control since you came here. Have you lost your mind?" he hissed.

Elise met his ire with a glare that made him flinch. "As much or as little as you have, Father."

"Is there a reason why you showed up here last night?" Tobias whispered sharply.

A muscle twitched in Elise's jaw. She frowned, her body tensing under his grip. "I want you to continue the search for Josi," Elise snapped.

Finally moving away from a heated discussion with several officers, Sterling stepped up to them. His expression was guarded. With all the tragedy surrounding them, he somehow still managed to hide his feelings. "We never stopped. I know this is an emotional time for everyone, but your anger and tears will not bring her back," Sterling said.

Elise lowered her eyes for a moment. It did not escape her that the last time she had seen him, he had been turning away from her after shooting a bullet into her heart. How far their friendship had fallen in the name of a man who would trade them both for a chance at ruling the city. Elise knew she would not get far without proper resources, but going back to her father felt like a betrayal of herself.

No amount of fear of the reapers who wanted her dead would force her back to this empire. "Clearly Sterling is not doing enough. I want to claim the Harlem lair. We can make them listen. I will make Layla listen." Elise spoke strongly.

Her father tensed beside her. "You finally speak like a true Saint."

"I'm doing this for Josi. Not for the empire."

Disgust wrinkled Tobias's nose. He dropped her arm and backed away. "I hardly recognize you. And to show up unannounced after months of leaving your mother to suffer heartbreak—she would hate this side of you."

Despite it all, Elise could not find it in herself to feel scathed by his words. She had spent so long learning how to remain standing beneath his fire, the blood from licking her own wounds tasted familiar. Elise recognized every part of this hurt, broken man. The shards that made up his losses held no reflection of her. She could only swallow the rise of tears in her throat, sensing the finality of her words not yet spoken. "It should have been you. Not her."

Elise turned away just as the pain broke across his face. She swiped the vial of venom from the table as she moved out of the garden. Dawn welcomed her at the garden gates, the early sun a necessary warmth in all the coldness.

Elise watched her blood fall into the sink. No amount of time spent hunched over the porcelain while nursing her self-inflicted wounds would ever make the process easier. From ruined nail beds due to her biting and open wounds on her hands from her clenched fists, there was always something to take care of. Violence, Elise found, was the only way she knew how to deal with herself. Choosing mercy had never been her instinct, despite her lending it to others. When it came to herself, she only knew how to be ruthless.

Until now.

She thought of the shock that had shone in Layla's eyes while her blade pierced her throat. It was a moment Elise had only ever dreamed of during their five years apart after Layla's turning. Never had she thought she would get the chance to act upon those violent desires—certainly not against a reaper.

Elise studied the venom in the vial that sat on the edge of her sink. She barely even remembered stealing it; at the time, her emotions had run so high, all she could think about was finding Layla. Now her impulses waned, but the desire to taste the venom and see how strong it could make her remained. If it gave her the control she so desperately craved, all pain that came with it would be worthy.

Before she could convince herself otherwise, Elise unscrewed the top of the vial and dipped her finger into the venom. The substance was slippery on her fingertip as she pulled it out and had a sickly-sweet smell to it. All things that might have given her pause months ago had no effect on her now. Elise pressed the tip of her finger into her mouth and swallowed.

In a world where poison dripped through every crack, lingering in every interaction, she wanted to be resistant to it. Maybe, she thought, if she kept up with regular microdoses, she would become used to it and eventually be made of poison herself. Or maybe it would kill her and all this would end.

The venom tore through her at first. Liquid flames seared through her veins, and she doubled over the sink, gritting her teeth to keep from screaming. Goose bumps rose across her flesh as her mouth filled with saliva. Her teeth bit down on her tongue so hard, twin wounds formed beneath her canines, spilling her own blood. An eternity might have passed before the pain finally subsided. She looked up, catching the red gleam of broken blood vessels surrounding her iris.

Movement behind her stole her focus. Elise turned to see Sterling standing in the bathroom doorway, his gaze traveling from the blood staining the sink to the vial of venom still open on the counter beside her. Shadows as dark as violets smudged beneath his eyes, which looked darker than the bright amber Elise remembered growing up with. "I'm surprised you came home. You insisted you no longer needed us," he said.

Home. This new brownstone deep in the heart of Harlem felt even less like her home than the Saint estate her father had abandoned in favor of greater obscurity from the public. There was nothing familiar about it. Even though her mother had taken the time to decorate rooms for her, Josi, and Charlotte, to keep their memories alive, the belongings had never been touched by them—no memories clung to the space between the walls. They might as well have lived in a hollow corpse.

"You have your motives; I have mine." Elise tried to speak clearly, but the poison, numb on her tongue, caused her to stumble over her words.

Sterling crossed his arms over his chest. "You and I both want the same thing. Your sister back and retribution for what happened to your mother. There is enough rage between us to get things done," he said roughly.

Elise scoffed. "I'm not sure I can trust that you won't try to kill me again."

A muscle tensed in Sterling's jaw. "Is there anything I can do to make you hate me less?" he asked. When Elise held tightly to her silence, he sighed, shifting on his feet. "I'd be careful with that venom if I were you. That particular strain is similar to the new drug devastating Harlem. Sometimes it works too well, and you don't know how close it is to killing you until it's too late. That's why they call it *karma*."

Marble grated against her palms as Elise dug her fingers into the sink. She ground her teeth together and glared at Sterling. The heat of her anger flourished in her, burning every inch of the much gentler guilt. This reaper's venom might have caused her rage to grow teeth. "There is one thing you can do for me: get me a gun."

9

LAYLA SCOWLED AT HER CRACKED REFLECTION IN the mirror. At some point, during one of her nightmares, she had shattered the glass. All she could remember was waking up with glass littering the carpet around her room and shards lodged beneath her skin after it had healed over.

"Are you coming down, Layla? We're waiting for you," Laure called through her bedroom door.

"One more minute," Layla replied.

The longer Layla sat there waiting, the more cowardly she likely appeared to her clan. The truth was, however, she did not fear losing to Julius. She feared what she would do to him if she allowed her anger to feed the poison inside her. The monster she would turn into would further strain her relationship with not just her clan mates but every reaper who heard about her brutal victory.

Another knock sounded at her door, and Layla bit back a growl of frustration. "I said—"

The door flew open so roughly, one of its hinges broke from the wall. Several Saint members and police officers barreled into her room, seizing her and securing her with chains before she could even fully realize what was happening. The Saint metal burned her wrists so badly, all she could do was hiss in pain and keep breathing so she did not pass out as they dragged her downstairs into the hotel foyer.

The center of the hotel had been turned into a dumping ground. Saint associates threw countless reaper belongings onto the growing pile of possessions. Several other reapers, chained and bloody, kneeled around the pile. Saint members held a gun to the backs of their heads. One Saint shoved Layla to the front of the group, just feet away from Julius.

The older reaper grumbled something beneath his breath, and the Saint standing behind him shoved his gun into his skull.

With the amount of blood filling the air, Layla struggled to ground herself. She searched the room, trying to find the Saint associate leading the raid. Sterling Walker stood by the bottom of the grand staircase, his gun out and finger poised on the trigger while he watched his men bring out more reapers. Nothing could have prepared Layla for what she saw next.

Elise Saint stood in the hotel entryway, covered in blood. It plastered her pretty brown curls to her head and stained her cheeks, which were much gaunter and hollower than Layla remembered them being. The absence of fine clothes looked strange on her—almost more than the blood soaking them. She still wore the same outfit from last night. Her eyes were what Layla could not get past. She had seen a lot of things in Elise, especially when they were younger, and Layla thought she would have died to give her the world. Never had she seen such violent turbulence in this girl's eyes before. It reminded her only of what a reaper's wrath was capable of conjuring. Looking at Elise, Layla felt like she was staring into the mirror the night she had been turned all those years ago. The girl standing before her had moved beyond hurt. She was on her way to choosing the path of destruction—a girl on the brink of disaster.

The intense display of Elise's departure from herself might have been the only reason why Layla did not become consumed with hunger at the sight of her. For once, her fangs stayed put and she could focus on things other than the tempting scent of Elise's blood beneath the carnage she wore.

No one could have anticipated Elise's next move. She was across the room and on top of Layla in an instant, her eyes wild and teeth bared in the most rage-filled expression Layla had ever seen on her. A Saint blade pressed into Layla's throat. Its iciness dug into her neck, the hard edge of the steel biting against her racing pulse.

Elise's hand shook around the knife, and anguish shone in the deep brown of her eyes. Even with the anger still sharpening her blood-soaked features, Layla could see only the hurt weighing down every part of her soul. Lips quivering, Elise spoke feverishly, her voice heavy and breaking over each word. "You've gone too far—"

"*Me?*" Layla managed to rasp out. Her throat bobbed against the knife, and it sliced into her soft skin with gentle ease, drawing blood. "I've kept to myself to ensure your safety. You have no idea the sacrifices I've made for you."

"There is no honor in your repeated violence. No matter the name in which you do it. Do not burden me with the responsibilities of your actions. Do not burden me with your blood. Again—" Her voice hitched, and Layla's blood leaked down her throat, weeping in tandem with the tears that had begun to leak down Elise's cheeks. "*How could you do this to me?*"

Layla couldn't bring herself to fight back. She recognized her old self in this version of the Saint heiress—grief-stricken and full of emotions too big to hold within. The tremor in Elise's hands grew too strong, and the knife fell from her grip. In turn she pounded into Layla's chest as she screamed over and over, "*You goddamn monster—*"

Layla's breath stuttered out of her, and all she could do was watch and take the Saint's hits. Beat after beat, the impacts grew weaker with each blow until eventually Sterling hauled her away. He pressed her arms to her chest and muttered furiously to her. But even Layla could tell his words did not reach her. Elise still watched Layla with a heated gaze, her chest rising and falling with an intensity that made Layla's own heart ache. Dried blood flaked over Elise's cheeks and fluttered down from her fingers, where her nails had been bitten down to painful-looking stubs. Her teeth created dark red divots from her biting ruthlessly into her lower lip. Even after her frenzied attack, Layla felt urged to be near Elise once more, if only to offer comfort. It went against all that Layla had put herself through the past few months. From the starvation to ensure she never turned herself into a monster by tearing apart another soul, to the forceful way her mind avoided all thoughts of the one person she knew she would otherwise be unable to keep herself away from. She had no choice but to return the ire and spite if it meant maintaining the distance that would keep Elise safe.

"I told you to let me handle this," Sterling almost barked out.

The heiress remained silent. She pulled the gun from her belt and dropped it with a quickness, as if the weapon had burned her skin. Her eyes roamed over the blood streaked across the handle and barrel. Just the sight of the barest tremble of her hand sent Layla's emotions returning to the surface. That yearning part of her wanted to go to Elise and take her hands in her own. She wanted to wipe the blood from her face and tell her it would be okay. But such a lie would only have worse consequences. She couldn't even tell whose blood stained her Saint gun—reaper or human. The sight made Layla tense with apprehension.

Layla fought to remember where her true loyalties lay. She gritted her teeth against the rising tide of guilt and directed every ounce of poison she could manage at the Saint heiress. "Call your Saints and the police off my clan. You've infected my lair like a plague. We had nothing to do with the attack at your estate," she insisted.

Elise regarded Layla with cold eyes. "We do not know that."

Layla ignored the sting of her words. Her brows furrowed as she pressed on. "You saw me leave—"

"You and your clan mate, who, by the way, had just said he wanted to kill me and my family hours before the attack. Am I supposed to assume you had no part in that plan? Why on earth would you show up and speak to me for the first time in months on the most important night for my family?" Elise said roughly.

Something bitter and painful pinched Layla's heart. She struggled to find her next words, her throat closing on the name she had fought so hard to keep herself from saying for the past two months. "I came to turn myself over to your father so his Saints would stop bothering my clan. *Elise.* Come on. I would never do something like this to you. You know that." The words came out like a plea for acceptance. Elise's previous accusation still echoed around her head, haunting her. *You goddamn monster.*

All Elise offered her was an expression of pure ice. "Not anymore."

Layla swallowed past a painful lump in her throat. She blinked through tears of frustration and hurt, forcing the guilt to subside as she settled on the one emotion that had faithfully carried her through the worst years of her life. "Fine. If you want to make me out to be a monster so that Harlem may have the drive to hunt me again, go ahead. I survived you once—I can do it again," she spat out.

Elise showed no reaction to Layla's anger before she was speaking again, this time with a shaky voice. "How dare you act small after showing us cruelty through mockery."

"What are you talking about?" Layla asked.

Elise stilled and shadows darkened her face. "The lotus flower left behind, painted in the blood." The pain in her shaky voice had

Layla moving forward without realizing it. Right as she made it close enough to touch Elise, Layla stopped, her hand outstretched as far as it could go with the chains, her fingers inches away from Elise. Her previous words still played in Layla's mind, along with the warnings from Karine and Julius. Despite all that they had been through together, Layla was still the very thing Elise's family sought to destroy.

"All that blood for nothing. My mother died for nothing." Elise's voice broke. She turned away from Layla and faced the window, her shoulders trembling.

Reapers stirred in their positions. Their blood had not even dried before Elise began weeping over Saint blood being spilled.

Layla had never been one to rationalize other reapers' behavior, but hearing Elise try to find some semblance of control made her think about her own mother's death. It had been five years ago now, but Layla still heard the screams as freshly as the day she'd lost her. Losing both her parents at the same time had been devastating, but she'd had no time to grieve because her own body—her very being—had been irrevocably altered with her newfound reaperhood, and she'd had to navigate that almost on her own. The only thing she remembered thinking in that moment was how much she wanted everyone else to hurt just like her. How much she wanted to see Elise share her misery. A life for a life. Elise had ruined hers, so Layla found it fit to do the same back to the Saint heiress.

Now all Layla wanted to do was show Elise a future version of herself, where the grief came in weaker waves and the pain felt less suffocating. But something bothered her about the description of the attack.

"I think you're right," Layla said quietly.

Elise faced her again. The golden evening light illuminated the tearstains on her cheeks like shimmering dew on a flower petal. "About what?"

"The attack being wasteful. Clearly someone wanted to leave a message, but if it were a reaper with a vendetta against your family, a simple kill would have sufficed." Layla ran a hand over her hair, wincing as the Saint steel dug into her burning flesh. In her stress, a few curls had come loose, springing back to frame her face even when she tried to tuck them behind her ears. "I truly do not know what would possess a reaper to brutalize someone in that way—unless they were overly passionate. Perhaps with a complicated emotional connection to…your mother. And the lotus symbol drawn in her blood," Layla swallowed, her mind racing as Elise's eyes narrowed. "What if this wasn't an attack by a reaper, but an attack by…a Saint?"

The Saint heiress reeled back like she had been slapped. Her eyes went wide, and she nearly shrieked, "Why would my father do this?"

Layla winced and contemplated whether she should speak her next words at all. They came out slowly, with deliberate carefulness. "Not your father. Your sister."

10

ELISE'S ENTIRE WORLD MIGHT AS WELL HAVE COME crashing down. For a long time, she could only stare at Layla and repeat one thing in her head over and over again: *Not Josephine. Not Josephine. Not Josephine. Not Josephine—*

"My sister is ten years old," Elise said in a voice so quiet, she was certain only Layla could hear it. By now she had forgotten that reapers and Saints were watching them nearby, though many carried on with their operations and ignored Layla and Elise entirely.

Layla shook her head. "The last time we saw her, Valeriya's venom had changed her. Reaperhood does not discriminate in its cruelty—"

"And what? My sister has turned into a monster capable of murdering her own mother?" Elise demanded. Her voice had returned, and this time, she put anger behind it with enough force to burn. "She would never do something like this; she could never be like…"

Her lip curled. It did not matter if she spoke the words—Elise knew Layla would hear them anyway. The absence of an explicit accusation seemed sting enough for Layla.

She dropped her hand and stepped back, her throat bobbing. "You need to find her before she hurts someone else or gets someone else in trouble."

Elise shot her a dangerous glare. "You cannot prove that this was her."

"And your people cannot prove that it was my clan either. I guess we both understand how unfair this system is now. If you do not find her, then I will go after her myself," Layla spat back.

With all her misery, Elise had hoped she would at least be able to take time to remember her mother and grieve her, but instead, her death had pulled Elise in even more directions.

"You should go home and clean up," Sterling said with a heavy sigh. He was finished gathering the reapers for interrogations. "You've done too much today."

Elise wanted to snap at him, but an older reaper lifted his head nearby, his lips baring to reveal a devilish smile. "You should have been nicer to Layla. It takes a reaper to understand reaper actions. Now how are you going to find your sister?"

A wave of profound sadness and rage began to break in Elise. She met Sterling's gaze and found reassurance in the way his expression seemed to wilt at her storminess. Facing the reaper again, she set her jaw. "I know my sister. She's still out there. I do not need a reaper's help to save her."

A rotten stench filled the air. Elise wrinkled her nose as she moved back, drawing closer to Sterling. "What is that?"

"Whatever they're hiding here. We've found bodies in reaper lairs before. I wouldn't be surprised if this was—"

The electric lights in the hotel winked out, throwing everything into an impenetrable darkness. There were a few murmurs of surprise, and Elise could hear the Saints discussing if they should investigate or remain guarding the reapers.

Elise tried not to let the thick tension get to her. She reached for the rifle Sterling had given her and lifted it. Even though she couldn't see through the dark, she still tracked the shifting shadows throughout the room.

"We should fall back," Sterling announced. "This feels like a trap."

A protest immediately landed on Elise's tongue. "No. They'll use this time to escape. We cannot let them go."

Sterling let out a frustrated huff. "And what? Let all my men die? Absolutely not. Let's go!"

Something creaked at the edge of the foyer. Elise's breath hitched as the familiar scent of a bittersweet poison crossed her senses. "Wait—"

A shriek tore like shards of glass through the room. Several Saints shouted, and moments later, blood sprayed, coupled with the guttural cries of pain and the sounds of flesh tearing. Bright red eyes flashed in the dark, and Elise found herself aiming her gun right between them as they charged for her.

She felt its breath and another gush of warm liquid on her face right as Sterling's hand wrapped around her arm and hauled her out of the hotel. It wasn't until they were outside, a few more Saints following suit, that Elise felt the pain piercing her chest. She reached up, feeling a lump of metal stuck in her flesh beneath her collarbone. As she pulled it free, the moonlight glinted on the front, revealing a bloodied Saint badge on her palm.

Then, from inside the hotel, the terror unfolded.

Death clung to the little spots of darkness that could be found around the city. Layla followed the faint scent of blood down the back alley of a club that was mostly dead during the day. No light shone through its windows, and silence wrapped around it with an eerie chill, but through the ground by its back entrance, Layla felt the pulse of the macabre lurking.

A young reaper woman let her in through the door after a slight roll of her eyes at the mention of Karine. Layla pushed her way through the dingy club basement, passing by curtained rooms where she knew blood spilled and alcohol passed between wanting lips. Finally, she found the largest room and ducked inside, letting the curtain swing shut behind her.

Karine's eyes slid to her slowly, her fingers tightening around the writhing victim on her lap. A young man twisted in her clutches. Blood smeared over her lips as she pulled away from him, her tongue tracing over the holes her fangs had left in his throat. The man slumped against the back of the couch they sat on, and Karine untangled him from her legs, moving into her own space. She wiped at the scarlet stain across her mouth and looked at Layla. "Is there a reason why you have interrupted me?"

Ignoring the man proved to be rather hard. The longer Layla looked away from him, the more she sensed his blood—its human heat almost called to her, begging to be noticed. She forced her hunger down, swallowing the pain of the thirst emerging in her throat. "What have you done with the youngest Saint girl?"

The older reaper sat forward, her eyes narrowing. She hesitated on Layla at first, then turned to the human at her side and gestured for him to leave. The man stood and did as he was told. A glassy look overcame him as he walked out of the room, his expression pale and desirous for Karine. Layla knew this ancient reaper remained underground during the day to avoid the sunlight, but the number of bodies she racked up remained a mystery.

"What is this about?" Karine asked slowly.

Layla noted her change in attitude, the softness of her voice. "The attacks. I have reason to believe she might be involved. If I find her, I can—"

Karine laughed. "You're so far off base, darling. She is a ten-year-old little girl—"

"If there's a chance she's been turned, she's no longer a little girl." Layla's voice went hard. "Not quite."

For a moment there was only silence. Then Karine sighed and shook her head. "I swore on Sena's grave that I would keep that little girl safe from any harm. The reason you have not seen her is not because she's running around, killing people in the dark. It's because she's hidden to stay safe from beings like you who wish to do her harm."

Being accused of harming innocent individuals more than once in the span of a few hours wounded Layla more than she cared to admit. Her remaining clan mates had only narrowly managed to escape the Clarice because of the bloody distraction that had taken out several Saint members and Harlem reapers. A ruthless beast now claimed their lair after tearing through the two groups. Who knew how much longer it would be before the Saints came back again, this time shooting without asking questions first? Layla reeled back, her lips twitching and eyes shining with hurt. "I would never—"

"Oh, but you're here, asking for her," Karine drawled.

Layla took in a shaky breath. "Julius wants to hurt her. If he gets to her first—"

"He won't. I have my ways to ensure that will never happen."

Nodding, Layla dropped the topic of Josephine Saint. She spoke in a lower voice this time, offering a less accusatory tone. "Do you have any hand in the new drug that has been going around? Karma, I think it's called."

A small smile spread across Karine's red lips. "A drug that hurts the people I make money off? You'll have to think harder than that, Layla. And as any wise businesswoman would say, I will not give out information for free. Especially not to someone who is becoming more and more of an enemy by the day. If you want my knowledge, you will have to work for it."

Exhaustion settled over Layla's shoulders, weighing down what little remained of her strength. "Sure."

"This blood house needs more patrons. If I have learned anything from running this place, it's that humans love a bloody show. Find me those who are willing to bleed." Karine's smile sent sparks of unease down Layla's spine.

She nodded once more and turned to leave, but the ancient reaper's voice followed her to the door. "A word of advice, Layla—never turn your back on a reaper. You have shown your weakness in more ways than one this week. Your whole clan might now see you as an opportunity rather than a challenge. If you end up choosing her over them, you might as well welcome death. You must forget your human past."

Layla hesitated by the door. She turned just enough to catch the older reaper's silhouette at the edge of her vision. What would have been an easy choice months ago felt impossible now. Layla's chest tightened at the thought of fully saying goodbye to every human part of her past and the things that remained in the present. Her brows furrowed as she clenched her jaw. "It's Julius…"

"And are you really so content with kneeling to a man? I would expect a reaper to make a puppet out of a human, not another reaper," Karine muttered.

Layla clenched her jaw, and a bitter taste filled her mouth. "I want him dead more than you do."

A low chuckle left Karine. "Take control by whatever means necessary. There is only one thing I am sure of now: this ends in blood."

No part of Layla wanted to make this choice. Playing in blood was always dangerous, but now that she was starved, it would be disastrous.

11

ANOTHER DOSE OF REAPER VENOM FROM THE stolen vial, a larger one this time, nearly brought Elise to her knees. A day after her first taste of it, she had already felt the effects wearing off. Instead of tension and adrenaline powering her muscles, all she sensed was a weakness growing within her. This time, as she sucked a spot of venom from her fingertip, she relished that sweet anticipatory burn before the pain began. Memories of the last time she had felt that familiar pain resurfaced in her mind. A time when Layla's lips had been pressed to her throat, her fangs triggering overwhelming pleasure in her system while agony chased it into oblivion.

The moment the blistering pain faded and Elise dropped her hand to the side, her finger still wet from the venom, she craved its burn again.

A soft knock on the automobile door had her shoving the vial into her pocket and smoothing her hands over her hair once, then twice before exiting.

Sterling gave her a stern look. "Elise, you cannot—"

"Where's Arendale?" she inquired roughly, shoving past him. Elise walked right into Harlem reaper territory. A normal person might have had fear—all Elise had was a rifle with nine Saint bullets and enough rage to start a fire in her chest. She half expected steam to rise from the sidewalk as she walked past the line of Saints and police officers readying their equipment in front of the Clarice.

The Hotel Clarice rose against the setting sun like a looming promise of death. It stared down at her with black windows, where shadows moved with the dying rays of the evening sun. The breeze, while cold from the snowflakes it carried, reminded her of the cigar smoke that had burned her eyes just hours earlier in her father's study. Despite the copious amounts of rancid burnt tobacco filling the air, Elise still could not escape the scent of blood hanging around that room, where a glass case holding her mother's remains stood in the corner. Her father had mercifully covered it with a sheet, but the presence alone and knowledge of what was inside the case had been enough to make Elise's stomach turn.

Arendale joined her on the walkway, with Tobias and Sterling watching nearby. "Police already swept the premises. The beast is gone. You will find nothing but bodies in there," the mayor said.

Elise glanced back at her father, who only stared straight into the Clarice with pure resentment. She met Arendale's gaze. There was no way to mention her sister without potentially endangering her.

Elise knew she had to search the Clarice on her own. "I just need to see for myself."

Even now Elise would not allow dark thoughts about her younger sister to grace her mind. Thinking about Josephine with a craving for blood and fangs for a smile made the possibility too real.

If her father suspected any use of the venom, he said nothing about it. As usual, he had no insight into her true nature. It was the mayor who leaned in to whisper to Elise, "You might be the most valuable human in Harlem, with your connection to the reapers and a vengeful desire to do them harm."

An acidic taste filled her mouth. Despite having walked the path of conflict between wondering whether reapers could be innocent or only the monstrous beings they had been made out to be, Elise had no more fight left in her for their cause. Not while her mother's remains sat locked in a box in her father's study and her younger sister's whereabouts were unknown. All because of her own proximity to reaperhood.

"At the end of the day, I am just a girl who was put in a difficult situation. I know enough to survive."

Mayor Arendale tilted his head to the side. "But…?"

"Surviving is no longer enough. I want blood for blood," Elise breathed.

The mayor nodded. A small smile twisted his lips, and satisfaction bloomed in his dark eyes. "Viciousness should be met with viciousness. For your family."

Pain gripped Elise's throat as she fought back tears. She had barely given herself a moment to grieve alone, yet this man found it fit to prod the wound that still lay open in her heart. "I would never expect a mayor to rally for vengeance. Rather prosperity and peace, not ruin."

"I want to propose a level playing field, where we all live separately but equal. But there is something hunting Harlem. So now, as you said, blood for blood."

All Elise could think about was the darkness encroaching on her now. Once a lethal enemy, now it served as a welcome guest as she stepped into the Hotel Clarice. Emptiness met her at the door, just as the police officers had promised. A few explosives, prepped and ready to detonate at the police chief's notice, covered the floor.

Snow dusted in across the floor with her boots. The rifle weighed down her arms more than she had been anticipating; weeks spent aiming on Jamie's windowsill and roof had not prepared her for this gun's heft. Elise passed through the vestibule and into the foyer. Her foot met blood almost instantly.

She froze, her shoulders tensing at the sudden prick of fear instigated by the hotel's stillness. Everywhere she looked, Elise found blood. On the walls, on the dusty furniture, covering the portraits and the melted candles. The coppery scent overwhelmed her senses, and Elise gripped the rifle hard enough to crack her nails to keep herself steady against the rise of bile in her throat.

Bodies littered the floor and the stairwell. It was impossible to tell which body part belonged to whom. Organs spilled from torn torsos whose legs were nowhere to be found. Police and Saint badges soaked in blood lay scattered across the lobby, their gleaming metals the only brightness in the room of shadows.

Her path of rage had been cut short. It appeared there was no one left to point a gun at.

Elise started to turn around, wondering where the beast had gone overnight, when a gurgle stopped her. She whirled on the sound and aimed the rifle at the mound of what she had thought was no more than rotting flesh.

A shaky hand reached up as a voice rang out, weak and painfully human. "Leave."

"What?" Elise called out. She approached slowly. A man lay at the bottom of the stairs with one hand pressed to his abdomen, where his organs spilled out of a large perforation. "You're still alive," she breathed.

He shook his head. The silver of his Saint badge glinted with each pained movement. "Hardly."

"I can call for help—"

"No. You need to leave. Before it gets too dark. It will come back, and it will kill you too," he wheezed.

Elise lowered her gun and leaned closer, struggling to catch his every word. "The reaper?"

Blood trickled from the man's mouth. A hiss of pain left him, but he coughed and continued anyway. "Not just a reaper. Death itself. A devil worse than anything Harlem has ever seen before. You must leave—"

The building groaned around them. Dust fell from the ceiling and billowed in great black clouds along the floor. Elise tried to reach for the man once more, but he shook his head as the roof seemed to tear open above. "RUN."

The few other Saints who had followed her inside raced for the door.

A grating pain in Elise's head slowed her down. She headed after them, but blood dripped from her nose, splashing onto the cracked wood beneath her. Elise cursed as her vision doubled, then tripled. Blood continued to stream from her nose. It ran over her hands in brilliant red streaks, staining the sleeves of her satin evening gown. Perhaps the dose of venom had been too much. The room swayed, and she stumbled, her hand coming out to steady her against the wall. Elise cursed under her breath. She should've been outside by now, away from the suffocating darkness and whatever lurked within.

"Lisey, don't let them hurt me." Her sister's voice echoed in her head, faint and distraught.

Elise began to wonder if side effects of the venom included auditory hallucinations when Josi's voice came back stronger.

"Please, Lisey. I'm scared," Josi whimpered. The quiver in her voice made Elise's heart drop.

The shock of hearing her sister gave Elise focus as she retreated from her crowded thoughts and listened to her surroundings. Sure enough, she could hear a distant crying just a few rooms over. Abandoning her plan to exit the lair, Elise ran toward the voice.

It led her to what appeared to be a music room. A sleek black grand piano sat in the back of the room by the floor-to-ceiling windows. Along the walls, where various portraits of composers hung, bodies of Saint members and police officers lay slumped. At first glance they looked almost normal—like they could have been sleeping off a heavy drug. But when Elise drew closer, she noticed the pink ribbons twisted so tightly around their necks, blood stained the satin.

"You found me!" Josi cried out.

Elise whirled, expecting to see her sister standing behind her, but all she found was a phonograph positioned in the middle of the room. A bow had been wrapped around the golden horn, the end of its tail trailing over the spinning record on the turntable.

Josi's voice echoed out from the speaker. "You still love me, right, Lisey?"

Even through the static, Elise heard the pain in her sister's voice. Tears welled in her eyes at the thought of her sister alone, speaking to herself and begging for a response. "Josi…"

"Promise me you'll still love me. Even if I'm different—" The record skipped, ending her sister's speech abruptly.

Elise marched over to the phonograph and snatched the needle from the disc. A scream rattled through the speaker, startling Elise so badly, she stumbled backward into one of the bodies. She watched in horror as the man shifted to the side and his head rolled right off his shoulders. The ribbon unraveled into an unceremonious bloody heap at her feet.

Static filled the air, and the record scratched again.

Then: "Don't let them hurt me, Lisey."

Elise backed away and broke into a full sprint. As she ran, she could feel heavy footsteps behind her, shaking the hotel corridor, shifting the floor. The pounding steps drew closer and closer, nearing a thunderous peak, until Elise finally turned and raised her gun. A taloned hand swiped out as she fired, sending her bullet through a stained glass window instead and bright white sunlight spilled into the hallway. The beast shrieked and shrank away, giving Elise enough time to reach an exit door. Outside, she doubled over, inhaling the snowflake-heavy and bloodless air of the alley. Her chest still heaved and her whole body shook with adrenaline.

Elise turned to glance back at the hotel.

Beyond the open doorway, where the sunlight faded into shadows, a massive figure looked back at her. It stood taller than any human, at least nine feet. Through the darkness, Elise could only make out its humanoid shape and long talons as it watched. Red eyes flashed in the shadows before the figure turned and charged out of sight, deeper into the gloom of the lair.

Hot, sticky blood seeped down Elise's arm from where the talons had sliced her. All Elise could do was press her knuckles against her mouth as her breathing grew heavy. There was no protecting Josi from Harlem—not anymore. Her sister, Elise had found, was the one Harlem needed protection against.

Her veins flared with heat—whether it was from the new reaper's assault or her abuse of the venom, she did not know. Elise welcomed the darkness that surrounded her as she collapsed on the frozen ground.

12

BLOOD CONSUMED LAYLA. EVERYWHERE SHE turned, it was all she could smell and taste. Humans passed her by with no knowledge that she may as well have been a ticking time bomb, waiting for the perfect moment to explode. Layla could not even remember the last time she'd fed. The longest she had gone without blood had been just over a week. Older reapers could teach themselves to go for longer and withstand the draining side effects of starvation. Layla remembered watching Valeriya function erratically with black eyes and pulsing veins for nearly a month when she deigned to make a point to the younger reapers. If Layla had starved herself for as long, she would have lost control only a week in.

Now Layla fought to keep her vision straight as she rushed through the street. A blood fury chased her waning control, turning her surroundings blurry and casting a red sheen over everything in sight. Her heart pounded so hard, her pulse became the only thing she heard. In this moment, there was nothing as lovely and delicious as blood, and Layla needed it desperately. Her fangs sank into her lower lip. Blood spilled into her mouth, calming her enough to slow her racing thoughts.

Two younger reapers waited outside the new reaper lair. Chosen and paid for by Julius, the space and all the reapers within were his now. Any other time, she might have stood back to admire the integrity and beauty of the abandoned cathedral they hid in. As their old hotel remained overrun with Saint members and overbearing police officers, it was the perfect location to lie low in.

Both the young reapers looked peeved—Laure especially so, with her arms crossed and foot tapping on the ground. Celie watched Layla with nervous eyes, her gaze flicking back and forth as if waiting for an adversary to spring out of the shadows at any moment.

"Thank you for meeting me. It's good to know not all of us can be bought out," Layla said under her breath.

Laure squinted at Layla, then nodded. "Of course. It's haunting in there." She nodded toward the cathedral. "I'm not sure how much longer I can keep myself from killing Julius. I have to physically hide Celie to keep her safe from him. I feel like a spy. He's gotten rid of anyone who remains loyal to you. He cannot know about us meeting."

Celie squirmed with discomfort, her lips twisting into a pout. "Laure wants to go back to being a rogue again. I convinced her that hearing you out would probably be better than that."

"I said we'd give you a chance." Laure's golden eyes turned molten as she stared Layla down. "Are you really going to kill the little Saint?"

Layla bristled, her skin growing tight with unease. "I need to find her and return her alive to the Saints. It could give me leverage."

Laure rolled her eyes. "Never trust a Saint—"

"There is one Saint I believe is crazy enough to do anything for Josephine. If I win her over, there's a chance this war ends before it can even begin. At the very least, I can ensure we receive a payment for turning Josi over. Imagine what you could do with that kind of money." Layla nodded to Celie. "You could go back home and work on reintegrating into your family. And you…" She looked at Laure. "You can start your own lair."

The younger reaper's eyes softened. "And you?"

"I'll flee this place. Go somewhere no one knows me and live out the rest of my long life in peace." Layla sighed. "What do you think?"

For a moment, both girls said nothing. Contemplation passed between them as they considered Layla's words silently. Then Laure spoke up. "Do you have any leads?"

"I'm almost positive karma and the younger Saint are connected somehow; that poison showed up the moment she went missing. As long as we lie low and don't draw attention to ourselves, we can trace the root of it, and then maybe we can find her."

Celie's face paled. "Before Julius."

Layla nodded. "Before Julius."

"Do you smell that? Smells like a bloodbath," Laure muttered.

Layla blinked. "You smell it too?"

"We're in a blood house. Of course you smell blood," Celie hissed. The young girl had grown increasingly pale the closer they got to the club. Now as they sat in the back room, waiting to be seen by the manager, she could not sit still. Celie practically vibrated out of her seat and soon began pacing around the dimly lit space.

Laure shook her head, eyeing the heavy red drapes that blocked this room off from the rest of the club basement. "It's not that. There's something else. I thought I was just hungry, but it's been in the air for a while now."

"It's not just you," Maria announced as she walked through the drapes. She stood by her desk, her arms folded over her chest and a look of disgust crossing her face. "Something is rotting in Harlem."

Interest piqued, Layla sat forward. She was glad to have something to focus on other than her hunger and the way it ate at every vulnerable part of her. "What do you know about karma?"

Maria blinked. Her throat bobbed, and she rubbed a shaky hand over her chest, where silvery scars streaked across her collarbones. "It's not quite understood by anyone as far as I know. Unfortunately it's making its way through my blood house."

"What does it do exactly?" Layla asked.

Both Celie and Laure watched with deep interest, their faces grave and shoulders tense.

The blood house manager leaned against her desk, sighing. "It appears to work at first the way opium does, causing euphoria.

Some reapers use it for that high, but it curbs their hunger for just a short time and makes them ravenous when they come down. Some call it 'the mortal drug' because it makes them feel almost human. But using too much of it can lead to death. For humans, it's worse. Taking it almost always leads to a brutal death, but it has a delayed reaction—hence why it's called karma. It hits much later after they take it." Maria gripped the edge of her desk so hard, her knuckles bulged. "After a few hours, a human will rot from the inside out. The warning signs are bloodshot eyes, darkened veins, fever."

"What does it look like?" Laure asked.

Maria opened her mouth to respond, but Celie beat her to it. "It's clear, like regular reaper venom." She covered her mouth and whimpered.

Everyone turned their gazes to her, at once curious and concerned. "Celie?" Layla warned.

"I didn't realize that's what it was," Celie gasped. "When I was working in a blood house before I joined the clan, the manager encouraged us to try it… He didn't give it a name. He just said it would make the bloodletting process more enjoyable. But I saw what it did to humans and reapers. That's why I left." Her hands clamped over the back of her neck as her breathing quickened. The ratty sleeves covering her arms fell back, revealing twisted scars on her wrists. Having spent time in handcuffs made of Saint steel plenty of times herself, Layla recognized the burn from the metal.

Her brows furrowed, and she shrank back, her hands clenching into fists on her legs. "Other reapers did this?"

Celie shook her head. "No. Gangsters. They weren't from here. They made that very clear."

Memories of the altercation between the gangsters and the Saint outside the blood house hit Layla and realization had her standing abruptly. "Patrons that are on karma and come here, upset that it wasn't working, unaware there is a delayed reaction."

Maria narrowed her eyes. "That would explain the sudden influx of infection in my blood house."

Layla turned to Celie. "Where did you used to work?"

"The Scarlet Lounge." Celie's tone grew hard with a warning. "You cannot enter unless you have business to sell or buy."

Layla lifted her chin. "I have plenty I want to buy. I want to buy karma."

13

Elise woke to a concerned face staring down at her. Sterling immediately backed away as she sat up. Her brow, sweaty and hot, furrowed while she took in the familiar surroundings of Jamie's apartment. All Elise could do was shake her head in confusion.

Sterling cleared his throat. "I threw out the venom. You were becoming dependent on it, and it was slowly killing you. You need to get it out of your system now. I figured you would want to do it away from your father—"

"I need it—"

"This is part of the drug people are using to feel bigger than they are, and it kills them, Elise. Let it go. Some of us don't want you to die," Sterling snapped.

Jamie folded his newspaper from where he sat at the kitchen

counter across the room. "She has no healthy fear of death," he muttered. "But I'm sure letting her bleed on my couch will fix that."

"You're not helping," Sterling bit out.

"Neither are you," Elise shot back.

His face twisted with anger. "Would you rather I have left you there? And let your father assume the worst? This doesn't reflect well on the empire, Elise."

"And you sidling up with a gangster does? Or do you only care about morals when they serve you?" Elise retorted.

Sterling glared. "It wasn't my idea—"

"He's right. I've been paid to look after you. Can't have you dying on these streets, as much as I would love to give up some responsibility," Jamie called.

Elise clenched her jaw. "I don't give a fuck about the empire. If neither of you will do anything, then I will do it myself."

"Why are you so impassioned by this all of a sudden?" Sterling demanded.

Elise's throat tightened as angry tears filled her eyes. "Why are you not? Our home is dying. Even if I had no personal stake in this, I would care. You should too. My father founded the empire to help, but he's done no such thing. You're no better than him, and he's the fucking worst, Sterling."

Hurt darkened his expression as his face fell. "What personal stake?"

Elise swallowed. She contemplated keeping the truth from him, but if there was one thing that would get him to see her perspective, it would be her younger sister. "Josi. Josi is doing this. Or she's involved with the beast somehow. I heard her voice in the hotel when that… thing attacked me."

Silence draped the room in stiff tension. Holding her breath, Elise waited for Sterling's next words. Even Jamie tensed in his seat. Elise's patience dried up the longer she sat on the couch with blood soaking through the bandages on her wrist. "Karma has been around for as long as Josi has been missing. I need the name of the club that young woman got her venom from."

14

THE SCARLET LOUNGE ROARED TO LIFE AT MIDNIGHT. When the streetlights came on and partygoers filled the streets with their drunken shouts and glittery getups, the beasts lurking in the shadows began to take their picks. Layla stood at the entrance to the lounge, her fingers twitching with anticipation by her sides. Celie and Laure flanked her. Each wore a weary expression that mirrored how Layla felt. The scent of rotting blood only increased as the night went on. For the past hour, Layla's head had been swimming, her thoughts becoming more difficult to pin down and vision narrowing as her heart rate increased with each wave of hunger.

The manager, this time a human gangster instead of a reaper, glanced down at her, suspicious. "You look like you would be a liability. When was the last time you fed? We cannot have any mishaps here," she said sharply.

Layla knew her appearance was damning. There was only so much she could do to cover the enlarged black veins that pulsed beneath her eyes and on her throat. By now her fangs could not retract, and she was distracted by every bloody temptation nearby. The busy crowd of people outside the alleyway only made things worse—she was certain she could have picked up on someone's paper cut from a block away if such a thing were to occur. Still, this starvation was better than the alternative—being at her strongest, when the poison had something to feed on.

"I assure you I have more self-control now than I have ever had in my entire life," Layla rasped.

Laure nodded. "It's true. She's studied under an ancient reaper. You have nothing to worry about."

The manager looked unconvinced. She scoffed and cracked the door open a bit wider. "There's a door fee."

"I am here to do business, not take it," Layla said. She lowered her voice for her next words. "I want to buy karma."

Celie shuddered by her side while amusement pulled a soft smile onto the manager's face. "Is that so? In that case, we have space for you." The gangster stepped back and opened the door wider for them to move inside.

Smoke greeted them as they walked through the doorway. Layla was grateful for the overbearing scent and its ability to cover up the old blood that lurked beneath the floorboards and in the walls. She allowed herself to breathe deeply for the first time all day, relishing in the thick, dissatisfying air. Her hunger remained at bay. It did not surge into her throat, and she ran her tongue over her fangs, feeling how dry they had gone from the lack of nearby temptations.

Celie's shoulder brushed her side, pulling Layla from her internal distractions. The younger girl's frame was rigid and tense, and she walked with a slight unease in her step. "Nothing good happens in these places," she muttered. Fear darkened her brown eyes, rendering them almost black.

Laure slid a hand over her arm and tucked a loose strand of hair behind her ear. "We're not going to let anything happen to you."

The younger reaper shuddered. Her brows knitted together, and she gave Laure a doubtful look. "What if they try to take me back?"

Her friend's expression softened. "Then I will break you out of here again. We'll be okay, Celie. Right, Layla?" Laure's voice went hard on Layla's name.

Layla couldn't ignore the accusation in her tone. The pure vitriol that sprang into her eyes bored into her. It went beyond a threat—Laure held a promise of violence in her gaze that Layla knew she would not survive should anything happen to this littler reaper. She nodded her agreement. "Of course."

They followed the gangster down a set of stairs in the back of the club. The air seemed to thicken with cold tension the farther they descended. As they neared the bottom of the staircase, Layla stopped, turning to her companions. "You two should stay up there. I don't want you to get hurt in case anything happens."

Celie's face, already ashen, paled even further. "Okay." She hurried back up the stairs without another word.

Laure looked after her, then sighed as she returned her gaze to Layla. "Be careful."

Layla waited for her to disappear after Celie before she continued down with the gangster. They stepped out into an open basement that would have been better suited being a dungeon. The walls shone with condensation and mold whose toxins stuffed the air until it grew hard to breathe. Layla stepped over decaying rodent bones, following the gangster to a tall cage at the back of the room. The bars making up the enclosure stretched from the floor to the ceiling and were covered in so much rust, Layla could imagine them being built around the same time that the city of New York had been erected.

The only light illuminating the room came from a tiny window at the top of the far wall. As they neared the dim cage, Layla caught sight of several glass vials littering the floor inside. She followed the trail of them to a hole in the wall, where pieces of brick had been blown out and scattered across the floor. Inside, something hidden in the shadows breathed.

Layla pressed closer to the bars, careful not to touch them. The moonlight did not reach inside the enclosure, but even if it did, she would have been unable to see the prisoner's face. Darkness covered them like a cloak, leaving only their hands visible. Chains trailed out from a hole to iron hooks that kept them planted firmly in the stone wall.

Amid all the mildew and rot, Layla smelled humanity. Mortal flesh and warm blood sat before her; she knew that much. Her breath left her in a startled gasp. "You're keeping a human down here? If the Saints find out—"

"Then it will not be my problem. I only take orders. I do not manage the production of the product. You will have to take any conversation on the topic up with the owner of this club," the gangster said. She nodded to the still human beneath the rags. "If you want karma, you have to take it here. It doesn't leave the premises."

Layla's lips parted. "I'm not sure I can do that."

The gangster shrugged and headed back to the stairs. "Then don't. You're free to go whenever you'd like. My men will collect payment at the door regardless of your decisions." She left, leaving Layla standing alone by the enclosure.

Layla eyed the vials of the drug. Her gaze flicked from the vials to the chains and back to the human in the middle of it all. "Where did you learn how to make this? And who is doing this to you?" she whispered. "Is it reapers? Or humans?" Layla drew closer, the end of her shirt brushing against the bars and her breath stirring the loose flakes of rust on the metal. "Is it the Saints?" She almost didn't get the words out.

The human moved so fast, darting out of the hole, Layla couldn't react in time to avoid their grabbing hand. In a flurry of ratty fabric and angry hisses, the human fisted Layla's shirt and yanked her into the bars. She slammed against the metal and cried out as it burned the skin on her shoulder. The Saint steel hissed around her melting flesh, drawing her blood and cauterizing it over and over again. In her fight to free herself from the surprisingly strong grip of the human, Layla failed to notice them moving closer. Until they sank their fangs into her throat.

Upon contact, they finally unlocked their grip on Layla's shirt. Layla stumbled back, her hand flying to the fresh bite mark in her neck. Already the creature had retreated into the shadows.

Layla stared at the darkness, shock running a tremor through her body. "Who are you—" she started, but the burning in her neck cut her off. Layla doubled over and scratched at the bite, where boils had already begun to form around the twin holes. The discomfort ran bone-deep within seconds of receiving this reaper's venom. Something felt off. She stumbled, her hand catching her against the wall before she could fall.

A familiar fury rose in Layla, and she snapped her gaze back to the cage. Her vision, narrowed and seeping with a red sheen, locked on the reaper inside. She took one step toward them, stopping only when a new scent filled the air.

Layla could have recognized that sweetness anywhere. The blood, painfully human and delicious, sang so closely to her heart, it might as well have beat with her own pulse. She tore her gaze away from the reaper and started up the stairs toward the arousing commotion.

The last time Elise had been this close to a reaper, she had been the one in control. Now she sat in a blood house, a stranger with fangs dragging his nose across her throat while he inhaled her scent. A shiver traveled down Elise's spine. She fought to keep her composure, knowing any wrong move could anger this reaper and put her life on the line.

He moved back, a sigh escaping his lips. "This should be fun for both of us. Miss Saint, I fear you seem uncomfortable." The reaper had beautiful brown skin and glowing dark eyes, a picture of true beauty. Perhaps under any other circumstance, Elise would marvel at the pretty face of this devil and his ability to captivate others while hiding lethality beneath the surface. For now, she could only swallow hard and bunch the lace of her dress in her fists to stop from fidgeting.

"I assure you, I am fine," she said through gritted teeth.

The reaper cracked a gentle smile. "I paid a large price for you, and I want it to be worth every penny." His hand came up to brush a curl out of her eye, then trailed over her cheek and down the slope of her neck. She clenched her jaw against the shudder that rose in her as he leaned closer. "Many believe fear makes blood taste better. It's why predators enjoy the chase before the kill. I can tell you right now, your racing heartbeat is only making this so much sweeter for me—"

The curtains covering the doorway of their private room flew open. In stepped Layla, expression wild and blood streaking down her neck. She locked eyes with the reaper who had jumped back from Elise, though he kept his hand on her throat. "Get your filthy fucking hands off her," Layla snarled.

In all her years of knowing her, Elise had never seen Layla look so unhinged. Her hair half spilled out of its simple clip, and the black veins lining her eyes seemed to swell as her anger increased. She bared her teeth, revealing her fangs dripping venom and blood.

The male reaper finally stood up, but he held his ground. "I paid for Saint blood."

Layla's eyes widened. "I don't care what you paid for. Get out."

This time the male reaper stepped forward. Elise heard the threat in his voice before he even spoke. Now, with two reapers standing before her on the verge of a bloody fight, she felt calmer than she had all night. She much preferred bloodshed to any man getting comfortable near her.

"I don't think you understand, little girl—"

Layla charged forward with a speed Elise had not known was even possible. She became a blur as she grabbed the man's shirt and threw him through the doorway. He crashed out of the curtains and into the wall opposite the room. Elise shot to her feet, her mouth hanging open in shock. Even Layla looked a little surprised. She blinked rapidly as if trying to bring herself back to reality, her eyes darting from the place the reaper had stood to the crumpled heap he had collapsed into on the floor. The wall caved in around him, and debris dusted his messy hair. Several cuts lined his face, but they began to heal almost immediately, leaving behind small smudges of blood.

A few heads poked out of rooms along the hallway. Curious murmurs filled the air, and the live music paused, rendering the club nearly silent.

Elise dragged the curtains shut and spun to face Layla. "What on earth is wrong with you?"

The reaper frowned. "I think what you meant to say is *thank you*."

"No!" Elise exploded. "You've drawn so much attention to us, they're never going to let us go. There was no reason for you to throw a man through a wall—"

Layla scoffed. "You were so uncomfortable, I could feel it practically chewing my skin off."

Elise blinked in confusion. "What? How could you feel anything from all the way—"

"It looks like quite the mess has been made in here." The gangster who had been manning the door earlier snatched the curtain back and walked into the room. She placed her hands on her hips, glaring at Layla and Elise. "Neither of you has brought me enough of a profit tonight to cause this much chaos and damage the property."

Layla lifted her hands in surrender. "Apologies. We were just leaving—"

"No, I don't think so. You will stay and repay what you have taken. Marco!" She snapped her fingers, and a small man with a nervous smile popped his head into the room. "Set up the stage. These two will be giving us a show."

"That is completely unnecessary. We can pay you. She has a lot of money. More than enough to cover any damages." Layla pointed to Elise, who slapped her hand away.

The manager shook her head. "You've already piqued many

patrons' interests with your outburst just now. I want you to give them a show. Many will pay good money to see a Saint tortured by a Harlem reaper." She gestured outside the room, where a few men ushered dancers from the small stage at the back of the main floor. "Get up there and break a leg."

Pure rage crossed Layla's face. She looked ready to argue this woman to death, but Elise had never felt more ready for an opportunity. In this moment, she had this reaper right where she needed her. Now Elise just had to convince her she needed her as well. Without another thought, Elise grabbed Layla's hand and pulled her over to the stage. Two seats sat on top of the wooden setup. She kicked one into the curtains at the back of the stage and turned to Layla.

The reaper still wore a perplexed and frustrated expression. Her mouth twitched like she had a million words for Elise but couldn't settle on just one thing to start with.

Elise pointed at the chair. "It's your turn to listen to me now."

Layla lifted a brow. "Excuse me?"

"Sit," Elise demanded.

Though she heard onlookers struggling to get close enough for a good look onstage, to Elise, the room might as well have been empty save for Layla. The look of pure stunned awe the reaper gave her captivated Elise. Something tender pulled at her chest as the corner of Layla's mouth ticked up briefly before she pursed her lips into a thin line. Elise sank onto her lap, her stomach already heating when Layla's hand came up to gently brush her back.

Elise's breath shuddered out of her as Layla's palm pressed more firmly against her spine, keeping her upright. "This has to look real to them. It shouldn't be weird."

Layla coughed out a laugh. "You're sitting on my lap in front of a room full of people and reapers. Two days—might I add—after you attacked me."

"Should I ask for forgiveness for how I behaved after witnessing my mother's brutal murder?" Elise leaned closer, snaking her arm around Layla's shoulders. "In that case, you should be on your knees begging for mine."

Pain shone in Layla's eyes, and a flicker of guilt pulsed in Elise's heart. "I guess we have matching wounds then. I would gladly accept you on your knees for me." Her fangs dug into her lower lip hard enough to draw blood. It pooled around her teeth, soaking her tongue until the inside of her mouth was entirely red. Layla's fingers pressed into Elise's back like she was hanging on to her self-control. "Why did you come here?" she asked.

Elise ducked her head to whisper into her ear. "I need you."

Layla stiffened beneath her. "What?" she asked, her voice choked.

Her reaction gave Elise pause. She furrowed her brows and hissed, "What is wrong with you?"

"*You*," Layla snapped. She swallowed, and Elise swore the veins on her face jumped. Her fangs seemed to grow even larger, drawing more blood.

Elise released a heavy breath. "You're starved." If she didn't know any better, she would have assumed Layla was losing her battle with what little self-control she had left.

"Don't mention it. There's enough blood in this place to drown a person. I just need to make it through this." Layla wrinkled her nose. "Stop moving so much."

All Elise had been doing the past few moments was breathing. She glanced down, only just noticing how much her body had shifted to be closer to Layla. Unconscious, like the dormant venom still sought to reunite with its maker. She swallowed past her dry throat and met Layla's dark gaze again. "You were right."

"About what?" Layla breathed. Her chest, rising and falling quickly, brushed against Elise's with each breath.

Elise's mouth soured before she spoke her next words. "It's my sister. I need your help finding her. That's why I came here. I needed to see you." The buzz of the watching crowd waned, and Elise grabbed Layla's chin, forcing her eyes back to her. She let her fingers trail over the reaper's cheek, her thumb brushing her jaw and smearing the blood pooling around her lips.

Layla's mouth opened slightly. Her eyes grew glassy as she watched Elise, her breath hot on her thumb. "So you made yourself into bait to get my attention?" she whispered.

"It worked, didn't it?"

A small laugh left Layla. Her smile looked almost delirious with her half-lidded eyes, drunk with anticipation. "You're driving me crazy."

Elise's lips twitched, but she did not smile. "Good." She liked being in control. Whether it was the remaining venom in her system steeling her against any improper emotions or just the confidence she felt sitting atop Layla, it did not matter. Elise had the upper hand now, and she would wield it to get what she needed. Damning her morals had never felt this good. Elise would have to be careful to not give in to such devious temptations in the future. She ran her fingers along the scar she had left on Layla's neck the other day. Goose bumps prickled beneath her fingertips, and Elise watched as Layla's throat bobbed with her touch. "I hope you like the scar I gave you. It matches the ones you gave me."

Layla grabbed her hand, stopping her delicate movements. Her golden eyes pierced into Elise's. *Wicked, violent creature.* How far Elise had fallen just to make herself feel something other than pain. In the end, hurting Layla had not made any difference. Elise had been flooded with guilt more than satisfaction, but she could not be sure that if circumstances were better, she would have done anything differently. Was that always how it would be? Them drawing blood and creating twin wounds? Until one gave up or someone died.

Layla's grip tightened on Elise's hand, bringing her back to the present. She focused on her fangs instead. A cruel craving twisted in her chest, hot and persistent like the hours after she had let Layla bite her the first time all those months ago.

"You remember how it felt when I took your blood?" Layla murmured.

Elise's stomach fluttered at the tease in her voice paired with the visceral memory. She could never forget the pleasure Layla had brought her through tender violence. The stirring in her core had her wilting a bit, and Layla dropped a hand to her thigh to steady her.

Layla continued, her voice a breathy promise in Elise's ear. "You can call me a monster all you want, but you let me at your throat and liked it." She was impossibly close now. Her breath stirred Elise's hair, and the tip of her nose brushed along the column of Elise's throat. Just a few more inches and her lips would touch her skin. Elise could imagine it now—the sweet heat of Layla's soft mouth against her throat, her fangs scraping along the delicate surface above her rushing pulse.

Layla inhaled, this time allowing her face to press into Elise. "You smell like…" Her hands tightened on Elise, who felt the possessiveness in her touch and heard the yearning in her voice.

Mine.

It offered a clear explanation for how Layla had felt her while being nowhere near her. Whatever venom Elise had consumed, Layla recognized it as her own.

Elise peered into Layla's eyes, studying the moving shadows and frequent sparks of adrenaline, no doubt from forcing her hunger down. "I'm still so angry with you," she muttered fiercely.

This time Layla broke into an easy smile. "Fine. If it will keep you looking at me like this, then be angry with me forever. Maybe you will hate me for an eternity. It's why we can never work together. Forget my immortality and your mortality making a terrible pairing—it's our strife. We cannot do this again."

I don't hate you, Elise wanted to shout. She glared and watched the easy amusement fall from Layla's face. "You can't even say it."

"Say what?" Layla inquired.

Elise swallowed. "That you hate me."

Layla's lips parted. She blinked up at her.

But before she could speak, Elise straightened, determined. "Say it. Tell me you hate me and I'll go away. You'll never have to see me again. I won't ask you for anything anymore. Just tell me to my face how much you can't stand me." Elise's voice shook. Tears burned in her eyes. She did not want to hope for Layla's silence, but the alternative terrified her so much more.

The reaper's eyes flicked down to Elise's lips, and for the briefest moment, Elise saw heartbreak in her gaze. Elise cupped Layla's jaw and leaned in, desperate to hear her every word.

Layla opened her mouth to speak, and the world fell apart around them.

It was a minor commotion at first. A young woman ran into the room, blood dripping from her face and neck. She stumbled around the audience and stopped only when one of the club managers rushed toward her. "Help me—"

A cloud of smoke engulfed her as dust and splintering wood exploded. Several patrons scrambled backward off their seats to avoid the hole that had opened into the floor by the stage. The woman screamed as the floorboards fell away beneath her. Some patrons gasped, while others kept silent, anticipating the crushing sound of the woman hitting the floor below. Instead, her screams cut off, and the sickening crunch of bones and flesh tearing between teeth sounded from the hole.

Elise jumped up, peering over the edge of the stage and into the depths. The soft lighting from the chandeliers above hardly reached far enough to reveal anything of substance, but she glimpsed gray flesh and talons stretching through a small patch of light. Blood smeared across the floor in its wake. Elise moved back, waving her arms. "Get out! Everyone needs to evacuate now!" The building shook again as people began to rush for the nearest exit. Elise turned to Layla, who was looking around frantically, searching for someone or something. Elise stepped toward her, her lips moving to form her name, but the floor creaked under her feet.

Then the wood was splitting once more, gaping and ravenous as it swallowed the stage and its contents. Elise reached for anything to hold on to, but her hands only closed around air. Her breath left her body as she fell. For a brief second, she was weightless, her only thought surrounding the anticipatory fear of being eaten alive by whatever waited in the dark below.

Gold flashed above her, and a firm hand clamped around her wrist. Her fall stopped abruptly, and Elise dangled in the space where the light faded to nothing, her eyes wide and scared on Layla.

The reaper stiffened above her, leaning over the edge of the cracking wood. Blood circled her eyes, which were as scared and relieved as they were determined. Her muscles grew taut when she tugged Elise back up onto the floor.

Elise could only try to make herself as weightless as possible, but when her dress caught on a splintered floorboard and she felt the air move by her dangling feet, she struggled and twisted to free herself. Finally Layla gave one sharp yank of her arm and pulled up so hard, Elise tore free and flew into her. Elise landed on top of Layla in a pile of dust and debris.

Layla exhaled roughly. Her hand fluttered by Elise's waist, and she glanced into her eyes, where desirous hunger still lurked. "Okay?"

Still flustered from her near-death fall, Elise could only nod shakily. She rolled off Layla and forced herself to her feet. A small patch of blood stained the front of her dress where she had torn herself free. It was a feeble price to pay for her survival. Even if it meant the reaper who'd saved her would look at her like a prized bit of prey for the rest of the night.

"Celie," Layla breathed. She brushed past Elise, still searching for someone.

Just then the gray beast launched into the room through the cavernous hole. It lunged for Layla, who was preoccupied with a young reaper cowering in a corner.

"Layla!" Elise screamed. She reached for her gun, but it was missing from its usual thigh holster beneath her skirt. So much for that security. *Thanks a lot, Sterling,* Elise cursed under her breath and ran for Layla.

Another figure flew past her, between the beast and Layla. The gray beast plowed right into the intercepting reaper and sank its talons through her chest. Layla watched with horror, her body shielding Celie from the sight. Blood sprayed across the floor and the walls, but the reaper continued to fight around the beast's claws. Her nails dug into the floorboards, scratching while the creature dragged her back to the hole. They disappeared into the darkness, leaving the room still and soaked in blood.

Layla shot to her feet. "It's back."

Elise thought back to the chaos at the Hotel Clarice. She cast a wary glance at all the carnage and whispered, "Its hunt is starting."

15

Layla watched Elise pace back and forth across Jamie's living room. She still wore her torn and bloody dress from the club and made no attempt to remove it despite the overwhelming scent of death clinging to its design.

"So, you're saying there's a new type of reaper hunting in Harlem? But no one knows exactly what it is—not even other reapers?" Jamie asked. He raised a finger. "Have we considered asking around?"

Elise grumbled under her breath, and Layla dragged her gaze away from the Saint heiress to look at the gangster. "Do you have people in mind you'd like to ask?" she inquired.

Sterling rolled his eyes. "The Saints won't help anymore. According to your father, it's not quite a pressing issue since it's mostly affecting reapers. My guess is we turn to the police and the mayor—"

"No," both Jamie and Layla said at the same time.

"Like they would care at all. There was a massacre at the club, yet the police are citing it as usual reaper violence. Never mind that humans died there too, and they are holding something captive in the basement—you people don't give a shit about anyone but yourselves," Layla spat.

Sterling glared and stepped forward, his hands fisting by his sides. "I went to the club and found nothing in that hole you mentioned. And I'm here right now trying to help, aren't I?"

Layla matched his ire and met him in the middle. She stood several inches shorter than him, but her own fury was enough to keep her strong in the face of his. "Only because of your own personal interests. If it were anyone else involved, you wouldn't care. But because it's Josi—"

"That's not true," Sterling seethed. "Even if Elise does not see herself as the true heir to the Saint empire, her actions still reflect on it and all government parties and powerful individuals associated with us. Someone has to keep her in line. I'm here for the greater good of Harlem as a whole."

Layla's body further heated with anger. She clenched her jaw so hard, her teeth began to ache and her fangs snapped out on impulse against the pain. "Bullshit."

Jamie pressed a hand to his face, sighing. "This is going so well already. Miss Saint, do you care to step in here? Since you've brought all your friends into my home and they are now giving me quite the headache."

"This is all wrong," Elise said. She stopped her incessant pacing and turned to face everyone. "We have to tell my father Josi is involved. Even if anyone else stepped in to help, they would stop at nothing to see her dead. I cannot let that happen." Pain shook her voice, and though she spoke with clarity, tears welled in her eyes.

Layla regarded her with pity. Her gaze softened, and she moved closer, her body itching to be near Elise. "It might be too late to save her. She could be too far gone." Layla spoke quietly, as if dealing such a lethal blow in a gentler voice would make any difference.

The Saint heiress reeled back and shoved past Layla, cursing. "No. She's not. Josi will be fine; we just need to find her and Dr. Gray, and we can fix her." Elise pointed at the messy map on the floor. "I found a pattern in the attacks. Shipments of karma must come to certain clubs at certain times. We can figure out which club is next and intercept it there. My father can mobilize his associates to help. If he knows about Josi, he will have to."

A painful lump rose in Layla's throat. Before her stood a girl on the edge of ruin, whose own thoughts were not in her control. Layla did not have the heart to tell her that if Tobias could be responsible for these things happening in the first place, why would he step up to fix anything at all? All she could do was nod as Elise kneeled by her map and began to put the pieces back together.

Jamie cleared his throat, and when Layla turned to face him, he gestured for her to leave the room with Sterling. Once they were out of sight and hearing range of Elise, Jamie shook his head. "We can't do this. There is a monster that is close to running rampant on the streets of Harlem, and she wants to not kill it but catch it? I've seen what that thing does to people. There's no way in hell any of us will survive it."

Images of the man severed in half at the dock resurfaced in Layla's mind. She understood Jamie's perspective—especially as someone who hardly knew Josi. Why rush headlong into danger for something that might not even be worth saving?

"I honestly don't think she's thinking clearly anyway. It's been months of this. You two have not seen how unwell she's gotten," Jamie muttered.

The thing was, Layla did see it. She saw the shadows that ran deep beneath Elise's eyes and the haunted look that never seemed to leave her face. She smelled the blood from the aggressive digging of her nails into her palms and peeled-back skin around her fingers. Layla wondered if she would bleed herself out without proper assurance.

Sterling crossed his arms. "Josephine is her sister. She's already lost one. We have to try."

Jamie fell silent for a long moment. Finally, he nodded, albeit with hesitation. "If you can get the Saints on board"—he looked at Layla—"and you can get the reapers involved, I will join in with my men."

"I can get Celie to help me convince Julius." Layla had no choice but to agree. She could not tell them that her clan was hardly her clan anymore. Finding Josephine and settling the tensions between reapers and the Saints might have been the only way forward.

For the first time in months, Elise felt small in the presence of her father. Returning to the Saint home could have been more of a regression than a plan for progression. If she could not get him to listen to her or see her side, she would have no choice but to become that begging, hopeful girl who needed her father. As much as it was against her will, Tobias had become her lifeline again.

"Home again already? Consider me surprised, given the way things ended last time." Tobias Saint leaned against a large mahogany desk in the back of his study. He had his arms crossed, his face a mask of unmoving stoicism.

"I do feel badly about that, Father. Especially now. Our neighborhood—our home—is on fire, and the Saint empire has only begun to burn with it. I was born with a duty to this family. I have to see to it that the business remains standing. There's so much left for us to achieve. I might not be your chosen heir, but Josi…" She swallowed past the rise of bile in her throat. "Josephine deserves a chance here. We should all be coming together in these times, rather than fighting."

Lying to her father was easier than Elise had thought it would be. Waiting for his reaction, however, was a different beast. The time in between her declaration and the shift in his expression made her palms sweat.

Her words were met with silence for a long stretch of time.

Tobias pushed himself off the desk so that he stood up straight and walked toward Elise, his hands clasped together in front of him. "And here I was believing you hated our empire and everything about its business."

"I like the loyalty of your associates, and I wish to have that back in my life. As for how the empire moves forward, we would have to discuss that in depth—"

"So I can hear how ungrateful you are for my care. And how much you hate me and wish I was dead," Tobias said slowly. He watched her face, no doubt looking for an obvious tell to decipher her emotions. "Is that right?"

But Elise kept her expression neutral. Even with anxiety crushing her chest and her heart slamming against her ribs, she did not break. "I was hoping to gauge whether you could ever trust me again. Because I have a proposition and I need your help."

Her father gave her a curious look. "You really do need me." Another smile emerged on his lips, and Elise's stomach turned at the thought of him believing he had her again. He nodded, still moving through the room. It felt massive with his slow steps and calculated movements. Several paces later and he was still far from her, despite his words brushing up against her like poison-tipped fingers, ready to drag her down with his frayed thinking. "*Trust*. It's such a familiar term, from petty situations between friends to forming global alliances. Trust between family might be what holds kin together. Trust between the Saint empire members is necessary to push our message and goals forward." Tobias stopped by the fireplace. It sat in the back wall, empty, but Tobias looked at it as if had the ability to compel magic to life. "Trust is not something reapers know well. Especially not with humans."

Elise thought about Layla, who believed she was better in isolation to protect people from her monstrous tendencies. Then she thought about every reaper out there still roaming the streets with no ties holding them down anymore. She thought of the Harlem reaper clan and how they had rallied behind one another and Layla even when she was working with a Saint. The reapers never had a problem with loyalty until it was broken. Humans had solidified the importance of loyalty, then continued to ruin it for centuries.

"I believe that is something we can change," Elise said firmly.

Her father's lips curled into a cruel smile. "A belief is only as strong as its experience. All reapers crave blood—especially the blood of their betrayers. But they will not forget your contributions to the cause of their eradication." Tobias finally stopped in front of her. This close up, with him towering over her, she felt their differences and distance even more. "You think working closely with one reaper will be the beginning of solving the human-reaper crisis. You think your love for her—your love for each other—will be enough to end the strife."

Elise shook her head. "No—"

"That wasn't a question, Elise. It was a fact. You're sick with love, and it's making you stupid." He twisted his wedding ring on his finger, his hands shaking a bit as he turned back to the desk. "I would know. I've spent hundreds—thousands—of dollars trying to make things right. Made a deal with Mayor Arendale to help track reapers and keep them in control as long as he helped me rebuild the empire. It was not so easy at first. Clearing my name was the worst part of it all. Then closing the mansion and halting business for a while turned out to be the only way I could stay on top of everything. I wouldn't be in this position if I had not been tempted by the devils that walk this earth. The one reaper I tried to work with poisoned me, and I still feel the effects of it now. Worse still, your sister..." His fingers worried the wedding band again. As his eyes traveled to the glass decanter of what Elise assumed was red wine on his desk, her throat tightened.

Elise saw an opportunity at that moment. She placed her hands on the desk, leaning over so he was forced to meet her eye. "Josephine is why I'm here."

Tobias paused. His eyes shifted as he considered his words. "What do you mean?"

Silence again. Elise chose her words carefully, not wanting to scare him into doing something destructive. "There is a new evil hunting Harlem. Neither reapers nor humans are safe. I have reason to believe it is Josi partaking in this violence. Valeriya's venom...it's changed her," she muttered.

Horror darkened his eyes. He stiffened, his shoulders going tense and his hands clenching the edge of his desk so hard, his knuckles grew ashen. "My Josephine... No, Valeriya said it would be temporary."

Elise blinked. "You knew she planned to hurt Josi?"

Tobias's hands shook as he raised them to pull at his hair. "It was not supposed to hurt her. It was supposed to keep her safe. I only agreed because the beast infected me with her blood first. It sounded right in the moment, and in the end, it did keep Josi alive." He cursed under his breath and shook his head. "But at what cost?"

"I believe Josi is okay. Beyond the monstrous being she's hiding behind. She's just…scared," Elise said. "You have to tell your associates to stop the patrols in case she shows up. Tell the police too. Perhaps changing the weapons to be ones that incapacitate rather than kill while Josi is still out there—"

Her father was already shaking his head. "If she really is so dangerous, then we should be protecting the city from her and not vice versa."

Elise's heart dropped. She could hardly bear what she was hearing, much less the insinuation coming from her father. "No. I have a plan. We just have to find her and Dr. Gray, and we can stop her—we can *fix* her."

"There is no fixing monstrosity, Elise. Once you've turned, you're too far gone—"

"She's not gone, and she's not a monster," Elise snapped. The moment the angry darkness returned to her father's eyes, she regretted her tone. But Elise would never regret standing up for her sister. She held her ground as her father stared her down, his lips pulling into the most vicious scowl.

Tobias crossed his arms and spoke in a hollow voice that somehow felt scarier than a strong threat. "You have clearly been influenced for as long as you've been gone. I can accept wanting to help Harlem, but understand that our actions reflect on the empire and the powerful people in the government and beyond who have invested in us. You cannot be reckless with this power and expect me to accept that."

Elise frowned. "The treatment reapers have endured for centuries, leaving them with no choice but to hurt, corrupt, and bleed people dry also reflects on us and the government. The only difference between us and them is that they have no choice when ours are endless," she said. Her breath left her in rough exhales, leaving her chest heaving and hot. "Will you really not help?"

Her father cast his gaze sideways. "I do not see a future where reapers and humans are ever coexisting productively or peacefully. You will always have a place here if you want to follow the way of the empire, Elise, but I cannot support this path you wish to take."

Elise's throat burned with unshed tears. She nodded anyway, knowing she had done all that she could to involve her father in this fight for her sister and a better future. Despite confronting what she had tried so hard to avoid and not be afraid of for the past few months, she had still come up against a dead end. "Right." Elise began to turn away and head out of the room, but his voice stopped her as she crossed the doorway.

"Elise."

She faced him again, already wary of what would come next.

Tobias had the decanter in his hand and was already pouring some of the red liquid into his matching glass. "I know you will go back to Layla, and I want to know why. There are so many other young women who you would match with much better. Layla… while I adored the joy she brought you as a child, those days are long behind her. I guarantee she's keeping more secrets than you could ever guess. Don't be so gentle with her this time." He took a sip of the liquid, its unnerving ruby red staining his lips upon contact.

Elise had no idea how to respond to his words. She liked to think she had no choice but to trust Layla now, whether she wanted to or not. There was no one else to cling to in these unprecedented times. In a place like Harlem, where the shadows held hell with poisoned fangs, there was no time to keep secrets from a beloved.

Without another word, Elise pushed out of the study and almost stumbled into Sterling, who stood blocking the hallway.

"Elise—"

She whirled on him, ignoring his pleading tone and the way his eyes filled with hurt. "Did you know?" Elise put every ounce of strength she had into the glare she gave him.

Sterling blinked. "Excuse me?"

Elise raised her voice. "Did you know they were poisoning Josi?"

The life seemed to rush out of him at once. Sterling paled, shaking his head, and held his hands up in defense. "No, Elise, I never—I never wanted her to be a part of any of this. They're monsters, and they're not to be trusted. I thought your father knew what he was doing." His throat bobbed, and Elise saw the devastation in his eyes.

Conflicting words popped into Elise's head. *He does, but he never does the right thing.* But she couldn't say them out loud. Because that would make them truer than she was ready to admit to herself. Though Sterling's words almost drove her to a state of breathlessness, the irritation never left her. She inhaled sharply, shoving the new emotions back down. "You have to choose. You cannot side with him and also help me. He only hurts me. Do you understand?"

Sterling stared at her, wide-eyed and perplexed. Elise couldn't wait for his answer. She turned and left, the embers of her anger igniting more with each step.

16

ABSOLUTELY NOT. AND FRANKLY, IT DISTURBS ME that you feel so comfortable coming back here after all the chaos you've caused. You abandoned your lair and lost your opportunity as a fair fight for clan leader when you sided with the Saint girl. I told you to stay away," Julius warned.

Layla stood in the cathedral vestibule, facing the new self-appointed Harlem clan leader. It was hard to look at him without malice, but she forced her expression to remain neutral while he stared down at her, knowing hostility would only hurt her chances at getting him to agree with her proposal. "The beast is attacking both humans and reapers. We would be smarter to fight it together."

Julius glanced back at the rows of pews leading up to the dais, where a few reapers sat and listened to their heated conversation. "You know how manipulative humans can be. They've created unspeakable horrors and committed violences that our world will never forget, but you expect me to believe they are small in the face of this beast? What, we do the work in protecting Harlem for them, and then they just go back to treating us like demons? I thought you were smarter than this. But suddenly because it's Elise Saint asking, you are willing to damn your reaper morals to help her and all the humans who have hated us for centuries?" he hissed.

His points were difficult to argue against. Layla knew exactly how he felt. Why should reapers lower their defenses and accept another partnership with humans after the devastating way things had ended last time? Why should they heed to their needs when reapers had been living beneath the mortal boot since they were conceived out of their selfish malevolence? Still, Layla could not give up so easily. Celie's tear-streaked face and pained cries flashed in her mind, along with the lingering scent of Laure's blood as she had been dragged away by the beast. It was not just a human problem. The whole of Harlem was in danger—reapers included.

"Helping humans helps us too. We need their numbers and their weapons to defeat something like this. The Saint—" she began, but Julius cut her off.

"I already said no," Julius snapped. "I do not give a damn if you find a friend in this Saint girl; she will never be ours. You bring her around here, or I catch a whiff of her on you again, you'll both be dead."

Layla could only stare after him as he walked away, back into the long shadows of the old building around them. A small figure emerged from behind him, and Layla caught Celie's eye. She lifted her chin, hoping for a sign of their loyalty to each other still being alive. But to her dismay, the girl only shook her head and continued after Julius.

The cathedral felt colder than it did holy. Layla was glad to finally leave it and step into the sunlight outside. However relieving it was, the feeling was short-lived as a familiar scent floated over to her in the breeze. She tracked it down with ease, then groaned when she found Elise Saint waiting for her in a covered alleyway at the edge of reaper territory. The Saint heiress leaned against the wall, one hip popped and displaying the gun strapped to her body. Layla would have to get used to seeing her carrying a weapon so confidently. When Elise had been using Sterling's gun months ago, the girl had been almost as uncomfortable as she was around the schoolboys who'd crushed on her when they were younger. The memory nearly made her smile, but then Layla noticed the way she straightened and instinctively reached for her weapon when she saw her.

"You shouldn't be here," Layla said coldly.

Elise dropped her hand and lowered her shoulders. "I'm assuming he said no."

"I can't blame them. Last time we tried to work together, it was a disaster," Layla muttered. She still warred with herself over whether working this closely with Elise on her own was a mistake.

"Things have changed. We're all in danger now. Does it really seem wise to hold on to grudges when there's something bigger than all of us threatening our lives? Are reapers really all so stubborn—"

"Stubbornness is a human trait. Reapers live too long to care that deeply," Layla said.

Elise rolled her eyes. "How much longer until *you* stop being stubborn?"

At this, another smile almost found its way onto Layla's lips. She looked away, her voice dropping as reality set in. "One hundred more years at least."

Elise's blood seemed to cool at that admission. She swallowed, her throat tensing. "Right."

Layla studied her face, taking in the narrowing of her cheeks and the hollow bruises beneath her eyes. Despite her recognizable scent, the heiress's essence seemed off. Something else wrestled within her, and Layla sensed it to be more than just her mental state. "What did you do?" she asked before she could think better of it.

The Saint's gaze flicked to her. "Pardon me?"

"You seem less afraid," Layla said.

Elise blinked. "We all have to grow up eventually. I figured you would appreciate me crying and complaining less. Jamie certainly does," she muttered.

Layla shook her head. "It's not that. You do not care about your life." She remembered Elise reaching for the gun when she entered the alleyway. Perhaps her sense of danger only arose when it came to Layla. A sinking feeling took over her chest, and she suddenly regretted asking Elise anything.

"My life does not matter anymore." Elise shrugged. "There's not much to look forward to nowadays, is there?"

Her words reminded Layla of herself. There had been a time, years ago, when Layla's own life had become collateral in her own motives for vengeance. The path she'd taken had brought her to darker places than Layla ever imagined. The thought of Elise taking the same descent scared her. If Layla had hardly survived it as a reaper, there was no hope for Elise.

"You don't have to worry about me. We're in this together only until we find my sister," Elise said.

Layla narrowed her eyes. "That's exactly why I have to care. You are my ticket out of here. So you cannot be reckless with your life because you have to stay alive long enough to vouch for my immunity after all this is over."

Elise pursed her lips. She hesitated, her mouth twisting while she thought. Finally, she nodded slowly and spoke again. "Allow me to be reckless once more. The last few attacks have been in places where public officials and Saint associates were around. If Josi really is targeting those people, we can set a trap for her."

A long sigh left Layla as she pressed a hand to her forehead. "You want to be bait again, don't you?"

"I would not say it's what I want, but it does seem necessary. We have no support outside of each other. Let's make the best use of ourselves."

Layla insisted on walking Elise back to more neutral territory, despite Elise's protests. "This is unnecessary."

The reaper looked up at the setting sun and shook her head.

"It's almost sundown. If what you said is true about the new beast, that sunlight deters it, then you'll be vulnerable when the sunlight disappears." They turned to go down a covered alley, a shortcut that would save time.

"*If* what I said is true..." Elise rolled her eyes. "What will it take for you to just take my word for it? I do believe if we are to be partners again, you should trust me. I have no reason to lie to you now."

"I'll trust you when you stop lying," Layla said sharply. She stopped walking and gave Elise an expectant look.

There wasn't much Elise could say that wouldn't make Layla treat her differently. Jamie and Sterling already looked at her like she was losing her mind. She didn't want to further strain their partnership before it properly began. "We do not have to make this personal. The less emotional investment you have in me and the decisions I make, the better the outcome will be when we inevitably have to part ways again. Would you not prefer that?"

Layla stiffened, and Elise sensed the striking fear she had made a mistake. The reaper held her hand up. "Shut up."

"Excuse you—" Elise started, but a shadow loomed from behind her. She began to turn, her hand resting on the grip of her gun. Before she could face the threat, Layla was slamming her into the nearest wall. Elise tumbled several feet away, rolling to a halt in a crouching position. A gasp of surprise tore from her as she spotted Layla with a massive chain thrown around her neck. An unfamiliar reaper held the other end, and while the metal dug into Layla's throat, burning her flesh until it melted into her collarbones, the reaper holding it had no reaction to the Saint steel.

Elise tried to stand, but someone pushed her into the wall, their forearm pressing into her throat while she pulled her gun from her holster. Julius loomed over her, his eyes dark and furious. "You two just cannot resist each other, can you? I'll give you one chance to tell me what you're planning before I rip your throat out."

"I thought you did not want to be involved?" Elise rasped. Her throat ached beneath the pressure of his arm, but he was too close for her to get her gun out.

"I want the Saints to stay out of reaper business," he spat. Julius removed his arm only to clamp his fingers around her throat. His nails, sharp and unrelenting, dug into her flesh. Blood leaked from the new cuts, pooling in her collarbones. "You're poison to Layla, and she's spreading it to my clan."

Layla could barely cough up a pained response. She clawed at the ground, leaving deep scratches while her blood leaked out of her throat. The chain continued to seep into her flesh with each passing moment.

Elise choked out a nervous laugh. "The poison has already existed in your reapers for centuries. Layla is the least of your worries."

Julius tightened his grip on her throat. Her eyes watered with the effort to breathe past his grasp, but he was ruthless in his claim over her. "You know nothing. You think you know her, but you couldn't be more wrong. The longer you sit here, posturing instead of giving me answers, the closer we get to that chain tearing her head off."

A gurgling noise left Layla. She lifted her head, revealing bloodshot eyes and pulsing black veins making their way across her face. "I'll kill you. Let her go—"

The reaper holding her yanked the chain back, and she collapsed.

With the last of the air remaining in her lungs, Elise scoffed at Julius. "Why would I ever trust you?"

"Because I know where your sister is, and she is not invincible. Layla knows as much." Julius's voice made her blood run cold.

Blood rushed out of Elise's face, and she stopped struggling against him, her body going slack with shock. "You—"

"Let her go." A stern voice boomed nearby.

For a moment, Julius's fingers only strengthened their hold on Elise. She saw her own death flash in his eyes, and as the darkness began to encroach on her vision, Elise went willingly into its depths. But then he released her and light returned to her eyes as well as air to her lungs. She slumped against the wall, her chest heaving while she struggled to catch her breath. When Elise looked up, she found an unfamiliar woman had approached. She wore lengthy garments that covered her from head to toe, leaving no skin exposed—as if she was afraid of the sun itself. Shadows hid her face beneath the massive hat she wore, rendering her completely unrecognizable.

Julius shot a fiery glare at the woman and snarled, "What are you doing here?"

"I do appreciate you finding her for me, but let's not forget we cannot make this look anything less than human," she said. Her attention turned to Layla, who had gone eerily still on the ground, surrounded by a puddle of her own blood. "Shame, Layla. You could have been so good by my side if only you'd listened to me."

Panic clawed up Elise's throat. She tried to keep herself together, but pain split her open, second by second, the longer Layla lay there unmoving.

The male reaper backed away from Elise, though he kept unwavering watch over her as the other woman moved closer.

"You will be happy to know that your mayor approached me the other day with an enticing offer. He wants to make good on his promise to you. Fewer punitive measures and more rehabilitation efforts to keep reaper and human relations stable. He understands that it takes a reaper to understand their habits and learn the best ways to…manage them. I am quite tempted to take him up on the partnership opportunity, though I do remember how the last attempted cooperation between reapers and humans ended up." She tilted her head to the side, and a flash of scarlet revealed itself beneath the shadows of her hat.

Elise lifted her gun again, this time alternating between aiming it at the woman and Julius. "Who are you?"

"I could say I'm a friend of Layla's, or I could say I'm a friend of your sister's. Either answer, I'm sure, only raises more questions for you," she murmured.

Elise narrowed her eyes. She remembered hearing about this reaper woman; Layla had mentioned her after Valeriya died. This must have been Karine—the one who had come all the way from France to be close to Valeriya. Elise's finger moved over the gun's trigger on instinct. She pointed it right at the reaper's heart, thinking only of the awful things Valeriya had said and done to her family. All the poison she had spilled and left in her absence. "Where is Josi?" Elise seethed.

"Surely you are not considering making the same mistake as last time? Killing an ancient reaper who is full of information that would only be useful to you. Granted, you will soon learn those Saint bullets have no effect on creatures that wear the night like armor." The reaper spoke slowly and with a calmness only immortal souls could possess. "My old friend is gone, Elise. And despite the reaper lair codes prohibiting reapers from killing one another, Layla seems to be protecting her murderer. I find it incredibly hard to believe. I do think, however, that you know more about it." She drew closer, her movements fluid and inhuman. "I can't help but notice how comfortable you are walking around unchaperoned. You are unafraid. You've seen what reapers did to your sister Charlotte, yet you are so unburdened by the lingering threat. Why is that?"

Elise ignored her, keeping her gun arm steady. Even with the gun between them, Karine pressed forward. She moved in so close, the gun sank into her chest, but she remained unbothered by its barrel resting right over her heart. The reaper swiped a finger down the column of Elise's throat, where it had grown sticky with blood. She lapped at the drying substance and grimaced. "You're poisonous. You know death is never the end for a reaper and things in Harlem never really stay dead. Between your siblings and Layla, you should know that better than anyone else. You should be angrier about what happened."

Conflict had never tasted so bitter. Elise swallowed past her unease and deepened her glare. "You have no idea how angry I am."

"Not angry enough to stop Layla from coming around and to keep the Harlem reapers from threatening you." Karine placed a hand on top of the gun, the pressure forcing Elise to relax her own stance. "It is time you learned reaper strength has no business being manipulated by humans."

As the final embers of the sun's glow retreated behind the alley's makeshift rooftop and darkness covered the space like a veil, the ancient reaper removed her hat. Golden eyes roamed over Elise, calculating and cruel, yet warm with intense hunger. Her lips split into a crimson smile that sent chills down Elise's spine. "Did you know that in France, reapers cannot survive the sunlight? Humans banished us to the darkness, yet they become weak when there is no light. Now shadows are less of a convenience and more lethal for you. When the world falls dark, you become blind, while we are stronger than ever. You have rendered half the time you spend alive dangerous to you. Your sister was remade in the shadows. She belongs to me now."

Julius made his way over to Layla. He reached down and grabbed her hair, pulling her head up. Blood covered the reaper's face; even her eyes had turned to a lethal shade of red. "All this starvation has made you weak. But I know you cannot resist the taste of a Saint. When you feel the blood fury, you'll have no choice but to kill her."

Julius pressed his fingertips, still drenched with Elise's blood, into Layla's mouth.

Elise watched with horror as Layla stirred. At the same time, she heard a scraping and saw the cover of a nearby maintenance hole being pulled back. A long gray arm reached out, and a beastly reaper hauled itself from the darkness beyond. Julius rolled a vial of some strange substance across the ground toward the reaper as more crawled from underground. He held a few more vials out, taunting the others. They each took a swig from the mysterious liquid, and almost instantly, their bones began to stretch beneath their skin, extending their limbs, growing their height.

Layla shot to her feet, a new ravenous strength driving her forward. Even with the chain still digging into her flesh, she continued to move as if it had no effect on her. She yanked the metal away from the reaper holding her captive, then pulled it off her throat.

The moment the new monstrous reapers stepped toward Elise, she pointed her gun upward and fired into the tin roof covering the alleyway. Bullets blew several holes into the cover, allowing the remaining sunlight of the evening to break through. It landed on the reapers' flesh like fire, burning right through them. They shrank back, shrieking in pain. Elise did not wait to see how long her assault would hold them. She sprinted down the alley and back into the dying sunlight, away from the darkness hunting her down.

Layla thundered after her, her snarls filling the frigid air behind Elise. The Saint heiress did not stop until they were close enough to Jamie's apartment. She screamed for him, hoping he had finished his duties for the day and was safely inside. Just as his window cracked open, Layla crashed into Elise, tackling her to the ground. The reaper's blood poured over Elise while venom dripped from her torn mouth. She hissed, sending more of it spraying into Elise's face. "What did you do?"

Elise winced as her nails dug deep into her shoulders, pinning them to the ground. "Whatever the hell is in you," Elise gritted out, "it's in me too."

The reaper's face went slack. Even with the black veins spiderwebbing across her cheeks and up her bloody and ruined throat, the devastation in her eyes looked painfully human in the dying evening light. She could only let out a whimper of realization before her eyes rolled back into her head and her body gave out on top of Elise.

17

"WHERE DID YOU GET THIS?" JAMIE EXAMINED THE vial of strange fluid Elise had handed him.

She looked over from the bloody mess of rags piling up in the bathroom sink. Layla continued to bleed out on the white tiles, crimson seeping into the grout and filling in the dusty corners of the room.

Elise pressed a clean rag to the wounds on Layla's throat, trying to ignore the fading beat of her pulse. "Julius and Karine had it. I think it might be karma."

Jamie's expression twisted into a doubtful frown. "You *think* it might be karma? And you want to try this on Layla?"

"It's either that, or she dies. The wounds from the Saint steel won't heal properly, if at all," Elise snapped. "If you want to leave while I give it to her, then fine. I'll deal with the consequences."

The gangster scoffed. "This is my house. I'm not going anywhere.

Frankly, I'm a little peeved you brought your problems here. Now there's a big mess—do you even know how hard it is to clean blood out of grout...?"

Elise shot him a piercing glare.

Jamie cleared his throat. "Are you certain no one followed you back?"

"No," Elise said flatly. She watched the faint flutter of Layla's eyelashes and cursed.

Jamie opened his mouth to speak again, but a loud banging at the front door turned him pale. He ran down the hall.

Elise turned back to the dying reaper before her. She grabbed the vial from the counter and popped the lid, preparing to pour its contents into Layla's mouth. As she reached forward to part her lips, someone yanked her arm back. Elise whirled to see Sterling and the small reaper girl from the club standing over her.

"Don't," Sterling said sternly. He nodded to Celie, who came forward with a small needle and syringe. Before Elise could even ask what it was, the small reaper was plunging the needle into Layla's chest. She stepped back, and they all waited, their breaths shallow and scared while they watched Layla.

For a long moment, she did not move. Her breathing continued to slow, and blood spread around her. Then Layla shot up suddenly. Her eyes were wide with panic, and her hands shot toward her throat, clawing at an invisible restraint.

Elise reached for her and clamped her fingers over her wrists, stopping her frantic movements. "You're okay," she whispered.

Sure enough, the wounds on Layla's neck began to heal. The flesh knit itself closed, and proper color slowly returned to her cheeks. She still breathed heavily, apprehension making a home out of her traumatized body.

Elise's cheeks heated as Layla's eyes roamed the cuts on her throat. "Did I hurt you?"

"No," Elise said roughly.

"What happened?" Laya asked.

Elise glanced up at Celie and Sterling, who shared a look.

Celie spoke up first. "I saw Julius leave after Layla, and I knew he wasn't going to do anything good. He's always working on things, so I took his medicine just in case. I figured he would try to hurt Layla the way he hurts other reapers he wants to make an example out of. But when I saw the Saint girl, I knew it would be worse. I found her brother, and he decided to help. I'm sorry. When I was human, I always went to my brother for help," Celie whispered. She wrapped her arms around her middle and stepped back.

Elise's heart softened at the mention of Sterling, who had been as much a brother to her as a friend. "What did you give her?"

"Whatever Julius uses to quell his own problems. I'm not sure where he gets it from," Celie said.

Layla struggled to her feet. She caught a glimpse of her reflection in the mirror and quickly looked away, her lips twisting in disgust. "He was a physician before he was turned, and he used to regularly continue practicing on reapers because he found them to be the perfect specimens. His words, not mine."

Elise followed her out into the living room, where Hendricks jumped up from his spot on the couch at the sight of her. He hissed, his tail and back fluffing in agitation. Layla bared her own fangs at him, and the cat scampered off, disappearing into Jamie's room.

She settled down by the window and inhaled the fresh air coming from outside. "The rot is not metaphorical."

"Excuse me?" Elise asked.

"There is something rotting underneath Harlem. The reapers Karine called from underground…they smelled dead. Like they had just emerged from their graves," Layla said.

Nothing in Harlem ever stays dead. Karine's words echoed in Elise's mind. She swallowed the rise of bile in her throat. Jamie pressed a hand to his mouth and left for the kitchen, while Sterling shook his head.

"That would explain their inability to tolerate the sun. If they've been dead in the ground for years," Elise muttered.

Celie's breath caught. "There is no way… Maybe they're just reapers who have been lost. I know some who, when they first turned, couldn't bear the thought of drinking human blood, so they locked themselves away to keep from hurting anyone. The dead cannot walk."

"If they were a reaper first, or God forbid, experimented on in their reaperhood, then tossed out for being an experiment gone wrong, anything is possible," Sterling said. "When Stephen Wayne still worked with your father, he used Saint members to help him dispose of reaper bodies that had succumbed to the experiments

Dr. Harding ran. It's possible these are the remainders that refuse to die."

"And Karine has somehow gotten her hands on them how? She has been in Harlem for only a couple of months. How does she already know the depths of its atrocities?" Elise asked.

Sterling shrugged. "She must have allies hidden all around."

Elise's eyes went wide. She returned to her map, where she had circled known blood houses and gang territories. They all overlapped with Saint territories, the ones politicians like Stephen Wayne and the new mayor had sought to influence during the election. "She has allies everywhere…" Elise looked at Sterling, whose face was still void of his usual confident color. "When is Arendale's next event?"

"Tomorrow evening. He's visiting one of the newer apartment buildings in Hamilton Heights to talk about fighting astronomical rent prices. I don't think he has a plan, but he just wants to make himself look good. Why?" Sterling asked.

"It seems Karine's hold on him has already begun. She mentioned he offered her a partnership to improve human and reaper relations. I cannot imagine that event will run smoothly. Every time the Saints rally with any important government leaders, something goes wrong. If Karine really wants to usurp human power over reapers, she will see this as an opportunity to strike," Elise said.

Jamie cleared his throat from where he stood behind them all in the kitchen. "Have you forgotten that we have no allies? If it's true that this reaper woman is plotting the downfall of humans and she has allies in high places, we are mincemeat in the face of her attacks.

The new monster she's rearing has already almost taken you out twice. What will make this event any different?"

Elise clenched her jaw as everyone turned to look at her. "Josi might be there. We have to try."

Sterling reached a hand toward Elise as if he meant to comfort her, but it fell, and his fingers clenched by his sides. "If it makes you feel any better, your father is losing control over his weapons supply, and his factories have been shutting down, so even if he wanted to fully arm the rest of us, he would barely be able to do so. The loss of the Saint empire on your side is really no loss at all."

"What happened to his weapons?" Elise asked.

"Total theft and seizure of one of the Saint training centers," Sterling said.

"By whom?"

"Criminals, Elise. Who else?"

Everyone looked at Jamie. The gangster lifted his hands and scoffed, his face turning red beneath their assuming gazes. "I did not do a damn thing. I've kept to myself per her orders." He gestured to Layla. "That's why it's so cold in here. I can hardly afford to heat this place. My son hates me for it. You're welcome."

Sterling choked back a laugh. He rubbed his hand over his face and cleared his throat when Elise scowled at him. "Can I trust you this time?" she wondered aloud.

The other Saint member sighed. He pulled his overcoat back, revealing empty and barren shirt lapels. Even his gun holsters were empty. Sterling produced them from his pockets instead, wrapped in protective cloth. "I was on my way to hand my badge and guns in to your father when Celie found me. As soon as we're done here, I'll go back and finish the job."

A smile spread across Elise's face. "Sure. But we need that badge for tomorrow."

18

SAINT BADGES HAD LESS AND LESS POWER IN Harlem these days. Sterling wore his proudly as they approached a line of police officers outside an apartment building. Elise stood close by, unable to stop staring at the cold metal of his badge. It was odd, seeing the shine of the Saint seal in the early-afternoon light, knowing that her home and its empire had been destroyed. Elise swallowed hard while Sterling introduced himself and gestured to their group. Though it was small at a glance and only consisted of her, Sterling, Jamie, and Layla for now, Jamie had his crew hiding out nearby for backup.

"You are not permitted to enter this event. It is invitation only, for the residents of this building," the police officer said in a flat voice.

Sterling blinked. "Do you not think if this man is to represent the people of this city, the people of the city should be invited to these events?"

The police officer's jaw tightened. He lowered his hand to the gun at his hip and sighed. "Look, kid, you should just go. Don't give us any trouble."

A young Black couple shuffled right past them. One of them, a man wearing a hat and a casual suit, stopped as Layla muttered something beneath her breath. He gave her a knowing smile, then handed Jamie something before continuing on with his girl. Layla nodded for Elise to come over, and she did, leaving Sterling to converse with the officer.

"What was that about?" Elise asked, gesturing to where the couple had disappeared into the building.

Layla nudged Jamie, and he brandished a small piece of paper with print that read, *You can wake up the devil, raise all the hell; no one will be there to go home and tell*, on top of address and time details. It appeared to be an invitation, though for what, Elise had yet to determine.

Jamie let out a low whistle. "This is nothing we should be getting involved in. I don't want to see you in such circumstances. We are not *that* close." He looked behind Elise at Sterling and lifted a brow. "He might enjoy it—"

"Jamie, what are you talking about?" Elise demanded.

His mouth gaped at her confusion as he lifted the card. "Is this not an invitation for a petting party?"

Elise's heart skipped a beat. "A *what*?"

Layla snatched the card from Jamie and grumbled. "No, it's not. This is an invitation for a rent party. You know, where people get together to help pay for rent." She sighed as Elise gave her a blank look. "Of course you don't know. Never mind that. Jamie, I told that man you would supply alcohol, so you will have to at least pretend to do that when we go in."

Elise blinked in confusion. "Why would Mayor Arendale be at a rent party?"

"He isn't," Layla said, her voice going hard with exasperation. "But he's in the courtyard of this building, intending to address its residents. Getting inside is our first step—"

"Step back!" the officer shouted, interrupting their seemingly endless back-and-forth. Elise whirled to see the man pointing his gun at Sterling, who had his hands up and eyes narrowed with anger. "You don't run things around here. I do."

Sterling's breath came out quickly but with considerable effort. "This is my neighborhood—"

"And I protect it. You were a Saint member. I know you understand the magnitude of the danger that has been running rampant in these streets. Your people left one hell of a job behind for us to clean up," the police officer spat.

Elise couldn't be sure if *your people* referred to Saints or Black people. Either way, she'd had enough. Stepping forward slowly, she took hold of Sterling's arm and gave the police officer an apologetic smile. "I am sorry, Officer. We are actually on our way to an event at our family friend's home. So sorry to bother you."

The officer leveled his deep glare on Elise, and a sharp fear shot through her at the intensity in her his gaze. Even without the gun pointed at her, Elise did not like being in this man's presence. He made her feel small in more ways than one, and just moments into being on the other end of his interrogative stare, Elise had her fingers digging into Sterling's arm to ground herself.

"Do you really expect me to believe you?" the officer demanded.

Before Elise could even open her mouth, Jamie was stepping forward with the small invitation. "Yes, sir."

The officer took one look at Jamie, then lowered his gun. He barely glanced at the invitation. Just stepped to the side and gestured for his police colleagues to stand down and let them pass.

"What pigs," Layla muttered once they were all inside. "I hate that you have to change your voice for them. This is all such bullshit."

Elise tried to reach for her, but she continued walking at a faster pace. As Layla departed on her own, Elise turned to Jamie and Sterling. "Maybe we should split up for a bit. Sterling, you go with Layla. Jamie and I will go to the party and try to warn everyone."

Jamie sighed. "What if you're wrong about this? Maybe nothing bad will happen at this event. Maybe the mayor really wants to help people."

All Elise could do was shrug. "Maybe he does. But Karine certainly doesn't. The moment she shows up, we have to be ready."

Elise barely had to show the invitation to the guests who opened the door to the party before she and Jamie were whisked inside.

Live music made up the majority of the commotion inside this tiny place of living. All the furniture had been pushed back against the walls, and people leaned on the edges of tables and chairs while they watched a jazz musician wield his saxophone in the middle of the room. Neighbors tapped along with this soulful song, some passing around a hat to place money inside. Despite the room's small size, it was still packed with people who wore smiles and had eyes that shone brighter than most crystals. Some danced together, taking up the little space available, bumping into others, who only laughed and joined in. Elise had never seen such genuine self-made joy. All the parties she had attended growing up had been ways to flaunt money and status; people walked in with their nicest jewelry and did not even bother to dance half the time. Or they attended to intoxicate themselves with the people's poison and drank until the room spun and they collapsed. Here there was only benevolence and camaraderie. It was a refreshing scene to experience, no matter how close to tragedy they all might have been.

The man who had opened the door for them spoke over the music. "You can make yourself at home here. We have refreshments and some food, but it's going pretty fast."

Elise nodded and gestured to the performer. "What's his name?"

"Wilson," the man replied. His eyes wrinkled as he gazed at the attendees around the room. "Rent is supposed to be ten dollars a month, but this place charges us folks more than the few white families they host." The man eyed Jamie with suspicion. "You are not a plainclothes police officer, are you?"

Jamie only smiled and shook his head. "I've got your refreshments covered."

The man gave him a delicate smile before turning away and reintegrating into the moving crowd nearby. Elise carefully stepped around a couple of kids coloring on one of the tables and dragged Jamie over to the window. Outside, the mayor's rally was beginning in the courtyard below. Layla was down among the hopeful audience, weaving in and out of the crowd to get closer to the stage. Sterling stood farther back, keeping an eye on the entire crowd from a distance. From up here, Elise could not hear what the mayor was saying, but she knew enough to believe it was all a rhetorical distraction.

"We need to get these people out of here," Elise murmured.

Jamie looked down at the growing crowd outside. "And what about them? Are you not also worried about Layla and Sterling being down there?"

She shook her head and turned back to the dancing room. "Let's worry about them first."

They couldn't wait for the saxophonist to finish his song. Jamie lifted his hands and shouted, "I am with the police!" He did not have to threaten to arrest people for having illegal liquor. The room exploded with chaos at the mention of police.

Elise began herding the people closest to her toward the door, calling out for everyone around them to evacuate. The party deflated like a dying balloon, all energy evaporating in an instant. Murmurs of needing the money to continue through the week followed Elise all the way out of the building. The things people would do for money…it made Elise wonder about all the ways people had turned into corpses just to hold their life's earnings with them in their graves. What was the use if one wasted their life to be able to afford it? If she let them stay and make more money, they could die in an attack planned for this building. But that was the problem, wasn't it? That people died to live at all.

Once outside, people gathered around the sidewalk, still grumbling and upset. A few tried to maintain the mood from inside, tapping their feet to whispered lyrics and swaying under the effects of the alcohol.

Elise pulled Jamie back into the building and toward the courtyard in the middle. The sun was already sinking below the horizon, and Mayor Arendale looked eager to introduce a new guest to the rally stage. Surprisingly, Elise caught no sign of her father. An event like this had his name written all over it, though he was nowhere to be found. She wanted to breathe easier because of it; it should have meant less to deal with on a personal level. But knowing Tobias, there was probably something sinister at the root of his absence.

Mayor Arendale grinned at the various crowd members waving posters of his face and political cartoons that depicted him in defiant exaggerated styles, lifting the state of New York on his back. He waved his hand to silence them as he began to speak. "We have lived for ages in New York because of the freedoms it offers us. But not all of us are truly free here. While the country has made mighty strides to keep its citizens safe and happy, there are many things still keeping us down. To name one thing, reapers are a significant blight on us here. We have tried for years to keep them in check. The Saint empire created methods to eliminate them, but after the tragedies that have occurred the past few months, we decided a new approach is needed."

Curious murmurs moved through the crowd as he continued. "I am introducing a new initiative that will hopefully settle the strife between humans and reapers. I specifically visited this complex because of several families here who have been impacted by reapers. When a human being turns into a reaper, they do not simply forget their human past. These families have lost sons, daughters, mothers, fathers; stigma has prevented them from seeing one another. In an ideal world, reapers and humans will be separate but equal. No more prejudices keeping families apart. To help me, I have partnered with a wise woman who sees a better world once all of us can get along. Please join me in welcoming Karine Dupont to our community."

Karine walked onto the stage, her smile wide enough to reveal her fangs. A few people in the crowd cried out, while others ran away, and even more still stayed to feed their morbid curiosity.

"Karine was turned in the early 1700s and was taken to France during the early 1800s to serve masters there. She knows how cruel humans can be to reapers and how that has only increased violence between the communities. She believes that together, we can make Harlem safe again. Reapers can have a leader in her as you all have a leader in me. This is the dawn of a new America."

Elise tried to listen, but she found Karine's eyes boring into her. The reaper held hundreds of lifetimes in her gaze, and Elise felt all of them ripping into her, passing more judgment than a divine being could ever muster. Elise wanted to scream at her, establish the truth that she was still alive despite this ancient reaper trying to end her life. But the ground trembled beneath her feet. Jamie stiffened beside her, and she reached for the gangster, tugging on his arm to get his attention. "Run—"

An explosion rocked the courtyard.

Layla tasted nothing but ash and blood. Even before the dust settled, she saw carnage moving through the yard, its gray body pulling itself from the ruins of the complex gardens to prey on vulnerable humans scrambling to process what had just occurred. Through the chaos, she found Elise hauling herself to her feet and lifting her gun to the beast. She fired once, only succeeding in blowing a chunk of flesh out of the thing's neck. It turned for the heiress this time, shrieking as it ran. Layla charged for the thing and rammed it into the ground. The beast skidded across the ground, smearing through the blood and countless bodies the blast had downed. She allowed the heat of her wrath to urge her forward until she was crouching over the beast with her hand outstretched and ready to strike. But as the dust cleared and Layla got a closer look at the beast, she saw something else instead. The thing had been replaced by a young boy with brown skin and fearful dark eyes who lay crumpled and whimpering, human again. Blood leaked from his throat where Elise's bullet had torn through. Layla hesitated over him and bit back a gasp.

People stampeded around her, fighting their way to the nearest exit. Too caught up in the young boy's horrific death before her, Layla did not register the swarm of new bodies approaching her until it was too late.

"Do not move!" several police officers shouted.

Layla dropped her hands and turned to face them. They pointed their guns at her and beyond where she was standing. Just a few feet away, Sterling stood, startled. He lifted his hands in defense, and Layla watched as Elise and Jamie skidded to a halt behind the officers.

Elise glanced up at the stage where Mayor Arendale descended with Karine trailing behind him. "Sir! Please, this is not—"

"What kind of monster are you?" Karine demanded. She moved closer to the officers, who held their guns steady on Layla and Sterling.

Elise blinked in surprise. "Excuse me?" She swiped at a piece of dirt that clung to her face and gasped when an officer turned his gun on her.

Karine pressed on, her expression cold and unfeeling. "You heard me. Choosing to work with this criminal reaper?" She jerked her chin toward Layla, whose own body had gone rigid with anger. "Attacking innocent humans together? Was this whole thing your plan?"

Elise was shocked. "What? No. This is you. *You're* the one who—"

"We found your letters to the esteemed Doctor Gray, by the way.

Did you know she was arrested in Switzerland for medical malpractice? And you want to work with her for what reason? To continue such treatments here in the States?" Karine gestured to where a crack in the ground had opened up and where countless bodies lay just beneath the surface of the dirt. A few appeared less human than the rest, like beasts among the dead. "Are these monsters your creation as well?"

The scent of death had become particularly overbearing now. Layla wrinkled her nose more and more with each shift of the wind. Whatever the explosion had unearthed had been dead for a long time. And now they stood at the center of it all.

"You all need to leave immediately, or we will use force." The police officers' voices rang out around the street, closing in on the nervous crowd gathered before them.

"The premises are not safe at the moment. Frankly, I'm starting to get a little frustrated with how you are treating former colleagues," Sterling said strongly.

While Layla knew he had grown used to managing authority as a Saint member, she did not understand how he still stood so defiantly in the face of a man who had pulled his gun on him. Sure, the Saints had worked with police officers—or rather worked to fill in the gaps police officers left—but that clearly did not make these officers of the law any softer toward them.

The closest officer scowled at Sterling. "Because you are a *former* colleague. We no longer work with the Saints. You mean nothing to me now. None of you do," he snarled. The man reached for his gun, but before he could fully draw it, another explosion shook the ground and everything around them.

Layla ducked with the rest of the crowd. Several moments of weighted panic passed as smoke filled the air and ash rained down. Layla looked back up and saw that the building's windows had been blown out and fires raged on every floor. In the courtyard, people cried out as they watched their homes burn.

Layla straightened, her eyes darting around the holes that continued to open in the courtyard. Bones surfaced in the dirt. Rotting caskets and burial decorations littered the ground, revealing a mass grave of long-dead humans.

The police officers looked on in horror. They lowered their guns and fell silent while the crowd began to scream again.

Jamie touched Layla's arm and signaled to Sterling and Elise. While the rest of the audience grappled with the atrocities exposed before them, she followed her companions out of the destruction.

19

Back at Jamie's apartment, they found the place ransacked. Jamie pulled his gun the moment Sterling noticed the busted front door, and the two men entered the apartment first, guns cocking as a full scene unfolded in Jamie's living room.

Several rogue reapers stood around the room, each one more menacing than the last. Layla stepped in front of Elise, who continued to peer over her shoulder at the reapers.

One of them held Hendricks, stroking the bristling cat's fur. Jamie pointed his gun at him and snarled, "What the hell are you doing in my home?"

The rogue jerked his head to one of his buddies, who came forward with a small vial. A tiny pink bow was wrapped around it, and Elise gasped behind Layla at the sight. "This was delivered to me late last night. We have seen that Karine is working with the mayor, and now you…are challenging them. We only want to know if we need to discuss new boundaries."

Layla narrowed her eyes in suspicion. "I thought rogues worked alone. Why are you together?"

"We no longer know who to trust. There has been word that a new poison is spreading and that something is hunting in Harlem. Collective confusion has brought us together. Your friend Celie has only confirmed the chaos."

Annoyance pricked at Layla. However, there was no time to wonder about Celie's loyalty when some of the most unpredictable reapers sat before her. "Karine is not on our side. She acts on her own. I would not trust anything that came from her, and that certainly did." Layla gestured to the vial.

The largest reaper stood, towering over Layla as he walked by with his companions. "Your actions reflect on all reapers; try not to get us involved again."

Even minutes after they left, the room still seemed to reel from their presence. Jamie hugged his cat to his chest and murmured sweet words to him while everyone else stared at one another in shock.

"Well, that was a disaster," Jamie said flatly. He frowned at the floor, where blood and dirt had been tracked all over in Elise's and Sterling's wake. Layla hung back in the kitchen, where her skin buzzed with adrenaline and her body tried to heal her wounds as quickly as possible. Minor scrapes turned to scars on her face, and the biggest cut from the evolved reaper began to close slowly but surely on her stomach. Still, the damage burned, and it did not help that the venom in her system ached for more blood.

Jamie shook his head and sighed. "I don't think the four of us should handle anything ever again."

Sterling looked like he wanted to say something, but Elise threw her holster on the floor and hurried down the hallway to the bathroom. He looked after her, then turned back to the kitchen, his lips pursed and gaze distraught. "You might be right, Jamie."

The gangster's jaw went slack. He pointed to the floors and threw his hands up. "Anyone with eyes can see that, Mr. Walker. My home is a mess because you all have brought your chaos in with you—"

"He meant you're right about Elise," Layla snapped. She wiped her blood onto her pants and straightened. "She's not doing well. Maybe we shouldn't have encouraged this, but I think it's best she saw the outcome for herself to understand we have to make better plans."

Sterling tried to start down the hallway, but Layla moved in front of him. He gazed at the bathroom door and frowned at her. "I can help her."

Layla gave him a tight smile that did not reach her eyes. "I don't think so."

"You were not in her life for a significant amount of time—do you honestly think you can handle how bad it gets?" Sterling demanded.

She studied his face, noting the way his teeth worried his lowered lip and how his amber eyes swam with apprehension. He clung to his old life with Elise so desperately, Layla recognized a piece of herself in that fear of losing everything. Still, the memory of reaching into the wound Sterling had left in Elise's chest kept Layla from budging when he tried again to move past her. "You are not allowed to tell me how to make her feel better when I am the one who dug your bullet out of her not even three months ago," she said coldly. Layla relished in the way he fell back, defeated. She turned for the bathroom door and pushed it open.

"*Get out*," Elise almost shouted. She stood over the sink, her hands clenching the ceramic so hard, her knuckles strained.

Layla shut the door behind her and folded her arms over her chest. "Should've locked the door if you didn't want anyone coming in." It took her a moment to realize Elise was staring hard not at her reflection in the mirror but the vial of venom that sat in front of it. Layla shot forward, reaching for the glass, but Elise snatched it up before she could grab it.

"Do not take that," Layla ordered.

"Why not? How long have you been starving yourself? I can't be self-destructive? It makes me feel better," Elise said shakily.

"Elise, that's crazy. Do you even hear how crazy you sound?" Layla hissed.

Elise's fingers tightened on the bottle so hard, Layla feared the glass would break and venom would spill directly into her veins. "I know I'm fucking crazy. You don't have to say it." Her voice was shrill, stuck between a whisper and a shriek.

Layla swallowed. Guilt beat at her heart, and her chest grew heavy as Elise's hands shook. "I didn't mean it like that."

"I know exactly what you meant. I know what Jamie and Sterling say too. You all look at me like I'm some disaster waiting to happen. I never should have asked any of you for help. I should have just done this on my own." Her voice broke, and she wiped at her eyes with her free hand. Elise twisted the top on the vial, and Layla immediately sprang forward again, this time successfully grabbing the venom. Still, the Saint heiress tried to pry it from her, but Layla yanked it out of her grasp.

"*Enough*," Layla huffed out. "I refuse to watch you ruin yourself like this."

Elise's grief turned to ire, her eyes narrowing to angry slits. "Since when do you care? You didn't think to stop by for two whole months and left me to rot here with Jamie. Now, all of a sudden, I'm such a damn burden to you—"

"Because every second with you is torture. I cannot control myself around you," Layla hissed. She could hardly understand the words coming out of her. For so long she had only thought them, never giving them voice. Now the object of her pervasive thoughts knew exactly how much she occupied her mind. Layla turned before she could say something even more reckless. Her head buzzed with anticipation, her throat dry and vision narrowing.

Elise's voice cut through the cloudiness. "I'm not done talking to you."

Layla had just managed to crack open the door when an irresistible scent filled the air. Blood—warm and fresh—swarmed her senses. Every reaper instinct kicked in instantly, and Layla whirled on Elise, her eyes finding the source of the bleeding. A considerable cut had been made in her palm, and the heiress let it bleed out, scarlet drops hitting the floor in rhythmic intervals.

All Layla could do was freeze. With blood rushing in her head and the violent urge to feed climbing up her throat, Layla feared getting too close to Elise. It was difficult to even process her words. All she could think about was the racing pulse in her jugular vein that contained everything Layla needed in that moment. She let out a heavy breath and pressed herself against the door. "Elise. I can't do this right now." Her fangs emerged again, and this time they would not retract, no matter how much Layla willed them to. Even her vision derailed. Red narrowed her sight to a pinpoint, searching for the new life suddenly prancing into the room.

"You…" Elise noticed Layla's shifting attention. A small meow sounded mere steps away, where Hendricks pawed his way into the room and sat beneath the counter to watch them.

Layla's lips parted at the sight of him. The blood fury didn't care what kind of blood she got, so long as it was fresh and filling. She took a step toward him, but Elise moved faster, scooping him into her arms and carrying him out of the room. Once he was gone and Elise returned, she was all Layla could focus on. The anger rolling off Elise stood no chance at stopping her. A red haze began to cover her eyes again, and her pupils dilated as Elise drew closer to her after shutting the door.

"You've always wanted to be the hero so badly—you make yourself responsible for too much—you cannot even realize how much danger you put yourself and others in," Layla said breathily.

Elise's brows furrowed. "Because I still have a family that I wish to take care of, that makes me a hero? What's so wrong with wanting a better life for my sister?"

"You shouldn't have to sacrifice yourself to achieve that," Layla snapped.

The Saint heiress let out an exasperated breath. "You hate me anyway. Why the hell do you care?"

Layla pursed her lips, for fear of what she would do if she opened them and caught a mouthful of Elise's blood. It was all she could think about now. Not the building anguish in Elise's eyes that nearly eclipsed the dark anger in them. Nor the way her chest rose and fell rapidly like she had been trying to catch her breath the entire time they had been talking. All Layla saw, tasted, and smelled was blood. When Elise stepped closer, her lips moving to form more words, Layla could not hold back.

She leaned forward and crashed her mouth onto Elise's. Biting her would have been gentler. Kinder. When Layla felt Elise's lips under hers, she kissed her with enough force to bruise. All adrenaline built up from her rising blood fury went into the kiss, but she began to pull back when her thoughts caught up with her actions.

But Elise's hands were moving behind Layla's head, pulling through her hair. Elise groaned into Layla's mouth, and Layla felt her fingers dig into the heiress's back involuntarily. Elise pressed closer to her, her lips parting over Layla's. She complied as Layla pushed her back on top of the sink, releasing her just long enough to steady herself on the ceramic. Her legs wrapped around Layla's waist, and she squeezed her knees against her hips, drawing her closer.

Kissing Elise Saint proved to be a worthy distraction from Layla's vicious hunger. She tasted all of the heiress, her tongue tracing the inside of her mouth, and a new hunger opened up within her. Layla's hands dipped beneath her shirt, her fingers trailing the warm expanse of skin beyond. Elise shuddered under her touch and arched into the mirror behind them. Her breath fanned out across Layla's face as she pulled back, baring her throat for her.

The rush of blood pulsing against her skin tempted Layla, but she refused to give in to her brutal desires. Instead, she pressed a hot kiss to the juncture between Elise's jaw and neck, savoring the soft moan she drew from her. With her fangs out and scraping against the delicate skin, Layla could not help but think of how such a thin barrier kept her from Elise's greatest arsenal. Her very essence— her existence was Layla's weakness. She hesitated while Elise's hands roamed up her shirt. Her lips lingered on the pulse point in Elise's neck, her breath hot against her flesh as she inhaled her sweet scent.

"Do it," Elise whispered. Her hands fumbled on the buttons of her blouse, a few of them popping as she rushed to open it.

Her desperation to bare herself to Layla only drove the desirous urges home stronger than ever. Even with the blood fury pulling all impulse control from her, its ravenous thirst driving all the years of practice and work against temptation from her system, Layla knew feeding from Elise was a reckless idea. She grabbed Elise's wrist, stopping her as she finished opening her blouse to allow Layla better access to her throat. Blood dripped from the wounds Layla's fangs had left in her own lips, and she let it fall between them. There was no greater rush than in the moment before her fangs found home in someone's flesh. The fury ravaging her self-control tore at her nerves, sending prickling want across her entire body. Even the sight of Elise turned from a portrait of mortal frailty to a picture of devouring beauty. Layla needed more than just her blood. She needed all of her. The pulse of her rushing artery against her throat was all Layla could focus on with her hand still wrapped around Elise's wrist, so close to the source.

"I'll kill you," Layla whispered, her voice tense with yearning. "Do you wish to turn me into a monster?"

Elise snatched her hand away and pulled Layla in by her waist. "You will do no such thing. I command it."

Layla's bloody smile turned vicious. The Saint girl could command all she wanted, but there was no control when it came to bloodless devils. For in this moment, Layla had become one. And she would not stop until she was full. Her hand curled around the back of Elise's head as she leaned in to sink her fangs into her neck. At once, the hostile hunger in Layla's core turned to something sweeter. With Elise's blood on her tongue, coating her mouth, and flowing down her throat, there was nothing else in the world that mattered. All she saw was the curve of Elise's spine as she again arched against the mirror and the bliss that made her eyes roll back. Her blood, her perfume, her humanity, her essence was all Layla smelled. The endless hunger before might have made her crave Elise more, but

Layla was certain nothing would ever compare to her. The taste of Elise stood closer to divinity than anything Layla had ever experienced. Her blood was a sacrament on her lips, the only thing Layla might ever get on her knees for. All morals be damned, Layla would find happiness in death if it meant dying with the taste of Elise on her tongue.

Elise's breath grew heavy in her ear, and Layla knew she should have stopped, but she couldn't find the strength to cut off the flow of blood between them. Between the urgency of Elise's nails dragging along her back and neck and the soft moans she let out, Layla had found heaven. When Elise dragged her leg over Layla's, Layla gripped her thigh to haul it farther around her waist. She pressed closer to Elise—into her. Until the flesh she drank from became ragged and Elise's breathing faint. Still now, Layla was hardly full, but when Elise drew a hand up to push her away, she complied and stepped back.

Blood dripped from both of them. It seeped from a messy bite mark in Elise's throat, paving a path of carnage over her collarbones and between her breasts. A long tear ruined the front of her blouse; Layla hadn't even noticed causing it due to her frenzy. Blood drenched her mouth, and her fangs remained out as her tongue curled over the leftovers of her feast. They were still close enough to touch, though Layla kept her distance, her fingers flexing while her eyes roamed Elise's appearance.

Besides her chest heaving to catch her breath, she seemed mostly okay. A spark of desire lit her eyes alongside the anger that she had greeted Layla with earlier. Elise pulled herself away from the sink and gripped Layla's chin. "You look feral," she spat out. Behind her, a crack had formed in the mirror.

"I am. Because of you," Layla breathed. Her blood heated again, yearning for a finale that would strike the hunger from her body indefinitely.

Elise shook her head and dropped her hand. "No, this has nothing to do with me." She began to walk away, pulling at the ruined parts of her blouse as she went.

Layla trailed after her. "Elise, please." Her voice came out like a desperate plea. Layla couldn't even curse herself for the desperation; in this moment, there was nothing she wanted more than the girl before her. Elise finally turned around again, and Layla wasted no time in dropping to a kneeling position at her feet. How magnificent it was that a human could bring her to her knees with just her blood.

"Lise." Layla's hand trailed up Elise's leg, feeling the heat of her blood beneath her flesh. The sensation had her fangs digging into her lips again and more blood spilling over her teeth. "I'll do anything for you. Anything you want. I need you." Her hand slid farther up, fingers curling around the back of her thigh. "I can make my apologies more repentant." Most days, Layla hated how weak she became when presented with the only thing she needed. Her affections for blood turned her into a fool. She could stomach it for Elise Saint only. Her blood had a hold on her like no other.

For the first time all night, the anger melted out of Elise's expression. Intrigue replaced it, and while she continued to frown, allure became visible in her trembling lower lip and glowing eyes. "I'll take you up on that offer some other time," she murmured. Then Elise exited the bathroom, leaving Layla desirous and kneeling by herself.

Eventually she collected her thoughts and got up to follow Elise down the hallway. Sterling and Jamie met them both with incredulous stares. Hendricks, who sat comfortably between the two young men on the couch, paused in licking his paw to peer up at the girls.

Jamie blinked. "What the hell kind of calming down did you do to her?"

A faint look of disgust darkened Sterling's face as he eyed the blood still spilling from the bite wound in Elise's neck and then the scarlet stain on Layla's mouth. "I would rather not know. Please do not answer his question," he grumbled.

Layla brushed the back of her hand over her mouth, wiping the blood away. With most of her hunger subsiding already, the cool, calming relief of a fresh feeding settled over her body. Her tense frame relaxed, her shoulders slumping and fangs retracting. "She's fine now," Layla said.

Elise nodded and crossed the room to pick up the vial with the bow. "I wonder if this would be enough to blackmail Karine with."

20

WITH LAYLA'S VENOM RUSHING THROUGH HER veins and marking her bite wound, Elise felt safer than she should have walking the streets of Harlem alone. It helped that she had just been ravaged by a reaper experiencing a blood fury and survived. The wound in her throat still wept, but she did not wrap it, if only to remind herself of the consequences that might occur if she was not careful executing her plans tonight.

At her destination, an elegant brick building loomed above her. Jazz music, loud and bumping, trailed from behind the walls, its presence so entrancing, it caused a thunderous vibration in the sidewalk outside. Elise hesitated as she glanced up at the light bursting from the windows. Being among people had never been easy for her, but since the accident with Charlotte and all that had happened with her family and every party she had attended between those times, she was especially wary of putting herself among drunken socialites. Danger thrived in places where the music rose to volumes loud enough to drown out screams and people drank enough to be unable to tell their right foot from their left. Elise couldn't tell if she had a death sentence or if she was so far buried beneath the guilt of losing Josi that doing anything to find her had become the only choice.

"Are you looking for the Renny?" someone asked nearby. A young Black couple passed by, the man stopping to look at her.

Elise nodded.

The young woman waved a hand toward the building. "There's so much to do, you'll be overwhelmed the moment you walk in, but just remind yourself you can always come back." Sparkles lined her eyes, and they fell into the white fur shrug draped over her shoulders. The sight of her carefully done makeup and nice dance outfit reminded Elise of nights when she would get dressed up and head out with Sterling. Those times no longer existed, and even with all her efforts to make things right, Elise feared she would never know a sense of normalcy again. The way people continued to drown the darkness out with alcohol while monsters in plain daylight and nighttime preyed on the vulnerable made Elise's stomach turn. She wasn't sure she could ever fall into their patterns.

A piece of paper flew across the ground, catching on her heel. Looking down, Elise found her own face staring up at her. Her face along with crass renderings of Layla, Jamie, and Sterling sat beneath a jarring WANTED. Elise picked it up and crumpled it in her fist before letting it blow away with the breeze.

As Elise stepped into the Renaissance Ballroom, she was immediately hit with the aroma of sweat and liquor associated with parties these days. She craved no part of it. Avoiding stray feathers from boas and the long trains of fabric from people's dresses proved difficult as she weaved her way through the crowds. The place had been a prime spot for entertainment for years, with a casino, a ballroom, a theater, and a basketball court. And wherever a crowd gathered, there was bound to be illicit behavior and activities. Elise knew the Renny was the perfect place for politicians to meet gangsters—or for any illegal opportunities. She'd also discovered her father frequented the place, though he had never been a dancer or a gambler, unless she counted him betting on others' lives. Tonight, however, she hoped not to find him but his previous partners in misdeeds.

Elise made her way to the casino, the best area for deals to take place under the table. Smoke weaved through the room as she surveilled the various people at each game table. Some leaned heavily against their seats, weighed down by liquor. Politicians placed bets on their cards while whispering to gangsters who stood behind them with loaded guns strapped to their bodies. Money spilled between fingers just as quickly as liquor flowed from cups into mouths. Elise might have been the most sober person there and reaper venom still wreaked havoc on her system.

She swallowed past a particularly intense wave of heat that radiated from her bite wound. Every time she blinked for a bit too long, Elise saw flashes of Layla's eyes, golden and desirous, gazing up at her in the darkness. She should have let Layla take her—consume every inch of her. Falling victim to a reaper's wants only ever felt right when it was Layla's desires Elise was satisfying.

Her heart pounded so hard, it threatened to bruise her ribs. Elise steadied herself against a nearby table as her vision blurred, and she let out a rough breath to level out her shallow breathing.

"Drink, miss?" asked a server at her elbow.

She waved him off but kept close behind on the path he cleared through the room until she finally caught sight of the figure she'd come here to find.

Karine sat at the edge of a booth just behind a gambling table. A glass of champagne sat between her slender fingers, and she sipped it slowly with one hand while she played with the hair of a young gentleman leaning against her.

Elise approached the table and sat in the empty seat by Karine.

The older reaper turned a surprised look onto her. "Elise Saint. Back from the dead, are you? You must be kept on a leash by that reaper lover of yours," Karine said in a low voice.

A few people at the table looked around, intrigued, but they continued their game. From the gun imprints along their waists and ribs, Elise knew they were gangsters, but it wouldn't surprise her if they still had some sense of loyalty toward the Saint name because of their quiet business with her father.

"Layla has no idea I'm here. She did tell me you would be, though," Elise replied. She spoke loud enough for only Karine to hear her above the ruckus of the party around them.

Karine lifted an eyebrow. "Oh? And, pray tell, how did you manage to outsmart a reaper?"

"She thinks I'm with my father. He was deeply upset by the way things ended at the mayor's rally. He does not appreciate the way his name is plastered everywhere now that I'm wanted by the police. I knew he would need to be assured that things would be okay, and Layla, of course, knew I had to be the one to tell him that. He hates you, and he is soon to hate the mayor as well. It's been well-documented what my father does to reapers he hates," Elise said. She gave the older reaper a cruel smile, remembering just how powerful she had felt when facing Valeriya mere months ago.

Karine swallowed. Her scowl did not let up, but the nervous gleam in her eye and slight quiver of her lip betrayed her tough facade.

"It's okay to be nervous. I lived under the same roof as him for eighteen years and his temper never got easier to deal with." Elise pressed a finger to her lips and reached into her pocket to pull out the vial of venom left behind by the rogue reapers. "I won't lie to you, though. Neither Layla nor I have much experience with rogue reapers. They are, however, unconvinced by your motives. I have half a mind to tell them just how dangerous you are to other reapers and subsequently let my father punish you."

Karine's eyes narrowed on the vial and the signature bow that tied it together. "You're far too involved in a place where you do not need to be."

Elise tightened her grip on the bottle. "You have made your

wrath everyone's problem. I wouldn't be here if you hadn't dragged the ones I love into this," she hissed.

Karine nodded. She lowered her glass and pushed the young man away from her. Two red dots lined his throat, and Elise felt her own bite mark hum with pain as if in response to the sight of his. The older reaper smiled, noticing Layla's mark on her neck. "I can smell Layla on you. You must enjoy being a patron for her if you can stand being around her for this long."

Elise's lips twisted into a frown. "Don't change the subject."

"Ma chère, I think I'll do whatever I want. Your father has brought much ruin to this neighborhood and state," Karine said. Ice lined her words, and Elise had to fight to roll her eyes at the feigned concern.

"You just got here two months ago. How could you possibly care about Harlem more than me or anyone else who has been here their whole lives?" Elise hissed.

Karine shrugged. "Because I'm French, I cannot care about countries other than my own?"

Elise coughed out a dry laugh. "Not because you're French, but because you're an outsider whose only motivation to come here in the first place was because you needed something from us. You have invited nothing but violence into our streets."

"You wish for peace in Harlem, but you ignore reapers in your pursuit of it. We have been living in hell for longer than you have cared to believe. Reapers deserve liberation from your mortal surveillance at the very least," Karine said.

Elise's brows furrowed in concentration. "If I can guarantee you that, you owe me my sister back."

The reaper studied Elise's gaze carefully, watching for every minute reaction. "She's changed, you know. Would you even like the new person she's become?" Karine asked. The false tenderness in her voice made Elise want to scream.

"I just want her back. In one piece," Elise ground out.

Karine leaned forward so she could speak more quietly. "Get me the Harlem reaper clan and Josi is yours."

Elise's skin prickled at her proximity and the metallic scent of blood still coating her breath. "Do you not already have it?"

"Not with Julius heading the place. Take his life for me, and I'll return your sister's intact." Karine spoke slowly.

Discussing her sister made Elise's heart pinch with guilt. "Is she okay?" She almost couldn't get the question out, afraid of how Karine would answer.

The older reaper's confidence returned in an instant, her eyes lighting up at Elise's discomfort. "*Okay*? Depends on how you'd define that word. As a woman who has been a reaper for centuries and seen how powerful we can become, I would say she is more than okay. She is phenomenal. But that's neither here nor there. I have no control over her or what she does. She looks to me for solace because she has no one else."

Elise's heart fell. She swallowed past the emotions threatening to choke her and had to look away briefly to collect herself.

"Don't look so defeated. It shouldn't be too hard. You've killed a clan leader before, and she was an ancient reaper. Anything is possible when your hands are covered with blood," Karine murmured.

Chills ran down Elise's spine. She knew Karine saw her as an enemy despite being a temporary ally. That Elise would lick the blood of a reaper before cleaning her hands of it just to prove she was capable of such a slaughter. She thought of the blood on her throat from Layla's bite and wondered if Karine found her crazy for keeping it on display.

"That was not…" Elise caught Karine eyeing her bite mark once again.

"Not what? You have a fondness for blood, whether you care to admit it or not. I want to make sure, before I make an ally out of you, if you are willing to die and kill for the cause." Karine tapped her fingers against the glass, the wild lights from above illuminating the blood beneath her sharpened nails.

Elise looked away. Surveying the room, she found a familiar face. Mayor Arendale stood around a game table with what she could only assume were gangsters. One of the gangsters turned to meet her eye. She stood out among the rest, being a young woman, but by the way she commanded herself around them, Elise wondered if she called herself their leader. Could anyone do such a thing? Would there always be blood involved in claiming a title and making a declaration?

She faced Karine again and nodded. "I'll do it."

On her way out of the Renny, all Elise could think about was Layla and this new task she had agreed to carry out. If Layla had known what Elise was planning, she would've offered to do it for her. But Elise could not let her. Not when Julius already expected it of her and not when Layla already believed herself to be a monster. Going against her own clan would be disastrous. In this time, where Elise didn't know how long she had with Layla, she refused to subject her to the consequences of her own actions again.

"A friend of Layla Quinn's? I'm surprised you are still alive." A smooth voice with a heavy Italian accent called out to her from the end of the alleyway. Night had not yet fallen, but the sun was getting close to its final hour. With the threat of the monster rising after sunset, Elise knew better than to be out so late.

Still, she could not help but turn to face the person. "Who's asking?" she demanded.

A young woman, the same gang leader Elise had seen inside, stepped out of the shadows. She wore a suit rather than the kind of shift dress many young women in New York wore these days. Thick leather gloves covered her hands, which remained on her hips and most likely close to the weapons she carried. "I am, of course. You have no reason to fear me unless you find yourself tied indefinitely to Miss Quinn. If you see her tonight, please let her know that if she shows her face around Harlem reaper territory again, I will take her life. Do not let me run into her."

A chill passed through Elise as the woman disappeared back into the shadows. "Who the hell are you?" she shouted after her, but the gangster was gone already, leaving behind nothing but an eerie promise. The whole way back to Jamie's apartment, Elise's mind continued to reel from the message.

She found both Sterling and Jamie standing around the kitchen counter, talking strategy for trapping and killing the monsters. Jamie looked intently at the former Saint member while he spoke, his eyes wide and bright with awe. Sterling stopped talking the moment the door shut behind Elise. He faced her, the lingering passion of his conversation with Jamie displayed in the flush of his cheeks.

"How did it go?" he asked.

Elise set the vial on the counter. Hendricks padded right up to it and rolled onto his back, his paw coming up to swat at the ribbon tied around the bottle. She glanced around, searching for any signs of Layla. "Is Layla back?"

Jamie shook his head. "She's still out looking for Celie. Trying to convince her to stay in the lair for long enough to keep eyes on Julius." He nodded to the vial. "What did Karine say?"

Sighing, Elise sat down on the couch across from them. "She wants a favor in exchange for Josi's whereabouts."

"Sounds suspicious and dangerous. Especially for a human," Sterling said.

Elise stepped around the shiny part of the floor, where the blood from previous days had been cleaned up. "I play her game, I get what I want."

"Or you play the game, you die. Maybe you should ask Layla for help," Sterling said strongly.

Jamie shrugged. "She's survived a surprising number of reaper games for being a human…"

Elise slammed her hand onto the table, frustrated. "Layla can't help me. Some gangster just swore to kill her if she showed her face around Harlem reaper territory. Jamie, you wouldn't happen to know—"

"I don't know every gangster just because I myself am a gangster—"

"She's Italian and she hates Layla. That should narrow it down for you," Elise shot back.

Jamie squinted, his hand coming up to rub over his hair. "Are you sure she's not just a friend of Karine's? Adding more rules to the ancient reaper's wicked games?"

Elise shook her head. "Whatever it is, Layla cannot be around her old territory."

"That's probably for the best," Sterling said. He gestured to Elise's map, which had new notes since her evening out. "The old Harlem reaper lair seems to be where the monster heads to most often. If we can isolate it there, we can strike. No more failed traps necessary. We use the nest against it. Before it can hunt anyone else…" A muscle feathered in his jaw while he thought.

"But?" Elise urged him forward.

Sterling pressed his knuckles to the table and shared a dismayed look with Jamie. "We don't have the proper weaponry. Even with Jamie's explosives and Saint bullets, it's a tough bet. The thing seems to thrive in chaos, as evidenced by the attacks it emerges from. We need to find a way to control the environment and incapacitate it. If we can gain access to the Saint compounds that have been taken over by gangsters, maybe we'll have a shot at finding resources that can help us fight this thing."

Jamie nodded along with his words. A slight smile turned his lips upward, and he chuckled softly. "It's fascinating, watching a trained Saint's mind work. Have you ever thought of joining the army?"

Sterling narrowed his gaze on the gangster. "No. And honestly, I take offense to that question."

Another laugh left Jamie. He pointed at Sterling, his smile broadening. "That was a trick question. And you passed my test."

Rolling her eyes, Elise left the two men to their own devices at her map. She swiped the vial from the cat, who had been trying to swat it off the counter during their conversation. "You might be the least insufferable one here right now, Hen."

21

Layla dreamed of Elise again. Even when she woke up, she still felt her fingers, soft as ever, on her face, and her voice whispering a sweet goodbye into her ear. She wore an outfit that took to the night. Swathed in black garments, she looked more like one of Layla's clan mates than the elite Saint heiress Layla had known her entire life. Still, Elise was a picture of true beauty without even trying. She had pulled her curls back into a golden hair clip, though a few tendrils hung by her sharp cheekbones and stuck in the gentle shine of her plump lips. It was a large turnaround from her usual dreams of the Saint heiress, where blood drenched her dying body like a veil. For once, Layla could touch her without causing her demise and hold her without having to say goodbye. The dream elevated her mood more than she cared to admit; the months of sleeping with only nightmares had been so long, Layla had forgotten what it felt like to dream peacefully.

She was eager to join the commotion in the living room early that morning if it meant she got to see Elise alive and well in the flesh. But when Layla left her bedroom and found only Jamie and Sterling arguing over guns, all earlier contentment was chased away with a quickness.

"Where is Elise?" she demanded, cutting right through their heated tiff.

Jamie pulled back first, though he maintained his scowl at Sterling. "She left to…complete a task."

Layla's heart rate picked up. Already, her mind filled with all the terrible things that could have been happening to Elise in that moment. If last night's announcement on the radio about them all being wanted by the police was not enough to fear, then images of the beast that lurked beneath Harlem's streets, waiting for a glimpse of darkness to strike, popped into her head next. "Why did no one tell me she was leaving?"

Sterling shoved a gun into his chest holster, grumbling, "I wasn't aware you owned her."

Rage consumed her. Snarling, Layla lunged for him, her hands going around his throat. Without his Saint guns and his Saint bullets, he might as well have been just another man taking up space under this roof. Layla had nothing preventing her from shutting him up permanently now, even if it cost her all the work she had done over the past few months to keep herself calm. Right as her fingers closed around his throat, Jamie's arms plucked her from the air and hauled her back against his chest.

"Enough. Both of you. We're supposed to be working together. Now is not the time for petty fights," Jamie ordered.

Layla strained in his arms hard enough to make him pant with the effort of keeping her contained. Somehow he managed to maintain his hold on her, and he didn't let her go until she went still, silently promising her commitment to his word.

The former Saint member lifted a brow. "She's planning a blood mission, just so you know. If she's willing to die for you, you should know how to stop her. I have never seen such an unbalanced relationship otherwise. She deserves so much better than you."

Jamie ran his fingers through his hair, restyling the pieces that had been knocked free by Layla's struggle. "Are you serious? I just calmed her down and you're going to say that?" He turned a gentler look to Layla, who had begun to vibrate with anger. "She said goodbye to you this morning. So maybe if you really—"

She was out of the living room and back in her bedroom before he could even finish his sentence. Layla leaned over the bed, remembering just where she had seen Elise in her dream. She should have known her unconscious state had been too good to be true. It took all of three seconds for Layla to trace Elise's scent and then find Karine's mixed in with it. The older reaper's essence was faint, but it was there. And that was enough for Layla to tear out of the room with the intention of starting a hunt.

"How dare you not tell me she had seen Karine. You don't know how dangerous she is," Layla seethed as she shoved her feet into her boots and failed miserably at every attempt to curb the thoughts of

Elise walking into a reaper bloodbath just to prove herself to some mutinous ancient reaper who had been in their neighborhood for no longer than a few months. Layla gripped the edge of the kitchen counter so hard, her nails left divots in the granite. Her heart thudded in her chest at the image of Elise covered in her own blood and choking on death. She watched as Jamie and Sterling exchanged a look. The fact they held a knowledge of Elise that she was not privy to sent a sharp spike of jealousy through her spine. Whether it was the blood they shared between them or just Layla's twisted desires causing this charge of emotions, she didn't care. Her brows furrowed into a dangerous glare while her fangs emerged, digging into her lower lip until blood spilled over her chin in thin rivulets.

Jamie looked over Sterling's shoulder, and his eyes widened. "What the hell is wrong with you?"

Sterling frowned, stopping abruptly when he saw Layla. He relaxed, his shoulders lowering as he placed another gun on his belt. "It's a strange possessive reaction some reapers have after drinking from a human. Although usually it's the human who experiences the urge to lay claim over the reaper. I wouldn't be surprised if she tore through Harlem just to find Elise."

She would. Layla knew just how volatile human blood made her, and Elise's absence only increased her adrenaline. What she would give to be near the Saint heiress now—what she would *kill* to keep her around. "We can save a lot of lives if you just tell me where she is," Layla muttered. She licked the blood from her lips and waited.

Sterling offered her a soft gaze full of pity. "I will not betray her on this," he murmured. "For once you get to taste the sins of your own flesh."

Though Elise had been gone from the apartment for a while, Layla still suffered the overwhelming sense of her. Beyond just her scent and her essence, Layla felt like she could still feel Elise in her—as if the blood between them had become something more tangible than just spilled promises and acts of vengeance. Her heart throbbed the farther Elise went from her, and all her thoughts came back to the Saint, no matter how hard she tried to direct them elsewhere.

Even as Jamie passed her by, Layla grabbed his arm, roughly holding him in place. He grunted and gave her a bewildered look. "What the hell?"

Layla looked up at him with as much malice as possible, urging every ounce of glowing anger she had into her eyes. "If she has a single hair out of place when I find her, it's death for you." She shot her glare at Sterling. "You too."

Jamie pulled away from her the moment she released her grip. He brushed off his coat and rolled his eyes, blowing out hot air. "I'll be damned. And I'd rather die than have a Saint get hurt on my watch. I know my boundaries. Have a little faith in her, Layla. She might surprise you."

But with a Saint's blood still cycling through her system and an Elise-shaped hole in her sinking chest, Layla knew faith would not keep her calm. Her crushing desire would end in no less blood than the Saint's lone mission would. This hunt was Layla's and Layla's alone. Consequences be damned.

Layla had never been good at tracking those she did not care for. The act came easiest to her when there was a blood she desired to recognize and trace, but this time, she was going purely based on her own rage and urge to hunt and kill.

Karine knew many people and reapers in Harlem. It was no surprise to Layla when one of her blood patrons mentioned the various allies Karine had been through in an attempt to settle in Harlem. The absolute pride with which her patrons spoke of Karine with while reeking of her made Layla's stomach turn. Along with the slight sheen of their eyes and the dreamlike state they seemed to function in that told Layla Karine's venom still ran through their veins.

She followed the faint scent she had grown to associate with Karine through the apartment building her blood patron had mentioned just hours earlier at a blood house. The moment she stepped in front of the door that held the most of her essence, it swung open, revealing the older reaper inside a dimly lit sitting room.

"I've been expecting you, Layla." Karine gestured for her to come inside, and as soon as Layla crossed the threshold, she shut the door.

Layla didn't even take in the apartment and all its luxurious grandeur before she whirled on Karine. "What have you done to Elise?"

Karine raised her brows. "You figured it out. Your proximity to that Saint girl is impressive. You would recognize her and any part of her without a face, wouldn't you?"

Frustration locked Layla's jaw. She swallowed past the prickling urge to let her fangs snap out and tear into Karine's flesh. "Where is she?"

"You don't get to know." A cool curiosity darkened Karine's face. She made her way to the bar cart off to the side of the room and began pouring herself a cocktail made of clear liquid. Even with the strong scent of alcohol filling Layla's senses, she still sensed the familiarity of the blood traces around the apartment and on Karine. While a large part of her remained starved and yearned for the taste of fresh blood more than almost anything, an even larger part of her stood in an anger so steep, her hands trembled and a red haze crept slowly over her vision.

Karine continued as if she didn't notice Layla's seething state. She lifted her glass, before stopping halfway to her lips. "I'm also quite impressed by your Saint girl. She came right to me and made a deal almost instantly. She seems more willing to get her hands dirty."

Something inside Layla snapped. She lunged for her. The hunger ravaging her system made it impossible to control her anger, but Layla relished in it anyway. A blood fury was quickly taking over, and all she could do was let it happen. Layla threw herself into Karine so hard, the glass went flying out of her hand and shattered on the wall. The scent of liquor coated the room, but Layla's senses honed in on the blood dripping from a new wound in Karine's face. She dug her nails into the older reaper's shoulders and slammed her into the wall again. The force of her back hitting it sent cracks into the paint and the foundation. Blood spilled from the piercing of Layla's nails in Karine's shoulders. She lifted a hand to Karine's face, slapping it so hard, blood flew from her mouth. On the second strike, Karine caught her hand and wrenched it back until Layla felt the bone pop.

Layla shrieked as pain flooded her senses. Red still covered her eyes, but black dots seeped over the rage the more her hand flopped on her injured wrist. Blood filled her mouth, and it was then she realized that her fangs had sprung free and were digging into her lower lip. This time her own blood had no calming effects on her rage. Layla yanked Karine away from the wall and delivered a crushing blow to her knee, sending her to the floor. While the older reaper hissed in pain and struggled to rise again, Layla crouched over her, pressing her knee into her chest. She spat a mouthful of bloody saliva onto the floor and reached for the Saint blade in her belt with her uninjured hand.

Karine's glowing gaze flashed vicious and angry as Layla lifted the knife above her head, poised to strike. She grabbed the swollen mess of Layla's wrist, squeezing until she screamed.

Layla's vision went black with pain. Her body pitched to the side, and Karine hovered over her. It wasn't until the adrenaline subsided along with the worst of the pain that her vision blinked back to life. Glass crunched beneath her back, and Layla coughed, swallowing blood as she looked up at Karine.

A lifetime's worth of rage simmered in the ancient reaper's golden eyes. With her blood-tipped fangs bared and her mouth wide in a vicious hiss, Karine overpowered Layla on a bed of shattered glass. "You're too late, Layla. I told Julius your girl is the one who killed Sena. She's on her way right now to interrupt his business at the Renny under my request. Poor girl thinks she stands a chance against him."

Layla was too weak to fully take in Karine's words. The short revelation she had let slip had the power to spark a wildfire among her clan mates and get Elise killed.

He knows.

Julius knows Elise killed Valeriya.

The look in Karine's eyes told Layla there would be nothing less than hell to pay for her friend's murder.

22

THE HARLEM REAPER LAIR WELCOMED ELISE AND Celie with much less malice than Elise had been anticipating. Every other time Elise had visited in the previous weeks, threats had been doled out and blood had soaked every surface. She wondered how her visit would fare this time.

"How did they take to you wanting to come back?" Elise asked quietly.

The young reaper shrugged, her fangs worrying her lower lip. "Julius wasn't here when I came last night. The others seemed fine with it, but Julius…no one is allowed to have their own opinions when he's around." She stopped at the entrance of the cathedral, peering into the window. "I'm glad you feel like you can trust me enough to help you here…but maybe you shouldn't. I can't really even fight," she muttered.

Elise watched the shifting shadows of reapers beyond. "I only need to get inside," she barely managed to huff out before the door swung open.

A young reaper with brown skin and a charming smile met her on the other side. "A Saint…who is still alive despite my best efforts. To what do I owe this pleasure? Or trap?" A few reapers moved behind him, curiosity looming in their shadowed eyes. The cathedral continued to be lit by candlelight, the faint flickers and dated velvet furniture among tall painted ceilings maintaining its vintage appearance.

Celie gave the reaper a smile so bright, it might have been genuine. "It's nice to see you again, Julius. I brought—"

"I assume you got word about Elise Saint's value. She is the talk of the town now, not just in human circles, but also reaper." He gave her a tight smile, then turned to Elise. All feigned mirth fell away while his gaze roamed her stance, his eyes growing dark with resentment. "Unless you are here to turn yourself in for the crimes against my clan, I do not wish to see you. We will give you a head start to run, of course; the chase is part of the fun when hunting."

Elise lifted her chin. "I am here to turn myself over to you, Julius."

A sinister smile spread across Julius's face. "Living in a place as debauched as New York, I have learned things, Miss Saint. Reapers hiding in dance halls, waiting for drunk partygoers to stumble into the darkness so they can drain them dry, gangsters sliding bloodstained money to politicians so they look the other way, people drowning their worries in alcohol that hurts more than it feels good—I can spot a lie from a mile away." He paused in the foyer, his voice going hard. "There are still reapers going missing and succumbing to the effects of karma. And you are running around with a reaper who betrayed my clan. So I will give you one more chance, Miss Saint, to tell me the truth. Why are you here?"

Elise blinked. She knew if she hesitated for too long and let his words sink in, fear would become her enemy. So she scoffed a bit, smiling. "I am not here because of Layla if that is why you are concerned."

"My concern is you being a Saint. Miss *Saint*," Julius bit out. He shooed a few reapers from a nearby couch, then threw himself onto it, lounging against the gold cushions while he stared up at Elise.

"Please don't call me that," Elise quipped.

Celie sucked in a sharp breath while Julius lifted a brow. "Oh? Have you somehow divorced yourself from your family? Name included?"

Elise opened her mouth to respond, but Julius continued. "I do not appreciate your tone. Is it all Saints who are like this, or is it just a problem with the women? Your father, surprisingly, was very polite to me. Now, we've only met once, but for a man who is so hell-bent on eradicating my kind, he really knew how to turn on the charm for a half dead beast like me." Julius nodded slowly. "You could learn a few things from him, Elise. Perhaps it's not such a good idea for you to denounce your position as his heir."

Irritation grated on Elise's nerves so violently, her body felt as if it had gone aflame. She clenched her jaw with enough strength to cause pain, and when she spoke, there was nothing but venom in her voice. "You think you know my father better than me?"

Celie stepped forward, lifting her hands in surrender. "I believe we're getting sidetracked now. Why don't we just stick to our original plan?"

"No, I'd like to hear Miss Saint's choice words for me. She's come into my home and has shown me more disrespect than kindness." Julius stood up, clasping his hands before him as he stepped closer to Elise. "Once again, you are in my home. You are a mere guest in this lair, and should the reapers decide to make a blood meal out of you, I will allow it. Many of them have yet to recover from your family's relentless attacks." The older reaper stood so close to Elise now, she could see the white scars on his face and throat. Though faded with age, they appeared no less brutal, serving as proof of his survival abilities.

Other reapers cowered around the area. They stood far enough back to not interrupt Elise and Celie's conquest, but close enough for Elise to see their obvious distress. Some hid behind one another, whispering back and forth, while others began scurrying off to more distant parts of the cathedral.

The place ran on fear and pure apprehension. Julius had no authority besides moralized harm.

Elise understood why Karine wanted him dead.

She shifted on her feet, feeling the weight of the gun against her hip. Julius's threat still hung between them, and Elise felt more determined than ever to execute her plan. "I know the danger of reapers, Julius. Multiple members of my family have been killed by them. While I understand your reluctance to trust me, I implore you to consider the state of this neighborhood and what would happen if we continued to work against each other."

Julius's jaw hardened. "What are *you* insinuating?"

"Elise," Celie warned.

Elise ignored him. "A truce. Not on behalf of the Saints, but on behalf of the countless innocent people who have been caught in the crossfire of this never-ending war between reapers, Saints, and gangsters. I don't have any viable power anymore, but I can get you protection from the greater forces that threaten your kind. Maybe together we can stop the beast that's hunting all of us."

"Why would I trust a Saint?" Julius asked, unimpressed.

Elise crossed her arms. "Half your clan has been eradicated, Julius. You will not last much longer against the beast without our weapons."

A slow smile spread across Julius's face. "You bargain just like your father." He spread his hands by his sides, gesturing to the cathedral around them. "I would be happy to make a deal with you if you offer me one thing."

"What?" Elise asked.

Julius leaned in, his finger catching one of her stray curls and twisting it until it sprang back against her cheek. "A blood bond between you and me." *So I can track your every move and feeling.* He did not have to say the words for Elise to know why he wanted the bond.

Everything about this seemed like a bad idea, but all Elise had to do was get close enough before she could act on her plans. Gaining his trust was her best option. No matter how much her spine tingled with unease and her gut twisted with apprehension, Elise nodded anyway. "Okay."

Music pounded through Layla's bones, and for the first time in ages, she did not feel compelled to dance. Her narrow escape from Karine had only been possible due to promising the ancient reaper Elise's capture and containment. So her hunt continued.

She watched a young Black man lean against the outside wall of the Renny and lift a cigarette to his mouth. Smoke swirled around his face, drifting into the street to intermingle with the chaos of West 133rd Street. Swing Street—or Jungle Alley—as some called it, had become something of a spectacle over the past few years. Prohibition had gangsters opening speakeasies in and between the dozens of jazz clubs and cabarets lining the streets. Tassel and sequin dresses shimmered against the night as women, giggling and delightfully intoxicated, decided where to go next. Men tipped their hats at the passing groups, some trying to entice them to enter the clubs. Various forms of music exploded into the night air, creating a bright cacophony of sound.

Layla pressed farther into the alley wall by the Nest Club. Blood still coated her body, and the final stages of the healing process consumed her wrist. Harlem had grown dark enough that few rational, life-loving humans chanced roaming the streets, allowing her to walk around the quieter parts of town without being stopped for her disheveled state. The worst part of the journey was the excruciatingly slow pace at which her arm healed. It no longer throbbed, but it remained puffy and felt as if someone had stuffed cotton between her flesh and her bone.

The man she had been watching dropped his cigarette when a familiar face emerged from the nearby doors. One of Julius's companions. They were far enough away that Layla couldn't hear the words being exchanged between them, but she crept closer again, ready to intercept them if only to beat some answers out of them.

Before she could get near enough, a commotion sounded behind her in the back of the alley. Layla turned and saw the outline of a few people struggling near the other end, where another street intersected. The scent of blood wafted down the dark alley, though none of it was human. Still, Layla could sense the presence of humans around it, their essence a fresh and dominating sensation. With one last look at Julius's companion, who was in the process of readying this man for his feeding, Layla snuck back into the alleyway. The scuffle seemed to settle down as a body collapsed and two other people began dragging it away.

She stepped into the streetlight before they could escape, her eyes lighting up when she recognized the faces of two reapers surrounding a fallen rogue reaper. While Julius was nowhere to be seen, his right-hand men stood with a body between them and gangsters preparing a car for their transport. Blood leaked from the reaper's head and mouth, and judging from the rate at which it flowed, Layla guessed the damage had been inflicted by Saint weapons.

Sure enough, a couple of gangsters stepped forward with guns drawn and blades made of Saint steel ready at their hips.

Layla eyed her two clan mates, Roy and Sam, young Black men who had been members of her clan for even longer than she had been. "What are you doing?" she demanded. Fire lit her nerves at the sight of her clan mates taking part in illicit activities against their own kind.

"Julius's orders." Sam spoke first, stumbling over his words. "He said this would help the clan and make life better for reapers."

"Killing other reapers?" Layla demanded.

One of the gangsters waved his gun and nodded toward the alley. "I suggest you leave before you get too deeply involved in something you shouldn't know about." He had a heavy Italian accent. But what business did an Italian gang have with the Harlem reapers? Layla wondered. Either Julius had done a suspiciously great job at going behind her back, or she had done an awful job at paying attention to the activities of her own clan.

"No, Bruno, it's too late for pleasantries. She's already seen too much." A young woman dressed in black stepped into the middle of the altercation. Wind funneled through the alley, lifting the long black hair from her shoulders and exposing her tanned skin. Though she spoke with a rather gentle tone, her words contained a threat that matched the unsatisfied frown on her face. Still, Layla dwelled on the fact that these seemingly new and foreign gangsters had Saint weapons, even though the Saint empire was all but closed for business at the moment.

It was then, with a belated and slightly embarrassing realization, that Layla realized her connection with the Saints might have been her only salvation. She relaxed her shoulders and willed her expression to slip from hostile to neutral. "I'm a friend of the Saints. I see you're using their weapons. I could get you more or have them cut you off. Kill me and your ties to some of the most lethal weaponry on this side of the United States is gone," Layla said in a low voice.

The young woman considered her words, various unidentifiable emotions flashing in her eyes. "You are a reaper, proudly affiliated with a business that wishes for your death? I find that very hard to believe."

Layla thought of Elise again and how each second spent here was wasted in her search for the heiress. "I'm sure you find a lot of aspects of New York very hard to believe. How long have you been here?" she asked.

A sharp laugh left the young woman. "The worst part of New York is how you monsters murdered my brother and his men in cold blood. There's not a single sense of morality or control in these streets. Every neighborhood in the city runs red with blood, and yet you expect everyone to take you seriously. This place is a lost cause."

Though the criticisms of her home raised in Layla a violent anger, she knew she could not do anything brash before she got significant information from these gangsters. Julius would likely lie about his involvement and find some way to turn the rest of their clan against her. Layla refused to let this lead die. "Why not just find the reapers who killed your brother? Why punish all of us?" she demanded.

"Nicoletta." One of the gangsters gestured toward the other end of the street, where a few police cars had materialized, no doubt to survey the activity in Jungle Alley.

Nicoletta lowered her gun. "Would you not do the same if your Saint was threatened?"

Hot anger flared in Layla's stomach. "Where is she?" Her voice went hard, despite her efforts to keep calm.

The gangster ignored her question. "You wouldn't happen to be friendly with the reapers who murdered my brother would you?" Nicoletta eyed the Saint gun she held, turning it over in her hands while she spoke. The chamber clicked, and she held the gun up again, facing Layla once more. "You can tell me the truth about the Diamond Dealers, Layla."

The blood froze in Layla's body at the mention of her name. Just by Nicoletta's knowing smirk, Layla knew she already had an idea of what had happened with the Diamond Dealers. Layla had not been the one to incite the fight that had left most of the gang dead, nor had she inflicted most of the violence. That had been another reaper's doing. But Layla knew that would not matter to someone like Nicoletta, who took vengeance seriously enough to travel across the world to enact it.

"I have my secrets and you have yours. Do you want to see what happens if I spill the details of your operation to my clan mates? Or should we just never speak of this again?" Layla tilted her head to the side and watched the heated anger rise in Nicoletta's eyes.

The lead gangster took in a deep breath, her jaw clenching. "You are absolutely right. I'd prefer to shut your mouth so we can never speak of this again." Nicoletta raised her gun and squeezed the trigger.

Layla moved faster than her aim. Having anticipated her attack, Layla lunged for the gangsters beside Nicoletta, knocking them into her hard enough to jostle the gun from her hand. Nicoletta cursed and reached for her belt, but Layla was already hovering over her with a Saint blade in her own hand. She nodded as Nicoletta flashed her a nervous grin. "I like your fear. It tells me I'm doing something right. But if you'd only told me what your plan was here, we could have avoided all this."

Nicoletta's smile widened. "I prefer mutiny while avenging my family." Her eye flicked to something behind Layla, and the tell was all she needed to strike against the approaching gangster.

Layla sank the blade into his gut and reached for his hand, twisting it so hard that the bones and muscles popped. He dropped the gun, but Layla kept wrenching his arm until the skin split and the muscles pulled away from the bone. Blood sprayed across her face as she yanked his hand free. It pulsed in Layla's own grip for a moment before she shoved it into Nicoletta's gaping mouth. The gangster choked on the ruined flesh and blood, her eyes going wide as Layla bared her fangs at her.

"Does this mutiny taste good?" Layla seethed.

Nicoletta gurgled around the hand but still tried to fight back.

She reached for Layla, grabbing onto her shirt and her belt, but coming up empty.

Layla gripped her wrist and glared. "Touch me again and I'll take your hand too."

A gun cocked behind her. When Layla turned, she saw the unmaimed gangster aiming his weapon right at her heart. Her clan mates, Roy and Sam, had vanished, leaving the rogue reaper's body behind on the street.

"Get off her," the gangster demanded. His comrade writhed on the ground by his feet in a pool of blood fountaining from where his hand used to be.

Layla rose, with blood flowing down her chin and chest. She faced the gangster and spat a mouthful of blood and saliva onto the ground. Already the presence of human blood in her system had her thoughts spiraling into oblivion and her skin prickling with adrenaline. "You are making a fool's bargain. Look around." Layla gestured to the fallen bodies between them. Even the police vehicles still idled at a safe distance by the end of the street.

The gangster's gun arm shook. He pressed his fist beneath his elbow, trying to steady it, but the fear in his eyes was nearly palpable. Layla relished it now. She felt her heart rate quicken, and her gaze narrowed to the throb of blood in his jugular. Even now, while mostly full, Layla craved the destruction that would bring the sweet satisfaction of his blood. She almost wanted him to shoot. To give her a concrete reason to lunge and tear his throat open until a geyser of blood poured down her throat.

"Leave it," Nicoletta grumbled. She finally got to her feet, wiping at the blood on her face. Without her weapons and confident attitude, she seemed much smaller, though she still stood a few inches taller than Layla. "We'll take care of this later."

"You will not," Layla warned. She eyed the gangster still cradling the bloody stump of his arm. "I suggest you leave town. Reapers never forget the blood of their betrayers. My clan mates and the rogue reapers will go after you, and I won't stop them."

Nicoletta gave her a fierce glare. Even her human eyes, full of mortal ignorance, challenged the ravenous spirit threatening to break from Layla. "We do not run."

Layla shrugged. "Fine. I'll kill you next time." She bent to hoist the fallen rogue reaper over her shoulder, then picked the gangster's hand up. Blood smeared over the gang-affiliated tattoo on his knuckles, but it was visible enough. She watched as Nicoletta and her colleague entered the nearby car and sped off into the night. The reaper on Layla's shoulder groaned, but remained unconscious. The lair, Layla realized, would have a feast on tonight's finds.

She disappeared into the alleyway just as the police vehicles sped by, blood trailing in her wake.

In all her rage, Layla didn't stop to talk to anyone or gauge the scene before she stepped into the cathedral lair. Reapers scattered, though they remained interested at the sight of her carrying a bleeding rogue and a severed hand whose blood had yet to dry. She stopped only when she made it to the wall by the staircase where Elise stood with Celie and Julius.

The older reaper turned, his face falling first into shock, then shifting to confusion when he saw her. "Layla, I'm sure no one wants your mess in here. You can go back to treating your girl like a sack of blood—"

"Shut up." Layla dropped the rogue reaper onto the floor between them, tossing the hand onto his chest. The tattooed gang symbol was face up and visible to everyone who crowded around them. She frowned at Julius. "You're a goddamn traitor. Selling out your own kind to gangsters for God knows what unethical reasons. You should have never been allowed to call yourself the head of this clan. You're a danger to us all."

Gasps filled the room. Their clan mates whispered as they conferred among themselves. Some met the declaration with pure shock and apprehension, while others claimed to have had an idea of Julius's crooked tendencies. Disruption quickly spread through the cathedral, and Layla was glad for it. Whether they were on her side or not, she didn't care. So long as there was enough chaos to feed her urge for violence.

Even Celie shifted on her feet and crossed her arms, unsettled beyond words.

Layla expected Julius to defend himself. With lies or sympathetic truths—whatever he took on, it didn't matter. What she had not anticipated was his cool and collected attitude, his eyes roaming lazily until they got to Elise.

Julius's fingers fiddled by his sides while he watched her. "Do her animalistic tendencies not bother you?"

It wasn't until Layla's gaze settled on Elise that she realized the scent of her blood permeated the room. Several puncture wounds lined her throat, still leaking from their freshness. Layla's body stilled at the sight. If darkness could become an emotion, it would have then, covering her nerves until every part of her had been consumed by its depths. Layla tore her gaze from Elise and leveled an icy stare on Julius. She hardly registered Celie and other reapers moving away from them. Layla's attention latched onto the older reaper before her, a red rage covering her vision until all she could properly think about was tearing into Julius's chest.

Elise shrugged at Julius's words. "She does only what she needs to do. No part of her *bothers* me."

Julius chuckled. He touched his chin, the usual brown of his eyes lighting up with a gold sheen as he studied her. "And what about me? Did offering yourself to me not make you feel as if you were betraying her?"

Layla didn't have to look at Elise to sense her discomfort. A rush of blood heated her cheeks and flowed quickly around her chest as her heart rate increased. That alone was enough to make Layla take a threatening step toward Julius. She held herself back only to ensure that Elise did not panic over her advancements.

Julius remained unfazed, his eyes glowing as he nodded to Layla. "I get why you're so obsessed with her. Her blood is delectable." He lifted his fingers to his lips, where he sucked the remainder of Elise's blood from the tips. A slight look of disgust emerged on his face, but he hid it with a smirk.

At this, Layla allowed her fangs to emerge. She stepped in front of Elise and hissed, taking satisfaction in the tension that arose in Julius. "Touch her again and I'll kill you. I'll break every bone in your body and let everyone watch while I drain you." Already, she could sense Elise's toxic blood weakening his body.

The male reaper lifted a hand, but his movement was slow and his eyes glazed over. Time seemed to lag for a moment. Layla felt Elise's hand on her back, a small whisper beginning to emerge from her lips.

Julius gave Layla a cruel grin and said, "Try me."

All Layla could do was return his smile. Then she pounced.

Julius turned out to be much less agile and prepared than Layla had anticipated. She had Elise's tainted blood to thank for that. After dodging a strong swipe of his arm, Layla took him down, pinning him to the bottom of the staircase behind them. He strained against her foot in his chest, but even with him tearing at her leg, she still overpowered him. Layla started first with the hand that had touched Elise. Just the idea of his grimy fingers digging into her throat and spilling her blood made every rational thought vanish from Layla's mind.

Her rage had turned cold by now, no longer spurred by a passionate feeling for someone else. Instead, she longed for the isolating feeling that pure monstrosity bred in her. Reminders of her time under the influence of Stephen's poison infiltrated her thoughts, and she imagined herself in that position again, impossibly strong and willed only by ire. Julius might have been pleading with her, but all Layla could hear was the rush of blood in her ears as she positioned his arm on the edge of one stair, then slammed her foot onto the bone. It gave way like a stick snapping in half. The feeling of his body crumpling beneath her coupled with his tormented screams only encouraged her. Layla bit back a bitter smile as she dug the heel of her boot into his other hand. Bones shattered under her pressure until his hand felt like a mass of swollen flesh beneath her. By now, Layla was certain he was panicking and begging for her mercy. To her benefit and his demise, her anger blocked him out easily as she grabbed him by his hair and dragged him to the top of the staircase. The carpet grew soaked with his blood from each one of her steps and his futile struggles. Below them, reapers watched, turning the landing she'd stopped on into a stage of frightening violence.

Layla could have stared into Julius's eyes as she ended his life and given him one final glance into her own version of humanity. But he didn't deserve a familiar face, even if it was worn by the devil. In that moment, Layla focused only on the rush of her own adrenaline and blood. She gripped his jaw and the back of his head, then pulled. It was as if all that held Julius together was treachery and lies. His skin tore into fleshy ribbons as his head came free from his shoulders. Blood and muscles spilled out of the gaping holes, his spine following after his head.

Covered in blood, Layla approached the edge of the stairs and lifted Julius's head above the crowd below. "From now on, you all answer to me. If anyone crosses me, you're fucking next," Layla snapped. She tossed the head down the steps, watching it thump along the velvet and leave crimson spots behind.

Despite all the bloodshed and self-indulgent violence, Layla still could not calm down. Her body shook with the aftermath of the adrenaline spike, and the traitorous blood covering her body only made her crave a sweeter taste. She almost didn't care what her clan mates thought of her show of dominance. Whether they accepted her as clan leader would only matter if she failed to settle the tensions ruining Harlem. Layla caught their expectant gazes switching from her to Elise.

The Saint heiress had not budged during the entire altercation, and now the reapers waited, watching for Layla's next move. Elise's own watchful expression was unwavering as the reaper descended the stairs and reached for her. Layla moved Elise through the silently deliberating crowd and out of the cathedral. They walked over Julius's leftover blood like it was nothing more than a wine stain on the carpet. Once outside in the fresh air, free from all blood besides the mess that covered them, Layla pulled Elise in to face her, examining her in the fading sunlight. She didn't realize how frantic she must have appeared until Elise grabbed her shaking hands and smiled softly.

"I'm okay," she whispered. "He didn't bite me."

A sigh of relief left Layla. Her body finally began to settle, tension and rage leaving her system with a cool sensation that made her want to move closer to Elise's warmth. This time, seeing the wounds along her neck made Layla's throat tighten with guilt. She should have been there, making sure Elise was safe.

Layla was so lost in the scent and feeling of Elise, she almost didn't notice the arrival of a new being. She pulled back the moment she recognized the essence. Elise startled a bit as Layla stepped in front of her again, this time keeping a firm grip on her waist.

Celie regarded Layla with pity. The corners of her lips turned down and pressed into a flat line. "The rest of them won't like that you're with her."

Layla wiped the smeared blood from her mouth and frowned at the young reaper. "They won't know. Because you will not tell them. Not until we have a proper plan," she said.

Celie nodded slowly. "If you cannot win them over, they will join the rogues, and they're close to siding with Karine. It's already not good having a mortal grow attached to your immortal soul. But now is the worst time. A reaper leader with a human lover. They will never fully trust you."

Layla's hand tightened on Elise. "Let me worry about that."

"I only want the best for us all." The smaller reaper sighed as she turned back to the cathedral entrance. Though the words were mostly harmless, Layla heard what she really meant. The unspoken roared just as loudly as the claims that had been spoken aloud. *You cannot run from your fate, Layla. A Saint and a reaper will never last...*

Elise touched Layla's chin, forcing her to look away from her injuries and into her eyes. "I know what you're thinking, and none of this is your responsibility. I chose to come here against your advice and wishes. I never would have been able to kill Julius on my own, but I owed it to myself and to Josi to do something. Even if that meant luring you here to get the job done. I cannot feel like I serve no purpose, especially when it comes to taking care of the ones I love. At the end of the day…" She sighed, and her throat bobbed with the effort of holding back her emotions. "I'm the reason we're in this mess."

"Karine knows you killed Valeriya. I think she sent you here to die. So as far as anyone is concerned, you're my prisoner now," Layla said. She could have told Elise that none of this was entirely her fault. That there were greater systems at play neither of them could even dream of defeating. But for now, all she wanted to do was drink in Elise's presence and the fact she was still standing despite facing an older reaper.

"Better yours than anyone else's." Elise's gaze dipped to the blood soaking Layla's shirt front and painting her face. "Do you feel better now?" She smiled, her teeth digging into her lower lip.

Heat spread between Layla's ribs as she noticed the intrigued tone in Elise's words. Still, she worried whether she had done too much—*been* too much. Her eyes darkened. "I had to do it," Layla muttered.

Then Elise did something Layla never would have expected: she dropped a hand onto Layla's chest and trailed her fingers through the blood. "I know. It was quite the show."

Layla let out a shaky laugh. Between coming down from her

exhilarated state and Elise watching her with eyes of lust so intense, Layla felt like they could have commanded her to do anything, she wasn't sure how she was still standing. *I would do anything for you.* She did not say the words out loud, for fear of being looked at like the monster she had just become.

Elise's smile widened anyway. "I love you even more like this."

Her lips were on Layla's a second later. Though shocked at first, Layla reacted quickly and returned the kiss, her hands coming up to grip Elise's waist. Already, Elise had parted her lips and cupped the back of Layla's head to deepen the kiss. If there was anything that might have been better than Elise's blood, it was her lips.

Kissing her was akin to what Layla thought being close to God would be like. Her entire body felt light while simultaneously grounded by Elise's touch. Being close to her like this matched every dream Layla had had of her in recent days. But even with them kissing like they wanted to consume each other, with Layla's core heating and her body vibrating with anticipation, it still wasn't enough. She wanted to press into Elise until they were one entity, a Saint and a reaper rolled into one sinful act. Layla might have allowed it to happen.

"We should stop," Elise gasped, her breath hot inside Layla's mouth. "They'll sense me on you, and they'll hate you for having me."

There were almost no better words to encourage Layla. In this moment, she did not give a damn about anything besides the girl in front of her. "Tell me to stop then," Layla murmured.

Another sigh of pleasure left Elise as Layla put more intensity behind her kiss. "No."

It was word enough for Layla. She walked Elise back until she was against a wall, the blood on her smearing between them while they continued to kiss. The cathedral watched them with its dark windows and cross-laden steeples casting shadows upon them, judging them as the saint and the damned they were. Layla was certain there was nothing more sacred than having Elise Saint in her arms, whispering her name like a prayer between their fevered kisses. If it was sacrilege, then Layla welcomed it. She pulled back just enough to peer into Elise's eyes. Her own had gone black with ravenous desire. "Lise…I need you."

Elise gave her a knowing smile, but she shook her head. "You just want my blood." Startling realization filled her eyes, and her face paled.

Layla touched her wrist, concerned. "What is it?"

"I just realized something. That reaper at the blood house all those weeks ago—he said he paid for a Saint, but he wasn't expecting me. He was expecting a different Saint."

23

"ARE YOU SURE YOU DON'T WANT ME TO HELP YOU with those?" Layla gestured to her throat. She had come out of the bathroom with wet hair and fresh clothes moments ago. Elise still sat at the kitchen counter, staring into space while she considered her options after the incident at the lair. She was glad to have something else to focus on when Layla approached her.

"I'm okay. I don't want to be responsible for your starvation again," Elise said with a slight smile.

Layla watched her intently. "You know my starvation is always worth it when it comes to you."

Elise stood from the chair and made her way to the couch. She tried to ignore the blossoming heat in her cheeks and throughout her body at the undertones of Layla's words. At this point, there was no part of her that did not want Layla. But Elise wondered if Celie had been right—that there was no use in sharing their lives when one of them was destined to outlive the other by an eternity. In the grand scheme of things, Elise would be a mere moment in Layla's impossibly long life. That had never been what Elise wanted—with Layla or anyone. Love to her had always been beyond just a grand gesture or a moment of bliss. It was a promise that refused to be broken against tumultuous times and lasted long enough to tell future generations what true romance was. It was akin to a myth, where belief belonged to those who were so consumed by their passion, they might as well have been made of it. While Elise had never been so close to anyone, she could not be certain that reaperhood would not change things.

Layla had always alluded to the idea that her reaperhood made her unable to love—or at least struggle to do so fully. If Elise's humanity would be a problem, she did not want to be in the way of Layla's happily ever after.

"Elise—"

"I'm okay," Elise said quickly, trying to shove the spiraling thoughts from her head. She always forgot how sensitive Layla was to her ever-changing emotions. Even more so now, the reaper seemed to pick up on her with increased precision. "I'm just thinking of my sister. If we don't find her soon…I'm not sure we'll ever be able to help her." Elise settled on the couch and pulled her knees up to her chest. She had not even arranged the sofa into a bed. More desperately than not, Elise hoped seeing her preparing for bed would help Layla take the hint and leave. Part of Elise wanted Layla to convince her to stay with her. Why not be like the thousands of Harlem residents who prowled the night like starved beasts in search of sinful pleasures? Why not allow herself to succumb to the darkest desires at work in her soul, which would not only lead to her inevitable demise but provide endless satisfaction in the moment? Though her last name had not changed, Elise had long since been unable to call herself a Saint. Looking at Layla only made her realize that more.

Layla stepped closer, and Elise's heart jumped at her sudden proximity. Layla tilted her head to the side, a small smile playing on her lips while she watched Elise. "We will find her, and we'll find Dr. Gray too, and everything will be okay. Tomorrow we confront the gangsters stealing your father's weapons to ensure we do not have another failed attempt to save your sister."

Elise wanted to ask her why she had so much personal investment in finding Josi, but she trusted that Layla cared because *Elise* cared. Josi was important to her and must have been important to Layla to some degree if she truly cared for Elise. That was enough for her.

"What are you doing out here anyway?" Layla asked.

Elise shrugged. She could barely bring herself to look at Layla, for fear of igniting in herself a naked want she would not be able to control. "Going to bed."

"On the couch?" Layla asked, lifting a brow.

The sigh that Elise let out had more feigned frustration in it than she meant to display "Thank you, truly, for noticing that I've been relegated to the couch for the past couple of nights since you returned and Sterling joined us. No one has even asked how my back is from sleeping on such a rickety thing. No one has even asked if I was comfortable—"

"You surprisingly have not complained about it." Layla crossed her arms and tapped a finger along the back of her wrist. "Sterling has no problem sharing a room with Jamie. You could have asked to sleep with me."

Elise almost choked. "You only *just* started talking to me properly!"

Layla pursed her lips. "You could have found some way to tempt me."

"Unbelievable," Elise huffed. "I hope you know I have a bad back now because of you and Jamie."

"You're eighteen. It can't possibly be that bad." Layla almost laughed.

Elise glowered at her and touched her lower back as if in defense. "I'm almost nineteen. And trust me, it is quite bad."

Layla moved even closer. Her knees were dangerously close to touching the couch and, by extension, Elise's legs. Layla lowered her arms and leaned against the edge of the cushion. "Would you like a massage?"

"No." Elise barely got the word out past her constricting throat. It was silly just how strongly she was reacting to Layla's presence. Despite having lived in the city of love for several years and met other incredible people, her heart's yearning somehow always came back to Layla. Most days now it went beyond yearning. That part of her was still difficult to admit to herself. Though Layla showed her desires plainly on her face and in every way she allowed them to touch, Elise still found caution in their interactions, if only because of what the world had to say about reapers and humans being together.

"No?" Layla feigned hurt. She pouted and opened her hands before herself. "I've been told I have very skilled hands."

"I'm sure you do." Elise's face flushed with heat. She didn't have to look at Layla to know she smirked after having sensed the rush of blood in her reaction.

Finally, Layla seemed to understand her hesitation, and she backed away toward her room, sighing. "I hope you don't break your back tonight…"

"Like you wouldn't love to hear me scream," Elise called after her.

A stunned laugh was all she heard in response.

Screams of pure terror tore Elise from her sleep. She sat up immediately, blinking against the dark while trying to place the whimpers nearby. The moment the sleep-riddled fog cleared her mind and she realized what was going on, Elise rushed down the hallway and into Layla's room.

The reaper sat with disheveled hair, her chest heaving as she caught her breath. Elise had never seen her so undone. Even her sleep shirt was a mess, with the hem torn and wet marks from what Elise could only assume were tears. They still streaked her cheeks now, glittering rivulets along her brown skin in the pale moonlight.

Elise shut the door behind her but remained by it. "Nightmares?" she asked.

Layla's hand shook as she ran her fingers through her hair, pulling some curls out of her eyes. Nodding, she wiped the wetness from her cheeks. "My nightly routine," Layla muttered.

Elise's fingers clenched the end of her nightgown. Every part of her wanted to rush forward and comfort Layla. She had never been the affectionate type, even when they were little. Layla had always been the one to comfort her, not vice versa. Elise remembered trying to on multiple occasions. Whether it had been after a particularly brutal rehearsal that Layla could not stop beating herself up over or a tense conversation with her parents, Layla had always turned away from Elise's affections. For so long, Elise wanted to understand why and make herself easier for Layla to accept, but eventually it just became normal. Layla welcomed her affection in other ways, and Elise tried not to put too much pressure on herself to be enough. But when it came to Layla, it wasn't just about being enough. She wanted to be everything for her.

"You know your screaming sounds like someone is trying to murder you, so I just had to check," Elise said.

Layla leaned back on her hands and looked up at her. "The fear really brings out the beast in me."

Elise nodded, holding back a smile. "I'll let you get back to sleep." She started turning for the door, but Layla's voice stopped her.

"Elise. Please stay."

If words could be adrenaline, these would be it. Elise felt her heart skip, and heat flooded her chest as she faced Layla again.

Layla moved over on the bed and pulled the blankets back, making room for Elise. It was far from the first time they had shared a bed, but the formal invitation made Elise buzz with anticipation. She climbed under the covers beside Layla and propped herself up on her elbow to watch her. Every part of Layla intrigued Elise. From the honey-gold curls mixing with the brown ones, to the sharp line of her jaw and the slope of her collarbones leading down to her breasts. Just hours ago there had been blood soaking her chest and face. While Layla was clean now, all blood scrubbed from her body, Elise remembered how she had looked at her, made of devotion while covered in blood.

"Do you want to talk about it?" she murmured.

Layla settled onto her side, leaning so close that their faces were mere inches apart. "I'd rather have a distraction."

"I think I know just the one." Elise's eyes dropped to her lips. The moment she saw them curving into a knowing smile, Elise kissed her. Layla was hesitant at first, her lips soft and slow on Elise's. But as Elise started to move away, worried, she was pulled back in. Layla's hand curved over the back of her head, deepening the kiss. The moment her tongue swept into Elise's mouth, Elise groaned. She dropped her hand to Layla's waist and felt bare skin. The shirt had ridden up in their frenzy. Elise smoothed her hand over Layla's waist, feeling the soft warmth of her. She drew her fingers upward and tensed as Layla shuddered.

"Is this okay?" Elise asked, breathless from their kiss.

"Yes." Layla nodded. Her eyes traveled over Elise's body, slowing where the hem of her nightgown had ridden up on her thighs. The dazed look in her eyes turned ravenous at once. "Lise…if we keep going, I'm not going to want to stop."

Elise laughed softly. "I don't want to stop."

"Good." Layla could barely get the word out before they were kissing again. This time Elise's hands strayed to other parts of her. One curved over her waist, while the other cupped her jaw. Layla kissed her harder, and Elise moaned into her mouth. Heat built up in her core as Layla moved her hand down to her thigh. Her fingers slipped beneath the hem of her nightgown, stroking up the tender skin on her inner thigh. Elise arched against the pillows, fisting Layla's shirt. Layla dropped several kisses along her throat while it was still bared to her. She kissed the pulse points in her neck, seemingly savoring the proximity to Elise's most precious arsenal.

Elise dragged a hand down her spine and exhaled. "You've done this before."

Layla paused in her kisses so she could look at Elise. "Does that bother you?" she asked.

"Not at all. I just noticed…you know what you're doing," Elise said, smiling.

A breathy laugh escaped Layla. "So do you." Her eyes glowed. "Can I touch you?"

Elise nodded. "Please." Tension knotted her core, and her lips parted as Layla slipped her hand between her thighs. Her thoughts vanished into a haze of immediate pleasure. Elise's spine curved, her head pressing into the pillows as Layla continued her precise movements.

Layla kissed her throat. Her fangs emerged to scrape against the heated skin, drawing a burning pleasure from Elise.

"Does that feel good?" Layla asked. Her lips closed over the soft skin just above Elise's chest.

Elise let out a breathy moan. "*Yes*. Keep going." With her stomach tightening and her chest heating, Elise tried to keep a steady hand on Layla's cheek. But every stroke of Layla's fingers had her self-control withering away bit by bit.

"You're so beautiful," Layla murmured. She kissed her again, swallowing every sound Elise made for her. "I missed you so much, Elise."

Just as she was picking up the pace, the door to the bedroom flew open. Layla pulled the blanket over a gasping Elise, and they both looked over to see Jamie standing in the doorway.

"Sterling has another brilliant idea—" He froze, eyeing their close positioning. "What are you two doing?"

"Nothing." Layla pulled away from Elise, glaring at the gangster.

Heat flushed Elise's cheeks, and despite the blanket covering her completely, she still crossed her legs, the pressure between her thighs a persistent and distracting variable.

Jamie frowned at them. "Do you think I'm stupid?"

"Yes," Layla said. At the same time, Elise shook her head and said, "No."

Silence stilled the room, neither girl moving nor breathing while Jamie stared down at them. Eventually, he shook his head, sighing, as he left the room. "You get blood on my sheets, you're out. Both of you."

The second he shut the door behind him, Elise covered her face with her hands. "How embarrassing," she groaned.

Layla only laughed. "He's seen much worse." Her smile fell away as realization crossed her expression. "Maybe you should go back to bed."

Elise blinked. "What? Why?" She touched Layla's arm before the reaper could withdraw again. "Is it your nightmares?"

"Worse," Layla whispered. "I'm afraid I'll hurt you. Sometimes when I wake up, I struggle to remember…but there's so much blood. I'm not safe to be around."

Elise sat up. The blanket fell back, revealing the sloping front of her nightgown while the straps hung down her shoulders. "I'm not afraid of you, Layla. If anything, you make me feel safe," she insisted.

Layla's face went slack with shock. Her hand settled on Elise's leg, and she nodded slowly, though her eyes remained dazed. "Really?"

"Layla. You are not a monster. I'm sorry for saying you were that day—I didn't mean it." Elise shuddered. A gentle smile lifted her lips, her hand coming up to tuck a strand of hair behind Layla's ear. "We can just sleep. If you have a nightmare, I'll be right here. Squeeze me if you need to. One day I *will* get to taste you like you always taste me."

Layla lifted a hand to stroke the side of Elise's face. She grinned as Elise kissed her palm and leaned into her touch. "One day."

24

WATER SPILLED OVER LAYLA'S SHAKING HANDS, and images of Elise's face, struck with horror, filled her mind. The hot water turned into blood, leaking across her body while she tried to hold Elise's limp body up. Her efforts were in vain, no matter how hard she tried. No reaper strength, reaper blood, no will could keep Elise's mortal life earthside for long enough. As her heart failed and every living essence faded from her body, Layla could only scream.

"Layla?" Elise's voice brought Layla back now, her mind returning to the hot water splashing over her hands in the kitchen sink and drowning the blood from beneath her nails.

She looked up to see Elise staring at her over the counter with concern furrowing her brows. "Did you sleep at all last night?"

Layla turned the water off and wiped her hands on a nearby towel. "Hardly."

Elise swallowed hard. "You were saying my name last night in your sleep and scratching yourself to death."

"Nightmare," Layla answered quickly. Though the scratching explained the blood under her nails night after night.

Elise's lips parted. All her concern was chased away by true shock. "Hell, I'm so evil, I'm in your nightmares?"

Layla gripped the edge of the sink so hard, her fingernails split and the steel dented beneath her force. "No, Lise." She paused before saying the next part out loud, as if her voice could give the words life. "I watch you die. Every time I try to save you, and every time I'm too late."

Silence seeped between them. The moment stretched on for so long, Layla wondered whether she should have kept her wretched imagination to herself. It wasn't that she wanted to see these things. Her mind had always been good at making her afraid of herself and everything she was capable of. Things had only worsened once she became afflicted with her reaperhood. Dreams quickly turned to nightmares, and in the five years that she had been turned, Layla had yet to figure out how to convert the darkness to anything somewhat light.

Finally, Elise moved, her fingers coming up to touch her lips. They tapped them once, twice, then continued until she reached a repetition of seven. It happened so quickly and with such nonchalance, Layla wondered if Elise even noticed herself doing it. The sight hurt Layla's heart nearly as much as the dismay in her eyes. She should have kept her thoughts to herself.

Layla looked away, sealing her statement with a definitive claim that could not have been interpreted in any way other than how it was said. "That's why it's hard for me to look at you. I hate seeing you dead."

More silence followed her words, but before Elise could respond, Jamie entered the kitchen area. He appeared to be ready for the day, with his coat thrown on over a suit and two guns resting along his hips. Elise still had her robe on over her nightgown, and Layla stood in her long shirt and shorts despite the morning being half over already.

Jamie splayed a hand on the counter between them, forcing their attention onto him. "As I tried to say last night, Sterling has an idea."

Layla glanced around the room for the man of the hour. "Well, where is he?"

The gangster paused, sucking in his cheeks. "Hendricks is sleeping on him, so he is not permitted to move from the bed right now, but I can fill you in."

"Diabolical." Elise tried to roll her eyes, but she leaned against the counter and yawned instead.

Jamie clenched his jaw, shaking his head. "Late morning and you're both still unreasonably exhausted. Serves you right for being awake until four o'clock in the morning. Had I known you were going to be up so late, I would have just called a meeting to go over today's plans."

Layla felt the heat of Elise's blush. She scoffed, ignoring Jamie's vexing statement. "Something else happened last night that I think you should know about."

Jamie paused, then shoved his guns away. "What is it?"

Elise leaned in closer as well, her interest piqued.

"I ran into a friend of the Diamond Dealers. She did try to kill me, but I think I scared her away for now," Layla said.

Sucking in a sharp breath, Jamie rocked back on his heels.

Elise blinked in confusion. "Why would the Diamond Dealers—or anyone related to them—want you dead? What do you have to do with them? I thought they were gone."

Layla shook her head. "I thought so too. The woman who threatened me—she's the sister of the Diamond Dealers' late leader. She wants my blood for killing him. Even though I did not kill him. Your gang policies surrounding blood for blood are starting to get out of hand."

Elise looked bewildered. "*Starting* to?"

Jamie dismissed her distress and turned to Layla. His jaw dropped as realization lit his eyes. "The Italian lady. I *have* met her. She's the one who said her name was Roma. Sold all my remaining booze from the Cotton Club to her. I didn't know she was still around. She made it seem like she was only here for quick business to take back to Italy."

Layla narrowed her eyes. "She told you all this? Doesn't that negate the purpose of an alias?"

"No, I had my men do some research on her. She leads the Diamantes. We still don't know exactly what she's doing here. It seems like she's establishing her territory," Jamie said.

"I know she's involved in the disappearances of reapers lately." Layla's gaze flicked to Elise, who now had a contemplative look on her face. "She and her men also had Saint weaponry, so it's either they're working with Tobias somehow, or they've lifted a bunch of his guns from the training compounds."

"That's exactly what I've been saying," Sterling said. He emerged from Jamie's bedroom with the cat under one arm. The feline was limp with a calmness that Layla had never seen in him. It being the most annoying Saint of all people to get Hendricks to relax made her want to curse. Sterling set the cat down and joined the rest of them around the kitchen counter. "I can arrest them for heading an illegal operation and trespassing. We should be in and out of the compound in minutes. As for Josi…" He sighed, and his expression softened as he faced Elise. "I don't think we need that much of a plan. If your sister misses you…she'll come to you."

"We tried baiting her before, and it didn't work," Elise said.

"What if we make her feel like she's summoning you?" Sterling asked.

"How?"

Layla thought back on every recent memory she had of Elise and her sister. She paused on one in particular that had made her feel things she had not felt since becoming a reaper. "I have an idea. But you're not going to like it."

Elise had never felt more like a fraud in her life. Sitting at the piano in front of an eager afternoon crowd at the Nest Club had her more nervous than she'd ever imagined a performance could make her. It had been ages since she last properly played—she found herself missing it less and less as time went on, but now her confidence in her ability to put on a decent performance had never been lower.

Layla caught her eye nearby. The reaper stood at the front of the crowd and had a small smile on her face. *Just focus on me.* Those four words from earlier stuck with Elise as she lifted her hands onto the keys.

There were a select few songs Elise had committed to memory. Two of which she had only played for special occasions. She chose one of those songs today. Part of her felt like a fraudulent pianist—picking a song no one knew so they could not call her out when she made a mistake. But at the end of the day, all that mattered was that Josi knew the song. Elise desperately hoped her sister had committed her symphony to memory just as she had. Otherwise, this performance would serve no greater purpose.

Even Elise could not convince herself of that.

She cleared her throat and bowed her head as she spoke, "This song is dedicated to my little sister."

The moment her fingers hit the keys and she began to play, she felt at home. Commanding the room with just her fingers dancing across the ivory instrument, Elise found more control than she had experienced in ages. She did not need to watch the crowd to know they went silent, their eyes alight with awe and wonder. Music fanned out around her as she produced the opening notes with a sense of shyness that clung to a childlike innocence. The song started out in a joyful tone, inspired by the memories Elise had made with Josi as a young girl. Eventually, her fingers stretched across the keys to reach a higher crescendo. The ascending scale took her through all the years she imagined for her younger sister. Invigorating highs and unexpected, but calm, lows that came along with growing and changing. With each note, Elise laid out a story only she knew. One she had clung to for years, hoping and praying she would never have to turn to music to feel her younger sister's presence instead of Josi herself. Elise had been forced to imagine Josi trying on her first pair of pointe shoes and taking the stage for the first time as a solo performer while she had been hidden away in France. She had missed out on so much of her baby sister's life. Now she spent more time grieving that than she did reminiscing about the memories they did have. The only comfort came in believing that another life had them together the whole time. No forceful separation to make them imagine what growing up with a sister would have been like.

Elise still remembered the day her parents had brought Josi home from the hospital, a tiny warm bundle of flushed skin and silken hair. Elise had fallen in love immediately. While holding her, Tobias had placed a gentle kiss on her brow and insisted, *You must take care of her.*

To Elise that had only meant one thing: *You cannot let anything happen to her.*

The responsibility had only compounded over the years, the longer Elise spent time away from her. Tears spilled down her cheeks now, hot and unforgiving as she closed out the song. Despite having played for the past couple of minutes, Elise could hardly recall the quality of her performance. All she saw was Josi's face when she closed her eyes and as the stage lights flashed in her eyes. The crowd erupted into applause, but Elise only heard her sister tearfully begging her not to leave her alone.

I don't want to be alone.

When it had come down to Elise to make a choice, she had left her sister alone. The one promise she had made to Josi, she had failed to keep.

Elise skipped the bow and moved right off the stage without thanking her audience. Her teachers back in France would have been appalled by such an exit, but life had a funny way of making things that used to be her whole world inconsequential and minute.

She bumped into a man passing her by. As Elise opened her mouth to apologize, several bottles fell from the box weighing him down. He cursed and gathered them, grumbling at the cracks that had formed in a few of the bottles Elise noticed a diamond tattoo on the side of his neck, and she called after him, "*Hey*. Where did you get those?"

The man ignored her and continued on his way out of the club. Elise hurried after him, vaguely aware of Layla catching up to her. "Elise—"

"Karma," Elise gasped.

The reaper's grip loosened on Elise's arm as she spotted the gangster with the vials. She stopped at the door and nodded to the space outside, where Sterling already stood, gun cocked and aimed at the fleeing man. Before he could shoot, the gangster hopped into a readied vehicle and sped away.

The roar of another vehicle started up as it approached. Elise glanced over and almost let out a joyful laugh. Jamie sat behind the wheel, his arm beckoning for the three of them to get in. They wasted no time in pulling themselves inside, and the gangster slammed his foot on the accelerator, veering them down the street after the other men.

"I told you—always be ready with a getaway car," Jamie called over the rush of wind.

Sterling gritted his teeth against a particularly sharp turn around a street corner. "What exactly is the plan now?"

"WE FOLLOW THEM," Jamie shouted. "I CAN'T HEAR YOU TOO WELL UP HERE."

Layla rolled her eyes, and Elise felt something bump against her foot as the car rolled over a pothole. Looking down, she found bullets scattered across the car floor. A few guns were even tucked beneath the seat she sat on. Elise pursed her lips and glanced at Layla, who was watching the two men bicker back and forth in the front seat.

"I have the feeling he's always wanted to do this."

"DO WHAT?" Jamie bellowed.

"A car chase!" Elise shouted back.

Sterling groaned. "We are not in a car chase!"

"IF I'M SPEEDING AFTER ONE CAR, WHAT WOULD YOU CALL IT THEN? SMART ASS—"

A round of bullets exploded through the roof of the car. Layla ducked, instinctively pulling Elise down with her. The loose bullets on the floor rolled beneath Elise, and she took up a handful of them, then grabbed one of the guns lodged between the seats. A quick look outside showed her another gang's car gaining on them from behind. She turned to Layla as she loaded the gun and gestured to the window. "Hold me."

"*What?*" Layla nearly shrieked.

"Hold me so I don't fall." Elise barely gave her time to process her words. She hauled herself off the floor and dragged her body through the open window. Layla's arms clamped down on her waist so she didn't topple over the edge, and Elise used that leverage to balance against the wind current and jarring turns Jamie took. The gangsters behind the wheel in the following car shouted in alarm. Their eyes widened, and a few tried to aim for her, but by then Elise was already pulling the trigger. Her single shot hit the front left wheel of the car, and the tire exploded, taking the driver by surprise. The car swerved so hard, it careened off the road and into an unlucky department store. Smoke bloomed from the engine as the store window shattered around the stalled vehicle.

Elise let out a satisfied scoff and allowed Layla to pull her back inside the car.

The reaper looked at her with wide eyes that held equal parts fury and relief. "Don't ever do something like that again."

All Elise could do was laugh as Jamie finally brought the vehicle to a steadier speed. A few blocks later, they approached a Saint training compound. Her lover's relief warmed a part of her that had not been touched since their separation. She had spent so long defending herself and others, yet no one had done the same for her until Layla. The tender concern in her eyes made Elise want to pull Layla into her arms and stay there until they were forced apart, but Jamie was clearing his throat and Sterling groaning nearby. She allowed Layla to release her and climbed out of the vehicle to face the building Jamie pointed at. The men they had followed were long gone now after having fled into the compound.

"It looks like it's mostly empty right now, but they have guards." He gestured to the two strange men standing just outside the door to the Saint training center—or whatever was left of it. While the building still stood, no more eager and determined men and women entered or exited the building with their shiny new badges and earned honor. Instead, it remained a tall brick building in the middle of Harlem. What had once been a factory was converted into a multistory building with various gyms and armories. Now Elise wondered if they were even used with the intruding gangsters having taken over.

"What is the etiquette for one gang approaching another?" Elise asked.

Sterling whipped his gaze to her. Though his expression remained mostly stoic, Elise noticed the flicker of apprehension in his hazel eyes. "Are you calling us a gang?"

"With Jamie leading us, who's to say we aren't one?" Layla muttered. She nodded to Jamie. "You two go ahead. Elise and I will take up the back in case they feel provoked." She waited back at the corner with Elise as the two men approached the building across the street. With them out of earshot, Layla turned her attention to Elise. "Don't you find it a little odd how easily your father's empire fell? Where there was once an insane man is now the shadow of an empire that was considered great."

Elise bit back a bitter laugh. "It wasn't exactly that easy. There was biological warfare and bad press involved. Bad press can take down anything. Especially if you were believed to be a failure from the beginning."

Layla considered her words carefully. "Sure, but…I think we should be cautious. What if he's planning something else, or someone else is planning something through him?"

"Then we'll stop him before the plans come to fruition," Elise said strongly.

"So confident."

"One of us has to be." Elise moved forward before Layla could respond to her jab.

Across the street, they met Jamie and Sterling at the entrance to the training center, where the two men appeared to be stuck in a heated conversation with the guarding gangsters.

"Do you take me for an idiot? We are not just letting anyone inside our property," one Italian gangster spat.

Jamie lifted his hands and coughed out a laugh. "Listen. I know you don't pay rent for this place. It's a fortress. I understand your frustration, though, because plenty of people call me dumb. But the trick is letting them underestimate you so you can—"

"This is not your property. We have alerted the Saints to your theft, and they will not take kindly to finding you all here when they arrive." Sterling pulled his coat back to reveal his guns, which had newly engraved crosses on the handles as tribute to his time as a Saint member.

The gangster did not seem impressed. His hand tightened on his gun, and he continued to glare, his dark eyes only filling with more irritation as Elise and Layla arrived. "That means nothing to me. If you want this place, you will have to take it from us. Judging by your small group, you would certainly die in any type of insurrection."

Jamie's easy smile dropped into a frown. "Well, it was never going to come to that, jester." He gestured to Layla, whose lips had pulled into an annoyed flat line. "This one will destroy you—won't you, Layla?"

Layla stared at him with a blank expression. "Never for you."

Elise bit back a groan of frustration. "Sir, please. It's in your best interest to work with us. You can tell Nicoletta—"

"*How do you know her name?*" The gangster shoved his gun under Elise's chin. The metal only grazed her skin before Layla shot between them, baring her fangs and hissing.

"Watch it," Layla snapped.

Her fury had the man stumbling back in shock, his arm shaking as he tried to point the gun at her. "Demone!" His voice quaked even while he used his native language to insult her.

Layla wrapped her hand around the barrel of the gun and wrenched so hard, his wrist twisted and popped. His fingers released the gun, and he collapsed, still staring up at her with horror-filled eyes.

"How are you here, in the sunlight? You look so…so human. What kind of sorcery do you practice in New York to hide monsters in plain sight?" he demanded. The gangster scrambled for the second gun at his belt, but Sterling and Jamie were already lifting their own to his heart.

Elise relished in the display of violence. Three beings stood in front of her, ready to spill blood to defend her. Whatever their true reasons for doing it were, she didn't care. All her life, she had wondered whether she would ever be worthy of such devotion. Today, she understood her humanity and ever-shifting morals did not make her a liability, but rather an asset worth protecting.

"You do not know this city or country well enough to want to run it. Just hear us out," Elise said.

The gangster cradled his arm in his hand and shook his head. "I'm not the one you need to talk to. My boss—she's not here right now. You can wait for her, or—"

"Oh, Vito, che hai fatto?" A feminine voice called out nearby.

Everyone turned to see a tall woman with dark hair approaching the entryway, two men following her. The same woman had approached Elise outside the Renny a couple of nights ago. She peeled leather gloves off her hands and bent toward Vito, pinching her fingers around his wrist. The gangster cried out as she forced him to his feet by dragging him up with two fingers around his injured arm.

"Scusa. Mi dispiace tantissimo." Vito wept.

The woman, who Elise could only assume was Nicoletta, shook her head and gave him a bitter smile. "Your apologies mean nothing to me now that you've made a fool of me and my business." She dropped his limp wrist and shoved him away. The man scampered back into the building, leaving his gun and his dignity behind.

Nicoletta turned to Elise and Layla, her eyes flicking to Jamie and Sterling briefly before returning to Layla. "I see you have a thing for hands."

Layla tilted her head to the side. "Not all of them."

While Elise remained baffled by that statement, she did not question either woman's history. "Why do you claim this stolen training compound as yours? Did you kill Saints to take it over?"

Nicoletta turned a bored look onto Elise. "Are you the Saint representative? As far as I'm concerned, you are mostly gone. Worthless now. Your name is already spreading abroad like a cautionary tale. *Never do business with Saints. Only take what is left of their empire to build your own.* It's so pathetic, I almost feel bad for you. Almost." She dropped one hand onto the handle of the gun at her hip and regarded all of them. "This property is mine now. As is everything within and all information surrounding it."

Layla ground her teeth. Her fangs had retracted once more, but Elise noticed a smudge of blood staining her lower lip from her earlier threat. "At least tell us who and what you are capturing reapers for and why you are distributing karma," Layla demanded.

The gang leader let out a low whistle and shook her head. "So you can steal my business? Absolutely not. I imagine we could have gotten along, you and me. If you had worked with Julius. He was so easy to work with."

"Because he was a traitor to his own kind," Layla spat.

Nicoletta ignored her and turned to Jamie. "As are you. Choosing the wrong side of this conflict for what? Are they your lovers?"

While Sterling choked at her words and Elise recoiled in disgust at the idea of seeing Sterling or Jamie in any way that was not platonic, Layla only curled her lip and rolled her eyes.

Jamie glared back at Nicoletta. "You hardly know how to do business in Harlem. It's not like Sicily. This place will eat you alive if you don't have the right allies."

Nicoletta gestured toward them. "And these are the right allies? A barely alive girl and a girl who looks like the sight of blood would kill her?"

Elise blinked at the insult.

"You're close to making enemies out of every reaper in Harlem," Layla hissed.

Laughter burst from Nicoletta. "If you're trying to threaten me, you should try much harder. I am the one with the weapons that can stop your immortal hearts."

Layla smiled coldly. "And I still beat you. And your men."

A calculating light filled Nicoletta's eyes as she considered Layla's words. She opened the door behind her and pointed to the WANTED poster that had all of their faces on it. Beneath the renderings, a new incentive had been added: *$1,000 REWARD*. "Harlem no longer belongs to just you. I could use some extra cash. I'm sure the mayor would appreciate me telling him of your whereabouts. It helps to be a little selfish sometimes. I only really want Layla. Perhaps I would take mercy on you if you handed her over to me. Make that decision and I have a ship that can take the rest of you anywhere you'd like if you need the escape."

Layla bristled by Elise's side. Her eyes could have lit fires with the burning rage illuminating them. While Elise never for one second considered agreeing to give Layla over to this strange gangster, she wondered if the gangster had considered what it would be like to have a reaper in her possession. Especially one as angry and volatile as Layla.

"If you want her, you'll have to catch her yourself," Elise bit out. She nodded to the others, gesturing for them to follow her as she walked back to the vehicle.

"Your sister is not long for this world, Elise. That Saint girl has a larger target on her back than anyone else in Harlem. Consider what you're willing to give up to save her," Nicoletta called out.

Elise stopped in her tracks. The glare she shot Nicoletta was lethal in its entirety, even before she began to speak. "What did you just—"

A song, its painfully familiar notes faint on the evening breeze, drifted out from the nearby sea. Elise's chest tightened with realization, and all blood drained from her face, rendering her stricken expression ashen and slack. She turned in the direction of the music and almost felt the notes envelop her.

Josi's face appeared in her mind, rippling with the movements of the song Elise had composed for her. Wicked happenings had been haunting Harlem for the past few months, but this was something she had to believe in. There were only two people who would have known that song and how to play it, two people who knew what it meant to Elise, and one of them stood by her side.

She took off running toward the music.

Elise did not wait to ensure her companions followed her. She tore through the streets of Harlem, her feet hitting the ground so hard, her bones rattled. The music grew louder and clearer as she passed building after building. Each step brought her closer to the dock, where ships came and went, passing like whispers side by side.

Her run came to a halt only when she made it to the dock. She stepped onto the sea-slick wood, her eyes watering as she moved through the mist. For a few feet, all she saw was the thick cloud of fog overtaking the long wooden walkway, save for a distant blinking light in the far distance. The current sucked below the dock, and the wood shifted beneath her feet. Elise squinted as the mist finally began to part, her song cresting with its crescendo of a finale.

In the middle, a small form became visible. The violent breeze crashing over the surrounding water stirred her long curls and the two pink ribbons that tied them back. Her skirt pressed around her legs with the wind, billowing out behind her as she trailed her delicate fingers over the edge of the phonograph sitting in the middle of the dock. The music faded out, and the spinning record slowed to a stop. She turned, her gaze widening as it settled on Elise.

Elise's eyes filled with tears at the sight of her sister. "Josi." Her voice broke as she came forward and pulled the little girl into her arms.

Josi was hesitant at first. Her body stiffened in Elise's hold, but soon after, as Elise's hands smoothed over her back and her hair, she melted into her touch. The wetness of her own tears dripped onto Elise's shirtfront, and her arms gripped Elise hard, like how she used to when she was little and still figuring out her strength. This time, Elise felt the intention behind her force and the possibility of even more. She pulled back a bit to study her sister's face. While her cheeks seemed a bit hollower and shadows caved in the space beneath her eyes, they were still the same soft brown they always had been.

"Elise?" Josi sniffed. Her hand came up to wipe at her eyes, and Elise noticed the scars lining her wrists and fingers. "Is this real?"

Elise's heart broke at those words. She cupped Josi's face and nodded, allowing her tears to fall freely now. "Of course. It's me. I'm here."

More tears spilled from Josi's eyes. "It's been so long. And I'm... I didn't think you would remember me because things have changed. Everything is different—I'm different now." She hiccupped as she cried, and Elise saw the little girl begging her not to leave all over again. More than anything, she wanted to take Josi into her arms and remove her from this world and all the hurt that came with it. If she had been kept away by Karine for this time, Elise could not even begin to imagine the horrors she had seen. All that work Elise had done to keep her safe might have been for nothing.

"You're still my dove. You're my sister, Josi, and nothing will ever change that. No matter how much time has passed, no matter how much distance there is between us. I'm so sorry for letting you go. I never should have left you. But I'm back now, and I promise it won't happen again," Elise said fiercely.

A creak sounded behind them, and they both looked over Elise's shoulder to find Layla standing at the edge of the dock. Sterling and Jamie stood farther back, though each man wore a look of awe and relief. Josi's face scrunched into an overwhelming mix of anger and betrayal. She backed away from Elise, her eyes darkening until the brown turned nearly bloodred. To Elise's dismay, black veins spread beneath her eyes and along her throat. Josi pulled a knife from the makeshift ribbon belt around her waist and held it up, her arm steady. "Why are they here? You said it would always be me and you," she demanded.

Layla stopped, her body tense and muscles bunched in a prepared stance.

Elise turned back to Josi and held her hand up. "We're friends now, Josi. She's not here to hurt you. No one is."

"She's still infected, Elise," Layla warned behind her.

"She's *fine*," Elise shouted back.

But Josi's eyes found Sterling and Jamie, and she took more steps away from Elise. "No...this is some sort of trick. You're not really here for me—you just want to turn me in," Josi snarled.

"No, Josi. I'm here for you and only you. I promise." Elise touched her arm, and Josi visibly relaxed. "I'm not going to let anyone hurt you."

Josi's eyes softened, and she looked like she wanted to respond, but a soft wailing sounded nearby.

Elise tried to pull Josi behind her, but the little girl showed surprising strength and stepped forward, out of her reach. Waves crashed over the edge of the dock as a storm picked up overhead. In the time they had been standing together, the sun had vanished from the sky. Darkness pillaged the once-blue expanse, and wind swept between them, driving them farther apart. The dock wavered beneath their feet, and when Elise looked over to the edge of the walkway, she saw a massive gray hand, slimy and scaly, emerging from the foamy black depths of the water.

"Josi…" Elise's voice came out in a breathy whisper, too horrified to find any strength.

The hand clamped down on the dock so hard, the wood creaked and cracked beneath the pressure. A head slowly rose next as the rest of the body hauled onto the dock. Water ran off of the emaciated yet lithe body of the beast, plastering its long dark hair to its head. Striking green eyes glared up at her like lights from a beacon through a storm. Though the thing crouched and contained more inhuman traits than human, Elise found a startling familiarity in its haunted face. But it wasn't until it opened its mouth to speak, revealing bloody fangs poking out past its black lips, that Elise realized why.

"Valeriya." Layla gave voice to Elise's thoughts before she could.

Elise pitched forward for Josi, but the ancient reaper shot forward, faster than a bullet. Her taloned hand swiped out and caught Elise in the chest, sending her flying over the edge of the dock. The last thing she heard before she hit the water was Josi's and Layla's screams echoing over the frothy waves.

Icy water crashed over her, the frigid temperature cutting her right to the bone. Elise kicked her way through the pain toward the surface. Her lungs, burning and empty, spurred on the brutal blow of her pounding heart against her chest. She reached her hand out as she neared the surface, seeing blood bloom like a flower over the reflection of the stormy sky above.

Something clamped over her ankle, and a scream erupted from her throat in a flurry of bubbles as it dragged her down. In all the darkness, she could make out only a flash of black talons and fangs, but several other shadows swarmed the water around her.

Elise kicked at the hand dragging her down, to no avail. Its talons sank deeper into her flesh, and her blood poured out in rivulets while they continued their descent. In a last desperate effort, Elise smeared her hand over the blood flowing from her and shoved it into the waiting mouth of the reaper. It released her almost instantly, her blood a drop of bitter poison on its tongue. The more the scarlet substance spread around her, the farther the other reapers strayed.

Finally, Elise broke the surface, gasping for air. She hauled herself back onto the dock just in time to see Josi pounce on a Saint member. Several members had the dock surrounded and aimed their guns at her and Valeriya. Their vehicles continued to run in their rushed attempt at quelling the chaos. Elise had no time to wonder why or how her father's men had come. Other reapers crawled from the water, clashing with Layla, Sterling, and Jamie, but Elise saw only her little sister attacking the Saint associate. Josi clung to the man's back and held his head with both hands and was twisting it until his flesh tore from his neck. She sprang from his shoulders, taking his head with her. Blood coated her mouth and the front of her dress, but she paid it no mind, only tossing the head into the water and turning to block a blow from another Saint member. No longer the fearful little girl Elise had left behind, Josephine took on men more than twice her size, leaving them in a pile of flesh and blood that even a reaper would not want to touch.

A few Saint members aimed for Valeriya, who had remained still, watching from the end of the dock until she locked eyes on Layla. The evolved ancient reaper lunged forward while Layla had her hands full with another reaper. Elise reached for her gun and fired at the beast right as she made contact with Layla.

She jerked back but kept her taloned hand around Layla's throat. Blood leaked from the fresh bullet wound in her shoulder, trailing all the way down her arms and into Layla's face. Her nails dug trenches in the wood beneath Layla, and the younger reaper coughed, spraying blood from her mouth as the pressure from above increased.

Josi let out a pained cry, and Elise searched for her through the chaos. She found her sister with her hand clamped over her shoulder and gritting her teeth in agony. Josi threw a frustrated look at Valeriya, who had yet to release Layla. The interaction gave Elise pause, and she lowered her gun as Valeriya lifted her talons, aiming them for Layla's head.

One Saint member nearby locked in on the scene and pointed his gun at Valeriya's chest.

Elise screamed as his finger readied the trigger. She threw herself into him as the gun went off. Blood sprayed over the dock, and Valeriya let out a shriek of pain. Looking up from her tangled position with the Saint, Elise found the beast stumbling back with blood pouring from a wound in her side. Josi crashed into Valeriya, nursing a matching wound in her stomach. She cried out, and Elise felt her heart crack as her voice broke under her pain.

Several reapers dropped to the ground while Valeriya retreated, still bleeding heavily. She dragged Josi away with her into the fog. Even after they had disappeared among the misty air, Elise swore she still heard Josi's agonized screams.

Nearby, Layla tried to drag herself to her feet, but something cracked in her chest, and more blood poured from her nose and mouth. She collapsed, and Elise crawled to her, placing a hand on her arm to get her to stay down. Shadows surrounded them as figures approached. Elise looked up, expecting to see Jamie and Sterling, but her heart dropped when she came face-to-face with none other than Tobias Saint.

25

"Four of my men dead, three buildings destroyed, and now my name—*my name* is being destroyed. You are making a mess of our city," Tobias Saint nearly shouted. He swiped a stack of newspapers from his desk, sending them fluttering to the floor in a messy pile. A few contained wanted ads with photos that stared up at Layla from the floor.

If someone had told her a few years ago that she would once again find herself in front of Tobias at the Saint residence, Layla would have called them a dirty liar. Now she sat in the Saint patriarch's study with her hands bound behind her by Saint chains. This new house she did not recognize from her childhood, but the threatening nature of this man's anger and all the sinister things he got up to in his office remained. Layla tried to concentrate on her battered body healing instead of Elise's pained tone while she spoke to her father.

"Don't you understand that the city is no longer ours? It was never ours to begin with. There are reapers with lives and people who deserve to live without the fear of what the government, or whatever self-proclaimed powerful man with money, is doing to poison them—" Elise tried to press on, but her father waved a dismissive hand at her.

"So you've taken it upon yourself to fix things? Without acknowledging how this reflects on our legacy and this empire—without acknowledging how this reflects on New York and the country?" Tobias snapped.

Elise's lips quivered. "The way you encourage the abuse of weaker individuals is the worst reflection of all. No one trusts you or this empire because of what you've done. If you really cared about Harlem, you would help us."

Tobias passed a hand over his face, sighing. The man might have aged twenty years since this conversation had started less than an hour ago. Lines deepened on his face, and his eyes grew so dark, they looked black in the low light. "I am not sure what you expect me to do. Foreign criminals have control over many of my assets now." He pressed his knuckles to the top of his desk and leaned against it, sighing. "The Mafia is not something you can just barter with. They've been here forever, and they only grow larger and more dangerous every year. It's no surprise they saw my success and decided to latch onto it. I'm shocked Sterling has never told you about them. My men have run into them countless times. One of their past bosses even approached me with a pitch for business many years ago. They're vicious. But this particular family that's just arrived from Sicily is hell-bent on revenge against your *girl*."

Layla shot him a dirty look but said nothing. The man wasn't worth wasting her breath.

He dropped his cigarette into an ashtray that was already stuffed full with others. "Let me tell you, Elise, I always hoped you would find a nice girl to settle down with peacefully. Layla is not that girl for you. She doesn't deserve you at all."

The words were nothing new to Layla. She had been telling herself that for years, even before she turned. Because what Saint had business with someone like Layla? Back when they were children, Layla was just a girl trying to find solace in dance, one who happened to be born to parents adored by the Saints. Elise saw something great in her that Layla never managed to see for herself. As a reaper, it became even harder to see herself in any position of honor or love. She had been taught, since turning, that she would have to earn good things. Such was the way of reaperhood. Remade into a tragedy, forced to work for anything more.

Elise's chest rose and fell quickly. Her lips twisted in frustration, and her brows bunched together as she thought. Layla wondered what of. Whether she was worth defending to Tobias anymore. While she sat, bound by chains in his study, covered in blood, proving to him that she was no more than the monster they all saw her as.

"I did not come here to hear what I deserve from you," Elise said.

Tobias sat in his chair and regarded her with less retained hostility. An impressed smile crossed his face. "Perhaps I underestimated your rightful presence as my heir. You could have done wonderful things, Elise. Give me a reason why I should not turn Layla in to the gang in exchange for my training bases back?"

Some time ago, those words might have delivered a gentleness to her battered heart. All the old Elise had ever wanted was her father's love and affection. But it had come with limitations and conditions that she could never manage. Now she faced him with a coldness that she had been trained to reserve only for reapers.

Elise shook her head. Layla sensed the quickening of her heart rate as her anxiety picked up. The heiress let out a heavy breath and straightened her shoulders. "The truth is I do not want to turn her in for my own selfish reasons. I do not want her to die because I care for her. I know, however, that you do not recognize such reasoning as legitimate. So I say we need Layla because she is integral to getting Josephine back. Since Josi was turned, she might only connect to another reaper."

The spike in her blood pressure informed Layla Elise had told a lie. If Josi's reaction to Layla had been any indication, the little girl certainly did not want to connect with her at all. But the lie seemed to work on Tobias, who leaned forward, nodding.

"If I can fix this, will you try again?" Elise asked.

Her father narrowed his eyes. "Try what?"

Elise swallowed hard. "To be a father and a leader. For Josi. We have reason to believe she's being used to help distribute karma among blood houses, and we can save her from there. But she will need you when she's back. I don't want to take her from you too,

Father. But I need you to promise me you can do the right things for her."

Tobias ran a shaky hand over his hair. He let out a rough breath, and before he even spoke, Layla knew a devastating blow was coming. "You mistake my motivations, Elise. I do not wish to house a monster. If you get Josi, you are to *fix* her. You will not return her to me as a beast. Do you understand me?"

Layla's fangs slid out at the threat in his voice. The rise of tears and helplessness in Elise's eyes made her strain against the Saint chains, no matter the blood the burning metal drew from her wrists.

Elise nodded and blinked past her anguish. "Understood."

26

GETTING DRESSED UP IN FANCY CLOTHES AND expensive jewelry took Layla back to a time when humanity ran through her veins as surely as her blood did. Going through Valeriya's old belongings had been a last-minute decision—as had deciding to take their night at the Nest Club seriously enough to warrant entirely new outfits. Especially since Sterling claimed they would be in and out in minutes—all they had to do was steal the gang's stash of karma.

"If I've learned anything the past few days, it's that anything that can go wrong will go wrong. Might as well prepare for that," Elise had grumbled then. The mood after leaving the Saint home had been low, and Layla knew only one way to present them with some excitement, no matter how fleeting.

The look of pure joy on Elise's face, however, when she saw the massive collection of luxury clothing and rare jewelry had been worth it. Layla sat on the edge of the bench in the closet and watched as Elise rummaged through the layers of clothes hung up around the room. A few wardrobes lined the hotel room that had been turned into a walk-in closet, with shoe racks and cabinets serving as extra storage where the external racks could not fit everything else. Elise had gone straight to the racks of gowns that looked more expensive than anything Layla had ever owned in her life. Her parents had been fine financially when they had been alive. Layla had never had to worry about where her next meal would come from, and she had been in dance classes multiple times a week. She knew back then that her parents had sacrificed a lot to get her into dance and afford her lessons and costumes. They had worked hard to guarantee her a future that most people would only ever dream of.

It turned out, Layla would soon become most people. Despite all that her parents had done, their hard work did not prevent her from being forced onto a path of damnation. Nothing anyone did could ever guarantee the future for anyone else. Even while Layla was close to Elise and her family, there had been nothing to prevent the direction in which their lives went. Layla had to wonder if there would always be an expectation of failure and ruin when it came to being Black in America. If one family got to be successful and ride the riches of their hard work, then another had to pay the debts of escape from bondage to the toxic patriotism of the U.S.

All that made Layla wonder how exactly Valeriya had come into possession of these beautiful items. She knew Valeriya could have paraded around as a socialite if she wanted to and that she had in the past. Some places beyond the United States obsessed over beings who were different from the norm. Valeriya may not have been kept like a creature in a zoo in those places, but their infatuation with her was enough of the same sentiment. Abroad, she was put on display for money, and she took enough of it to make a more permanent home in New York. But perhaps Layla had the story wrong and Valeriya had earned these luxury items through different avenues. When the Clarice had still been operating as a hotel, her old mentor had haunted the halls until the patrons became too afraid to book and effectively drove the place out of business. Maybe Valeriya had just kept whatever was left behind. Maybe she had more discreet means that Layla would never know about because she was dead and the ancient reaper had been far less honest and more of an enigma than Layla had ever realized.

Now Layla shook her head, rubbing at her brow as the thoughts finally dissipated from her mind. Elise stood in front of her holding a long baby-blue gown in one hand and a pearl necklace in the other. "What do you think?"

Layla blinked and sat up straight. "Is that what you're going to wear?"

"No, silly. It's for you. I figured you would want something less flashy." Elise held it up to Layla, eyeing how the gown looked against her skin and frame. "Maybe not this color."

"Are you a professional stylist and I just never knew?" Layla asked in a teasing tone.

Elise sighed and hung the dress up before pushing around the rest of the garments for another option. "This is the most normal thing I've done in ages. I'm just happy to be doing something that will not result in pain, distress, or blood." She hesitated, her search slowing while she thought. "Is it not strange, though? Rummaging through her belongings knowing she's out there…alive, but different?"

Layla nodded slowly. Already the excitement on Elise's face had dwindled in the few minutes that they had been in the closet. "We only have a little while until sundown, and this place still might be her nest. Let's not think about that for now." She pursed her lips as Elise's fingers faltered in the racks. "I will wear anything you choose for me."

Elise's smile returned. She thrust a white dress with lace and a stacked pearl necklace at Layla. "Try this. I'll go put mine on."

Layla could only smile after her as she disappeared behind the changing screen to dress. Her own dress was thankfully made of a light material that hardly weighed down her shoulders and fit her well enough to make her wonder if Valeriya chose clothes with little regard for how they framed her. Layla had been far from her mentor's size, with Valeriya being several inches taller than her. But this dress fit her as if it were made for her, and after piling the stacked pearls onto her throat and admiring herself in the mirror, Layla felt fit to dine with the divine.

"Oh my god, Layla, it's perfect. You're perfect." Elise spoke almost breathlessly.

Layla had to agree. She had never been one for fancy dresses, but seeing the way this dress fit her and hearing the way Elise reacted to it made her want to wear one all the time. Layla turned, expecting to see Elise poking her head out of the side of the changing screen, but instead, she was stopped in her tracks at the sight of Elise in a shorter golden flapper dress. A rope of pearls hung around her neck and a shimmering headdress sat on her head, keeping her fluffy curls away from her face. In an instant, Layla forgot all about her own dress and how good it made her feel. She could only stare at Elise. The way that even though her dress sparkled with impressive intensity in low lighting, her bare legs still outshone it. Layla didn't realize just how moved she was until Elise came up to her and touched her jaw with a gloved hand.

"You're going to swallow a fly," Elise murmured, giggling slightly.

Layla shut her mouth and swallowed, her eyes roaming the gentle way the fabric hugged Elise's body. The Saint girl had always been magnificent, but tonight, knowing they would be out together, with Elise by her side…the thought was enough to make Layla's mouth go dry. The only other times they'd had to dress up and put on a show with their appearance had been as children, when they were expected to act as children. Layla had never appreciated the beauty then, but she had always admired how carefully Elise did herself up, as if trying to make the gods of beauty jealous of her own. Even back at the fundraising gala hosted by Tobias and Stephen all those weeks ago, Layla had not been allowed to properly acknowledge Elise. It was a miracle she didn't lose her mind in the alley afterward, when her fangs sank into her throat and she finally got a taste of Elise's sweet, sweet blood. All night had been torture, just craving her second after second. Layla wondered if it would be similar tonight—or if she would be calmer if only because she was allowed to touch Elise now.

"Remind me of our plans at the Nest Club tonight. What roles must we assume so we do not stick out unpleasantly?" Elise asked.

Though she spoke clearly, Layla struggled to hold on to each of her words. If she could, she would just watch Elise and listen to her talk every day, even if it meant getting lost in her eyes and the sound of her voice without retaining any information. Layla turned away, trying to ignore Elise's surprised expression. "They have dancers who perform every night because it's a cabaret. I think one of us will have to go as a dancer and the other a musician. That way we will get the full experience and maximum visibility to find Josi and whoever is producing and spreading karma. Jamie and Sterling will go as gangsters," Layla said. When she turned back to Elise, she was happy to find her leaning over the vanity chair to adjust the strap of her heel. Staring straight at her might have sent Layla into a distracted spiral once again, and now was the worst time for that.

Elise sat up again and tugged at the headdress she wore. "You will be the dancer, of course. Unless…do you not know cabaret?"

Layla tilted her head to the side. "Well, I do not have to actually do it. I just have to get backstage. But I've had some training." She narrowed her eyes. "What would you say if I did not know cabaret?"

"Nothing. I would just be shocked. You danced everything. At least that's how I remembered it," Elise said.

"Mostly ballet. But there is already less of that in Harlem, unfortunately," Layla said.

Elise nodded. "Just like Josi. You know...differences and circumstances aside, I think she would really like you. I hope she doesn't remember too much of this time of her life when she gets older."

Layla could have told her that five years would not make her remember less pain. Both of them knew that. Their lives had been changed irrevocably when they were only a few years older than Josi was now, and both of them still wore scars that bled whenever their minds decided to punish them. But Layla just nodded. "You played beautifully earlier, by the way. I know you were nervous, but you were exquisite."

A tender hope mixed with sadness filled Elise's eyes. "It's been so long... Thank you, Layla." She lowered her gaze. "I feel awful for leaving her. She's been alone this whole time, taken care of by God knows what kind of deranged ancient reaper traditions... Now she's different, and I wasn't there to help her through any of it."

Layla touched Elise's arm and spoke softly. "When I was turned and I came here, I couldn't sleep alone in my own bed because I was so scared. I kept bothering Valeriya for comfort even though she was the least warm reaper I've ever met. She raised me as a reaper, and I turned out okay. All that to say, I believe Josi will be all right."

Tears rose in Elise's eyes. "What if everyone else is right and she's too far gone?"

"You cannot give up now. Not when we've come this far. We have to hope." Layla drew closer to Elise, pressing her palms to her cheeks before any tears could fall. "We will bring her home. And then, when everything is calmer here, we can run off to Paris together. We will get Josi back into ballet and you back into piano. We will do whatever we want."

Elise nodded and breathed through her tears. "Oh mon Dieu. S'il te plaît, laisse-moi mourir en premier."

Layla smiled at her shaky French. It had been ages since she'd heard Elise speak it. Even before Elise's last-minute move to France, she had studied it with a private tutor at the Saint estate per her father's request. Layla remembered her own parents trying to encourage her to join Elise's lessons. Tobias Saint had constantly insisted that one should always know more than one language. *Better to know what other people are saying, especially your enemies*, he'd say. As a child, Layla had assumed she had no enemies. But now...

"What does that mean?" Layla asked.

Elise only pulled away, wiping at her face. Before Layla could ask if she had overstepped somehow, Elise was reaching for a pin in her updo. She pulled it free, allowing her curls to tumble down her shoulders. A delicate arrangement of diamonds made up the end of the silver pin. Elise slipped the pretty thing into Layla's bundle of curls at the back of her head. As she finished and moved away, Layla grabbed her hand and pressed a kiss to her palm first, then her knuckles.

"You're beautiful," she murmured.

Elise could only smile in return, and the answering joy that chased away the previous darkness in her eyes was enough for Layla.

A hundred feet east of Seventh Avenue, any screams were drowned out by the sound of live music and exhilarated dancers. Layla understood now why some rogue reapers preferred to hunt around Lenox Avenue and Jungle Alley. There people were too busy choking down liquor and heading to the dance floor to even consider the dangers that lurked in the shadows just beyond a club's front doors.

A couple of women stumbled out of another nearby club, narrowly avoiding bumping into Layla and Jamie while they laughed. Smoke flowed from the ladies' mouths, and they held cigarettes between their gloved fingers as they waved back to the men who called after them. The scent of liquor followed them down the street, and Layla wrinkled her nose, wondering how they were still standing.

"How much money do you think gangs make from the speakeasies here?" Sterling asked. He looked particularly scandalized seeing the number of people smoking out in the open, the women in their revealing dresses, the men leaning heavily against the walls from their inebriation. He kept turning his nose up and rolling his eyes whenever they came across such a scene.

"Will you somehow turn this into a legal thing and get everyone arrested?" Jamie replied as he walked beside Layla.

Behind them, Elise laughed. She had her hands tucked away beneath her large fur shrug, and though the mass of white fluff covered a significant portion of her dress, she still shone in a way that outdid the light of the stars above. It was a shame Layla walked in front of her; she wished she could stare at Elise all night long.

Sterling grumbled something unintelligible, then spoke up. "When you said we would be parading as gangsters, I thought you meant the kind who do quiet business with politicians. Not the… loud kind who create chaos in clubs to get what they want while everyone is screaming."

Jamie threw him a sideways glance. "Which one do you think I am, Sterling?"

"Considering the number of speakeasies you have run and how many people have been killed under your lead, I would say the worst kind."

"Maybe you two should keep your criminal activities and combative theories to a minimum when we go inside," Layla suggested. They had reached the entrance to the Nest Club. While plenty of clubs in Harlem were Black owned or allowed racial mixing, it still shocked Layla when she was allowed inside without extensive questioning or having to offer a part of herself. She'd also tried to avoid establishments where humanity was put on display for everyone to see. To her these buildings seemed less like spectacles and more like coffins with people desperate to hang on to life inside.

The bouncer outside the Nest Club surveyed them with cautious black eyes. He paused on Jamie, his face lighting up. "Vex. Wonderful to see you again. Though business has never been as good as when you ran this place."

Jamie smiled a charming yet vacant smile. "Even the best have to move on eventually. I'm back for pleasure this time. What have you got for us tonight?"

"Cabaret is starting in a few. The restaurant on this floor is pretty packed, so I wouldn't expect any openings for a while," the bouncer said.

"And what if I said I was here for blood and karma?" Jamie asked.

A cold look crossed the bouncer's face. He glanced behind him back into the darkness of the hallway before leaning toward Jamie. "Are you taking or giving?"

Jamie laughed softly. "Maybe a bit of both."

"All right, well, I'm not the one to talk to. But I can let the boss know you're here, and he might give you some special treatment. Do not tell anyone else." The bouncer gestured to Layla and the others. "Are they with you?"

"They are," Jamie said.

The bouncer eyed Layla so hard, each roaming look made her skin prickle with an irritated heat.

"All human by the way. I know you've been wary of them since the last incident." Jamie shook his head, sighing. "I cannot wait until the blood house fad passes. They're turning worse than the Cotton Club."

The bouncer gave him a sympathetic nod. "If you ever need a new place to post up or a new job, we've got you. As long as you don't cause any trouble tonight. We've seen your posters around—don't turn us into snitches."

Layla nudged Jamie with her elbow before he could dive into another lengthy conversation with this man. She was relieved when the bouncer waved them all inside. Layla rolled her jaw out and exhaled the moment they were hidden by the shadows. She felt Elise's hand close over hers as they moved from the darkness of the hallway into the open restaurant on the first floor. Scents of barbecue wafted around them, and Layla was glad for a distraction.

"Are you okay?" Elise asked, her voice slightly raised to cut through the loud music.

Even though Layla nodded, all she really wanted was to go back to the front of the club outside and tear every WANTED poster down. "I'm good," she muttered.

Jamie tugged on his lapels as he surveyed the room. He dressed the part of a gangster almost too well—he looked more gangster than he did in his everyday life. The black pinstripe suit he wore and the hat he refused to take off were the same kind worn by others at the Nest Club tonight, though he somehow still stood out against everyone else. Sterling hardly matched him. If anything, the Saint member looked more like a young aspiring politician with his expensive suit and even flashier cuff links. Even Elise had gawked at his chosen attire when they had first met up an hour ago.

"We should all take our own areas to scout out and maybe talk to people. Layla, I think you will have the best luck at finding the blood rooms," Jamie said.

Layla bristled at his statement. He was not wrong, but some part of her hated being acknowledged as the one who could most easily sniff out blood. As it was, the room they currently stood in had such a strong aroma of barbecue, Layla could not smell anything beyond it. She felt as if her nose had been coated with the stuff, and it didn't help that everywhere she looked, there were people sharing plates of marinated meat or flagging down servers carrying trays of it.

"Assuming we're close to some of the blood rooms, it's not safe for Elise and Sterling to be alone. The patrons might have a strong craving for Saint blood," Layla said. She watched with gentle amusement as Sterling stepped closer to Jamie, rolling his eyes all the while. He had a Saint gun strapped to his body, but Layla could still see the apprehension tightening his shoulders and pulling the corners of his lips down. Elise, on the other hand, pressed into Layla's side with something akin to excitement. As the group finally split up, with Elise following Layla into a less crowded part of the club, Layla understood why.

It had been years since they had both attended a function like this with better intentions. At the fundraiser gala, they had both been on edge, with no chance to enjoy the energy or each other's company. Now, however, Layla threaded her fingers through Elise's and pulled her through the crowd with a soft smile on her face.

Elise leaned in beside her, a hushed excitement riding her words as she spoke. "It's almost like old times, don't you think? When our parents would bring us along to these parties, we would get a chance to dance and be away from the chaos at my house. I never thought I missed this until now. Back then, it was always about appearing good enough in my father's eyes, but now, even as we're sneaking around,

I feel better about it. Because I have you." Elise's voice had lowered to a near whisper at the end, as if she wanted only Layla to hear her small confessions.

Layla stopped at the edge of the crowd, where people were dancing to a live rendition of "Black Bottom Stomp". She released Elise's hand only to point to the piano. "You should go next."

Panic flickered across Elise's pretty face. "Excuse me?"

"You were great last time, and I think they might even recognize you now because of it," Layla said. "I miss hearing you play. And like you said, it's been an eternity since we could be normal, so maybe we take that chance now."

Though Layla hoped Elise might have found some confidence in her words, she looked more unsure than ever. Elise kept glancing back at the pianist and then at Layla, her mouth pursing and teeth grinding, sometimes on her lower lip. "I did not say it had been an eternity," Elise hissed.

Layla shrugged and pushed Elise toward the piano. "Five years? Close enough."

Despite her utter mortification and shaky nerves, Elise did not back down. She approached the piano as the band began to move off the stage and sat down on the bench without a word. The room, while still rowdy from applauding the previous band, seemed to settle down enough for her. Layla watched with piercing eyes. Elise had never been more captivating to her than when she was in her place, with her hands perched on a piano and face struck with concentration. It was in moments like these that Layla remembered the most from childhood. Watching her best friend do what she did best and make every song she played fall in love with her right back. Then, Layla had been unable to keep her eyes and dreams away from Elise. Now it was no different. Layla stood in front of the crowd with her fingers clasped in front of her and eyes bright on Elise's quickly turning expression.

Apprehension turned into joy, and Elise relaxed as she settled into a gentle melody. As the song continued, she seemed to pick up more confidence, her fingers coming down more violently on the keys and her head bobbing slightly to the music. Even as the crowd began to cheer, she remained focused on the notes she followed in her head. The peak of the song came around, and the room fell away from Layla. For a beautiful moment, it was only her and Elise in the room—Layla listening to Elise pour her heart out at the piano and watching her with awestruck eyes. Her body vibrated under the intensity of Elise's music. Layla grew half convinced that the thudding of her heart made up the pounding in the floorboards beneath her feet. She might have gotten carried away with her wide smile and shining eyes if Elise hadn't ended the song.

The moment her hands stilled on the keys, the crowd erupted into a round of applause that seemed to shake the room. Layla was the first one to catch Elise's eye. She gave the audience a quick bow, then hurried out of the spotlight. While people resumed their dancing and excited chatter about the night, Layla could feel only Elise's trembling body against her own. Her heart raced from pure adrenaline of being put on the spot, and Layla could have sworn her own heart beat just at the sight of her fully returned happiness. It was more than a spontaneous performance—it was a reminder of all they had been through to get to this point and all that stood beyond the stage, waiting for them.

"Was it okay?" Elise asked. Her cheeks flushed with a frantic sort of energy, though she smiled.

Layla touched her hand and nodded. "You were magnificent."

"I just played what I knew, and it felt right." Elise tucked a curl behind her ear, and Layla noticed the blossoming blush on her cheeks. "That was the first time I didn't mess up your song."

Something in Layla's stomach fluttered. "That was the first time I heard it all the way through."

A moment of silence passed between them. From the vulnerability in Elise's eyes and the aching of her heart in Layla's chest, she felt like she was brushing up against something beyond either of them. In the five years of being a reaper, all Layla had tried to do was forget the human feelings she had been torn away from. As a reaper, there was no love for her parents, no love for human activities, no love for her best friend. Until now. She stood in the middle of a crowded club with her, servers and dancers pressing in around all sides, yet all Layla could think about was how much she no longer cared about the damnation of it all. Hell could close in on the world, and she would still turn to Elise, even if the only path left had her soul destined for ruination. Darkness she had become, and darkness she would return to. Even if she lived forever, this one part of her life would remain forever light. The rest of it could have been shrouded in dullness for all she cared. People would move on, people would die, the world would build new life, new meanings, and rules, but Layla would always stay the same. If this was the moment she understood herself the most, then this was how she wanted to be defined. By her love, not the loss of it.

So, when Elise pulled her into her arms and coaxed her into a slow dance, Layla went willingly with her. At first their hands were clasped, with Layla's other hand on Elise's shoulder while Elise's hand rested on her waist. When trying to move closer to her proved futile, Layla frowned. "You hold me at a distance," she said.

Elise laughed softly. "I hold you in the proper ballroom pose. I think we look dashing and blend in well."

"We are two women dancing and looking as if we want to devour each other. We do not blend in at all." Layla rested her hands on Elise's hips and sighed with contentment as Elise slung her arms around her shoulders. "Much better. And a proper ballroom stance is different."

"Dance master, are you?" Elise tsk-tsked under her breath and rolled her eyes.

Layla gave her a smug smile. "It is the one thing I was ever good at."

Elise's expression softened. "You were great at being my friend." She scooted closer to Layla to avoid bumping into a spinning woman from behind. Layla's hands tightened on her waist as their chests pressed together, their hearts beating so close, it might have been impossible to tell them apart.

"Until I was not. And I became the devil," Layla said. She

remembered her rage-induced hunt from all those years ago and how vicious she had wanted to be if only to scare Elise into never seeing her ever again. Layla had never anticipated having such easy access to her. Climbing her wall and tumbling through her window in the middle of the night had shocked them both, but while Elise had frozen in her bed, Layla had taken advantage of her surprise and yanked her out of it. Before she could even process being on the wrong side of her best friend's affections, Layla had thrown herself over Elise and began tearing at her throat and chest.

Elise's soft voice brought her back to the present. "If I must be tricked by the devil, let it be one that wears a familiar, pretty face."

"I don't think that's how that quote goes." Layla laughed softly.

Something dark flickered in Elise's gaze, and Layla felt her arms stiffen around her shoulders. "I was thinking…five years ago, if you had really wanted to kill me, you would have, right? I mean, you were a new reaper; you could not control your urges and your strength then. You obviously wanted me dead, but you didn't succeed. Why?"

Blood soaked Layla's vision again. Images of Elise lying limp beneath her with blood seeping through the carpet as it spilled from her chest and dripped from Layla's shirtfront after it had sprayed in a wild display of violence. All she could think in that moment was how much more she wanted. And Layla wanted it all from Elise. She wanted her ruin, she wanted her blood, she wanted every part of her—even if it was to snuff her out with a single squeeze of her fist around her rapidly beating heart. Layla had licked the blood from her mouth that night and promised herself a feast built on vengeance and brutality.

"Sterling and your father came in," Layla muttered, her mind still locked into the past.

Elise shook her head. "You would not have needed more than a few seconds, but you hesitated—"

"Do you want me to tell you it's because I remembered our friendship and suddenly could not follow through on my anger-induced promise? Because that's not the case," Layla said sharply. She already regretted her tone, but seeing the images of Elise bloody and dying by her hand made her lose touch with her warmth. Coldness swept through her body, and Layla considered pulling away, but Elise kept a firm grip on her. "Elise."

"You deserved to be angry, Layla. I don't want to take that away from you or change the narrative," Elise said. If she was hurt by Layla's sudden switch in tone, she did not show it. Instead, she spoke with a strong sureness that only made Layla want to stay close. "That night was a tragedy for both of us, and I want to understand why you did not put an end to the bringer of your suffering. I want to understand why I'm still here and no one else is."

Layla's breath caught. Her chest stilled against Elise's, and the sight of burning tears in Elise's eyes nearly did her in. She thought back to the night she had intended to kill Elise, when her hands had moved between her throat and her chest, Layla's eyes, which had gone red with blood and fury, could not focus on a single part of the bruised and broken body before her. "I could not decide which part of you to hurt first. There was so much pain, I could not make a decision. Before I figured out what I wanted to do, Sterling was pulling me off you."

"And what was that decision?" Elise asked in a soft whisper. By now the noise of the crowd had fallen away as they locked in on each other's every word and expression.

Layla swallowed. "I wanted to turn you. I realized death was too easy for you. I wanted you to suffer in damnation with me." She remembered her hand closing over Sterling's gun in his holster before breaking out of his arms and leaping from the window. The Saint bullets, she believed, would have put an end to all her misery. To be a reaper, stuck in a sort of torturous purgatory for an eternity, without the chance for relief—there had never been a more terrifying fate for Layla then. Maybe dragging Elise with her might have at least lessened some of her pain or given her something to hold, even if her hands grew talons and made her bleed. Elise owed her that much. To bleed for her, to become ruined by darkness.

For so long, Layla wondered what her place in the world was as a reaper. Confined to the darkest parts of society without descending into hell itself or having a chance to ascend above. Death forever chasing her but never taking a lethal bite. It was clear she was no creature of God, but an abominable thing not worthy of even hell. Reapers wandered like purveyors of death, their rich feasts and bloody tendencies as immortal as their lives. While others thought themselves gods and killed indiscriminately, Layla fell into an in-between pit of despair that brought with it more moral confusion than she had ever been able to understand. She came to realize that there was no philosophy or moral truth in suffering. Only loneliness had made itself her companion during it all and become the sole promise of reaperhood.

"Neither of us would have stood a chance. Not if we were together as reapers," Layla said.

Elise shook her head. A dark sadness had deepened her expression, but only certainty rode her words. "Even the most monstrous beings find love in the darkest depths of hell."

Layla clenched her jaw. "Love does not guarantee anything, nor does it solve anything."

"No, but it brings light to the darkness." Elise's arms tightened around Layla. "I already told you, I love your darkness as much as I love your light. Every part of you that craves blood and seeks carnage has found its way to my heart. If you must be monstrous, then you should be. There are far worse monsters in the world that do not suffer from a centuries-old affliction that leads everyone on an inevitable path of damnation. You are not the worst creation out there. Men who think themselves gods and act as monsters without reaperhood in their blood—they are the worst."

This time, true laughter broke past Layla's dismay. She leaned her face into the crook of Elise's neck and inhaled, the familiar intoxicating scent of her returning Layla's messy nerves to a state of calmness. Her heart beat so hard, Layla believed at first that she felt it in her toes. But the music had died down, and Layla knew it had to be something else causing the bumping beneath her feet.

She pulled away from Elise and looked down, watching the floorboards jump every few seconds. Now that Elise's perfume had cleared the heady scent of food from her senses, Layla could smell fresh blood. The banging stopped briefly, then started up again, as if someone were beneath the floorboards, desperate to claw their way out.

"Do you hear that?" Layla asked as she straightened.

Elise looked confused. "No? What is it?"

Layla tried to glance between the floorboards, but she saw only darkness. "I cannot be positive. But I think the blood rooms are beneath us." She tried to walk to the edge of the room, but Elise held her wrist to stop her.

"We should go. Find someone to talk to about karma." Elise led her through the throng of people. The next room over was not as packed with people, and Elise quickly found a booth with space beside two reapers. They eyed her with curiosity, then hungry desire. "May we join you gentlemen tonight?" Elise asked.

Layla tightened her hand on Elise's, not liking the predatory look these reapers maintained on her. "Elise…"

One reaper nodded and patted the open space next to him. "Always for a Saint."

A rush of hot blood flushing Elise's cheeks had Layla shaking her head. She tried to pull the Saint back, but she settled in the seat anyway, dropping her hand. "Can you tell us where we can find karma?"

As the other reaper leaned over the edge of the booth to whisper to someone out of sight, Layla wanted to grab Elise and remind her of the dangers that came with not sticking to a plan. But the Saint heiress looked perfectly comfortable flying by the seat of her pants; Layla couldn't help but wonder how long her luck would last, if it did at all.

"Karma will be all around us soon. This is the room where the magic happens." One of the reapers winked.

As if on cue, all doors that served as exits and entrances to the room slammed shut. Elise jumped in her seat and looked around as bouncers stepped in front of the doors for extra assurance that no one could come or go. She leaned in to whisper to Layla and nodded toward the stage. "Your turn. See if you can get a better look at everything from there. I'll continue talking."

Layla complied, albeit with hesitation. She made her way toward the stage and tried not to think of any of the reapers getting too close to Elise. Soon all Layla could think about was the state of the blood rooms beneath them. If the scent was this strong through the floor, Layla could only imagine how depraved it was in the actual rooms. She pushed past a group of people at the bottom of the staircase and hurried upstairs. Eventually she made it into the backstage area, where dancers lined up and rehearsed behind the curtain. They ranged from middle-aged women to girls younger than Layla. Some stretched their long limbs by the wall, brown skin glistening with stage makeup even in the low lighting of the small space. Others paced by the curtain, muttering eight counts beneath their breath as they blocked their routines. It had been so long since Layla had been in the presence of other dancers just before a show, and she relished in the buzz of their energy. She wanted to pretend, just for the night, that she was one of them, that she was destined to end up on the stage and maybe even catch the eye of a scout who wanted to hire her to dance forever. But for now, all Layla could do was watch and hope. As a reaper, she was no more destined for a better future than an illness the entire world wanted to eradicate.

To distract herself from the bitter emotions, Layla poked her head out of the side of the curtain and began surveying the crowd beyond. Her gaze found Elise in the booth with the reapers, who all looked at Elise with an interest that bordered on predatory. The sight made Layla's eye twitch, and she found herself almost moving out from behind the curtains. Every part of her craved to be near Elise now, her heart picking up the pace and skin lighting on fire as she thought of another being—specifically a reaper—laying a hand on her.

Until Layla sensed the presence of other reapers, this time closer to her. She turned. Even with all the costumed performers pressing in around her and the scent of powdered makeup in the air, she smelled the ancient blood twisting among the youthful human essence of the younger dancers.

A spotlight lit the stage, and a young man stepped out to face the audience. "Thank you all for attending tonight. As you may have heard, this show is far from ordinary. You will become absolutely bewitched. May I welcome to the stage a volunteer who wishes to be the first to partake?"

Shouts rang out across the room, and several audience members shot their hands up to offer themselves. But Layla was already walking onto the stage, her face a mask of cool confidence. A few disappointed cries erupted from the crowd, and even the announcer gave her a stunned look. "Very well then. One more volunteer and we'll be all set."

An eager but somewhat shy man with hunched shoulders and a wide smile was brought onstage next. Then a blood so familiar filled her senses, Layla almost whirled, expecting Elise to have followed her behind the curtains. But instead, she came face-to-face with the littlest Saint.

Josephine Saint, wearing the red horns of a devil, stared up at Layla. Her brown eyes flashed with recognition, and she stayed put, not moving a muscle or even flinching as Layla leaned in closer to make sure her eyes did not deceive her.

"Josephine Saint…" Layla whispered. This interaction contrasted greatly from the first time they had seen each other in years. Before breaking into the Saint estate on the night of the party two months ago, the only image Layla had of Josi had been one of a girl barely out of her infancy. With eyes so full of childlike innocence and skin softer than a rose petal, the youngest Saint daughter had only ever filled Layla with the urge to protect. Until the night of the Saint party, when she crept into her room and hid in the shadows with the intention of striking fear deep into her heart. Truthfully, Layla had been aiming for Elise. When she realized it was Josi she'd happened upon, it was too late to turn away. The little girl had already seen her. Fear lit her eyes immediately, and a bloodcurdling scream that still echoed in Layla's bones had rattled the room. Layla did not think she would ever be able to shake the realization that she was the monster under the bed, the thing lurking in shadows that made everyone warn girls not to take nighttime walks.

The girl looked older now in her stage makeup, which painted her mostly red to match the glittery dance costume and headpiece she wore. A devil. They had dressed this little girl like a devil. Layla's fangs threatened to break free at the startling realization. But the curtains were already pulling back, and another human had settled beside her, with one hand held out. Without looking, Layla could still sense Josi on the other side of her with her own human partner. The stage lights were so bright, at first all Layla saw were blurry white flashes while she took the man's hand and stepped onto the stage. It was not until the music began and her vision adjusted to the lights that Layla even knew what to do.

Before she could process the familiar jazz song blaring throughout the room, the man was swinging her into a stiff stance. Layla faced him, noticing the sheen of sweat covering his exposed throat and arms. For a long time, she had always assumed it would be a cold day in hell before she ever experienced stage fright. Growing up, the stage had been one of her few safe havens, and stepping onto had it felt like coming home. But now, after these startling moments, all Layla could think about were the countless ways she could fail during this performance. Her grip tightened on the man's shoulders as he pulled her across the stage, their feet moving in perfect sync with the music. Jazz had never been Layla's preferred dance style. Her toes stepped on her partner's during various quick turns, and her back arched a bit too far on certain dips, but for the most part, she kept up. Even as she began to sweat and the smell of blood became more pronounced the longer the dance went on, Layla became grateful for the relentless training her dance instructors had forced her through.

After one particularly prolonged spin ended in a pose, Layla took the moment to stare into the crowd. While many in the audience applauded the way she and Josi held their positions, Layla locked in on the sight of Elise in the clutches of the two reapers at the booth. One held her in place with an arm wrapped around Elise's waist while the other gripped her chin, leaning in to sniff her throat. It might have appeared scandalous in the way most people perceived flappers to be, with their short dresses and casual naked vulnerability, but in a place like this, where no one knew of mercies and blood flowed freely beneath the floor they stood on, Layla knew there was nothing but sin being planned between the reapers' blushing faces and roaming hands. Elise smiled at both of them, but the smallest flicker of fear in her eyes sent a spark of fire up Layla's spine.

Just that one look had her digging her nails into her dance partner's shoulders. His movements hesitated, bringing her face-to-face with the younger Saint girl.

"Where is the karma?" Layla whispered just loudly enough for Josi to hear over the music.

A devious look filled the girl's eyes, and she laughed. "It's me. I'm karma." She twisted back, launching herself out of her partner's arms.

The man startled, confused. Josi landed in a crouched position on her feet, one hand on the dusty floor while she glared up at him. The intensity of Josephine's displeasure might have been strong enough to start several wars in another life. In this one, however, her nose dripped blood that leaked down her mouth and over her jaw. The audience gasped as they watched the broken dance routine fall apart before them. Layla's partner released her, and she was glad to see that the halted performance had baffled the spectators so much that even the reapers with Elise stopped what they were doing to look toward the stage.

Layla felt something shift in the air. But though the crowd murmured about the show, she knew it had nothing to do with the onlookers. A violent chill swept through her senses, and she turned to the small Saint girl. Josi now stood facing her partner, who looked desperately contrite. Apologies spilled from his lips, but only a faint roaring filled Layla's ears as she watched Josi's gaze turn into something more lethal. As soon as Layla recognized Josi's expression, the Saint girl lunged for her partner. Despite being much shorter than the man, she knocked him over with the precision and quickness of an experienced predator. Josi slammed the man onto the floor and was upon him in seconds. Blood sprayed across the stage, and screams erupted from the audience as she tore into his throat. Flesh fell away from the man's body, which had gone eerily still in only moments. Josi appeared to not be drinking from him but rather playing in his blood; a smile split her lips while she pressed her palms into the blood spilling across the stage and gripped her partner's face with rough hands.

The roaring in Layla's ears only continued as she approached the girl, her hand outstretched. With the chaos of the room exploding around her, she stayed intent on reaching Josi. By the time she did, the man was far beyond dead. His glassy eyes stared up at the ceiling, mouth and chest agape from Josi's assault. Layla tried to reach for her, but a clear voice, desperate and lovely, cut through the commotion.

"JOSI."

Layla dropped her hand and turned to see Elise approaching the front of the stage. Their eyes met for a moment before Josi stood, the blood soaking her dance costume shining a brilliant crimson in the light. She looked like a princess of death, crowned by her baptism into violence. Josi waved a bloody hand at her sister. If the horror in Elise's face bothered her, she didn't show it. Instead, the little girl descended the stage steps. She cut a path through the crowd easily, with people stepping away from her and yanking their dresses and shoes out of her way to keep themselves from becoming soiled with her carnage.

"Lisey," Josi said in a light voice.

As the sisters neared each other, Layla snapped out of her shock and followed Josi toward Elise. One of the reapers who had been at the booth with Elise emerged from the crowd. His eyes flitted from Josi to Elise, calculating, until realization settled into a cold darkness in his expression. He was closer to her—Layla realized with a panicked gasp. She moved faster, but another man came between them, this time reaching for Josi. He hauled her up by her waist and flung her over his shoulder. Josi let out a screech loud enough to make people in the crowd duck and cover their ears.

After all that Josi had done to the man onstage, Layla knew the girl was more than capable of holding her own. Meanwhile, Elise had become surrounded by several reapers now, all watching her with more-than-hungry eyes. Whether it was greed or true craving that drove them to her, it didn't matter to Layla. She needed to get closer.

New blood filled the air; Josi had managed to grab the arm of the man carrying her and twist it until it dislocated. As she dropped from his shoulder, she took his arm with her, tearing the remaining flesh apart as she went. Blood trailed her quick movements through the crowd. Josi passed Layla in a heartbeat, approaching Elise. The girl did not utter a word as she dropped the arm and rushed to her sister.

Layla tensed at the scene. But the two male reapers who had been pursuing Elise backed off, as if threatened by the violence Josi carried with her. Layla did not stand down until they had disappeared into the crowd. Even with the remaining audience members still screaming while scrambling to get away, the girl hugged her sister like Elise was the only thing in the world that mattered. Elise hugged her back, tears streaming down her face while she kissed her cheeks and whispered into her blood-soaked curls.

On any other day, Layla might have watched them with tender awe and slight envy. But tonight all she could think about was getting them out alive and finding Jamie and Sterling, wherever they were. Layla placed a gentle hand on Elise's shoulder and leaned down so she could hear her. "I hate to interrupt this beautiful reunion, but we really need to leave. Our cover is blown. I give us maybe two more minutes until the police, or someone, or *something worse* shows up for us."

Josi pulled away from her sister, frowning. The defiant pout might have made her look years younger if it had not been for the blood of several grown men covering her from nearly head to toe. "Sena and Karine will always find me. I cannot be free."

Free. The word sent chills through Layla. No matter how much she wanted to understand what the little girl meant by that, there was no time to unpack it. "I understand, but we are not safe—"

"We are never safe!" Josephine screamed.

Elise's eyes, still shining with tears, widened. She looked at Layla as she stood, her hands clasped with Josi's. "We need to find a way out."

Josi tugged on her hand. "I know how to help." She began pulling Elise toward one of the back doors with Layla following.

But a familiar scent filled Layla's nose, and she stopped in her tracks. Elise looked back, concerned. "What is it?"

Layla waved her on with Josi. "Keep going. There's someone here. You all need to get out as soon as possible. Do not wait for me." She spotted Jamie and Sterling emerging near the doorway and waved them over. "Josi, stay with Elise. Jamie, Sterling, keep them safe. Find an exit and leave. I'll distract the gangsters." She turned away before any of them could protest, walking back to the edge of the room. Just moments after Elise and Josi made their respective escapes—one outside with Jamie, the other downstairs with Sterling—a familiar figure emerged from behind the curtains on the stage.

Nicoletta held her hands up, glancing around the room. "Where has the show gone? I was promised excitement and delirious thrills. All I see is a nasty little monster with a death wish." She dropped her hands and glared at Layla.

"How funny," Layla bit out. She saw the glint of a Saint gun inside Nicoletta's coat, and a horrifying thought crossed her mind: that all this might be for nothing and she would meet her end in this very club. It was a strange feeling, to understand the fear that filled her system during a fight. Never had it been like this; before, Layla had always felt attached to death, as if she were a part of it. The concept never scared her because she lived so closely with it, and since becoming a reaper, she knew there were much worse things to experience. But with all she had been through with Elise and all that they had promised to each other, Layla knew she had more to lose now.

The gang leader slowly walked down the steps. Layla's heart rate slowed as she drew closer. At the end of the day, Saint gun or not, Nicoletta was just a human. Weak and frail and painfully mortal. As Layla inhaled the scent of her sweet human blood thrumming through her veins, she reminded herself of the fact. There were worse monsters than Nicoletta, and Layla had survived them all.

"I told you I would return the favor, Layla. Blood for blood, death for death. It's a shame, really, because I am positive we could have made a great team. Your reaperhood is fascinating when you are not attempting to take the lives of innocent people," Nicoletta said.

Layla narrowed her eyes. "*Innocent people*? I would not call you or your men *innocent*. Nor any of the people you work with. Is that what life and death are all about for you? Moral high grounds and what's right and wrong? Because I can guarantee you, when you are faced with eternal damnation and immortality, all that becomes trivial. There is nothing you can say that will change that."

Nicoletta nodded slowly. One hand reached for her gun and pulled it out. She aimed it at Layla, a smile stretching her lips. "Then I guess we should just stop talking." As her finger began to squeeze the trigger, a bullet exploded through her hand. Nicoletta screamed and her gun went flying. It hit the floor smoking, a hole shot clean through the handle and barrel.

Following the line of the shot, Layla found Elise on the balcony above. The Saint heiress aimed her gun at the gangster, who was still doubled over and howling in pain. Blood dripped from her injured hand and made a mess of the floor around her.

Layla's gaze flickered nervously from Nicoletta to Elise, who used the gangster's moment of distraction to come down from the balcony. She was nearing Layla when a steady rumbling shook the room. It started beneath the floorboards, where she hoped Josi, Sterling, and Jamie had found an exit and were on their way to safety. Then it continued beyond the curtains. The large swaths of velvet vibrated and swayed as if they were harboring a sinister secret. Layla caught the bittersweet scent of a familiar poison before Nicoletta spoke again.

"Elise," Layla muttered. "Leave. Now."

But the Saint girl only pressed closer to her side. She lifted her gun again and looked toward the curtains, where the commotion increased. "No. We stay together."

Even Nicoletta appeared alarmed by the approaching chaos. Her eyes widened, and she disregarded her bleeding hand to watch the curtains. Layla half expected them to part with their usual creaking, as if to properly open a show. But instead, rotting reapers ripped through them, tearing gaping holes in the fabric as they thundered into the room. Layla had only a split second to drag herself and Elise away from their oncoming attack. The one closest to her careened into a booth so hard, the table splintered into a mess of wood and broken glass. The evolved reapers surrounded Layla as she steadied herself against her rushing adrenaline.

Nicoletta laughed softly from the stage. "What a gift. My own men, turned, just to help me with you. Horrifying, aren't they?" She shot the reapers a stern look and snapped, "Do not kill her. Bring her to me once you've gotten her incapacitated. Do whatever you'd like with the Saint."

For the few seconds that the evolved reapers took to gather themselves, Layla considered their drastically different appearances. She had never known them as humans or regular reapers. But these modified beasts were just that—monsters. Skin, gray and sagging, hung off their enlarged bones while their eyes, red with blood and popped vessels, struggled to focus on anything around them. Even their talons seemed to have a mind of their own. They stretched, wide and long, scraping along the floor as the reapers moved. Layla stood slowly, already tensing for another fight. Her dress dragged the whole way. She had never been a huge fan of skirts, but tonight made them her enemy. When she pulled herself together after the first lunge, the reapers trained their gazes back on her and bared their fangs. They were wicked sharp, several inches bigger than Layla's. She felt her own prodding against her lips, but without any weapons, all she had was her speed to aid her natural strength.

Elise fired a few shots into the reapers, but they merely absorbed the bullets and kept moving. Her lips parted in shock, and Layla buzzed with anticipation as she reached into her dress for something.

"Have fun," Nicoletta crooned from the stage.

Layla whipped her focus back to her. If the gang leader had been able to stand around and command these reapers, then they had to have a controlled target. But with a little redirection, perhaps Layla could use their power to her advantage. She sprinted for the stage, beating Nicoletta behind the curtains. Grabbing the gangster while she was distracted and high on her early victory proved to be rather painless. Nicoletta struggled at first, reaching for her gun with her good hand while she whirled, but Layla already had her fingers locked around her throat. She kicked the gun from her hand and dragged her across the stage.

Just as she thought, the reapers paused in their tracks at the sight of Nicoletta. Layla tightened her fingers around the gangster's throat as she clawed at her arm. "You want me. I know you want me. You'll have to kill her to get to me, though. But you can't do that, can you?"

"Kill her. I changed my mind. KILL THE SAINT," Nicoletta managed to screech out.

Layla snarled and lifted her foot to kick her in the ribs, but the woman met her attack with a worse punishment. Nicoletta pulled a Saint blade from her belt. The silver hilt winked, sharp and deadly, in the faint light above them before it sank into Layla's thigh.

Layla let out an agonized shriek and wrenched herself away from Nicoletta. She stumbled across the stage, blood dripping from her leg as she struggled to stay upright against the brutal waves of pain rolling through her.

Already, the reapers were making their way toward Elise. The Saint knelt on the ground, fumbling with something in her hands. A few bullets rolled away from her, and Layla groaned, agony grinding into agitation. "*Elise!*"

To her relief, the Saint stood right as the closest reaper got within striking range. She fired the gun into his face, and this time the bullet actually tore through his eye. The thing screamed and began clawing at his face, his talons shredding what was left of his flesh. A satisfied smile spread across Elise's face. She lifted her gun to aim at the next reaper, but it approached her too fast. The thing knocked the gun from her hand and then slammed Elise to the ground. The Saint heiress struggled at first, her arms shaking under her weight before she collapsed. Reapers surrounded her, and Layla felt a rise of pure fear drowning out every logical path in her mind.

"Elise! Get up!" she screamed. But to no avail. Elise had gone still. Layla sensed her slowing heartbeat and the rapid pooling of blood beneath the large cut in her temple.

Layla knew taking the knife out would be a death sentence, but she couldn't move with it lodged in her nerve. So after heaving out a breath, she tore the thing free and watched in horror as blood gushed from a gaping wound. It pooled around her, which only attracted the evolved reapers.

"Not so strong against Saint creations, are you?" Nicoletta hissed. She pulled herself into a standing position as Layla continued to limp to the edge of the stage. "All this devotion and affection for one Saint has gotten you what, exactly?"

Layla threw herself from the stage. The moment her injured leg touched down, it buckled, sending her sprawling on the floor. She was met with the warmth of her own blood as it spread beneath her. Still, Layla dug her fingers into the floor as she dragged herself along the grimy carpet, tugging herself toward Elise. The light reflecting off the powdery shimmer on Elise's outstretched hand drove her forward, its distant glow a mocking reminder of how far she still was. Crimson smeared behind her, leaving behind a trail of mutiny. She didn't have to look behind herself to know the reapers crept along. They moved slower now, as if they knew she was barely alive enough to be prey worth hunting down. Each blink sent her into a longer and longer stretch of darkness no matter how hard she pushed herself forward. Even her heart began to beat slower, and soon all Layla had dragging her toward Elise was spite.

One reaper wrapped his talon-tipped hands around her throat

and hauled her off the floor. Layla used the rest of her strength to kick at him, trying to put some distance between herself and the violence in his eyes. Her neck strained beneath his grip and every muscle in her body ached as he held her up.

Nicoletta stood behind him, her own expression ripe with amusement. A wicked smile split her face, and she stepped closer. In her hand, the Saint blade still sat, dripping with Layla's blood. "The one you love will be what kills you. How have you not realized that yet, Layla? You have already met your fate, when you were turned all those years ago because of her. Just because you love her, that will change nothing. You are a tragedy in the making."

Layla wheezed out a breath. The reaper clenched his fist around her throat, and black spots flickered over her vision as he cut the rest of her air off. "Rot in hell," she managed to choke out.

The gangster only shook her head. Her smile fell into a bitter frown, and she spat out, "You first."

Never had Layla wanted to fight more than in this moment. But she had been bled dry. Her heart slowed as she took her last breath and fell into darkness.

27

ELISE PULLED HERSELF FROM THE DARKNESS WITH little strength. Sharp pain pounded through her head, and warm, sticky blood spilled down the side of her face as she sat up. The room around her had been torn to pieces. Curtains hung in tatters over the stage, and gangster bodies littered the floor amid blood and chunks of flesh. Elise struggled to her feet, the world swaying as her head pulsed. She found her gun several feet away, smeared in blood just like the rest of the room. It held only two bullets while the others remained scattered across the floor. Her foot crunched on an empty glass vial and splintered wooden remains of tables and floorboards as she continued to move around the room.

The fight that had ended in this carnage flashed through her mind like bloody pictures from a horror show. All she heard was Layla's screams over and over, each reminder of her pain digging into her heart. The reaper was nowhere to be found now, and with the amount of blood that covered the floor and the walls, Elise could only assume the worst. It was as if hell had broken loose and rampaged through the room. What disturbed Elise the most was the blood that stretched from one side of the room to another, before it ended in a puddle, still damp with heat and ripe in scent, just feet away from where she had woken up. In the middle of it, Elise recognized the silver hairpin she had given Layla. Crimson covered almost all of it, but a tiny patch of silver peeked out from the slaughter. The pin Elise had placed gently in Layla's hair and gazed upon with admiration only a couple of hours ago now sat in a pool of enough blood to stop her heart.

Tears threatened to spill past Elise's eyes, but she blinked them back, turning to look for any clues as to where Layla could have been or been taken to. The only hope she held that kept her moving forward was knowledge that Layla was no human. She had survived worse. What might have killed a human would have had to be doubled to even wind Layla. How devoted Elise must have been to throw herself into uncertain danger for Layla—the blade of understanding twisted deeper in her chest. Layla never would have let Elise get in between her and a fight that was her own.

Elise bent to pick up the hairpin, and the sound of a door opening nearby had her swinging around to aim at the intruders. She lowered her gun when she saw Josi, quickly followed by Jamie and Sterling. They wore matching expressions of torment, their faces pale as they looked around the room. It was Josi, little Josi, who bounced up to

Elise in a state of frenzied excitement, her teeth gleaming while she grinned.

"My venom worked!" Josi cheered. She gestured to the dead gangsters, whose bodies had been ravaged by advanced reaperhood.

Elise's heart stuttered in her chest. Eyes dull and tired, she slid her gaze to Josi and demanded, "What did you just say?"

Josi's smile fell. "It normally takes a few hours to work, but this time it worked right away. I poisoned them so they wouldn't help Nicoletta. I…"

Elise's expression hardened.

"I wanted to help. Karine always says I can use my venom to help… I thought I was helping."

Silence filled the room for what felt like an eternity. Eventually, when the quiet of the night became too still and suffocating to bear, Elise moved forward. She wiped at her face, where her hair had fallen into her eyes. Blood smeared over her cheek, and she couldn't be bothered to acknowledge who it belonged to. She focused on Josi, her lips trembling. "You did this?" Elise's voice came out flat and lifeless. Out of the corner of her eye, she saw Sterling burying his face in his hands and Jamie turning to rake his fingers through his hair. Only Josi remained in her spot, still and with her gaze trained on the pool of Layla's blood.

Josi sniffed and finally lifted her eyes to Elise. True guilt shadowed the usually warm brown of her gaze. "I'm sorry, Lisey. I tried to help. They were just supposed to die—I didn't want them to hurt you," Josi cried. A heavy breath shuddered out of her, curving her spine and her shoulders until she curled into the fetal position on the blood-soaked floor.

Even with her words to guide her through her misery, Elise could not find it in her to feel sorry. Not now. Not when her entire life had been upended in a matter of moments just seconds after she thought she had pieced it back together. A calm fury spread through her body, taking to her blood like ice and fire until she could no longer feel the brush of the outside air flowing in through the open door.

Her younger sister continued to sob. She looked smaller than ever. Her newly evolved strength had vanished in an instant with the emergence of her tears. The little girl Elise had remembered before everything had come crashing down slowly returned, yet all Elise could think of was how every bad thing had been attached to Josi's arrival. She stormed forward and gripped Josi's chin so hard, the girl was forced to her knees in front of Elise.

"*You did this?*" Elise screamed. She pointed at Layla's final struggle marked in blood; her finger, bloody and trembling, was a devastated accusation.

Josi cried harder. She reached for Elise's hand and tried to pry her fingers away from her face. Even with her new strength, her grief seemed to overpower her. Elise kept a firm grip on her chin to the point that red indentations began to form along Josi's jaw. "You've ruined everything. Do you understand? You're cursed," Elise screamed again. Fear struck across Josi's expression then, but with every furious emotion overtaking Elise now, she had no will to stop.

She might have continued if it weren't for Sterling throwing his arms around her waist and hauling her away from Josi.

"That's enough," he gritted into her ear.

Elise wrenched herself out of his arms and picked up the bullets she had left on the ground. "Take Josi home. I'm going to get Layla—"

"You don't even know where she is—" Jamie started.

But Elise was already halfway out of the alleyway. She heard Sterling mutter something about going with her and the shuffling of feet before Jamie was by her side again. With one final stormy look at her sister, Elise tore out of the area, leaving the calamitous death behind.

28

Layla dreamed of her again. This time she spun around an empty dance floor with the angel of death that had haunted her rare sleeps since she had made the violent transition to reaperhood. Layla stared into Elise Saint's brown eyes with soft affection even as she swung her across the ballroom and lowered her into a swaying dip. Despite it all—the eeriness of the quiet environment and the grace with which they moved to the point it seemed like neither of them was actually touching the floor—Layla loved every second of it. For so long, she had dreamed only of the haunting music Elise had composed and the back of her while she sat at the piano and refused to turn no matter how much Layla screamed for her to look at her. All those years of her begging for Elise's attention, and now she had it so wholly. Things might have been perfect.

A searing pain exploded in her thigh, and Layla's legs buckled beneath her. Elise tried to hold her up, but the floor had opened up underneath her, and suddenly their fingers were slipping apart and Layla was falling, falling, until all she could see of Elise was a tiny speck of light amid the darkness. The fall should have been endless. In dreams, they usually were. But Layla's head slammed into something so hard, her ears rang and black dots danced along her vision.

She jolted upright, gasping as her surroundings came into focus. Slowly, four metal walls materialized around her, and she breathed easier, her heart rate settling just the slightest bit. Salt stung her nose on each inhale, and the room swayed despite her sitting still. While no windows covered either of the walls, Layla knew she had to be on a boat. She tried to move and get a better look around her, but her thigh screamed in pain and chains cut into her wrists behind her.

Looking down, her eyes caught sight of a ragged white fabric tied around her thigh. Blood seeped through the tie and began to drip onto the floor beneath her. In her struggle, she must have loosened the tourniquet—the pain of her wound circled her mind now, crushing her thoughts and any previous ideas she'd had about freeing herself. Still, Layla tried to move again. Her wrists burned against the hot metal cuffs, and she winced, her muscles throbbing with the exertion. Hunger too, Layla realized, with a slight panic. Her memories returned to her in a flood, slamming into one another as she tried to concentrate on something other than the misery in her thigh. All the blood she had lost at the Nest Club—it would need to be replenished before she did something she regretted. Layla tried one final time to switch her position, but the sharp movement only tore at her shoulder, causing a new ache to worry about.

"There's no use in fighting. It's Saint steel." A voice called out nearby.

She stopped struggling and lifted her eyes to the small door at the other end of the room. Nicoletta stood in the doorway, her arms crossed and face fixed with a smug expression. The hand Elise had shot back at the club looked completely healed, much to Layla's shock. Her gaze swept the room, passing over the chains and other holding spots Layla had failed to notice in her freshly awoken state. If she trained her attention more, she could hear the panic and frenzied activities of nearby reapers. The scent of their blood seeped through the walls around her, creating a hotbox of suffering and torture.

Bile rose in Layla's throat. She looked away and clenched her jaw, her throat burning as she fought to keep her disgust down. "What did you do?" Layla managed to grit out once the nausea had finally passed.

Nicoletta shrugged. She stepped farther into the holding room and leaned against the wall opposite Layla. "You put up a decent fight, but in the end, it wasn't enough." Nicoletta tapped her chin, as if pondering. "All your allies and your Saint girl and her family... they have suffered worse fates by now. Look at the mess you have caused." Nicoletta chuckled, and the sound sent a burning fury through Layla's body.

Her heart pounded at the thought of Elise and everyone she

had left behind at the club. While her memories were still piecing themselves back together, she could not help but borrow grief from simply not knowing enough. Whether Elise and Josi were okay. If Layla had left them to die an even worse death than she had narrowly escaped.

A slow smile spread across Nicoletta's face. "You're worried about your girl. While I cannot assure you that she's okay, you should know that she knew you tried to save her. Valiant efforts, truly."

Layla glared. She wanted to lunge forward, strike her, tear into her throat—anything at all to get her to stop talking. Her words were a far worse torture than the slowly healing wound in her thigh. "I'll kill you. If you touch her, I'll kill you and your entire crew just like I killed your brother."

Her words seemed to hit Nicoletta. The gang leader finally frowned.

The sight of her true self revealed beyond the layers of brute strength made Layla smile. "I enjoyed watching the life leave his eyes and feeling his blood run between my fingers. I'm curious to know if your blood is as bitter as his."

Nicoletta raised a fist to the door and banged on it. She shouted something at passing workers, but Layla could only focus on the growing knot of hunger in her system. The sound of Nicoletta's fist against the metal rattled Layla's head, making her wince and sit back as the severity of her starvation emerged once more. Her ears continued to ring even as the room fell quiet once more, and every time Layla blinked, it spun.

Somehow Nicoletta appeared in front of her and spoke loudly enough to stop Layla's ravenous desires. "I thought about convincing her to keep you alive, but you've lost your chance." The gang leader left, slamming the door after her, leaving Layla with a never-ending ringing of hell, before she could even ask who Nicoletta was referring to.

Ignoring the searing pain, Layla pulled her knees up to her chest and leaned her head against her thighs, hoping and praying for death to come swiftly.

Elise eyed the ship leaving the port. She had arrived just as the departure had been announced and was held back by Jamie before she could execute a hasty decision to chase after it.

"In the short time I have known you, you have had many terrible ideas, Saint, but I believe this might be one of the worst ones. Especially without backup," Jamie murmured as they crouched behind some shipping crates just beyond the dock.

Rolling her eyes, Elise checked her revolver once more to ensure that she had at least a few rounds of ammunition. After she snapped it shut, she looked up at Jamie with a slight frown. "I actually think it's a much better idea for me to do this on my own. I'm not sure why Sterling sent you."

Jamie blinked. "Because he doesn't want you to die, Elise. Whether it's to stay in your father's good graces, or whether it's because he genuinely cares about you, I don't know. But now I've been dragged into things, and you're giving me orders like I asked to be here. I will have you know, I never let my men speak to me like this," he huffed.

Elise studied his exasperated expression. A small fleck of dried blood stained his chin, but beyond a few droplets, she found him to be quite spotless for someone who had witnessed a near massacre. "I find that very hard to believe. I've never seen you raise your voice at anyone—"

"You've never seen me with my men," Jamie said. He glanced over his shoulder as if expecting someone's arrival.

"I guess I will see you in action tonight." Elise already had half a thought as to what he had planned during their trek to the port. She had a plan of her own, and even though Jamie had insisted on calling his men to assist, she had refused simply because he could not agree with her on one condition.

"I told you not to call your men for help unless you brought a bomb, by the way," Elise mumbled. She peered out from behind the cartons, and once she noticed that the port's guards had moved out of her line of sight, she stood, brushing her dress off before starting toward the dock.

Jamie hurried beside her and whispered roughly, "I do not have bombs. No one just has bombs. Grenades maybe. But bombs? You'd have better luck asking your father for some."

Elise ignored his quip. "Just have your men ready at my signal."

"Which is?" Jamie asked.

"You will know." Elise waved as the guards spotted them. She stood calmly despite them pulling their guns on her and Jamie when they approached.

One worked more aggressively, shoving his gun into her sternum, while the other eyed Jamie with suspicion and pointed the gun at him from a distance. "Who the hell are you?" the first man demanded. "What business do you have here?"

"She's a Saint, you idiot," the other man whispered.

Elise's brow furrowed at the ease he made his claim with. Was it that she looked like a Saint, or was it that they had committed her face to memory? Either reasoning made her spine tingle with relative distress. She held her hands up and spoke in a calm voice. "There is no need for any of this. I have a delivery."

"I don't see a package," one guard said, glancing around her and Jamie.

"It's monetary. One need not walk around with hundreds of dollars in view," Elise said. "I have business with Nicoletta. I suggest you stop that ship so she can get paid, or it will be hell for everyone involved in keeping her from her money."

Both guards stared at each other for far longer than Elise thought was necessary. Her jaw ached from the irritated grinding of her teeth before they finally split apart. One ran down the dock to converse with another man in charge, while the other stayed back, still pointing his gun between Jamie and Elise. After what felt like ages, the first man finally returned, winded and breathing hard.

"We will take you to the ship. May I ask what this delivery is for?" he asked.

Elise shared a look with Jamie. He gave her an almost imperceptible shake of his head, and she turned back to the man, sighing. "If I told Nicoletta you inquired about her money, would she be happy? Because I can tell her as soon as I board the ship, and we can all be privy to her thoughts on the matter."

The man's mouth gaped. "I…I—well, we would…"

Elise shook her head before he could stutter his way into a trap. "I understand. Why don't we keep our business affairs private then? You work for the port. I work with her." She nodded to the ship, which had stopped only a few yards away from the dock they stood near. "Take me to her."

The boat ride to the ship was swift and somewhat unnerving. Elise had asked Jamie to stay on land so that he might keep watch in case anything went awry. Really, she needed him ready with his own arsenal. Elise knew he had much better resources than her. The moment Nicoletta saw her, the ship would erupt into chaos. And that was if she was lucky. There was always a chance Nicoletta could shoot her on sight. After the mess she had left at the Nest Club, Elise had her doubts.

As the small motorboat pulled up to the larger ship, Elise's body buzzed with anticipation and residual anger. The closer they got to the ship, the more she tuned her surroundings out and only thought of what it would be like to finally confirm that Layla lived. She had to have survived the attack at the Nest Club. There was no other way for things to continue if she had not. Elise was not even sure she could return to her family with Layla alive after the way she had exploded on her own sister. There had been no love in how she had screamed or what she had said. All this time Elise had been missing her sister and assumed all would be right when she reunited with her family, but that could not have been further from the truth. That, she had come to realize, was the most difficult part of all this. Understanding that the truth often caused more grief than it did relief. And that no matter how intensely she planned anything out, life would always take her fate into its own hands. Elise did not want to believe she had been born a tragedy, but the world had taught her that in fewer instances in only eighteen years than most people experienced in their lifetime. When, she wondered, would she ever catch the relief of a normal life that most people complained about?

One of the crew members helped her onto the ship, and she turned away from the waves lapping up against the rusting metal as the smaller boat pulled back toward the docks.

"You can wait here. I will bring Nicoletta to you," he said before hurrying down the side of the ship.

Already, Elise knew she had walked into a trap. The only thing that kept her upright and calm was the knowledge that she had planned at least half of it. Nicoletta did not intend to let her leave this ship, dead or alive. Not when the boat that brought her was already yards away, halfway to its journey back to land. Not when she knew Layla remained in one of the many rooms that made up this massive ship. Elise would be stuck until she found her or until Nicoletta managed to kill them. Whichever one came first.

She ignored the man's instructions and made her way down the corridor opposite from the one he had left through. With her gun in hand and her quick steps, she felt comfortable moving through an enemy's territory. Once she arrived at the first block of rooms, Elise pushed the doors open one by one. The first couple of holding rooms were empty, with chains still littering the floor. A couple of rooms down, she opened the door to find a few reapers slumped against the walls. Bound and starved to the point where their fangs remained out and eyes had gone black, they could barely lift their heads when they saw her, despite the evident shock jumping across their pale expressions.

Elise glanced around the ship's corridor quickly to make sure no one had spotted her before walking into the holding room. "Were you all captured by Nicoletta?"

"Who?" the reaper closest to her asked.

"The woman leading this ship. She's tall, dark hair, Italian—"

"She tricked us. I…I was going for a hunt, and she said she had bodies that needed moving. We offered to take care of them for her. But when we arrived at the scene, she attacked us. Then we woke up here." The reaper looked around at his comrades. One of them leaned to the side so heavily with his eyes closed, Elise thought he might have already been gone.

She shuddered and knelt before the reaper nearby. "What did she do to you?"

He shook his head, sighing while he rested his head against the wall. "I only remember her having a Saint knife and using it to bleed us. Maybe she thought it would be better if we were weak."

Elise fumbled with her hairpin, trying to figure out how to open it so she could pick the lock holding the chains around his wrists. "But a blood fury—" she began.

"It's only triggered by fresh blood," he interrupted. His eyes flashed while they roamed her face. "You look familiar."

Reminders of the two guards at the port immediately recognizing her Saint heritage made her chest tighten. Elise pushed a stray piece of hair behind her ear and continued working on the lock. "I'm going to free you because I need your help. We're a little way away from the dock by now, but if you're a strong enough swimmer, we can make it back—that's if things go wrong. If they go right, we can figure out how to turn this boat around. I just need you to promise me something first." She held his gaze, her heart rate kicking up when she noticed the light leaving his eyes.

"What's that?" the reaper asked.

"Help me find Layla," Elise whispered.

Shock flickered across his gaze. He lifted his head from the wall and frowned. "You're a Saint. Here you are, freeing a reaper, asking us to help you." The reaper shook his head and laughed slightly—or tried to; it came out as a cough.

Elise pulled back, her brows furrowing. "I'm hardly a Saint anymore. And how do you even know?"

"You look just like your father."

Every muscle in Elise's body tensed, and her heart sank. Her blood might have gone cold and her surroundings wavered as she processed his words. Elise had never seen herself as a reflection of either of her parents, but now, with her mother's death still fresh on her mind and every complicated emotion under the sun plaguing each thought of her father, she could not figure out how to embrace having her father's looks. Her voice came out like a whisper, the words barely clawing their way out of her throat: "Don't say that."

The reaper continued, seemingly unfazed by her adverse reaction. "I've seen him all over the papers and in town with his buddy Stephen. Or at least I used to. The man is more mad widower than business mogul now…" His eyes grew glassy, and after a long beat of silence, Elise's shoulders seized with panic, thinking he had died.

She leaned forward and slapped his cheeks until he shuddered awake. "The Saint empire is done. I'm not with him anymore. I'm here for Layla. Do you know where she is? Or do you at least know what's going on here?"

The faint sound of footsteps and shouting voices arose nearby. Elise looked toward the door, where thankfully no gangsters had yet to pass by. But she knew it was only a matter of time before they discovered her freeing these reapers.

"They're taking us somewhere," the reaper breathed.

Elise stuck her hairpin in the lock and began turning it. "Yes, I got that. Where are they taking you?"

"I have heard…some island. For testing."

There was a sharp click, and then the lock opened. Elise tugged it off the chains and helped the reaper up just as a commotion exploded across the ship. Loud voices emerged even closer than before, this time accompanied with the ship's alarm. It blared as Elise made her way to the other reapers and freed them as well. Her hairpin grew jagged, the jewels already scraping off as the scratches wore down the true silver. She cursed as the final lock challenged the weakening pin, but she eventually got it free. Once all the reapers had struggled to their feet and looked at Elise for direction, she nodded.

"Find Layla for me."

She followed them out of the holding room and kept her gun clutched in her hand the whole way down the corridor. Gangsters slammed down nearby hallways, shoving open doors and shouting at prisoners. Elise winced every time their noises got closer and each time they opened a door. All she could do was hope and pray that she got to Layla first. Her confidence waned as they approached the end of the corridor and the last door. She prepared herself for disappointment when the reapers pushed the door open. But the moment they stepped back and looked at her, her heart nearly fell into pieces.

There was Layla, chained and pale inside. Elise ran right to her, dropping her gun on the floor between them. She kneeled before Layla and cupped her cheeks in her hands, her eyes already welling with tears of relief. Layla looked at her and tried to smile, but her head, heavy as it was in Elise's hands without the proper strength to hold it up on her own, lolled to the side. Still, her eyes seemed to smile and shine as Elise held her and grinned through her tears.

"Lisey? You came," Layla said in a faint voice.

Elise rubbed her thumbs over her cheeks and nodded. "Of course." She quickly assessed Layla's body, noticing the bloody tourniquet on her leg and the chains still holding her down. "I'm going to get you out. Just do me a favor and stay alive. I cannot have come this far just to have you die on me." When she dropped her hands and moved to take hold of the chains, she felt blood seep into her dress around her knees and slip between her fingers. The wound on Layla's leg still wept. Surprisingly, the reaper's face was void of any pain, though she was frightfully pale. Elise knew they had only so much time before either Layla bled out or the gangsters found them all. She looked up at the other reapers she had freed, still standing by the door.

"How do you get a reaper to stop bleeding after suffering a wound from a Saint weapon?" Elise asked. She stuck her hairpin into the lock and began working it against the gears.

The other reapers looked at one another, mumbling.

Layla cleared her throat and nudged Elise with her good leg. "You can't stop the bleeding. That's the point of the Saint weaponry."

Elise hissed as the hairpin snagged on something in the lock and got stuck. "I know, I know. But isn't there anything that will help? If we move you, you'll bleed out."

Layla leaned her head against the wall. "I need more blood."

The hairpin snapped in Elise's hands. Half of it remained between her fingers, while the other half sat, still stuck, in the lock. "Fuck," she muttered. Before Elise could figure something else out, gunfire went off around the ship.

One reaper at the door looked out at the hallway, then back at Elise. "They're coming. You need to hurry."

Panic seized Elise's chest like a fiery fist. Her heart thudded so hard and fast, she thought it might catch on fire or explode. She leaned over Layla, searching for a release, or something to use behind her where the chains were bound to a bar set in the wooden floor.

Layla swallowed and shifted uncomfortably. More blood poured from her wound, her leg trembling as she adjusted her position. Elise felt Layla's face by her throat and a sharp wince before she turned away. "Don't do that."

Elise sat back on her heels. Her brows furrowed at Layla's twisted expression. Her fangs dug into her lips, but only a thin stream of blood ran from the new cuts in her mouth. "Don't do what?"

"You can't be this close to me right now. I'm…" Layla swallowed, and her pupils dilated while her chest heaved with a deep breath. "I'll kill you." She watched Elise with a gaze that went beyond hunger. She had moved past ravenous and now regarded Elise like a downright predator eyeing their prey. Her eyes, black and glassy, no longer had a trace of her familiar gold.

Elise's throat tightened and went dry at the sight. She took a deep breath, pulling herself back while her hand closed over her gun. If Layla noticed her defensive retreat, she did not say anything. She continued to watch Elise with those eyes, her muscles straining while her arms fought against the restraints.

"Now!" one of the reapers at the door called.

Elise gripped the gun hard and pulled herself back to her original position by Layla. She ignored her desperate gaze and nodded to the open floor nearby. "Get as far away as you can. I'm going to shoot this thing off."

"Just shoot. I trust you," Layla rasped.

Elise could only roll her eyes. "You really have a death wish, don't you?" She aimed for the wood around the metal bar on which Layla was chained and fired. A gunshot would no doubt draw more crew members and gangsters toward them, but the only thing Elise cared about in this moment was Layla and getting her free. Once the wood splintered into pieces and part of the floor fell away, Elise reached down to pull the metal bar up. She slipped the chain off it and helped Layla into a standing position after the reaper managed to pull her bound wrists in front of herself. Dried blood crusted around deep burns on her wrists where the cuffs dug in. Still, the reaper made no complaints and only breathed heavily while Elise tried to move them forward.

Layla swung an arm around her shoulder and leaned heavily on Elise, her injured leg dragging between them. "You need to go. I'm only slowing you down." Layla.

Elise rolled her eyes again. "Say something like that again and I will make Hendricks sleep in your room tonight." Layla's head shake and faint smile made her heart slow to a calmer rhythm. If only for a moment. Elise crouched to tear a piece of her dress off and wrap it haphazardly around Layla's leg. The bleeding seemed to weaken under the applied pressure, though Layla still struggled to stand on it. When they faced the door, however, all the reapers had disappeared. Instead, a seething young woman stared down at them.

"What have you done?" Nicoletta growled.

Despite the chaos erupting around the boat, from the gunshots to shouting gangsters, Elise still heard the rush of water increasing beneath their shoes. Her gunfire had no doubt gone all the way through the ship, no matter how unintentionally. Elise was glad for it, seeing the panic and true ire on Nicoletta's face. She opened her revolver and saw the final bullet in its chamber. Then Elise met Nicoletta's eye and smiled sweetly. "We're sinking your operation."

Nicoletta barked out a humorless laugh. "You will drown. We all will."

Elise shook her head. "No. You'll die before you can touch the water." Before Nicoletta could properly react to her threat, Elise lifted her gun and fired off her last round.

The bullet barely grazed Nicoletta's arm. It skimmed right over her, leaving her bare shoulder red with a line of blood and burnt flesh. Her sinister smile widened on Elise, and she reached for her own gun, stepping forward. "You missed me, you fool."

Though the gang leader seethed, Elise did not have to respond to her anger. Layla had already stepped away from her. The reaper's eyes, sharp and black, honed in on the crimson leaking down Nicoletta's arm, and her fangs dripped her own blood as her lips parted. She inhaled, more blood spilling from her mouth.

Nicoletta's expression fell into fear. She backed up and tried to lift her gun, but Layla was already charging forward.

29

Nicoletta closed the door, but Layla burst through it like a bullet through flesh. She caught up to Nicoletta in the corridor and slammed her into the ground. The moment Elise's bullet had split the gang leader's skin, exposing her blood to the atmosphere, it had been all Layla could focus on. For some time, she had feared she might give in to her urges to drink from Elise. It would have been forceful and messy. Even more than that—violent. Layla did not like to think about it. But the whole time Elise had been near her, all she could smell was her sweet blood. This Saint girl, she would never understand just how much of a hold she had over Layla. Elise had worked with her most precious life force pulsing only inches from Layla's begging teeth. It was a miracle they'd both made it out of that room with just Layla's blood covering them.

Now, however, Layla relished in the spray of another human's blood. She dug into Nicoletta's chest and throat, tearing at her flesh until her muscles and tendons stuck between her fingers and beneath her nails. The gang leader gurgled on her own blood, her mouth hanging open while she stared up at the dark sky above them. Still, Layla did not drink from her. Though blood found its way down her throat from her messy slaying, she refused to fill herself with this gangster's rotten essence. By now, after getting her fill of violence and shedding some of her angry instincts, most of her blood fury had subsided from uncontrollable urges. Every once in a while, the snapping restriction between her arms reminded her of the Saint chains she still wore, and Layla snarled with frustration as she squeezed bits of Nicoletta's flesh in her hands.

The gang leader let out a shuddering breath. Despite the deep gashes in her chest and at the base of her throat, she still lived. Layla had been careful to avoid any major arteries or organs. She wanted the woman to suffer for as long as possible.

Nicoletta opened her mouth as if to speak, but before any words came out, a bullet whizzed by Layla's ear. She snapped her head up and turned, finding the culprit. One of Nicoletta's men stood by the corner of the corridor, gun in hand and aimed at her. Layla rose and charged for him. He ducked back behind the wall, but she got to him before he could lift his gun again. She shoved her nails into his throat and tore it open, sending his blood across the floor and windows along the wall in a brilliant red fountain. Layla let his body slump onto the damp floor and continued down the corridor, chasing the other gangsters. They tried to run from her, but with the water seeping over the deck coupled with her fury-led speed, she caught up to each of them and killed them even faster. By the time she had gone through them all, tearing throats open and reaching right into their ribs to pull their beating hearts from their bodies, blood covered her body from head to toe.

Layla panted as she rounded more corners. The massacre ran the boat red. Her hands appeared gloved in scarlet. They shook as she lifted them before her, the chains hanging between her wrists. Even the Saint metal had been tainted with all the carnage. Some stringy flesh clung to one of the metal links, and Layla's throat bobbed at the thought of leaving all that fresh human blood wasted and ready to rot on the sinking ship around her.

Water spilled over her feet, and she stumbled as the ship swayed. Layla reached for a grip on the wall, her heart skipping a beat when she remembered Elise. With all the blood around her, it was difficult to parse out Elise's scent, but she found it and followed it out to the upper deck. The farther she traveled, the faster the water seemed to fill the ship. It careened violently to one side every few seconds, and Layla had to grip the wall several times to prevent herself from falling over.

"*Elise!*" Layla shouted. She hoped to see the Saint poke her head around one corner, smiling and relieved. But even as Layla continued to call for her, she found no one.

Horror struck through her at one particularly vicious thought. What if one of the bodies she had left behind had been Elise's? What if through all her rage and starvation, she had failed to realize that she took Elise's life? Had failed to recognize her face in the midst of her ravenous drive for destruction?

Layla's throat tightened and she shook her head. *No. No, no, no.* She would retrace all her steps—cover every inch of the ship if she had to. Layla refused to find Elise dead. Her Elise—

An explosion rocked the ship. Layla was thrown into a nearby wall, hitting it so hard, her vision swam. It continued for a long moment, and all she could think about was the blood around her and how starved she had been for a taste of a particular human's essence. She struggled to stand, her hands slipping on the blood- and water-slicked deck. Eventually, Layla found purchase and forced herself to her feet.

She stood alone on a ghost ship full of bodies and blood. Layla let out a heavy breath and braced herself against the onslaught of sudden emotions. A sob rose in her chest, but she clenched her jaw against it, bearing the pain to keep herself together. Crying would not solve any of her problems. It would not get her off this sinking ship, and it certainly would not find Elise.

She pushed herself away from the wall and began walking the corridor again, but not even moments after she righted herself, a gun went off nearby. The bullet burrowed into her chest, shoving her back against the wall. Layla pressed her hand to her ribs, and blood came away, crimson and deadly in the moonlight. Her knees buckled at the sight, and she slid down the wall, her blood trailing along the corroded metal behind her. On the floor, her vision distorted, her hunger rising again and rearing its head like a beast within. Every part of her body ached, and keeping herself alert and awake only got more difficult with each passing moment.

Layla felt her lips moving and words spilling from her mouth while she tried to utter something. An apology, perhaps, for all those she had failed and let down. Her death had been a long time coming—this much she knew. But as long as Layla had lived as a reaper, she had hoped she would find a new purpose in life and reason to keep going. Something that would make her more okay with being half dead until she eventually had to be put to rest permanently.

She swallowed back a mouthful of blood and opened her eyes to the night sky. Tears emerged again, and this time she did not stop them from falling.

One wicked thing interrupted her grief into her own death. The blood of sin and stubborn perseverance that filled her senses and forced her to look away from the bleeding sky. Nicoletta stood at the end of the corridor, her hand, shaking and bloody, on her gun. "It's over for you." The woman could barely limp along the sliding, slippery floor. The water was up past her ankles, and she gripped the wall so hard, Layla half expected to see marks in the metal. Despite the gaping wounds in her chest and the blood covering more than half her body, Nicoletta still managed to approach Layla on her own two feet. She gave her a bloody smile and raised her gun again, pointing it directly at Layla's face. "You have ruined everything."

With a hand pressed to her own weeping chest, Layla laughed breathlessly. It felt as if blood swam in her lungs. She coughed, and more of it spilled over her lips, leaving a sticky, salty taste on her tongue. "Harlem will never trust you to run its streets. You should have just listened to us."

Nicoletta's mouth twisted into a frown, her brows furrowing beneath the blood caking her face. The gun shook with her arms, and for a moment, Layla thought she might drop it. "You don't get it. I have no choice. I have to find the quickest path to power, or I am nothing. My brother is gone and now so is my property. I have only my reputation left, and I will not let you control that too—" Her finger moved to the trigger, and Layla braced herself for the impact of another bullet.

But the voice she had been waiting forever to hear rang out. "I don't think so."

Layla looked up to see Elise on the upper deck just a few yards away. Even with the considerable distance between them, Layla still tried to assess her, noting the blood on her hands and her dress and relaxing with relief when she realized none of it was hers. Elise stood strong, holding her own gun with a firmness that only an uninjured person could muster. She faced Nicoletta, though her eyes flicked down to Layla occasionally. With her gun pointed at Nicoletta, Elise scowled and said, "You try anything against her, I kill you."

"What does it matter? She'll be dead by the time you even realize I pulled the trigger again." Nicoletta laughed maniacally. The force of her laughter caused her to stumble back a few feet, but she righted herself against the wall and smiled up at Elise. "That's the beautiful thing about your family's invention. The bullets do most of the work for you. Now we just get to sit back and watch her bleed."

"No," Elise countered. She reached into her bodice and pulled a handful of silver bullets out, holding them up for the gang leader to see. "I can't believe you didn't realize I had switched out your bullets." Now Elise wore a smug smile of her own, one that chased Nicoletta's previous mirth right from her face.

Nicoletta's mouth gaped. She shakily opened her revolver and poured out the bullets in the chamber. They dropped into the water and rolled along the deck, regular lead bullets in the ocean pouring itself into the ship. "No," she croaked. Her voice, hoarse and quiet, was so unlike her usual commanding tone, Layla could not help but look up at Elise with a spark of awe in her eyes. Elise met her gaze for a second, mirroring her relief.

The pressure in Layla's chest lightened, and she knew it was not just because of her wound knitting itself back together. Though when she pulled her hand away from her chest, where the bullet had lodged itself, she found fresh skin already forming over the new injury. She swallowed hard, relief crashing into her in waves that rivaled the intensity of the ones rocking the ship around them. Part of her wondered how much of it truly was the ship versus her own hunger working in tandem with her budding anger. She stood slowly, letting her nerves settle before she faced Nicoletta.

The gang leader dropped her gun. It sank into the water swirling around her legs, and she kicked it off of the ship before holding her hands up in surrender. A gentle look had appeared on her face, but the more Layla watched her, the more suspicious she became. "Fine. You win. Take the compound back. Just let me go."

Despite her sudden yielding making Layla doubt Nicoletta's every move, she could not have agreed more with such a bold offer. At the end of the day, that was what they had confronted her for. And all Layla really wanted now was to get off this ship with Elise and go back to their regular adversaries.

But Elise had other plans. "No," she said roughly, moving closer on the upper level.

"No?" Nicoletta asked, bewildered.

"Elise," Layla warned.

"You knowingly helped run an operation that exploited my baby sister. How dare you," Elise hissed.

Nicoletta laughed. It was a wicked, cruel sound that had Layla's muscles bunching with the urge to silence her. "What can I say? Her asking price was astronomical." Elise's gun hand shook, but she let Nicoletta continue. "Reapers and humans paid a pretty penny for her blood and venom. It would have been the same for your mother if only we had managed to keep her alive. I understand your despair, Elise, I truly do. It must be awful, right? Feeling responsible for the death of a loved one?"

Elise sniffed. Layla watched with horror as the glimmer of fresh tears arose in her eyes. She did not wait to hear what Elise said in response to Nicoletta's cruelty. Layla was already throwing herself into Nicoletta by the time her anger fully registered. She pinned the gang leader to the floor and relished in the strength her blood fury gave her in assistance with her rage. All Layla saw was red. Even as she faced Nicoletta, even as she tore into her fresh wounds, rehashing old pains and turning them into worse pits of hell. She tasted only satisfaction as she sank her fangs into her own wrist and held it over Nicoletta's mouth, forcing her to swallow mouthfuls of her blood. Her hunger increased with the loss of blood, but Layla continued, shoving Nicoletta's mouth closed and then tearing her throat out. She waited for a moment as the gang leader's breathing stilled beneath her. Eventually, her heartbeat stopped, and Layla noticed her blood flow coming to a complete halt. The gang leader stared up at the night sky with glassy eyes, her face stuck in a permanent state of pure terror. She had died, gurgling and choking on Layla's blood. While it was certainly one of the most vicious displays of violence Layla could claim, it was not her coldest. This had been an act she had imagined for many years, just not being done to Nicoletta.

Her heart stuttered as she stood and blood rushed from her head. The adrenaline of the night had begun to wear off, leaving Layla a body of sore muscles and aching cravings. She tried to walk away from Nicoletta, but Elise, having climbed down from the upper deck, appeared, her eyes soft and wild at once on Layla. "Are you okay?"

Layla could barely nod. The world spun around her, and she saw three Elises bend down to pick up the keys from Nicoletta's belt. Even as she pulled the chains around Layla's wrists into her hands to unlock them, Layla still couldn't focus on her. While the red haze had left her vision, several black spots danced across it now, and Elise and the sounds of the ships collapsing beneath them sounded impossibly far away. Once the chains came off and fell into the water that quickly climbed up their legs, Layla leaned heavily against Elise. Despite the blood of many gangsters filling the water and covering the interior of the ship around them, all Layla could smell and taste was Elise's. The pulse of her blood beneath her delicate skin brushed against her lips, and Layla closed her eyes, imagining the sweet sanctity sliding over her tongue and exploding into her mouth.

Elise pulled back to press her hands to Layla's cheeks. Her mouth moved, but Layla could barely hear her. Every word sounded like glorified static in her rushing ears. "…Layla…"

Layla's vision slid back to Nicoletta, whose body now floated in the filthy water around them. She turned to Elise once more, her own gaze fixated on the dead gang leader. "She'll be back," Layla whispered.

"I know." A distinct sadness darkened Elise's eyes.

Layla gripped her wrist hard enough to feel her pulse flutter beneath her fingertips. "How are you? Are you hurt?"

At this, Elise almost laughed. "I'm just fine, Layla. We need to get you off the ship—" Another explosion interrupted her. The boat rocked violently, but Elise held Layla steady in her arms. Once their environment slowed to a gentle swaying, Elise loosened her hold on Layla. She groaned as she looked out over the black water lapping up against the side of the ship. "I told Jamie only one bomb…"

But Layla did not hear the end of her statement. The world went sideways as she pitched over the edge of the ship, her fading vision catching sight of Elise's panicked expression among the stars before Layla plummeted into the dark water beyond.

30

Layla woke to a divine being dragging her along the sandy shore. She had been trapped in a nightmare just moments before, where the environment had been a sentient black beast pressing around her like a blanket of ice. It occurred to her that it might have been the ocean only when the divinity pulled her out of the darkness and hauled her onto a steady surface. Layla would have shown her gratitude could she move. But her muscles remained frozen even as lighter, warmer air brushed over her and her salvation leaned over her.

She might have been a lovely siren or an angel pulling her to her death. But Layla would have been glad to die in the presence of such sweet beauty. All she could do was stare as the face came into more clarity.

The siren rolled her onto her back and slapped her cheeks. It was gentle enough to not hurt, but she couldn't ignore the gesture either.

Layla forced her eyes open wider and saw a Saint hovering over her. The night sky surrounded her. She looked as if she wore the stars as a crown, their twinkling lights incomparable to the glow of her pretty eyes. "Layla," she said sharply. *Elise.* Her Elise.

Layla tried to smile, but even her face was too tired to comply. "Yes, angel." Despite the ache of her muscles and the imminent weakness she faced, Layla still managed to sense the quickening of Elise's pulse and the flush of heated blood in her cheeks.

Water flowed from Elise's body, and Layla noticed it lapping at her own feet just beyond. The rushing water urged her memories to piece themselves back together. "Did you jump us off the boat?" Layla asked.

Elise's brows knitted together in confusion. "No. I jumped after you."

"I dove? But I hate swimming," Layla muttered.

"Oh, Layla. We didn't just go swimming." Elise looked around, as if searching for something. Her gaze settled on Layla's again. "What happens if you don't feed for too long? I thought you were supposed to be extremely volatile right now. This is the quietest I've ever seen you."

Layla nodded slowly. "Death."

Panic lit Elise's eyes. "Can you sit up?"

"No," Layla breathed. "I'm not sure I can move."

Elise let out a heavy breath of concern and barely contained panic. She reached into her bodice, and the gesture reminded Layla of when she had done the same thing earlier. But this time she pulled out a knife instead of bullets.

Layla tried to laugh, but she was too weak for it to come out as anything more than a heavy breath. "What else do you have in there?"

The Saint girl ignored her question. She grimaced as she cut into her palm, drawing a thick stream of blood from her flesh. Then she held it over Layla's mouth and allowed the blood to drip into her face. "Shut up and drink. Please."

Layla did not need to be commanded more than once. The moment the blood hit her lips and she lapped at it, her heart rate picked up. More and more strength returned to her body with each swallow, despite her only managing to get a few drops of blood. It was not enough. Layla worried it never would be when it came to Elise. Truthfully, she could have fed on her for an eternity and never been satisfied. Her blood restarted her heart and any long-dead hopes Layla had once had.

Once her strength had returned enough, she sat up, grabbing Elise's hand. Layla ran her tongue along her fingers first, where the blood had streamlined into her mouth, then once all of it had been licked up, she followed the trail to the cut in her palm. Layla could have remained like this forever. If cravings were an act of devotion, Layla would have sat at Elise's altar for an eternity. She looked up from the heiress's hand and regarded Elise with a look of ravenous desire. Their eyes met with lust, Elise's soft and brown, Layla's molten gold. She pressed a kiss to Elise's wrist, lingering on the pulse point and the way her blood pressure seemed to jump beneath her touch. The way Elise tasted and felt—Layla was certain she would never tire of any of it.

She tugged on Elise's hand, pulling her down to her. The moment their bodies met, with Layla's back against the damp sand and Elise sprawled on top of her, Layla sank her fangs into her throat. That familiar liberation and blinding pleasure filled her again as Elise's blood flowed into her mouth. No matter her almost dying moments ago, and her fear of losing Elise, Layla isolated herself in this moment and blocked out everything that distracted her from this pleasure. With her linked to Elise like this, her blood the very thing holding them together, Layla could have died happy. She felt Elise writhing above her, her hand coming down to fist in the sand beside them. Layla dragged her fingers down from the nape of Elise's neck to her spine, feeling the way her muscles bunched and tensed while her back curved under her own bliss.

A soft moan fluttered in Layla's ear, and she retracted her fangs to kiss Elise's throat. It was just faint enough to be a gentle reminder that Layla was in control and their frenzy was more than just carnality. She let Elise pull back to look at her, but the girl's arms buckled, and she fell onto Layla, laughing breathlessly. Every bit of exposed skin Layla's fingers brushed over felt hot and feverish. Her own nerves heated at the thought of Elise enjoying herself just as much as she was, and suddenly, all she wanted was Elise's pleasure on her tongue. Even with the taste of her blood still filling her mouth, all Layla could think about was the way Elise had reacted to her bite—how her body had curled into Layla's and begged for more without uttering a single word. Now she needed all of Elise.

"Feeling better, I assume?" Elise asked. A smile curved her lips, and the light in her eyes flared like stars.

Layla finally managed to smile back properly. She gripped Elise's hips, her fingers brushing over the curves as she leaned into her. "What told you that?"

"I thought you might consume me. It was a powerful bite." Elise lowered her mouth to Layla's ear and whispered, "I liked it."

Layla was at the mercy of Elise's words and actions. She knew if she let Elise do anything else to her, they would both end up in a less-than-holy position tonight. But if the events of the last few hours had told Layla anything, it was that nothing was guaranteed—most of all the future. If Layla believed she might not wake up to another day where she could secure more memories with Elise and see her pretty smile again, then she wanted to make the most of this moment they were in now. So, when Elise moved back to look at Layla again, Layla lunged forward to capture her mouth with her own. Their kisses turned frantic in an instant, the blood on Layla's lips slipping between their mouths. She might have inhaled Elise, relishing in every groan she released in response to Layla's touches. Her hands roamed Elise's body, and she felt her own core heating with an impatient desire that only increased as Elise kissed her harder. Her lips had parted now, and Layla traced her with her tongue, feeling every part of Elise's heat.

Layla pulled back only to drop her lips to Elise's throat once more. She trailed over the fresh bite mark, lapping up the stray drops of blood and sealing the two holes with a gentle lick. The fabric of her dress tickled her chin, and Layla released a grunt of frustration. Without thinking, she reached up to grip the edge of Elise's bodice and tore it. While the thing still remained on her body to cover her in necessary areas, the confinement had been released, and it no longer obstructed Layla's path to Elise's collarbones. Elise gasped at the act of desperation, then laughed. The sound was among the most beautiful forms of music to Layla's ears, rivaled only by the compositions Elise herself had made.

Layla quickly drowned her senses in the softness of Elise's skin. Her lips trailed over her collarbones, her teeth scraping over them and drawing soft moans from Elise. When she got to her throat again and the path of blood that had fallen from the bite mark into the space between her breasts, Layla's stomach clenched.

She looked up at Elise, pressing her fingers into the juncture between her neck and collarbones, then slowly circling her throat. Elise smiled down at her and leaned her head back. She let her hair fall over her shoulders so the moon could shine down on her bare skin—mostly bare. The blood had covered a large deal of it, and Layla thought she had never seen anything more magnificent than the sight of her Elise covered in it.

Her fingers tightened around her throat, feeling the fluttering pulse of her blood beneath her warm skin. "*Elise*," Layla murmured.

Elise's smile widened. She placed her hands on Layla's chest, stroking over the ends of her collarbones. "You're stunning," she said on a heavy breath.

Hearing those words from Elise and seeing her on top of her

while wearing blood like it was her armor did things to Layla that she wasn't sure she could explain. The slight swell of her lips and the messiness of her hair from Layla's ravishing made every part of her body heat to indescribable levels. She smirked, and her teeth dug into her lower lip. "Nice girl. You're sinfully sweet. Such a saint."

Elise leaned down again, letting her lips brush Layla's throat as she whispered, "I let a monster at my throat, and I liked it. I'm not a saint."

Layla laughed. She pulled Elise closer to her and breathed, "You taste so good, my love. I truly believe just your love is enough to quench my thirst forever." Her tongue flicked out to lick the trail of blood between her breasts. Elise shivered beneath her touch, and Layla felt her heart race on the tip of her tongue.

"Forever?" Elise asked shakily.

Layla heard the lasting apprehension in her voice—the same apprehension she had heard when they had spoken outside the lair only a few days ago. But this time, Layla did not feel fear or hesitation in promising Elise an eternity. Their forever began with each other. The clock of eternity had struck its start when they had first met each other, and it would not fail them. "Forever," Layla breathed back as she kissed Elise again. This time, she flipped them over to guide the kiss. And as she pressed Elise into the sand and promised her beauty in the things they did beneath the moonlight, Layla tried hard not to think about the amount of her own blood that Elise might have consumed.

Forever would be different for them. But it would exist in its own time. And that was all that mattered.

Elise's heart raced long after they emerged from the beach. Even as they walked the dock in heated silence, Layla strolling calmly with her hands hidden beneath the pleats of her gown and Elise biting her lip at the thought of everything those particular hands had been doing to her just minutes ago, Elise could not force her blushing to relax.

She cleared her throat, guiding Layla's eyes to her. "You ripped my dress." The once-brilliant golden fabric hung in pitiful bloody tatters around her body. Elise did not care about the state of her dress, truly, but she did want to hear Layla's voice again.

The smile Layla let slip onto her face made Elise's heart rate pick up again. "Can't control myself around you, I guess."

"You shockingly exercised an immense amount of control on the boat."

"Did she?" Jamie asked.

They both turned to look over the edge of the dock and found Jamie sitting beside one of his men in a fast boat by the dock. Even in the darkness, he looked peeved, his cheeks red and his lips downturned.

Elise's face lit up as she remembered how Layla had torn through the boat and every gangster who got in her way. The sight of Jamie's annoyance could not dull her excitement. After all, their plan had worked. "You should've seen her, Jamie. She was amazing."

Layla rolled her eyes, but her cheeks filled with a dark red blush. "I was not the one doing the rescuing." Her amusement wilted as a realization dawned on her. She looked around, frowning. "Where is your sister?"

Everything in Elise went still. Her eyes darkened, and she looked away as her lungs deflated of all air.

Layla touched her hand. "Elise?"

31

The entire way back to Jamie's apartment, Layla would not stop looking at Elise. Not in the way of adoration and awe that she had reserved for her back at the port, but this time with concern and a bit of pity. The switch between two moods had been rather startling—almost as much as Layla reminding Elise of the atrocities that had taken place at the Nest Club. Before, the events of the ship had been at the top of her mind, the only things Elise could process. Now her mind returned to the Nest Club, where her panic had exploded into something severe enough to scar. Josi, poor thing, had only wanted to help. Elise understood that desperation all too well. But Elise's alliances had shifted so much, she had gotten her wires crossed in the process. Elise had never imagined herself getting so short with Josi. Layla might have been in pieces on the ground between them, and yet all Elise could think of in that moment was how angry she felt and how badly she wanted all her pain to disappear. In the end, she had taken everything out on Josi. And the guilt Elise dealt with now weighed on her more heavily than the tattered remains of her dress and bloodstained jewelry.

The moment they arrived at the door to Jamie's, Sterling opened it, poking out his head to see them. He clenched his jaw as he gave them all a once-over. Finally, after their bloody clothes and rumpled appearances had been examined, he let them in. Elise might have commented on the backward nature of this greeting, considering it was Jamie's apartment and not Sterling's, but all she could really focus on was the rate her heart raced, to the point of pain in chest. She expected it to crack ribs beneath its force, and even taking in ample air became difficult the longer they stood at the edge of the apartment with Josi facing the other direction by the window on the far side.

Jamie stopped inside the door and rubbed his fingers into his forehead. He was the first one to break the silence after the long walk back. "I told Josi and Sterling to go to my place because I figured it was better than bringing them to your father."

Layla shook her head. Soft amusement lit her features, and her eyes kept darting to Elise to see whether she was picking up on any of her attempts to lighten the mood. "I can't believe this. You invited more people into your home. How sweet."

"This is not a permanent solution," Sterling said sternly. His lips twisted as he thought. "I have not been able to get Josi to talk. She just…stares and cries." He paused, looking at the state of Elise's and Layla's dresses. "You should change before you see her. She doesn't need to see more blood."

Layla scoffed. "She's not exactly human, you know. I'm pretty sure she *likes* blood now."

Elise's body tensed at her words. Her veins turned to ice, and she felt rows of goose bumps pop up all over her flesh while they moved farther into the apartment, toward Josi. The younger girl sat by the window in her blood-soaked dance costume. She faced the night outside, her chin resting on her knees, which had been drawn up to her chest. Elise left the rest of the group and approached her sister. She waited to for Josi to stir or acknowledge her presence in some way, but the little girl did not budge. Slowly, Elise sat, facing Josi.

She spoke softly at first, not wanting to startle her. "Josi."

Josi's shoulders shuddered. The bow fastened to the end of her bun fluttered as she trembled. Through it all, however, she kept her gaze trained beyond the window, remaining silent.

When Elise spoke again, she took on a rougher, louder tone. "Josi. Please look at me."

Finally, her younger sister met her gaze. Weeping despair filled her red-lined eyes, and Elise saw the depth of the guilt amid it all. Her lips had been bitten to the point of drawing blood, which dried into cracks along her mouth. Scarlet still stained her cheeks, but her face otherwise remained mostly clear. Her pallid expression especially concerned Elise. It was as if all color had been drained from her. She wondered for a brief moment if she was experiencing a reaper-like state of starvation. Elise could not even begin to grasp this new version of her sister—not quite turned, but not fully human.

"You're angry with me," Josi whispered.

"I'm not—"

"I can sense it. Your blood is hot. And your pulse quickened just then when you lied about it," Josi bit out.

Elise swallowed. "I am happy to see you again. And I am really sorry I lost my temper with you at the club."

Josi's arms tightened around her knees, pressing them into her chest. "I was scared. The past few weeks, I've been so scared. I just didn't want to be alone. I've been locked up and hungry and forced to bleed for everyone. I only stayed alive for you, Lisey. But then you came back to me and left again, and I thought if I could help, it would make you stay. It's my fault—"

"No, it's not—" Elise choked on her own distress. Tears filled her eyes, and her throat tightened to the point of pain. She touched Josi's chin, pulling her gaze up to hers. "It's not your fault. There are bad people in this world who want to hurt you. The gangsters and reapers…they would have done whatever they wanted, regardless of what you did." Keeping hold of her sister's chin, Elise held Josi's hand with her free one. "I need you to understand that I am not angry with you. I did not mean any of the things I said. I was just hurt. I'm sorry it's taken me so long to come find you. And I'm sorry for whatever these awful people and Karine and Valeriya did to you. I'm sorry for it all. And I promise you, I won't let anything else happen to you. I won't let anyone or anything else come between us ever again. But you have to promise me you will try your hardest to be safe. And be honest with me, okay?"

Josi nodded. She sniffed and wiped at her tears. "I promise."

"Did you have anything to do with the attacks and people dying around Harlem?" Elise asked.

Her little sister stiffened. She was quiet for a moment, her mouth quivering while she contemplated her next words. "I only went to the gardens because I wanted to see you and Mommy, but Sena killed Mommy to help Karine punish me. Karine made us both hurt that night," Josi whimpered. "I can feel Sena all the time. When Sena is angry, I'm angry. And I can't control it."

A painful lump rose in Elise's throat. "You didn't mean to do… any of those horrible things, did you?"

Josi shook her head. A shadow crossed her eyes. "Is this hurt because of me? I don't want you to hurt because of me."

Elise tucked Josi's head into her chest before she could see her cry. She kissed the top of her head and let her tears fall silently as she hugged her. This embrace was the closest she had been to feeling like she was truly home in forever. In a strange apartment, full of people who had never all worked together before now, the thing that mattered most was her younger sister being alive and well in her arms.

Moments later, they pulled apart, and Elise felt content in letting Josi go off to bathe herself and get ready for bed.

Sterling stood with Jamie and Layla in the kitchen when Elise returned to them. "I think she'll be okay. For now at least. I will eventually have to talk to her about everything she's been through."

Layla's jaw clenched. She shook her head and pressed her knuckles against the counter. "She's lying."

Elise blinked. "What? She's not a liar."

"I sensed it from here, Elise. She's done all those terrible things and probably more," Layla said in a low voice.

While part of Elise had already somewhat convinced herself that her sister might have been on the other side of these attacks, she couldn't stop the venom seeping into her tone. "She's attacking your enemies. Why do you care?"

Layla's eyes widened. "Why don't you care? There are probably a million lethal targets on your sister's head right now. Our association with her puts us at risk. Her actions have already gotten my clan into trouble. She has to stop."

"She's here with us now. I can't imagine that she would continue."

"You heard her. When Valeriya is angry, so is she. We need to find Valeriya before she snaps."

"That's a you problem," Elise grumbled.

Layla's expression went cold. "Is it? Really? You killed her and are probably the reason why she's evolved the way she has."

"*You* are the one who sold her body to Karine," Elise shot back.

Layla went still. "I did no such thing."

A searing glare darkened Elise's face. She turned to leave, but Layla's voice chased after her.

"And what about Josi? If she's really linked to Valeriya, don't you worry that killing her will kill your sister too? Don't you wonder what their blood connection means for us and our shared blood?" Layla demanded.

Elise waited for her heated rage to simmer before she responded in a level voice. "We need to find her, and we need to find the person who is responsible for doing this to them. Maybe they can reverse the effects. Karine is no scientist, so surely she has outside help. I'm sure whoever is on the island Nicoletta was taking you to has more answers."

"Daddy's old friend." Josi's voice sounded from the hallway.

Paling, Elise shared a look with her little sister. "Do you mean Dr. Gray?"

Elise helped Josi into Layla's bed and stood in her doorway until she was sure she had fallen asleep. Even after that, when she came to the living room to sit with Layla by the window, all Elise could think about was how tiny Josi looked beneath the blankets.

Layla shifted as Elise settled beside her. "How is she? I figured she would want a bed. Who knows what Karine had her sleeping on—if she let her sleep at all?" Layla said.

A buzzing that had started at the beginning of the night in the apartment continued now, making Elise's thoughts hard to keep track of and even conversation threads with Layla difficult to follow. "Fine, thank you." She blinked as Layla furrowed her brows at her. "Sorry…reapers don't have to sleep?"

"Technically no. But we would be so much more miserable if we didn't. Sleep deprivation severely inhibits our impulse control. If Karine was keeping Josi from sleeping, that could explain her erratic behavior," Layla said. Her eyes roamed Elise's face, picking up on all the distress she wore. "Then again, she's newly turned, so who knows? Maybe she just needs more training. I've never seen anything like her before; I would assume it has to do with Valeriya's ancient blood and venom being what changed her."

Elise looked at her then, an idea coming to her. "Could you train her?"

Layla nodded. "Once I know exactly what she needs. If she's as in-between as Karine and other reapers say she is, then Josi probably doesn't need blood. So I can just teach her how to control her emotions—especially anger. For now, I think it's best if we starve her and go from there."

A loud meow cut between them, and they both turned to see Hendricks pawing at the door to where Josi slept. While Elise had no energy to shoo the cat away, Layla bared her fangs at him. Much to their surprise, the door opened, and the cat trotted in before it closed again.

Elise tensed at the thought of her younger sister alone with that cat. By now she was convinced he was more demon than feline— perhaps an abomination created in the shadows of the earth. Elise could not remember a time where she had been more afraid than when she was home alone with Hendricks the first for the first time and he would not let her leave the kitchen area. The cat had crouched on the counter and watched her with sharp green eyes, hissing and swatting at her whenever she tried to pass. He might have been worse than the most dangerous of reapers. Even then, Elise had faced off against an ancient one and survived, but whenever she came face-to-face with Hendricks on a bad day, she had to remind herself that there was no worse fate than being torn to ribbons by his tiny razor-sharp claws.

Another day, Elise might have laughed at the cat's threatening presence. But tonight she had been drained of all her energy. Even sitting up, talking to someone she loved more than anything in this world, felt like too much. Elise looked down at her hands, her fingers twisting in patterned intervals of seven. No matter how distracting a conversation might have been, her mind was always elsewhere, working overtime to protect itself from her.

Moving closer, Layla reached a hand out to rest on Elise's. Her fingers stopped immediately, and she looked up at Layla, seeing the remnants of a soft understanding in her eyes. Elise only hoped she looked as grateful as she felt.

"You were so good back on the ship. It was very impressive. You saved so many of us," Layla said quietly.

Elise sniffed. Tears rose in her throat, and no matter how hard she fought to keep them back, they still spilled onto her cheeks. "You almost died."

"But I didn't," Layla said firmly. She tried to wipe Elise's tears, but Elise moved away and stood.

"I couldn't save my mother. She's gone, and Josi will grow up with one parent. I'm sorry. I'm so sorry for all this," Elise whispered.

Layla followed her around the room, stepping in front of her to stop her obsessive pacing. "It's not your fault. Karine is to blame."

Elise shook her head. "No. I started this. Five years ago. When

I told my father everything I promised I would keep as your secret. I made his fears worse, and I've been feeding them ever since. He ruined your life and ruined mine, and nothing has ever been the same."

"This didn't start with you. This whole situation is bigger than us." Though Layla spoke calmly, Elise could hear the undertones of ire in her voice. Whether it was in response to the situation or bringing up her parents' murder, Elise couldn't be sure. But she regretted sharing this many of her thoughts anyway. That same little girl had been alone then, with no one to turn to for help wiping her tears and understanding her grief. It had all been too premature. Both of them had been too young to deal with anything like this. And now they remained stuck in the past in moments like these, when Elise could not stop remembering the pain and feeling it so clearly now that she thought she had gone back in time.

Elise dropped her head into hands and cried. Tears poured out of her while her heart cleaved in two in her chest. "I'm sorry. I'm sorry, I'm so sorry, Layla."

She felt Layla's arms around her and the frantic tension in her muscles while she cupped her cheeks and whispered, "*I know,*" into her ear over and over.

32

"HOW DO YOU FEEL?" LAYLA ASKED.

The younger Saint girl nuzzled her face into Hendricks's fur, her lips stretching into the biggest smile Layla had ever seen on her. "In love."

Layla bit back a smile. The only thing keeping her from this particular joy was knowing how volatile both this cat and Josi could be. There was no way to tell how Josi's cravings affected her; one scratch from this cat could send her into a rage that tore the cat apart in seconds. Holding the cat was a sort of impulse-control test of its own. Luckily, Hendricks appeared quite content in Josi's arms. He leaned into her touch, squinting with satisfaction as he purred.

Layla nodded, though her heart stumbled through her own sadness. Childhood. It was a fleeting thing to begin with, but nearly impossible to retrieve once it had vanished. "So, when you feel Sena… does it come out of nowhere? Or do you know when it's coming?"

"I feel...bad a lot of the time. Like my heart wants to beat out of my chest. I don't know what to do with all these feelings. It's like they just came on all of a sudden. When we were on the dock, that was the maddest she's been in a while. I'm sorry I was rude to you. Sena was angry, and I think...it hurt me seeing my sister with someone else at first. But you've helped me, and I know you're not bad," Josi whispered.

Wonderful. Layla let out a long exhale. "Do you miss your old life too?"

The joy on Josi's face fell into dark despair. "People look at me differently—including Elise. I don't know if she loves me anymore. Not like she used to."

Years of pent-up emotions seemed to spill into Layla at once, and her shoulders slumped. It was not too long ago that she had been dealing with the same feelings as this little girl. Experiencing them herself had been one thing, but to see someone much younger going through it now—Layla felt like her heart had been pierced. She willed her voice to be strong even though her body had gone tense with the effort to keep her true feelings at bay. "And what about your cravings and your hunger?"

Josi pouted. "I'm not hungry. I'm just sad."

A wave of relief crashed over Layla. She sat up straighter, her shoulders relaxing. "Has there been anything that has made you feel even a little better?"

"The cat!" Josi cheered. Her smile returned, and no matter how much Layla hated that damn cat, she was glad for him if it meant Josi's joy coming back to her.

Layla laughed. "Hendricks."

"He doesn't treat me like I'm different. He just wants pets." Josi rubbed her hand over his head, and the cat let out a happy chirp.

Watching the younger Saint now, Layla felt the most hope she had in ages.

"Relax a bit. Unless you're planning on shooting someone, there's no need for all that tension," Jamie demanded.

Elise could have told him she had never been able to relax a moment in her life, but instead, she settled on sighing and forcing her shoulders down. The rifle lowered in her hand, but she kept a steady eye on the entrance to the Saint compound. It being midday, the establishment was mostly quiet. But few passersby entered after whispered exchanges with the guarding gangsters who watched the door.

"Crazy idea, but why don't you just let me go inside? I could actually see what they're doing in there," Jamie said.

Elise shook her head. "Last time was a disaster. Besides, I don't want them to know we're here."

"I think this is just a distraction to you. You don't want to be around your sister, do you?"

Her hands trembled on the gun, but Elise kept it raised, her gaze sharp through the scope. "That's not why I'm here. We have to keep tabs on Nicoletta in case she seeks vengeance. I know she's still alive. Someone like that doesn't just die," Elise muttered bitterly.

Jamie pulled his sleeve back to check his watch. "We have about an hour until sundown, so if you were going to find something, you would have already. Also, my explosives last night were top of the shelf. There is no way she survived those. Layla barely survived."

Elise hated being reminded of the fact. A muscle tensed in her jaw, and she swallowed back a sharp response. Right as she was preparing to ignore him for the rest of the evening, a few gangsters appeared in the windows, moving frantically while they covered the glass with various blockades. With anything from wood scraps to metal pieces, each window was covered—protected—from some outside force. As the guarding gangster disappeared inside, Elise finally caught a glimpse of Nicoletta beyond the doorway. The woman looked darker than the approaching night, her eyes downcast and lips pulled into a seemingly permanent frown. Reaperhood was devastating on her. Elise lowered her gun as the door shut behind them. She looked at Jamie, who wore a bored expression beside her.

"I think they're preparing for Sena," Elise breathed.

Jamie raised his brows. "Did you want to help them, or—"

"No, but Josi might be impacted by this. If they have a connection, she will react." Elise tucked the gun beneath her arm and stood. "We have to go back."

Layla fought back a gag as Sterling dumped canned tuna into a bowl. The scent filled the apartment so thoroughly, Layla could not have escaped it if she tried. Even Josi dropped her crayon on top of her coloring page and covered her nose.

"Gross," she groaned.

Sterling paid her no mind. He scooped Hendricks into his arms off the counter and carried him to the food bowl. The cat rubbed his body against Sterling's legs once he was back on the floor—never in her life had Layla seen this feline delay his meal for human affection. It was truly a spectacle to watch. For a brief moment, Layla felt almost normal. Like a girl watching her friend feed his cat in his apartment on a regular weekend afternoon. But like all good things did, the peace had to end.

The smell of blood tainted the air. Layla's spine straightened as she sensed it, her fangs sliding out on instinct.

Sterling cursed and moved back to the kitchen. A thin stream of crimson trailed down his arm, dripping along the counter as he ran it under the water in the sink.

Layla snapped her focus to Josi, who now stood. "Josi—"

The little girl shuddered. "I feel her."

Before Layla could even rise to her feet, the smaller Saint was tearing through the living room and barreling outside. Sterling yanked his gun from his holster and ran after her, Layla hot on his heels.

"You're *running*. I don't understand why you're running—the sun is still up," Jamie shouted. He trailed few steps behind Elise as she sprinted down the streets of Harlem back to his apartment.

The moment they arrived at the building, Elise knew something was wrong. Spotting a familiar figure nearby, she stopped, her heart sinking. "Sterling?"

He turned to her with panic darkening his features. "She's gone. I don't know what happened. She's just gone—"

Elise looked around, noting the quickly darkening sky and the empty streets around them. She again faced Sterling, whose throat bobbed as he held back a barrage of emotions. "And Layla?"

"She's so much faster than me—she chased Josi down, but they're long gone," Sterling said quietly.

All Elise could do was pull the revolver from her coat while she made her way into the apartment. "Go find Celie," she ordered. Then Elise was tearing back down the street, toward where she could only hope death did not wait for her.

Layla had been in a state of frantic searching for the better part of an hour now. The sun sank dangerously low in the sky, and she knew by the time it set, there would be more blood soaking the streets if she did not find Josi. Tracking her grew harder the later it got and the more her scent faded. The little girl had run like she was possessed and outpaced Layla soon into their chase. Now all Layla could do was stick to her scent as she rushed through the outskirts of Harlem.

The one path that seemed ripe with her scent carried with it the distinct sourness of rot. Layla followed it with no hesitation, knowing there were things worse than demons in the city that would swallow a little girl alive, new reaper abilities or not. The thought of any more gangsters or evolved reapers getting their hands on Josi made Layla sprint faster. Caring for other people had not been her specialty the past few years. But Josi...there were people who would cease to live if anything happened to her, and Layla refused to let their worst nightmares come to life.

Eventually, she came up on the old Saint training compound. The little Saint stood in front of the building. Her head was tipped back, and she let out the most guttural, piercing screams Layla had ever heard. "HELP. PLEASE HELP ME."

Layla watched for movement inside. The gangsters knew of Josi's inhuman state. Whatever kind of messed-up trap this might have been, Layla did not want to be blamed for it again, however it affected the Diamantes. She ran forward just as the entrance cracked open. Layla threw herself into Josi, shoving her out of the way.

The massive beast that they had all come to know as Sena crashed down from the roof of the Saint compound, landing right where Josi had been standing. The gangster who'd opened the door screamed and tried to shut it, but Sena reached a taloned hand in, dragging him back out. From where she crouched with Josi, just out of sight around the corner of the building, Layla watched Sena tear into the man. She flayed his flesh until his organs spilled out, and even then, she continued, mincing him into no more than a bloody pulp. Layla kept a firm grip on Josi, who squirmed and hissed in her arms. Several other gangsters emerged from inside and fired rounds at Sena. The ones who stayed back passed around what appeared to be a vial of venom, taking turns drinking from it before joining the fight.

It was fascinating to watch these newly turned reapers engage in inhuman fighting. The venom, which Layla could only assume was left over from their exploitation of Josi, seemed to give them an extra edge. She remembered what Maria had told her in the blood house weeks ago—increased strength, sharper focus, severe agitation. All things exhibited in the reaper gangsters who tried to take Sena down. None of it was enough.

Sena tore them apart one by one, dropping bodies and spilling blood like it was her calling. With each second that passed, the Saint girl grew hotter and hotter in Layla's arms. Her skin scorched Layla's own flesh as if it had been lit aflame. She struggled to keep a good hold on her the more she kicked and fought.

Until something shifted behind Layla. She stiffened and turned to the alley behind them, searching the darkness for the other body that had appeared during her period of distraction.

"How are you finding your new body-turned-grave?" she asked the shadows.

Eventually, Nicoletta stepped out of the shadows. Red circled her piercing blue eyes, and they darted around wildly, her throat bobbing with a roughly contained ire. "If I never see you again, it will be too soon," the new reaper hissed.

No matter how cruel and malicious it might have been, Layla enjoyed the new reaper scent on her. The slower beat of her heart and the dull scent of her ruined blood—it all reminded Layla of how brutal she had been to Nicoletta on the boat. It felt good seeing the results of her violence speaking for themselves.

"Don't hold your breath." She tucked Josi into her chest, trying to ignore the girl's fevered whimpers.

Nicoletta's lip curled. Her fangs scraped her lips, and a tiny speck of blood fell into the corner of her mouth. Layla expected her to throw out another thinly veiled threat, but instead, the reaper raised her voice, calling out to Sena: "Your bait is here!" Nicoletta grabbed Josi's arm, wrenching her from Layla.

Alarmed, Layla tried to pull Josi back into her, but the gangster hissed and shoved her against the wall with incredible strength. Black veins stretched out beneath her eyes and out from her irises, indicating a variable intoxication. Layla stood no chance beneath the weight of Nicoletta's new strength. With the reaper's forearm crushing her throat, all she could do was watch, gasping for air, as Sena tossed a gangster's body to the side and stalked toward them.

The beast peered at Josi with glowing red eyes. Blood covered more of Sena's gray skin than it didn't, rendering her a monster cloaked in carnage.

Layla did not recognize the creature that approached her. Her old clan leader had been a wondrous beauty, both devastating and ancient. This thing was a manifestation of nightmares and sin. Layla had to fight to keep her eyes open against the gangster's assault as Josi screamed and kicked in Nicoletta's grasp and Sena drew nearer.

The beast moved so fast, for a few seconds, all Layla registered was blood after Sena struck. Nicoletta fell to her knees, her hands pressed to a gaping wound in her throat. Finally free, Layla coughed, trying to force air into her deprived lungs as she staggered toward Josi. Sena reached a taloned hand for the little Saint, and Josi whimpered, her hands fisting in the front of her shirt.

A round of bullets flew through the air and sank into Sena's back. The beast stumbled under the attack, shaking her head. She let out a piercing roar that shook the ground and building they stood beside.

Layla winced at Josi's pained cry and glanced over her shoulder to find Elise racing down the street with several others following her. Shock loosened Layla's jaw as she recognized many faces of her own clan members. Celie stood closest to Elise with Jamie and Sterling on either side of her. She shared a worried look with Layla as Sena rose to her feet once more and faced the new arrivals.

"Keep your nasty hands off my sister," Elise snapped. She lifted her gun again, aiming for Sena's chest.

The reaper reared back so hard, everyone held their breath, anticipating her final collapse. But she righted herself and dodged the flying bullet. Layla's heart stopped as Sena rushed for Elise. The Saint tried to escape her advance, but the reaper was faster. She snatched Elise into her grasp and took off with her into the night.

33

IN THE JAWS OF A BEAST, ELISE LOST ALL TRACK OF time and space. She had fired all her tranquilizer rounds into Sena's mouth, but the reaper had yet to slow down on her deadly rampage through Harlem. Eventually Sena dumped her into a pile of dirt and, to Elise's dismay, human remains. She scrabbled against the ground, trying to find purchase to stand, and her hands slipped over various bones. A human skull clipped against her fingers, and all Elise could do was let out a shaky breath as Sena drew closer to her in the darkness. Whatever graveyard Sena had dropped her in, she intended it to be Elise's final resting place. There was no escape out here—in the middle of a makeshift cemetery with no one around—no one to hear her scream. She faced the beast, her own expression growing sharp.

She did not wear a human face, but Elise could still see the cold rage in Sena's expression. The essence of the reaper's character remained through all her vicious transformations. Elise recognized the shaking hatred the damned creature moved with and all the spite she carried with her that had lasted centuries. A soul did not live forever and never change. This one had allowed itself to necrotize with time, growing cold and unforgiving. Elise could not fault her for it. If she had been forced to endure the turmoil of her short life and all the pain that came with it for an eternity, she would have let the darkness consume her sooner rather than later.

"I know you're angry with me. It was an undignified death that even you did not see coming. But I would have done something else had I had more power. For all you did to my sister, you deserve worse than hell." Elise swallowed past the lump in her throat. Not from nerves but instinctual disgust at her own violent thoughts. They were Saint words—things she had never felt comfortable spewing. A true Saint might have found comfort in degrading their prey, but Elise had only ever mourned hers. Forcing herself as far from her mind as possible was the only way she saw herself making it through this standoff. "I would kill you a thousand times over if it meant my sister was safe. Whatever grave you bury me in tonight, I will be sure to haunt you from it for an eternity. I promise you that."

The reaper bristled at her words. Such a reaction was enough for Elise to find satisfaction in the final moments she had before Sena lunged for her again, this time sinking her fangs into her throat.

The world became a blur around Elise. She went limp in the reaper's grasp, feeling her blood leak down her chest and over her face. Consciousness came and went, driving Elise through various forms of darkness until the reaper finally released her. By then, she had carved out a shallow grave for the Saint. Sena's venom fought the existing strain in Elise's body, rendering her stiff with feverish pain. She remained frozen in place as the reaper covered her with dirt and extinguished every last bit of light. The stars above winked out. In just a few horrifying moments, Elise was left in the dark, suffocating pressure and death closing in from all sides.

Elise might have been down in the dirt for an eternity. With her arms trapped by her sides and the earth crushing her chest, her breathing became shallow. She could only hope and pray that the venom was enough to overcome the substance in her system and take her out with a merciful swiftness.

A distant rumbling started nearby. Then the earth began to shake around her. Dirt shifted on her face and her arms, and soon, there was enough alleviation of the pressure for her to move. She reached up, clawing at the earth until she brushed something soft and cool. A brown hand reached into the darkness and gripped her arm. It hauled her out of the dirt with a grace only an inhuman being could muster.

Gasping, Elise broke out of the grave. She coughed up mouthfuls of dirt and wiped at her eyes while it poured over her legs. Sitting up and blinking against the cloudiness in her vision, Elise caught sight of the several beings surrounding her. Reapers, rogue and determined, stared back at her.

She didn't have the energy to be scared or even startled. Instead, Elise coughed out a broken laugh and shook her head. "You saved me."

Then she collapsed, falling back onto the grave.

"Sena meant to turn her. I think my tainted venom in Elise's system stopped Sena's," Layla muttered. She kept one hand on Elise's throat, watching her flesh knit itself back together beneath the stream of Celie's blood. Per Layla's instruction, everyone had settled in the new reaper lair after finding Elise. In the hour since bringing her back, she had yet to wake up. The steady beat of her pulse beneath Layla's fingers was the only thing keeping Layla upright and hopeful about the situation.

Once done treating Elise's wounds, Celie tucked her sleeve back over her arm. She glanced out across the entryway, where a few gangsters had gathered around Nicoletta. The reaper's blood coated the cathedral steps and pooled beneath her now. Whatever wounds Sena had left had been deep enough to require extensive healing time.

One of Nicoletta's men called over. "Thank you, again, for letting us rest here."

Layla nodded. "As long as you remain allied to us and not Karine."

"We've seen what she does to noncooperative humans and reapers. We want no part of that."

Layla had seen an opportunity in the tense moment after Sena's attack. With the Saint compound covered in Nicoletta's blood, the gangsters had to choose between staying and risking certain death or yielding to Layla's word. Even close to death, these newly turned gangsters chose life. Layla had never anticipated the new lair growing quite so crowded. Nor could she have anticipated rogue reapers saving a Saint's life. But Layla had dropped to her knees when she saw them pulling Elise from the dirt in Washington Square Park.

The Saint had been buried among thousands of other bodies. It was a miracle she emerged still breathing with all the blood loss she had endured.

"Is she going to wake up?" Josi asked. She had been sitting on the stairs with Sterling and Jamie, but she moved into the free space beside Layla. The younger Saint regarded her sister's limp body on the velvet couch with considerable concern. Her brows furrowed, and her lips poked out in a fearful pout. "I felt Sena calling me. I had to go. She gets so angry when I don't listen to her. I think if you had not held me down, I would have been worse."

Layla swallowed hard. She took Josi's hand and slipped it into Elise's. "If she'll wake up for anyone, it will be you."

Josi dropped to her knees beside her sister. She bent over her, murmuring something inaudible to Elise. Tears glistened on her cheeks as she spoke, and Layla turned away to give them a moment of privacy.

A few rogue reapers caught her eye, and she shook her head after reading their questioning expressions. "I have never known rogues to care for a Saint."

One rogue pulled his gaze from Elise to look at Layla. "She saved our lives on the ship. It felt unwise to move on as if things have not changed between reapers and humans. Incurable debts aside, we are on the brink of something more monstrous than history itself. Rogues would rather be on the side that sees us as worthy enough to live. So we will return the favor as long as we are acknowledged."

Layla's lips parted in silent awe. With the way things had gone over the past few days, Layla had no idea what either of them would do once Elise woke up. But to see such folks from different walks of life crowding in a cathedral together in the middle of the night—it felt like more than a coincidence. A calling, perhaps, if Layla believed in those things.

"Oh, dove. Please don't cry." Elise's hushed voice drew Layla back to her.

She spun around and found Elise hugging her sister back. Her eyes were bright with tears that refused to fall. As Layla neared, Elise's gaze settled on her. Elise reached for her hand and squeezed it, a soft smile gracing her lips. Watching Elise smile even while covered in blood and on the verge of anguish felt like watching the early-morning sunlight break across the sky.

"I hate that you're a part of this. I really wish you would just go hide with Sterling until all this is over," Layla murmured. She wiped her blood away from the freshly healed wounds in Elise's throat. For once, they were alone, tucked away in her room upstairs. "Maybe it was better when my clan hated you and didn't want you around."

The Saint groaned. "I wish you wouldn't do that. It's progress that your clan accepts me now for saving you and other reapers. We cannot discount that."

Layla's jaw clenched in frustration. She dropped the bloody rag into the bin by her sink and followed Elise out to her bedroom. "This is progress, but it has a cost. It's naive to assume reapers will continue to accept Saints just because of today. Not to mention you nearly died."

Elise whirled on her, ire creasing her brows and casting darkness across her expression. "And that was my choice. My whole life, I have had things decided for me. Everyone has made choices on my behalf. And now you're doing it too. You assume I do not want you in my life and assume I am better off without you. You keep me at a distance, and it drives me insane. I don't understand why you insist on being like this. Hot and then cold. Avoiding me, but needing my approval and my confirmation."

"You really have to ask me this?" Layla drew closer to her, her voice hard.

"Evidently. Why are you so stubborn when it comes to me and me only? What end are you searching for?" Elise ground out.

Layla was so close now, she could feel the heat of Elise's anger rolling off her. "One with you."

Pain blanched Elise's face, and for a moment, Layla regretted her words. No amount of protection on her behalf would be worth the anguish it eventually pulled from the Saint. "Are you trying to mock me? Trying to remind me why we can't be together because you will live forever and I won't?" Her voice broke. "Layla—"

"I'm trying to tell you I fucking love you," Layla almost shouted. Her body stilled as Elise's eyes grew shiny with awe.

Elise blinked slowly, and then a quiet smile stretched across her lips. "You could have just said that."

"It's hard, Lise. You're right. We don't have forever—not even close. No amount of time with you would ever be enough…" Layla's breath shuddered out of her, and when Elise touched her cheek, she covered her hand with her own.

"We don't have to think of that yet. So let's not." Elise's thumb stroked over the silent tear that streaked Layla's cheek. "There are a million little forevers in every moment we have. We can make our own eternity out of this time." She let out a little breath, and beneath it, Layla heard her mutter, "Laisse-moi mourir en premier."

Layla squeezed her hand. "You keep saying that. What does it mean?"

Elise's eyes crinkled and she spoke quietly. "*Let me die first.*"

The realization of her statement sank in like a physical blow. Layla swallowed past her pained shock, and she held Elise tighter. "No."

34

"WHY HERE?" ELISE ASKED. SHE STEPPED AROUND a broken piece of human skull, noticing as she walked past that the jaw contained fangs, rather than a set of true human teeth. Washington Square Park rose around her and Josi like a proper graveyard. What had once been a beautiful park full of fresh greenery and colorful flowers had faded into a gray wasteland since becoming home to Karine's and Sena's most brutal desires. A thick fog rolled in across the land, swallowing all the pitiful sunlight the winter had to offer. Various headstones erected in the ground leaned so heavily to the side, it was a wonder they had not collapsed already. The terrors of Harlem had disturbed the beds where souls had been laid to rest for an eternity. Even the dead were not safe here.

Josi wrapped her arms around her middle and frowned. Her shoulders had caved in with each step that brought them farther into the park. The wind stirred the white bows Elise had carefully tied onto the ends of her braids, and whenever the white satin poked out amid the soft brown of her curls, Elise could not help but think of the mountains of bones scattered across the dark earth they stood atop now. "Karine told me the people here are forgotten. That it's been so long since they died, no one would care if we used them." She swallowed hard and sniffed. "This is where my friends are."

Elise blinked, her stomach twisting. "What?"

"When she freed me from the dark to let me go to the clubs, I wanted to make friends, but they kept dying. She never told me my venom was bad. I only wanted to have more girls like me. I hated being alone. But they all died. She used me to get rid of humans." Josi pointed to the various piles of dirt that indicated recently dug graves. "We buried them here. On top of the rest of the dead."

Harlem was made of death.

Elise shuddered. "When you say Karine wants to use these bodies…what do you mean by that?"

Josi shrugged. Her eyes darkened, and when she spoke again, her voice shook. "She uses Sena's blood and her own blood to wake them up. She said she wants reapers to have their own freedoms and not live under humans."

"And she intends to take their liberation by force," Elise breathed. She looked out over the graveyard. "Whether the dead want it or not."

If anyone had seen the gathering of rogue reapers and humans in the Harlem reaper lair, they might have believed they were seeing something out of another reality. There was still an apparent divide between the groups. Most Harlem reapers kept to the middle of the room while gangsters stood on one side and rogue reapers took up the opposite side. But what mattered and relieved Elise was that they had all shown up despite their differences. If this was indicative of anything, then perhaps they all did have something better than death to look forward to.

Elise stood on the dais in front of the pews making up the main floor of the cathedral. Layla stood by her side with Jamie, Josi, and Sterling taking up the back. Looking out over the crowd of rogues, Harlem reapers, and gangsters filled her with anticipatory pride. The struggle of the past few weeks had brought them to this moment, and Elise was determined to make things last for the better.

"Tonight we survived a new evil that has been terrorizing all of us for the past few weeks. I believe our continued survival depends on working together, rather than against one another. No more secrets, no more bloodshed. I ask you, not as a Saint but as a human being who longs for a better future, to meet me on this promise," Elise said. Her voice was steadier than she felt internally, but she was grateful for it. To face a suspicious group with any ounce of uncertainty would have been disastrous at best. "I propose we lead an offense against Sena and Karine. With Sena still available to Karine, she will have a chance to raise an army of the dead and destroy Harlem as we know it. There is no telling when she will stop if she succeeds in her mission. We have to neutralize Sena before Karine can execute the rest of her plans. We do have an advantage with most reapers on our side now that Nicoletta is no longer working with Karine to abduct them. But I need to make sure we are all in this together. We must swear loyalty to one another."

Several voices chimed in from the crowd. Most Harlem reapers seemed to agree with Elise, and a few gangsters and rogues nodded along with them. It was a decent start—much better than she had been anticipating and astounding considering where they had all been just a few weeks ago.

Nicoletta spoke up once Elise went quiet. "Sena is immune to the Saint steel. How will we kill her?"

Elise shared a look with Josi, whose face had been a mask of discomfort throughout the whole speech. "We cannot kill her. Not until we figure out a way to end the bond between her and my sister. We just need to incapacitate her for now. Josi seems to think the antivenom will work. I know you have plenty at the compound from your previous work with Karine."

The gangster gave her a wicked smile. "How much will you pay me for it?"

35

DAYS OF CONTINUOUS PLANNING BETWEEN GROUPS and tense night watches to ensure Sena and Karine did not arrive unannounced had everyone on edge. Even Hendricks had been brought in to keep the littlest Saint occupied while everyone else readied defenses and offenses against Karine.

"Oh, come on. I've already apologized twice for giving you to her. Three times if you count this," Nicoletta grumbled, while pointing to the massive scar on her throat from Sena's attack. "You're the only one in here who still has a problem with me."

Josi pouted and continued to scratch Hendricks's ears. Even the cat turned his nose up at the gangster.

Sterling scoffed. "You threw her to Sena. She's allowed to be upset."

"We're allies now. All past strife is forgotten." Nicoletta's face lit up at the sound of Jamie explaining one of her explosives to a group of rogues nearby. "I'll finally teach you how to use my explosives?" She plucked the weapon from Jamie, who blinked in confusion.

"She's ten years old," Sterling said sternly. He tried to take the weapon from her, but Nicoletta ducked away.

"It's better for her. Right, tiny one?" Nicoletta asked.

Josi nodded eagerly. She released the cat and moved closer to the gangster. "I'm scared of my venom."

Jamie glanced between them. "We could use more of those."

Nicoletta eyed the sleek metal of the explosive while nodding. "Karine initially wanted to blow the graves out of the ground with poison-tainted grenades so it was easier to get to the dead, but the blast was too strong and destroyed many of the bodies. So, instead, she had me create an emergency detonation system for her island. We can find the rest of them there or scavenge the bombs left scattered around the city."

"What is she hiding on that island...?" Jamie's voice trailed off.

"Layla? Are you paying attention?" Celie's voice brought Layla back. She stared down at the vials of venom she had taken from her dresser at Celie's command. "Elise had the idea to roll Saint bullets in her tainted blood to create a sedative. We combined it with the antivenom, and we're sure it will slow Sena down enough for us to capture her."

Layla nodded, but her mind stuck on only one thing. "Where is Elise now?"

"Oh..." Celie glanced toward the stairs that lead down to the cathedral's sanctuary. "She said something about doing her rituals—"

Layla was out of the sitting room and down the stairs in an instant. She expected to find Elise deep in her harmful self-soothing rituals; Layla never could have guessed what the Saint put together in the sanctuary.

The holy space, full of pews and stained glass, had been turned into one of the most beautiful rooms Layla had ever seen. Lit candles covered the surface of the altar, casting a delicate glow over the space. Elise jumped, dropping the extinguished match when the door closed behind Layla. She frowned and placed her hands on her hips. "You weren't supposed to see this yet."

White drapes hung on the cross and saint statues, some dangerously close to the candle flames heating the altar. The sun had just begun to set, casting a golden glow around the place that only added to the lovely sparkle in Elise's eye. Even while peeved, she looked so beautiful, Layla wanted to cry. Her mouth stretched into the biggest smile while her eyes roamed the capped-sleeve white gown that hugged her body and shone the most pristine pearlescent shade in the evening light. She wore a pearl headpiece and matching earrings, her face a painting crafted with the carefulness of a loving god. No matter how good the red lipstick looked, Layla could think only of kissing it off her. She was sure her jaw had been unhinged for far too long and her eyes were wide enough to move the planets, but Layla continued to stare while Elise spoke.

"Do you remember when we were little and you used to be afraid of the dark, so whenever our parents would turn out the big light, I would light a candle for you?" Elise asked.

Layla nodded, forcing her gaze away from Elise and to the space between two large candles, where various jewelry pieces sat. "Of course I remember. I remember everything." It was a twisted blessing to be able to say that. In this moment, Layla was glad for all the human lives she had taken to use their blood to keep her human memories. She might have been an unfeeling beast that withered away to bone dust with time by now otherwise. But, instead, her best friend stood before her, and Layla recognized all parts of her and the past that hung between them because of her taste for humanity.

Elise led her to the altar and gestured to a candle. "Remember how I told you I would always light a candle for you?"

Layla pursed her lips against the rise of tears in her eyes. "You said you did it because you loved me."

"Because I love you." Elise trailed a finger along a thick dripping of wax. "I'm sorry I broke that promise on your darkest night. I know we're years past that time, but I want you to know I never intend to leave you in the dark again. I promise, for as long as we are together, I will do my best to bring you light."

"Oh, Elise," Layla said quietly. She eyed the jewelry covering the wooden surface before them. It had all belonged to Sena, the collector of all things luxurious and beautiful. She wondered if Sena had collected her earnings through vengeful acts of self-reclamation. Her taking of the Clarice had been vicious and coldhearted, but in the end, it had brought to life a place for reapers to stay. A place where they would never have to sell themselves just to live. Now Layla sniffled a bit as she recalled the things she had done to keep herself alive. Everything—whether cruel or kind—had brought her to this moment with the person she loved the most. Elise Saint, her one constant, even through all the pain and darkness. Layla took Elise's hand into her own. "You are my light, Elise. You always have been."

Elise let out a shaky breath. "Layla."

Layla could practically feel Elise's blood pulsing against her flesh. "Why are you so nervous?" she asked.

"Because I am about to sin on sacred ground," Elise whispered.

Layla wanted to tell her that her that she did not believe in God, not like she believed in Elise. And her sins were always sweet to Layla, no matter the severity. Instead, she stepped closer to Elise and lifted her hand to her lips, kissing her knuckles.

Elise released a heavy sigh. One of bitter expectations and unjust weight. "I know things are not ideal now. But I'm in no rush to create our life together. We have time. We may not have forever, but we do have time."

"The mortality of our time makes it just a bit sweeter. We will never be better than we are in this moment," Layla said in agreement.

"Exactly." Elise asked Layla to pick out a ring for her, and Layla chose the one she found the most beautiful—a sapphire ring to match the loveliness that was her best friend. Elise chose an amethyst one for Layla, and even after she slipped it onto her ring finger, she continued to hold her hand, admiring the sight of them intertwined and connected with two promises set in brilliant stone.

Layla's gaze lingered on Elise's dress again. "Is there a particular reason why you got to dress up properly and I didn't?"

"You interrupted my plans. But don't worry." Elise gave her the most innocent smile. "I intend to have you rip this off me in a moment."

Layla swallowed as her mouth went dry with hot anticipation. "As you wish."

Elise squeezed her hand. "You are my favorite person."

Affection sprang into Layla's chest like the warmth she had been waiting years for, since reaperhood's frigid hold on her life. She returned Elise's smile and tugged her closer. "You are my best everything."

They closed the remaining distance between them with a kiss that started fires in Layla's stomach. She knew none of this was a permanent fix for any of their problems. They would emerge from this kiss and from this room to a world that was still on the brink of war. Humans would still die, and reapers would still suffer all the same. But Layla knew, with Elise by her side and her promise tied to her heart, that she could die happy. And that was all she needed.

36

WE CANNOT KILL HER. FOR JOSI TO LIVE, WE MUST keep Sena *alive*.

Layla was amazed by everyone's quickness to adapt. She stood over the massive grave in Washington Square Park across from Celie and some rogue reapers. A few Diamantes stood along the perimeter of the area, watching and waiting.

She twisted the ring on her finger and tried not to worry about Elise heading things on her own by the old reaper lair. It was bad enough the Saint had nearly died trying to help keep Sena away, but now she was intent on drawing her out of her lair and directly to her.

Everyone, rogues and gangsters alike, watched the sun disappear behind the horizon and bring with it the dark cloak of night. The moment stars blinked into the sky, Layla sensed the sour necrotized scent and heat of Sena's presence. As the ground rumbled beneath her feet, Layla crouched by the edge of the large grave they had dug for the beast. One shot. That was all they had to take her down. In another life, Elise might have been a true gun-wielding, reaper-hunting Saint. In this one, she was Layla's greatest love and someone willing to do the worst for her.

The littlest Saint came sprinting up the nearby hill by the entrance to the park. Her white hair bows flapped in the wind, her speed impressive to even the older reapers standing watch around the grave. Behind her, Sena emerged, massive and haunting in her relentless pursuit of the little girl. Dirt pounded beneath her talons as she hauled herself forward on all fours. Josi jumped over the grave right as Elise approached from several yards away. She aimed her gun as Sena prepared to follow the smaller Saint over the burial plot.

Layla's lips parted, feeling the tremble of the earth again. Adrenaline buzzed through her at the sight of clawed hands reaching out around Elise. She tore herself away from her position and ran right for the Saint. Several other gangsters surrounded the undead, their guns pointed and their faces pinched with confusion. Distantly, Layla heard the younger Saint shouting something.

"Don't touch them!" Her voice, breathless and exhausted, was tinged with panic.

By the time Layla made it to Elise, the undead had already surfaced. Gangsters fired into them, managing to down the ones closest to the Saint. But as Sena continued to move and Elise struggled to get a clear shot at her, the undead only continued their rise. Layla shoved a human gangster—one of Jamie's men—out of the way of one's swiping hand. Its head popped out of the earth and sank its fangs into her calf instead. Layla cried out and stomped her foot into its face hard enough to cave its bones in. She limped away, her blood bubbling and thick from where it poured out of the fresh wound. The gangster she had shoved away struggled back to his feet, and as he looked to give her a nod of thanks, another undead emerged behind him. Layla opened her mouth to warn him, but the beast was already lunging. It yanked him back to the ground with impressive speed and tore into his throat until blood sprayed. Within seconds, black veins spread across this man's face and neck. His skin grayed and withered away, necrotizing with the undead's venom.

Layla's own leg tingled as she watched the brutal death. She limped closer to Elise, who was gesturing for Josi to come back. "We have to go. It's too dangerous." Layla winced.

Elise didn't even spare her a look. She was too focused on her sister's retreat, which led Sena back toward the grave. "I've almost got her."

All Layla could do was wait. Even as the dead closed in around them and the smaller Saint faltered in her run, Layla waited. She chose to have faith in Elise because there was nothing else she wanted to devote her beliefs to. So, when Josi stumbled by the grave and lost momentum, sending her careening toward the edge, Layla was there when Elise hesitated. She was there when Elise ran for her sister as Sena gained on her at the opposite edge of the grave. When Elise dropped her gun to help her sister back to her feet and when Layla was the only one closest to it, she picked it up and screamed Elise's name.

Elise held her hand out, and Layla tossed the gun to her. She watched with bated breath as Elise slid to one knee and caught the gun, then fired a single round into Sena right when she launched herself over the grave. The beast jerked in midair and slammed into the earth. "Now!" Elise called.

Jamie and Sterling jumped into the grave and pulled a Saint chain around her throat. Once secured, they climbed out and began replacing the dirt in the hole. The remaining gangsters and rogues helped shovel. They did not stop until Sena's heaving, bleeding body was completely covered. And when they leaned back, breathing hard, dirt caking their nails and smudging their faces, they realized the dead had fallen back to their graves.

In the quiet of the dawn, she rose. Layla sensed it between Josephine's tearful wails, which penetrated the walls of the cathedral, and Elise's hushed whispers intended to calm her. It was a miracle the girl had not descended into something worse, given Sena's lengthy comatose state. Layla sat on the cathedral steps, waiting. Just before sunrise, a shadow emerged across the courtyard, taking with it the final darkness of the night. A woman covered in dirt and mud crept toward the stairs.

The gangsters who had been guarding her grave walked behind her, weapons out and ready in case she tried to flee. But the woman was weak in her new state—Layla could tell just by the sound of her slow, labored breathing that increased as she neared.

Layla stood to greet her and almost smiled when she saw her familiar face.

Albeit battered and decrepit, Sena's human form stepped up to Layla. The Saint chain dragged behind her, filling the air with the eerie sound of metal grating over stone. Blood dripped from the burns in her throat, where the chain had dug into her flesh, soaking her black hair. She gave Layla a cruel smile as she stopped just inches from her. "It worked. Reversing my monstrous state only to bring me back to suffering. Tell me, was it your idea to make me walk the streets barefoot and choking half to death to get to you?" she gritted out.

"It was hers," Elise said. She moved into the cathedral entryway, leaving space for Josi to fill in beside her. Together, they stood by Layla, expressions stern and determined. "I've heard you did worse to my sister. It seemed only right to give her retribution for your abuse of her."

Sena smiled at Josi, but instead of malice, there was only sadness in her eyes. "The bond between us is fraying; otherwise I would have taken you down with me. If you do not learn to bear suffering early on, it will only crush you when you're least expecting it." She raised her gaze to Elise. "I suppose I can expect my death again. This time final. Since come next sundown, I will return to my worst form and you will be no match against me. I will make sure of it this time."

Elise narrowed her eyes. "No. We have something much worse in store for you."

37

I T HAD BEEN DAYS SINCE ELISE HAD GOTTEN A PROPER night's sleep, and the last thing she wanted to do was confront her father early in the morning. The only thing keeping her from turning back and leaving his new house was Josi's hand intertwined with hers and Sterling's red-rimmed eyes. As much as this was her responsibility, it was also their burden to bear. She was not the only one who had been impacted by Analia's death, and she refused to leave her sister alone in her misery again.

The moment Tobias opened the doors to this study, Josi ran into his arms. He kneeled for her and pulled her into him. Tears fell between both of them, and Elise could not help the pang of jealousy that rocked through her system at the sight. For so long, she had hoped she would have such a bond with her father. Perhaps it was better for Josi to have it than her. She would grow up knowing he was good to her and that he loved her. Elise had survived his wrath and the cold knowledge that she was nothing more than a project for him. As long as Josi never felt the burden of his expectations, Elise would shoulder the pain of being less wanted.

"I've missed you, my angel," Tobias said in a shaky voice. He touched Josi's chin and regarded her with tear-filled eyes and a weepy smile. "You look so much like your mother. You know she loved you so much."

Sterling and Elise shared a look.

Tobias spoke before either of them could. "I want to have a proper funeral for her. It will be intimate, so you do not have to worry about performing." Her father stood with Josi still in his arms and looked at Elise. "Your mother—the most magnificent woman I've ever known—will now remain in a box for eternity." His gaze flicked up to Josi, whose expression only further wilted at the knowledge of her mother's homecoming. "I fear what I want to do will only further wake the beast feeding on the heart of this city. I might not have the power I once did before, but I still love our neighborhood. I do not want things to be destroyed. My family..." His sharp intake of air cut his words off. Tobias's jaw clenched, and he looked at the floor in silence for a moment before continuing. "I can no longer protect any of you. And now you are too far gone."

"We're here now, Daddy," Josi said softly. She touched his cheek and gave him a gentle smile, but Tobias only took her hand from his face and set her back on the floor. The devastating fall of her expression sparked a hot rage in Elise's chest. But instead of letting her most vile insults fly at her father, she pulled Josi against her legs.

"You aren't. Not quite. You are…" Tobias pinched his brow and sighed before settling a dark gaze on his youngest daughter. "You are hardly my little girl."

Josi's eyes filled with tears. "I am."

"Father," Elise warned. "We had a deal."

"And you said you would fix her," Tobias shot back. "I have nothing else going for me now. No more children to carry on my legacy. All my heirs have been traitorous to me. A monster lurks, and I have no means to destroy it—"

"We already caught her. And we got your Saint compound back," Elise said sharply. She fought past the blow his words dealt to her heart. Even as her chest felt like it was caving in at her father's admission of not seeing her as his daughter any longer, she pressed on, voice strong. "Karine will come looking for her and Josi soon. With them as leverage, she will have to give us Dr. Gray's location. I have no doubt that she can help Josi and all of Harlem. Things are so much worse than we ever could have anticipated. But there is still something you can do to help."

Elise could not ignore the glare of disgust Layla dealt the mayor and her father as they entered the cathedral. She shot the reaper a stern look and leaned down to whisper in her ear. "Will you behave just for a few minutes? We need them to listen to us."

Layla's glare deepened. "I'm not sure why. We caught Sena ourselves. We can deal with Karine ourselves."

"Not if they see a value in continuing to partner with her. We have to ensure they know how dangerous she is. Karine is not the reaper they should be trusting," Elise said softly.

At this, the ire faded from Layla's expression. Her lips parted, and she looked at Elise with tender awe. "And who do you propose they should trust?" she asked.

Elise's mouth stretched into a smile. "You know who." She stepped away from Layla as Arendale and her father approached the small cage made of Saint steel that had been containing Sena for the past few hours, all thanks to Nicoletta and her full surrender of the Saint compound because of the reapers' and Elise's assistance in freeing them of Sena. The ancient reaper sat in the middle of the enclosure, a silk robe draped over her straight shoulders and her hands in her lap while she watched everyone surround the steel bars to peer down at her.

"So this is how reapers live now…" Mayor Arendale glanced around the cathedral, his dark eyes alight with wonder.

Layla gave him an unimpressed look. "I'm surprised Karine didn't give you a rundown."

The mayor stopped by the enclosure, staring down at Sena. "If your accusation is correct, she did not tell me about a lot of her actions. This is Valeriya?" he asked.

"Sena is her true name." Tobias nodded. His expression filled with a sad regret. Elise wondered how much of his interactions with the ancient reaper he even remembered, if so many of them were tainted by her poison, and how he even looked back on them with anything besides pure vitriol. "You've taken so much from me, and still you continue? When will it ever be enough?"

"I could ask the same of you," Sena muttered. She shot a piercing glare at Tobias Saint, who only returned the ire tenfold with his own scowl. "Pity to be woken from a vicious slumber only to be met with disappointment and used over and over again. I have been used my whole life. These experiments, whether you pay for them or not, will never end. You fight one side, they will always retaliate. I have seen every iteration of war and every perceived offer of peace. There is nothing you can do to change someone when they've already made up their mind about the way things should be. You say I changed your daughter, but I had her for only a month. You raised her. You made her into what she's become. Both of them," Sena said strongly. "Maybe it's time you all took responsibility for the state of our world too."

Elise had never seen someone confront her father with so much hostility. It made her wonder just how intense their conversations had been in the past, in the quiet darkness of privacy. "You must feel betrayed by your friend. She brought you back only to use you to sow more violence."

"I do not have the energy to feel much of anything anymore. I was willing to do what Karine wanted of me because I had a chance to take care of your sister. It was Karine who encouraged her to follow her impulses. I simply wished to protect her," Sena said.

Tobias shot forward, his fists clenched around the bars. "She was perfectly safe."

A low chuckle left Sena. "You gave her to a reaper. And after the lengths Elise went to keep her from you…there is no way you still believe yourself."

"Elise knows nothing—"

"Has anyone ever told you that you talk too damn much?" Layla snapped. She stiffened next to Elise as she turned to face Tobias. "*Shut up*. Your daughter has done more for everyone in this neighborhood in the past few days than you have done in your little empire's ten-year-run. If you sat back and looked beyond your ego, you would know that."

Wide-eyed, mouth agape, for a moment, Tobias was stunned into silence. Eventually he released the tension from his fists and turned away from Layla, ignoring her searing words.

Elise could only press her fingertips to her mouth to keep from smiling. Layla continued to shoot daggers at her father even with his back turned on her.

Sterling cleared his throat, drawing attention to him. "The reason we called you all here was to demonstrate that partnering with reapers can work. We could not have stopped Sena's violent rampage if it were not for the help of the Diamantes and the rogues. You have a chance to do the right thing and dismiss Karine as your partner. Choose someone else to lead reapers into a liberation movement."

Mayor Arendale crossed his arms and stepped away from the enclosure. "Perhaps I can negotiate with Karine. She seems sensible and willing to find a compromise as long as reapers benefit—"

Layla interrupted. "I don't think you understand. There is no negotiating with Karine. We tried with her, and when she refused, she turned to raising the dead for an army. She will not let even those who have been gone for decades rest. We have to act against her, and we have to do it before she realizes that we've met."

Silence filled the room for far too long. The mayor and Tobias continued to watch her with contemplative expressions, neither of them making a move toward a decision.

Layla shook her head, cursing beneath her breath. "Forget it. Do whatever you want, but don't ask reapers for help." She made her way to the back of the building and disappeared downstairs.

Elise let out a tired sigh. She faced her father, careful not to make her expression too vulnerable, lest he see an opportunity in her. "Please. You've said it yourself—you have nothing left. Let this be the one thing you choose to be a part of."

Tobias passed a look to Arendale, who still seemed rather unmoved. He turned back to his daughter, and to her surprise, she saw resolve in his dark eyes. "If the only way out of this is a war, then we must make sure we can support that. Give us a day to decide."

38

Layla found peace in the quiet cold beneath the cathedral. The stone arches making up the walkways and bridging the rifts between the walls felt like another type of cage, albeit much more beautiful than the one Sena resided in. While all the bodies in this space had been buried forever ago, Layla couldn't help but wonder if they would be affected by Karine's plans should she make them more widespread. If she figured out a way to spread Sena's blood without needing her directly, the consequences would be catastrophic. How would Karine even control such a large army of lawless beings?

Suddenly all of the ancient reaper's past musings to Layla made more sense. She had wanted Layla to step up and be a leader to reapers months ago. Maybe, if Layla had done so, they would not be in this position. Perhaps Karine would have found more satisfaction in Layla's rule had she actually tried. This whole time, Layla had been too concerned about hurting people with her reaperhood—she should have been more concerned about taking care of that side of her to ensure her community remained safe.

Now it was too late.

All the work that had been done would be wiped away in an instant if Karine had her way.

Layla considered how Elise had finally begun to smile and sleep properly since being reunited with her sister. Layla could not burden the Saints with this vicious path she knew she needed to take.

She stood, intending to go back upstairs and sneak out to find Karine on her own. But an icy chill swept through the underground space, followed by the heavy tension of another presence.

"How did I know to find you in the most unholy part of a holy place—where all the death gathers in the dark?" Karine's voice filled the room.

Layla turned and saw the ancient reaper standing by a small door at the end of the crypt, near rows of hidden graves. The cold settled over her shoulders when she looked into Karine's eyes. Her head began to spin. Even with the blurry edges encroaching on her vision, she still recognized the sensation of blood proximity, the inexplicable draw Layla felt toward Karine and the way her skin prickled the closer she came. With the blood she had shared with Elise, she wondered if the Saint girl could feel it now.

"You're back. For no good reason, I assume," Layla said.

Dressed in fitted pants and a silk blouse, Karine appeared to have distanced herself from her usual glamour, which only indicated further trouble. She flashed a bitter smile and stepped closer. "I believe you've run this place into the ground."

Layla scoffed. "Please—"

"How many reapers have you lost in the past few months?" Karine pressed.

Layla frowned. "Because of you. We know what you're doing to reapers and humans alike. You have no more allies here in Harlem. You might as well give up." She breathed past her swimming vision. The bite wound in her calf had yet to fully heal; it pulsed now, the venom from the undead wrestling beneath her skin as her anger increased.

"Not when there is still this clan, in desperate need of better leadership," Karine said.

Cold fury rolled down Layla's spine. She let out a shaky breath and glared. "This will never be your home."

"I would not recommend fighting me while you're at your weakest."

"I'm not at my weakest." Layla laughed sharply. "You had to wait until I had been poisoned to challenge me. Some ancient reaper you are. Pathetic." The last time they had fought, she had nearly lost and escaped with her life only due to Karine's mercy. Now Layla had a newfound rage to challenge her with.

Karine threw the first blow. She lunged for Layla, but Layla dodged her move, grabbing her throat to slam her against the wall. Karine gasped as Layla's hands tightened around her neck. Black veins sprang out around her eyes and throat like roots desperate for water. As the veins in her face began to pop and vessels exploded in her eyes, sending black and crimson spilling over the white, Layla's heart pounded so hard, she almost couldn't hear Karine's choked cursing.

A million voices clamored in her head, most of them screaming at her to stop. But the loudest of them all came from a rage that had been lying dormant for far too long. All that Layla had done to keep herself as human as possible rested in the control she forced herself to have. Unleashing this anger—this brutal monstrosity within, took more than a simple decision.

Karine's hands closed around Layla's wrist. Her eyes had no more white left; only red and black covered them like a bloody bruise. Still, she smiled and bared her dripping fangs. "You forget one thing. You cannot kill the monster that made you."

Layla's gaze narrowed in confusion for a moment. Then, in a split second, as Karine's eyes flashed, she was thrown back to the past. When she had been a thirteen-year-old girl, lying broken on damp grass with no one to take her gently into death. When a tall figure of darkness had hovered over her and forced a bittersweet taste onto her tongue. There had been no words at the time, but Layla recognized the ancient aura in the reaper before her. Years of blocking out the moment she had turned only brought her to this painful period of revelation.

All those years ago, Layla had been making herself forget Karine. The one who had cursed her with every moment of suffering and torment.

Layla's breath caught. In that small second of hesitation, when her fingers loosened and her guard lowered, Karine dropped her hands. Layla did not register her movements until she felt the pain they caused. When she looked down, Karine's hand had disappeared into her chest. Layla stumbled back, or tried to—Karine held her up with a fist pushing between her ribs.

Pain exploded through Layla's body. It cleaved her in half, splitting every inch of her with fiery blades that only amplified with each twitch of Karine's fingers in her chest. Blood poured between them, and Layla's vision flickered in and out. She maintained eye contact with Karine anyway, ignoring the heat of her own blood seeping down her stomach and onto her feet. "It was you," Layla breathed. The metallic tang of copper filled her mouth, and she let it trickle over her lower lip.

With her fangs retracted, Karine's smile looked less malicious. But the blood covering her eyes showed Layla no mercy even as she kneeled and allowed Layla's body to collapse before her. "You've known all this time. You just refused to face it."

"No," Layla coughed out. She knew Karine understood possibly more than anyone else—part of a reaper's survival instinct involved forcing themselves to forget the darkness. So much of their souls became lost against their will. Layla swallowed a mouthful of blood and used the last of her strength to harden her expression. "Sena killed the reapers who killed me."

Karine let out a dark laugh. "So she did. But they were my children, and she incurred an impossible debt, for which Harlem will now pay." She flashed one last bloody smile before she began to squeeze Layla's heart.

But the pressure was brief. A small figure slammed between them, shoving Karine back against the stairs so hard, the entire room seemed to shake with her impact. Layla coughed with relief as she sat up, free of Karine's hand in her chest. While a gaping hole still remained, she could breathe more clearly now, and the pain quickly dulled as the flesh started to heal itself. Her breath hitched in her throat when she laid eyes on who stood before Karine.

Josi towered over her, blood splashed across her face from the blow she had dealt the older reaper. Karine sat with a crooked jaw and bloody face. She tried to hiss back at Josephine, but her jaw flopped uselessly with each movement. Josi tilted her head to the side and sat down in front of her. "You don't get to come into people's homes and ruin everything. That's not polite."

Karine heaved out a sigh. "Now you remember our lessons?" She stood and, limping slightly, made her way to the door. "When I return, Josephine, I want you to remember who really took care of you when things escalated between the reapers and the Saints. Because it certainly was not your sister. Nor was it Layla." She met Layla's eye, then turned her gaze up at the entryway overlooking the whole scene, where Elise stood, watching. "With ancient blood in her, she's more mine than she is yours."

"We can discuss a trade," Layla said quickly.

The older reaper raised her eyebrows but said nothing.

"Dr. Gray for Josi. You bring us to her, and we'll give you the Saint."

39

The betrayal cut deeper than Layla anticipated. Elise nursed an irritated mood the entire morning and during the ride to the dock. Others sensed the tension quickly—Jamie couldn't help muttering to Sterling as they approached his fast boat. "Trouble in paradise already."

"No one is surprised," Sterling quipped back.

Celie punched his shoulder. "That's so rude."

Layla narrowed her gaze at both men, then turned to Elise when Jamie drew the boat closer to the dock. "Elise—"

"I'm not angry at you; I'm just scared," Elise whispered fiercely.

The tension released from Layla's system, and her shoulders relaxed. "We're not actually going to give Josi to Karine. I don't think she would go willingly anyway."

Josi balanced on the edge of the dock, her leg lifting behind her into an arabesque. Sterling held tightly to the back of her dress, though the little girl never faltered or struggled to stay upright. The sight of dance made Layla feel guilty. All those years she had dedicated to ballet, only to hang up her slippers for blood. Layla wondered where she would be if she had never given in to her rage and continued with her true passion.

Jamie sat at the helm, pulling leather gloves on while he watched everyone board his boat.

Sterling stopped beside him and eyed his arsenal of several guns and grenades. "Nice supply." His gaze roamed to the leather gloves. "Classy."

"Unexpected?" Jamie asked.

"Just nice," Sterling answered. He turned to find his seat right as a small smile lifted Jamie's lips.

The gangster pointed toward the dark horizon, where storm clouds had lowered and begun to hover over the barely visible island in the distance. "Nicoletta said it's a fast ride. I warn you against treating this as a fun journey. If you do not hold on, you will fall off, and I will not come back for you."

"What a gentleman," Celie muttered behind Elise.

"I never claimed to be one," Jamie called back. He shot a fierce look at Elise, who sat squished between Sterling and Celie. "Do not mess up the leather."

Elise waved him off, instead looking for Layla, who had yet to enter the boat. She stood at the edge of the craft and glared down at everyone. "I would rather swim than fit into whatever this is."

Jamie started up the engine, sending a rough rumbling through the boat. Elise reached across the aisle for Layla's hand, pulling her onto the craft. The moment the boat began to move, Layla had no choice but to settle on Elise's lap. She felt good with Elise pressed against her, no matter how much she blushed and refused to meet her eye.

Water sprayed around them as the boat sped off along the ocean. The salty sting of the heavy air whipped curls around Elise's face, forcing her to press her face into the back of Layla's coat. She folded her arms around Layla's waist and leaned in to whisper, "In any other circumstance, I would enjoy this."

Layla coughed out a rough laugh. "Remind me to take you on a boat when we are not on the brink of war."

Elise smiled and dropped her forehead against the back of her shoulders. "Away from here."

"Wherever you want," Layla murmured. Eventually she leaned back into Elise's touch and relaxed. Her shoulders slumped while one of her legs threaded between Elise's, and she rested her hands over Elise's arms. Even as it grew too loud to properly speak, Layla still understood all of Elise's cues, the gentle stroke of her fingers over her knuckles and the feeling of her leg brushing against her thigh. Layla wanted to pause the moment, find some way to bottle the charged energy between them so she could save it for whenever they were separated. What she wanted was a real future with Elise. One without heartbreak and inevitable tragedy. One where they could say yes to a forever and not be disrupted by outside forces.

What she wanted was impossible. It was easier to not think about it at all. Otherwise her mind would circle countless infeasible ideas to ensure their future.

The thought made her heart skip a beat and crumble in her chest.

Elise's breathing kicked up the slightest bit, and though she tried to steady it to level out her pounding heart, Layla still sensed her distress. She turned and pressed a hand to Elise's chest. The coolness of her skin against the panic-driven heat that threatened to consume her made Elise exhale in relief. "How can you lie to Karine without her detecting it?"

Layla shrugged. "Years of learning how to regulate my nervous system to prevent blood furies, and Sena taught our clan how to lie to rogues."

Elise let out a grateful sigh when tall concrete walls rose up around them as the boat made it to the island. Though they had passed the clouds a while ago, a thick white mist still hung around the area, washing the island in a dreary gray chill. The whole place looked far from an elite establishment intended to change their city's fate. *Hart Island.* A place meant to bring entertainment and joy to people had been rendered gray and full of death once the plans for an amusement park were abandoned and much of the land turned into a cemetery.

The sour scent of rot rode the air. Layla wrinkled her nose, and she watched the younger Saint cover her mouth as they stepped out of the boat. Goose bumps rose across Elise's flesh the moment her feet touched the ground, and she rubbed her arms, casting a doubtful glance as she searched the place. Jamie seemed less unsettled, but he kept a watchful eye on Sterling, whose shoulders remained tense and his hands reaching toward his gun. They approached a building that seemed more modern than most back home but remained modest in size and scope. Even walking inside, away from the freezing sea breeze, did not alleviate Layla's frigid nerves. A new round of chills roused her body as she took a sweeping look over the immediate interior.

The foyer seemed to open into what could only be described as a prison. Several reapers and humans sat behind locked doors with bars over the windows. All wore metal collars, though while some sat up, watching the group with dull, lifeless eyes, others remained slumped against the concrete walls they were kept in.

Layla buzzed with apprehension. The place might as well have been a ticking time bomb. Not just for them and their visit, despite being unable to trust Karine's intentions, but also for the captive patients subject to this ancient reaper's wrath whenever she felt so inclined.

Josi tugged on Elise's hand with the one she wasn't using to cover her nose. "This is worse than the graveyard in the park."

The thought of the countless dead bodies being disturbed in their rest and innocent reapers and humans being added to the carnage made Layla's chest hurt. She gently brushed past Josi and looked ahead, hoping for some reprieve, but all she came face-to-face with was more concrete and imprisoned reapers.

Celie looked horrified. All blood had left her face, leaving her cheeks pale and her mouth agape. "What on earth—"

"Consider this my lair," a dark voice announced. Everyone turned to see Karine entering the foyer from a back room. She spread her hands by her sides and gave Layla a sad smile. "You know I was always hoping to see you here, Layla. I tried to tell you so many times how much you could have accomplished if only you weren't so afraid of a little blood. Maybe I would not have gone this route if you had done right by your lair. Instead, you chose a human. With how weak and mortal as Elise is, I'm not sure what you see in her. She holds you back, and thus your love holds every reaper in Harlem back. We deserve a better place in this world," Karine said strongly.

Layla's jaw tightened, her skin prickling at the accusation in Karine's voice. "So you believe that taking lives is the best way to free reapers from human authority?"

"Those who refuse to acknowledge us as beings capable of leading ourselves, yes. We are faster, stronger, and more powerful than humans by an enormous margin. It makes no sense to be relegated to subservience," Karine said.

It would not be the first time a reaper had insisted on rising against the law to establish their own freedoms. Plenty of reapers held the same belief—rogue reapers especially. Those who had tried in the past, however, were left with a label more dangerous than Saint weapons against reaper flesh. Subsequent generations bore that burden now, of being the ruthless monsters every human believed them to be because some had previously used violence to find liberation.

Layla almost laughed. "You speak of strength, yet you cannot even go in the sun without almost withering away. And even if you do succeed—say you kill every politician and Saint you have a problem with—what then? You think more humans won't see us as worse creatures that deserve even worse extermination efforts?"

"I know what you're thinking. They will only see us as the monsters they could never get rid of. But our violence is not the same as theirs; therefore, they cannot apply the same morality to it. I feel no qualms about taking advantage of the claws and fangs they forced upon us. They made something monstrous and are now upset that we show our teeth." Karine's gaze slid to Josi, who backed behind Elise's legs. "Your mayor is considering my side now. If we do not want war, then all he wants is Sena and Josi in exchange for reaper freedom. No more human-imposed rules on lairs and restrictions on employment and housing. If only I give him you." Karine's voice lowered to a cruel grating.

Josi fisted the fabric of Elise's pants in her hands. She peered around her legs with wide, fearful eyes, but she did not break Karine's gaze when she met it. "I won't go. Not to you and not to the mayor."

"That is no longer up to you. You are my experiment and now considered a weapon of the state. I hate to open a new age of reaperhood with such a dehumanizing effort, but you understand that some sacrifices must be made, right?" Karine asked. Her voice was a wicked taunt that made Josi tremble into Elise's side.

"You keep scaring her and the deal is off," Layla warned.

"Let us not delay then." A sinister smile stretched the older reaper's lips as she pulled the door open.

Elise stared directly at a ghost from her past. Dr. Gray stood in the middle of a lab surrounded by expensive equipment and empty exam tables. She looked up the moment the door swung open, and her hands fumbled on the glass containers she held. An almost-fearful recognition filled her soft brown eyes, and her lower lip trembled the longer everyone stared.

She looked just like her daughter, Thalia, with her dark hair and determined brown eyes. Dr. Gray's brown skin stood out against her lab coat, and the little mannerisms she exhibited while she cleaned up her area and approached the group only made Elise think she was looking at her old friend again. The sight nearly brought tears to her eyes.

Sterling gasped beside her, his hand coming up to cover his mouth. "Dr. Gray." It was as if every emotion from his past with Thalia had come rushing back to him. He lowered his shaky hand and gave her a watery smile.

Dr. Gray stopped in front of the group, her eyes straying to Josi. "I am happy to see you're doing well, Josephine," she said in a cool voice.

Josi pressed closer to Elise. The little girl's hand squeezed her older sister's, and she looked up at Dr. Gray with anguish dampening her eyes.

Karine nodded. She shot a look at Elise. "Make good on your promise and hand her over."

Elise knew none of this would be permanent. Not if things went well. But she couldn't help her hesitation, especially as Josi's fear began to verge on panic. The little girl shook her head, and her eyes welled with tears.

Dr. Gray held a hand up. "It's best to not scare her. The way the ancient reaper venom interacts with her nervous system can cause incredible emotional dysregulation. Infected with ancient reaper blood and turned without having to die…her blood properties are different—"

"More valuable," Karine said. She turned away just as Dr. Gray pursed her lips in disapproval. "She is my most expensive investment yet. I want to ensure her good health before you give her my blood to keep her bound to me and me only."

Elise's jaw clenched. "Go." She released Josi and allowed her to go off with Dr. Gray. For the most part, Josi seemed okay as long as she was within reach of her. Though apprehension brightened her eyes and stiffened her body, she did not protest when Dr. Gray lifted her onto the examination table. While Elise had gone over their plan again and again, she still worried about whether Josi could stick to it.

Elise tried to block out the varying reactions around her. From Layla pulling away and shaking her head, to Sterling coming closer just to grumble something under his breath. Celie and Jamie both remained frozen in shock a few feet away. Elise pressed her fingertips to her thighs to keep her hands from shaking.

An assistant emerged from one of the doors at the back of the room. Without a word, he grabbed Josi from Dr. Gray, preparing to strap her down to the table. Shrieking, Josi kicked her legs out and tried to pull away from him. As much as it pained Elise to watch, she could only breathe through the sharp aches in her heart and do nothing.

"*Elise*," Sterling warned.

Josi continued to struggle against the medical assistant. He grunted when her knee dug into his sternum, but managed to snap a metal restraint over one of her wrists.

Karine laughed a bit while she spoke to Dr. Gray. "Ces Américains sont tellement stupides; ils ne considèrent pas la vérité, ou toute autre option. Ils vont juste pour ce qu'ils pensent être la jugulaire." Her French was quick and perfect, but Elise understood it all. What she meant to be a coded language against Elise and her group had been a second tongue for her for many years. She fought the urge to roll her eyes as she mulled Karine's words over in her head.

Dr. Gray said nothing, though her assistant barked out a laugh and replied, "Ils abandonnent l'or pur."

Elise could no longer hold back. Her words came out sharp as she spoke. "Ou, sang, c'est pareil pour toi, non?" she interjected.

Karine's jaw went slack, her brows shooting up in shock.

Elise continued. "I've got no language of my own because my people were taken from their homes and forced to learn your ways, but that doesn't mean I can't turn the tongue against you." She looked at Josi, who had finally stopped struggling and only watched her sister with an expectant gaze.

"Aller pour la jugulaire," she told her.

Elise turned back and nodded to everyone else, just as Josi lunged for the medical assistant. She heard the chaos taking place behind her, the snap of her sister breaking free from the metal restraints and the medical assistant's gurgling screams as Josi tore into his throat. Just as Elise had asked.

Karine took off, shrieking for the guards outside.

"We have to go. Now," Elise said quickly.

Layla did not have time to register everyone's shocked expressions. All she could do was hope everyone followed suit as Elise grabbed Dr. Gray's arm and tugged her away from the lab. Alarms began blaring and doors slammed shut, forcing them to a grinding halt.

"Close down the lab and make sure they cannot go anywhere," another lab assistant breathed to his partner.

Layla looked to the countless imprisoned reapers and humans in the cells. "We have to free them." She shared a look with Elise, who kept glancing nervously at the door. "Everyone else go. I'll catch up with you later."

Elise's eyes went wide. "Layla, no—"

"I'll stay and help." Celie nodded to Layla.

Layla could have cried with relief. "Sterling, cover us from the guards. Jamie, you go with Elise. Make sure Dr. Gray gets out okay. Josi—"

But the littlest Saint was already moving toward the cells and reaching for the chains. Layla gave Elise a reassuring look before her panic could begin. "I'll keep her safe. Please go." Relief flooded her tense muscles as the Saint heiress finally took the last exit out with Jamie and Dr. Gray.

The other assistant moved toward Josi, but Sterling pulled a gun out and aimed it right at his chest. "Do not move."

"I'm just doing my job." the assistant closest to Josi said shakily. "Please don't kill me."

Sterling's eyes narrowed. "Don't give me a reason to."

While the blood drained from the men's faces, Josi took advantage of their frozen shock and crossed the room to the imprisoned reapers. She grabbed the Saint steel bars with her bare hands, making Layla wince. "You'll hurt yourself," she gritted out as blood dripped around the reapers' wrists from the pressure of the Saint metal against their skin.

Josi shook her head. Her hands, still gripping the metal, had yet to see a single mark of suffering from the specialized metal. Before she could begin to pry the bars apart, the chained reaper closest to her shook her head. "We cannot be free. It's not safe. Not in the water, not off the island."

Layla tore her gaze away from where Sterling was chasing down guards by the entrance to frown at the reaper. "You'll die in here."

"No. Karine wants us to live. She's connected us to her through blood." The reaper winced as she looked out the window towards the cloud covered sky. "We'll die out there." Other reapers shifted around her, chains tugging at their wounds while they nodded their agreement.

Josi whimpered. "But I want to help—"

"We have to go." Layla tugged the little Saint up a set of stairs nearby as more guards spilled into the room.

Josi opened her mouth to protest, but gunfire tore their attention away so they could see Celie stumbling up the stairs, her hand pressed to a fresh gunshot wound in her chest. She hissed at the approaching guards holding guns and pulled her hand back. Blood spilled down her chest, but it slowed as the seconds passed and her wound knit itself back together.

Layla rested a gentle hand on Josi's shoulder. "Forget your impulse training, Josi. I want you to be your worst self, okay?"

The little girl nodded eagerly. Layla pointed to the lab and the sudden rush of guards closing in around the chaos. "Don't stop until they cannot come after us. Understand?"

Josi gave her a bright smile. "Understood."

Layla let her go.

A baby reaper tearing into grown men had to be one of the most glorious things Layla had seen in a while. She would have stayed and regarded Josi's carnage for longer if it were not for the sudden blare of emergency alarms and the repeated command to shut the island down. After shouting at Josi to follow them, Layla pushed Celie out of the room and bolted for the exit.

Several guards, however, had already begun to crowd the

entrance to the lab building. Most of them held Saint guns, and they raised them as Layla came to an abrupt halt with Celie by her side.

"This way!" Josi shouted behind them.

There was no time to question the ten-year-old's judgment. Layla gave Celie one look, and then they both took off down the hall in the direction of the Saint girl. After scaling several narrow staircases at the back of the building, they found her near the top floor. She stood by a tall window that the glass had been knocked out of. Thousands of shards scattered across the floor and stuck out at jagged angles from the window frame.

"What is this?" Layla hissed. She glanced back down the staircase as the sounds of racing footsteps and panicked shouts neared.

"We jump now." Josi pointed out the window. Several yards below, ocean waves crashed against rocks. The sea was a pit of blackness, drowned out only by the angry spray of sea-foam. Jumping to avoid the rocks would be difficult, but not impossible. Continuing to swim after being impaled by a rock or shattering a bone on one was what concerned Layla. She already hated water. Not to mention the last time she had been in the ocean, she had been on the brink of death.

She nodded to Celie. "You first."

The younger reaper gave her an incredulous look. Blood stained her face, and her fangs emerged on impulse, but the fear in her eyes betrayed any lasting intimidation.

Layla sighed. The storm of guards was deathly nearby now, their shouts only seconds away. She glared as she gestured to the window.

"You stay here, you die. You jump far enough out, you only have to worry about swimming."

Celie gave one last shake of her head before cursing beneath her breath. She stepped onto the stone ledge and launched herself from the window. Layla did not look to see if she landed well. She only helped Josi onto the ledge before hauling herself up next. Right as the men broke onto the landing they stood on, they jumped.

The fall felt endlessly long. Layla was aware of the wind whistling by her ears enough to reconsider her decision to jump. By the time she thought better of it, her feet were slicing through the water and the ocean had swallowed her whole. She kicked around to bring herself to the surface, but her leg caught on something in the murky depths. As Layla peered down through the water, she tore her leg free of the black thing clinging to her. The murkiness cleared briefly, and her eyes widened at the sight of an evolved reaper staring up at her. She startled at first, trying to back away from it, but went still when the thing did not move. It remained frozen, a chain circling its body and holding it captive to the ocean floor. Talons stretched up toward the surface of the water, and its mouth hung open in an agonized silent scream. Layla could only watch as its eyes moved toward her. Then it lunged, the chain rattling while it tried to reach for her. She moved back once more, waiting for the sand to settle so she could be positive she was not imagining things. When the water cleared, Layla found a nightmare one could hope only to imagine.

Hundreds of evolved reapers sat chained to the ocean floor. All of them alive and screaming in their watery prisons.

Among the newer, more sinister beasts, Layla found more human-looking faces. One of them, a reaper she thought she would never see again.

She kicked back to the surface and found Celie and Josi waving down Jamie and the rest in his boat. "Laure is here!" Layla called.

Celie snapped her head back. "What?"

"I need help getting her free. Make sure Josi gets on the boat first." It was the last thing she said before diving back beneath the water. Layla narrowly avoided the swipe of the evolved reapers' talons as she swam to Laure. The reaper's eyes were closed, and she floated at the end of the chain binding her to the ocean floor. Layla tried not to think about the air squeezing out of her lungs as she grabbed the chain. The Saint steel burned through her flesh, sending her blood flowing into the water. She gritted her teeth against the blistering pain and continued tugging on the metal, to no avail. A new presence swam up next to her, and to her surprise, when she looked over, she saw the younger Saint reaching for the chains. Josi pulled them apart with relative ease, though she grimaced as Laure's wrists and ankles became visible without the chains. They had been worn down to the bone. The messy flesh had been cauterized by the metal, but as it shifted off her, old wounds reopened, spilling her blood and bits of her skin into the water.

Josi grabbed one arm and Layla the other. Together, they hauled her to the surface. Jamie waited with his boat, both Elise and Sterling leaning over the edge to help pull Laure up. Once everyone was in,

Elise brushed Josi's hair from her face and pressed her palms to her cheeks. "Are you okay?"

Most of the blood had been washed away in the sea, but some still stained her mouth and her throat. Josi grinned, revealing her blood-soaked fangs. "I am great. That was amazing."

Layla might have shared her joy if it weren't for Laure, still unconscious and bleeding on the boat floor. Celie kneeled by her as Jamie propelled the boat toward shore. "What did you do to her?" Celie asked, her voice small.

A shadow crossed Dr. Gray's face. Wrinkles formed by her eyes as her brows furrowed, and she gave Celie a dismayed look. "Whatever Karine wanted. Saint associates and reapers who refused Karine's orders became this. You shouldn't have moved her from the water."

Layla remembered the Saint associate who had stumbled to the club, soaking wet and panicked all those weeks ago. Then the one who had emerged from the water to attack that man who'd purchased her venom and the ones who now acted as guards for Karine's new lair. With the Saint empire crumbling, they had been forced to choose between guarding a reaper or a fate worse than death in her army.

Celie frowned. "Why not?"

Dr. Gray looked up at the sky, where dawn was just beginning to break across the horizon. "She's not been remade for civilized living."

Layla opened her mouth to speak, but Laure was suddenly coughing up water, her body heaving as she came to. Whimpering, the older reaper shot up. She glanced around at everyone, her eyes settling on Celie the moment she found her. Celie went right into Laure's arms. Despite her smaller size, she still almost knocked her over with the force of her affection.

"I thought you were gone forever," Celie breathed into her hair.

Laure wrapped her arms around Celie and pressed her face into her neck. "I'm here now. You all saved me."

"We have to do something about the others," Layla said. "Karine has a whole army on the ocean floor."

Elise shook her head. "I don't even understand how she's funding this. And who in their right mind would trust a reaper to conduct such experiments?"

Dr. Gray cleared her throat. "Previous partners have been rather dangerous and inconsistent. I promise you, I let her take me here only because she insisted she wanted to help reapers. I wanted to help you. I did not know she was planning on abducting reapers and humans. Or planning on violently overtaking the city. My commitment as a physician researcher is to advance scientific knowledge and medical education, but never at the expense of other souls." Her voice went thick, and she pursed her lips, her eyes filling with tears. "I made a mistake. You have my endless apologies. I will spend the rest of my life making it up to you—to everyone."

The boat slowed as they made it back to the dock. Far behind them, the island sat in the thick fog, lights still glinting through the mist as if they were winking at those who had caused chaos and managed to escape. Clouds overhead parted and sunlight spilled into the atmosphere, lighting up the dock and the boat.

Celie reached back to help Laure out of the boat. With one hand raised, she waited for the other reaper to take it in her own.

"What are we going to do—" Laure stopped midsentence as she stared at her still-raised hand, her eyes widening. Black veins spiderwebbed across her skin. They crept along her arm, then exploded across her throat and her face. Laure collapsed with no more than a whimper and a choking sound fighting out of her throat. Celie and Dr. Gray dropped to their knees beside her while Elise covered her mouth with her hands.

"The sun," Dr. Gray muttered.

There was nowhere to go, nowhere to shield her from the light. They were out in the open, with nothing but water and a deserted shipyard around them.

All the blood drained from Layla's face, and she faced the doctor with true horror darkening her expression. "*Save her*," she demanded.

But deep down she knew, as she watched Laure writhe between them, her flesh turning black and falling to bits around her skeleton, that it was too late. The young reaper rotted into foul-smelling chunks of ruined flesh and blood before their eyes. Pieces of Laure fell through Celie's fingers, and the reaper could only look on in pure shock. The scent of poison and rotting flesh turned Layla's stomach, though neither worked as powerfully as the sight of defeat on Celie's pale face.

Dr. Gray shook her head slowly. She closed her hand over Celie's trembling shoulder before moving closer to Laure. Sorrow shadowed her eyes, and she reached forward with a shaking hand to tuck a piece of Laure's hair behind her ear as the remaining bulk of her body finally went still. "After they're dosed with the ancient reaper's blood, the sun becomes ruinous the moment it touches a reaper's flesh. There is no hope if there is no darkness to use as a shield." Though the doctor spoke of a reaper who had been a stranger to her, Layla watched a flicker of recognition in Elise's eyes and all the loss and devastation that filled it. She knew then that the Saint thought of her older sister dying at the hands of a different poison, her heart unable to start again even with Dr. Gray's cure filling her veins.

40

So many automobiles and people surrounded the old Saint estate, Elise almost believed she had been thrown back in time to the empire's golden days. She shut the curtain of her father's study and turned to face him, her heart already racing at the thought of being spoken about by the Saint patriarch once again. It was as if they had gone back to their old ways—Tobias presenting her as his perfect heir and expecting perfect behavior from her and unmatched results from the audience.

Tobias wore a nice black suit and had smoothed his curls down for the press conference. This tailored version of him was the most done up and prepared Elise had seen him since the fall of the Saint empire. While her father had once appeared grand in his suits and worn confidence like a shield, that part of him was almost nowhere to be seen now. He fiddled with his watch band, his fingers twisting the metal first, then moving to adjust his cufflinks. It reminded Elise so much of her mother's flighty nerves—the way she used to adjust her hairpieces and tuck invisible loose stands away. Elise found herself doing the same now, fussing with her hair even though not a piece of it had moved out of place. Her hands did not shake as much as they used to; standing so close to her father, a man who had refused to see her for so many years, who now appeared as nervous and broken as Elise had been for so long, she felt more at peace.

"How many people did you invite?" Elise asked.

Tobias ran a hand over his hair, sighing. "Everyone I have ever done business with. Could be hundreds. Could be thousands."

Sterling and Layla appeared in the doorway to the study. Layla leaned against the doorframe, her hands in her pockets, while Sterling stood with his arms crossed. Both were dressed in all black, though it looked odd seeing Sterling without his Saint badge proudly on display, pinned to his chest, despite how long it had been since he'd discarded it

"We have cleared the area, posted some guards and reapers on the perimeter. No one should be able to sneak in. Mayor Arendale is already ready outside, addressing the crowd," Sterling said.

"Dr. Gray and Josephine are ready?" Tobias asked.

"Yes. They'd love to see you if you are…willing," Sterling said.

Tobias shook his head. "No. It's probably best we remain separate. This is a situation I never thought I would find myself in. My daughters…safe with reapers." He glanced at Elise. "You look unwell."

Elise pursed her lips. The memory of exchanging blood with

Josi earlier weighed heavily on her mind. "I gave my blood to Josi to hopefully counteract her bond with Sena. In case anything happens."

"Thinking like a reaper…" Tobias muttered.

"Father—"

He held his hand up, effectively quieting Elise. She looked away and clenched her jaw even as he spoke again. "You do not have to tell me that things have changed. I knew it the moment I found your letter denouncing your admission to the Paris Conservatory. I saw myself in you then, Elise. Willing to do whatever was necessary to protect your sister."

Something sharp twisted in Elise's chest. Her lips parted, and her throat went dry as she met her father's devastated gaze. "I would never be as reckless as you. I understand fearing loss and loving us hard enough to change the world, but what you did to me—that was never love."

After years of his unrelenting passion, Elise finally understood him now. It did not matter that after tearing the soul from her, he gazed upon her with affection. He had a heart that felt too much even for himself. The constant, consuming hunger for safety had only further terrified him and chased away every good thing. All perfection he had created had been fitted with exquisite cruelty that he might not ever acknowledge. Elise had borne the burden of his faulty expectations for far too long. But her battered heart no longer wanted the guilt and distress. She wanted to let it all go. A bittersweet truth sworn in blood and false promises. A starving love she would no longer carry with her.

Even in her own defense, Elise felt a crushing guilt. She had never been able to stop feeling; the hyper-perception could be her own undoing one day. For now, she could only look at her father and tell herself for assurance that though he had fostered her personal hell for years, he had other companions. The devil was never alone in his desolation.

Tobias's gaze slid to Layla, whose expression had turned more murderous the longer he stood before Elise. "I suppose what she gives you is love?" He glanced back at Elise. "Are you with her now? Officially?"

Elise's teeth dug into her lower lip before she answered, "Always."

A muscle ticked in her father's jaw, and he dropped his hands to his sides. "Pray you go together. Burying the love of your life is the worst punishment imaginable." Tobias brushed past all of them as he left the room.

Elise twisted the ring around her finger, the tension working her system up waning with his departure. Through it all, she could think only of how her father had looked a few weeks ago, blood covering his shirtfront as he held her mother for the last time. On his knees and bent over her body like he was making a sacrifice. But Elise knew the violence that had brought him to this moment. It was strange, how in moments of intense grief and suffering, all previous revelations nearly vanished. Elise had not been far from her father's position then. She might have done the same with her mother's corpse if her father had not gotten to her faster. Now he walked out again like a ghost.

For all the things Elise faulted him for, accepting her truth was never one of them. Part of her wondered if he had always known she loved Layla as more than a friend. He never participated when her mother asked her about what she wanted her future wedding to a man to look like. While Elise was uncomfortable, she only countered with wanting to wear a matching dress with her bride. Analia's eyes lit up with surprise then, and Tobias's expression softened. *Just make sure she asks for my blessing* was all Tobias said. After that, her parents only ever addressed her as she was—a young woman who loved other women. Or one woman in particular. That was where Tobias had found his greatest strategy. To use Elise's heart against Layla.

She grabbed Elise's hand as they began to follow Tobias out of the estate. "I'm glad I never asked that man for his blessing," Layla hissed.

A small smile stretched across Elise's face. "How scandalous of you, Miss Quinn. You are sure to make us Quinns the talk of the town if you keep up this behavior."

Layla's cheeks filled with a dark red blush that Elise knew all too well. "I dare them to talk about my wife."

Elise could only squeeze her hand before pulling away and moving to stand by her father at the podium outside. For the first time in ages, hope burned as brilliantly within her as love.

Watching Tobias speak in the Saint estate courtyard before hundreds of onlookers, all desperate for a tragedy to turn into a beautiful story, felt like watching a ghost lingering by an open grave. While the house still stood rather proudly with its untouched white columns and massive exterior, what had once represented an empire predicted to change the world for better eternities, now resembled a gutted corpse. Fallen leaves that no one had bothered to sweep up littered the courtyard and crunched under the crowd's restless feet. Some of the house's windows held large cracks, and though many of their curtains had been pulled back, they revealed a deeper darkness within. Inside, dust covered the furniture and beautiful marble floors. Some of the family portraits had been slashed, and blood even stained a few of the ornate rugs and painted new scenes on various walls.

Though the crowd watching Tobias now had not gone inside, Layla recognized their bright and curious eyes. Many of them journalists, they waited in front of Tobias with their pens poised over their blank notepads. Other lower-ranking politicians and less public businessmen regarded Tobias with less respect and more doubt. They hung around the edge of the crowd, standing with crossed arms and furrowed brows while Sterling and Jamie pulled a chained and bound Sena from inside. A few gasps sounded throughout the yard as the ancient reaper lifted her head to stare them down.

Dark shadows coupled with black veins shifted beneath her green eyes. They were an unusual shade, like they had once been another color and only cruelly forced into this new violent green. Hunger darkened them, and Elise's mind went to every version of disaster that could ensue if the chains around her wrists were to break.

Josi moved into place beside Elise by Mayor Arendale near the podium. Layla stood behind Sena a few yards away, but she kept flicking her gaze between Elise and the ancient reaper.

"Many of you know me as a family man. A man who came from Texas with nothing more than a dream for the future. Before I even founded my metalworking company—before I even knew what I wanted to do with my life, I found purpose in the love I had for my lovely wife. With her from Louisiana and me from Texas, it was truly fate that we met at all. She followed me through every iteration of my hopes and dreams. She gave me the family I always wanted—my three beautiful daughters, who then shifted everything for me." Tobias's fingers gripped the edge of the podium as he let out a heavy breath. "As I stand here now, I have no wife and only two daughters left. One of them has been changed irrevocably by the venom of a reaper. In my line of work, I have seen only death and destruction. No matter how successful my empire was when it was at its best for so many years, there was still no relief from the suffering reaperhood caused. I know it will only get worse. Any choice to further spread that venom and take advantage of its properties is an immoral one."

The crowd shifted with unease. Some people murmured heatedly to their neighbors, while others scribbled notes in their notebooks, not wanting to miss a word of the commotion.

Tobias lifted a hand to ask for everyone's silence. As the courtyard fell quiet again, he continued, his face pale and eyes dark with a haunting so severe, Layla wondered if he had truly survived the death of his wife at all. "We must face our mistakes as a nation in creating monstrosities and blaming them for what they ended up being capable of after such horrific treatment. That is why I endorse the destruction of these new reaper venom markets. Instead of giving those crooked businesses money, I vow to support the scientific endeavors for a true cure, from someone who has been just as impacted by reaperhood as I have. Dr. Gray is a scientist who specializes in virology and has worked all over the world. She has returned to Harlem, and we hope to use her research for good.

"Previously, Mayor Arendale wanted a working partnership with Karine, an older reaper from abroad, to help steady human and reaper relations here. But since then, we have learned of her desire to use the worst kinds of venom to make reapers more vengeful. Sena, or Valeriya, the old Harlem reaper leader, is an example. She has been terrorizing Harlem for the past few weeks and even took my wife's life. It is only thanks to my daughter Elise and her partnership with the Harlem reapers, and some rogues and gangsters, that Sena was captured. They have uncovered a diabolical plan Karine has in the works to take over New York by any means. We believe it is necessary for everyone to come together—whether it be reapers, humans, gangsters, Saints. We are better together. It might have taken a few years, but I am grateful to my daughter for showing me that. Maybe we can prevent more deaths and collateral damage in this way. Reapers should have someone they can look to. Someone who understands them and their way of living. If my daughter trusts Layla Quinn to be that reaper, then so do I."

Mayor Arendale nodded. "And so does the city of New York."

Pride softened Tobias's grief. "May Elise and Layla's legacy better us all."

Layla watched a proud smile spread across Elise's face. She caught her eye then, the Saint girl nodding at her. Elise stood just beneath the stage, several yards from the entrance of the estate and even farther from her, but Layla still felt her gaze. She wanted to stay like that, wearing matching expressions of hope.

But a jolt shifted the ground beneath her feet, and as Layla looked past Elise into the house, she saw fire exploding beyond the walls. She moved as fast as she could toward Elise, but not even her reaper speed could outrun the explosion that rocked the Saint estate.

Fire licked up Layla's back, scorching her skin until it melted beneath her shirt. Through the pain, she sensed blood—her own, Elise's, everyone's around her. The thought of opening her eyes scared her. Before the explosion had hit the courtyard, Layla had run for Elise and managed to tackle her to the ground as the windows exploded behind her. But the overwhelming scent of her blood beneath her now told Layla she had failed at keeping her safe.

Finally, after a long moment of crackling silence filled only by the fire and the interspersed sounds of the estate collapsing brick by brick, Layla opened her eyes. She hovered above Elise, who blinked debris and blood away.

"Oh my God..." Elise's eyes widened, and her hands came up to cup Layla's face. "What happened? You're bleeding everywhere."

Layla had not examined her own body yet, but judging by the burning pain raging through it, she had taken most of the blow to shield Elise. Her own wounds didn't matter, though. Not while she watched blood spill from a gash in Elise's forehead. "You're hurt."

"*You're on fire*," Elise said sharply. Panic brightened her eyes. "Josi." She pulled herself out from beneath Layla, and the moment she was gone, Layla collapsed. Shrapnel lodged in her flesh sank deeper as she hit the ground. Beyond the burning, Layla felt something stirring in her. It was a feeling she could not ignore, no matter how much her burned back protested with her movements. Poison that had been dormant came to life in her system. Burning, angry, and begging to be fed. Layla smelled the poison before she felt it. The bittersweet scent coupled with its familiarity clued her in to the rush of heat and rage pummeling her system.

Layla watched as Josi ran up to Elise, and then the two of them bent to tend to Layla's wounds. But she yanked herself away, hissing. "Don't touch me. There was poison in the explosion. Most likely from Nicoletta's leftover grenades." Her voice came out strained and guttural. The veins on her hands darkened and bulged, as if black snakes writhed beneath her skin. Layla winced as her body seized with pain, her vision growing hazy. No matter how much she tried to breathe through it all, her racing heart only increased its pace, coursing whatever poison cursed her blood faster through her body.

Elise took a step back, and Layla glanced around, noticing the flattened crowd of people. Many of them had run for the gates and avoided the worst of the blast, but those in the front had begun to groan and stir. It sounded inhuman; each rumble a pain emerging from the depths of dark monstrosity. Through the ruined gates, a figure emerged. Layla sensed the ancient reaper before she became visible, her eyes golden and glowing through the smoke.

Karine surveyed the courtyard with level contentment. A small smile lifted the edge of her lips when she found the front area, where the blast had freed Sena from her jailors. Layla's heart dropped as the two ancient reapers eyed each other. A cry of fear shot through the wounded crowd as Sena's chains jolted with her movements. Sterling and Jamie had been thrown to the side, no longer in control of her restraints. They thrashed under the strength of the venom, their humanity fading as they began to turn. Just like with Layla, Sena's veins bulged, a strong indication of the new poison battling her system.

Karine watched proudly as people began to rise, their new reaperhood stretching their bones and drawing pained groans from their throats. Sena was barely recognizable by the time Karine made it to her. Her skin had gone gray, and talons erupted through her fingers the longer she stood with the poison taking over. Layla tried to shove herself to her feet, but the pain made her sway, and she could only drag herself a few yards before her talons tore into the ground.

The original ancient reaper yanked the gun from Sterling's holster and shoved the barrel into her own temple. Karine reached for Sena, alarm widening her eyes, but even she was too slow. The gun went off, and as Sena's body fell to the ground, the younger Saint did too.

Elise screamed. It was a wretched sound, tortured and devastated. She rushed to catch her sister and cradled her limp body in her shaking arms.

Layla wished her final moments of clarity involved the girl she loved in any other state. She squeezed her eyes shut, memorizing her face and all the beauty of her as she succumbed to the poison.

The next few moments passed by quickly. Layla rose under her newfound strength and found evolved reapers facing off in the courtyard. While some she recognized as previous human members of Tobias's crowd, others were complete strangers. They all aimed for the innocent beings left standing. A fresh rage crashed over Layla, and she tore into them. Killing had never been easier. Especially in defense of those she cared about. In her new altered flesh, she was a merciless warrior, driving her talons into anything that moved before her. When her hands became too full with one opponent, she used her teeth. Her larger fangs bit into flesh like it was nothing, tearing throats into brutal shreds and letting the blood paint her face and body. In this form, there was no remorse, no logical thinking. All that existed was the drive to destroy, the urge to kill. Even the thought of her time running out did not faze Layla. She would go until she collapsed—until her heart stopped, gorged on others' blood.

But Layla never got to that point. Minutes passed, and she eventually stood in the middle of a courtyard covered in bodies. Her final blow came from her fists. When she pulled her arm back, the talons had gone. Even her vision had returned to its normal scope, all blanketing redness and blurriness gone. Jamie and Sterling stood nearby in a similar state. Both covered in blood and reeling from the recent events. Sterling dropped his gaze and swallowed hard.

When Layla looked down, she found the only body that had not been destroyed by evolved reapers.

Tobias Saint lay beside the podium, dead. He had sustained too much of the blast, and his heart had given out before the poison could alter his body. Staring at his bloody and burned body did not rouse the satisfaction in her that Layla had been hoping for these past years. Instead, she felt nothing.

Mayor Arendale emerged from beneath the podium, bloody but alive and human.

Glass was shattered in the windows behind the stage, and in the reflection of the final shard, Layla saw herself standing among the flames inside. She looked like a normal girl, no more talons, only a regular human back to her usual height. Her breath stilled in her chest, and for a moment, Layla thought the poison might have irrevocably changed her body for the better. But when she stuck a finger in her mouth, she felt the point of her retracted fangs among her teeth. Disappointment had only just begun to darken her expression and squeeze her chest when she heard Elise cry out behind her.

The Saint girl sat curled in on herself while Dr. Gray bent over her younger sister. She whimpered, keeping her gaze down even as Layla, Jamie, and Sterling approached. Arendale stood over them, his eyes wide with astonishment. "You all…lived," he breathed.

Elise blinked through her tears as she surveyed Layla and her other friends. "You're okay."

But Layla was not okay. She had become a monster again and, in the end, remained a reaper. Even in her aim to take down only the evolved reapers to protect the innocent people caught in the crowd and ensure Elise would be safe, Layla had created immeasurable collateral damage.

"Elise…" Sterling said softly. His voice was so gentle, it almost sounded broken.

As Elise turned to face him, she found him kneeling by her father's dead body. Layla sensed the tensing of her muscles and the rush of her blood as her heart rate spiked. Elise buried her face in her hands, her body shaking with violent breaths taken to calm herself. When Elise looked up, Layla was surprised to see that her face had dried from tears. Red lined her eyes, but she did not cry. And when she spoke, her voice was an empty declaration that rang through Layla's hollow bones. "It's over."

"No." Dr. Gray placed two fingers on Josi's neck, feeling for her pulse. "You were smart to give Josi your blood earlier. She's bound to you for now, though the severing of her bond with Sena was violent enough to send her into shock. Now we must prepare. When night falls, all hell will break loose."

41

Hours later, Layla still smelled blood. Despite scrubbing herself raw in her bathroom at the cathedral and throwing her clothes away, she could not shake the veil of death that had been hanging over her since she emerged from her evolved reaper state. She checked on a sleeping Elise in the spare bedroom across from hers. The Saint girl had curled around her younger sister in the middle of the bed. Jamie had brought Hendricks to keep Josi company and Layla desperately hoped the grumpy cat, pressed into her side, would bring the little girl comfort through her dreams. Even in sleep, the Saints looked too fragile to be in such a place. Layla had been tempted to draw closer and stroke the unmarred skin beneath the fresh bruises covering her body, but she knew an important meeting awaited her arrival in the crypt.

The scent of old bones and stale blood hit her immediately.

While many of the bodies had been cleared out over time, their presence remained like a haunting.

"What a disaster," Jamie said. He leaned against the wall with Sterling and Nicoletta flanking his sides. The rain outside had plastered their hair to their temples. Even their clothes looked soaked, though none of it seemed to bother them. The older gangster lounged in the one seat with her shoulders back and her elbows on the dusty tabletop like she owned the place. The rain had settled to a nearly soundless drizzle outside, but Nicoletta still seemed to carry the worst of it in her damp clothes and wet, glittering lashes.

"So, this is how you lived. Sharing blood," Layla said, glancing between the three of them. "How long has this been going on?"

Sterling's cheeks bloomed red with embarrassed heat. He looked toward Dr. Gray, who'd made a quiet entrance into the underground space. The turn only made the bite scar in his neck more visible, and Layla felt a sharp annoyance tugging at her for all the judgment Sterling had put her through only to end up in the same position as her. "It was Dr. Gray's idea."

Dr. Gray's face was ashen, and her dark eyes were shadowed with concern. "Josephine is stable now. Still unconscious, but breathing. Introducing Elise's blood to her seems to have forced her body to let go of the bond she had with Sena. Speaking of…" She glanced at the recently buried tomb where the ancient reaper had been laid to rest. "It was not only Sena's blood waking the dead but also Karine's. While most of her army affected by Sena's blood should be down now, we have to worry about those raised by Karine's blood. We should focus our efforts on stopping her to prevent the assault. It will be difficult to kill her, so polluting her blood with antivenom to keep it from being useful is our best bet. We'll only need one shot."

A shaky pain flared in Layla's arm. It rippled down to her hand, and as she turned her wrist over, her breath hitched. Black veins rolled beneath her skin. They looked especially large in the glow of the moonlight, their constricting movements mimicking the hunger pulsing in Layla's stomach. She tried to force back her own shock but could only manage a wet cough. Blood dripped from her mouth and sprayed her hands.

Dr. Gray regarded her with genuine sorrow. The rain continued to hum in the background as Layla swallowed her own rotten blood. "The poison has been idle, but it's reemerging now. The good news is humans and reapers can use blood to bond and protect one another from potential attacks. Despite being poisoned and attacked by the dead's lethal bites, you all turned back to your regular states because of the blood you shared with another. We can use that to our advantage if we have to fight. I have seen in recent observations that overuse of the poison can cause lethal withdrawal symptoms. This should only be a one-time thing."

Sterling crossed his arms. "What if the poison never leaves us?"

Dr. Gray pursed her lips. "I'll work hard to keep you lucid for as long as I can."

The following hours were full of long announcements and attempts at assuring the clan. Reminding everyone that they could be stronger than evolved reapers together, even if it seemed impossible. That Layla had somehow miraculously survived an attack that should have killed her was a sign in itself. But even she was unconvinced. After she walked away from her clan mates shaking their heads and murmuring their doubts, Layla nearly collapsed in her bathroom. She retched until her stomach hurt and blood dripped from her eyes. While the bulbous veins from last night had gone away, there was a choking pit of discomfort in Layla's system that had failed to disperse. She felt it in her chest, her head, and her stomach—a slight burning like the beginnings of a muscle ache. But it never went away. Throughout the afternoon, she became restless, sometimes coughing up blood. Turning the radio on to listen to the news as a distraction helped for only so long.

Static filled the room at first as she tuned it to a station. Then a broadcaster's voice rang out, loudly breaking the static silence: *"This just in, Mayor Arendale has announced his plans to put Harlem on a lockdown and curfew. He has deemed the area unsafe and volatile after the major explosion at the Saint estate that killed Tobias Saint and several other citizens. With the recent explosions and poisonous attacks led by ancient reaper Karine, Harlem is a truly lawless place. Hopefully Mayor Arendale can get everything under control…"*

Eventually, her door creaked open and Elise came in. Her hair was messy from sleep, her eyes puffy with past tears. But she pulled Layla into the bathroom without a word and took a rag from the shelf before kneeling to wipe the blood from Layla's face. "I can feel your pain. It's like a burning in my chest. Are you starved?" Elise asked.

"Not at all. Dr. Gray said the poison makes a bigger home in you each time you're exposed to it. I think it's just my time." Layla swallowed past the rise of bloody bile in her throat. She passed a hand over her face and winced as the pain grew strong enough to send black spots over her vision. "Maybe it would be best if I died. I could relieve you of this pain."

"No, Layla. There would only be worse pain if you died. I've already lost everyone. We will not add you to that list." Elise wiped a hand over her forehead, and Layla noticed the sweat beading on her brow. Through all her own suffering, she had failed to notice the feverish heat raging through Elise.

"You're sick too," Layla said. She tried to sit up, but her stomach lurched, and she had to grit her teeth to keep from passing out.

Elise shrugged. "I think it's just our blood bond. Being close to you is helping. And honestly, I wasn't sure how much longer I could sit around, begging Josi to wake up. We'll be okay. We have to be." A shiver passed through her, and Layla's heart dropped.

"I have an idea," she whispered.

Layla watched the ripples of Elise's reflection in the shallow pool of holy water. The two sat side by side in the cathedral's sanctuary, water glistening on their skin in the low light. The brief dip had cooled them enough to settle their minds and nerves. Though only a few moments into their holy water escape, Elise was pulling Layla into her and begging for a new distraction.

It had been a while since she'd last coughed up blood or had an episode from the poison. Still, exhaust shadowed her eyes. Her veins were turning purple, and even her movements were much slower than usual. Elise raised a palm to her cheek, wincing at the unnatural warmth of her skin. Every other time, Layla had been cool to the touch, as all reapers were. Now she felt closer to a furnace. Burning with a malignant force tearing her up inside.

Layla threaded her fingers through Elise's and let out a shaky breath. "Thank you for staying with me."

All the heat that had been flushing Elise's cheeks dissipated, and she groaned as chills shook her body. "In sickness and in health."

"'Til death…" Layla muttered, her eyes falling to Elise's shivering form. She unthreaded their fingers and pulled Elise closer to her. She pressed her face into the heated junction between her chin and chest, sighing with relief as her warmth chased away her frigidity.

Layla still had brutal nightmares that involved Elise dying in every horrific way imaginable all because she failed to save her. She woke up with Elise's French words in her mouth, choking her like sawdust coating her throat.

Laisse-moi mourir en premier.

Let me die first. Let me die first. Let me die first.

"What if there were a way to escape this, but it meant abandoning all that we've started?" Elise said softly.

Layla peered up at her, curiosity returning the light to her eyes. "A Saint wanting to abandon her responsibilities? Do enlighten me."

"Your last name becoming ours is the only responsibility that matters now." Elise smiled, and Layla felt her heart crack at the sight.

Maybe there was a better way to think of things. She could live in blissful ignorance and assume that neither of them would die. Never mind the fact that Layla was a guaranteed immortal unless she got caught up in a fight against immeasurable Saint steel and poisons capable of starting wars. Never mind the fact that she and Elise had been through more near-death experiences in the past few months than most others had in a lifetime. Never mind the fact that Elise was a fragile thing in this war of malevolence and incomprehensible powers. As far as Layla was concerned, their separation was a matter of when, not if. There were very few things that could be done to keep them together for a time that Layla would find ample. She did not want Elise to be a small part of her life. She had known her since birth. All parts of her were tangled with Elise, her essence deeply interwoven with the threads of her life. She could not hear the piano without thinking of her; she could not drink blood without thinking of her; she could not laugh without thinking about how she laughed the most with her.

There was no life without Elise Saint.

42

WITH SAINTS, REAPERS, AND GANGSTERS GATHering in a holy place, Layla began to believe they were indicative of something greater. That perhaps they all did have something better than death to look forward to.

Dr. Gray stood at the front of the room with a syringe and a small glass test bottle in her hands. "The idea behind this science is that the poison acts as a sort of controlling agent to make anyone who ingests it angrier and more volatile. It would work in a similar way to reaper venom, where once a human is bitten, they are drawn to the reaper who bit them and feel an indescribable urge to serve them." A few murmurs of disgust and apprehension rumbled through the crowd as Dr. Gray paused. When she continued, they fell silent again, attentive and fully engaged. "After witnessing several attacks and responses to the poison, I have reason to believe that tethers will make the poison survivable. If a reaper takes the poison after having fed from a human, their tether to the human will keep them alive, even after the effects of the poison wear off. Karine was mostly using Sena's blood to raise the dead and turn reapers and humans into worse creatures. She will use her own blood now, even if it means her life is more vulnerable. So as long as we can get to her and neutralize her blood, or any potential human tether she is using to ground herself, maybe the war will not be so devastating. My research—including a newer working cure—remains at the lab. We need Karine gone so that I may continue to work on it and hopefully help Harlem heal. That being said, our partnership is imperative. You might be able to overcome an army of evolved reapers and raised dead by allowing yourselves to descend into the viciousness you've fought so hard to not become."

An eruption of disbelief seemed to barrel through the room. From reapers to gangsters, everyone had a different option to voice. None of whom were particularly thrilled. Layla made her way to the front of the room and stood beside Dr. Gray. Her presence acted as a calming agent. The crowd went silent while they watched her, eyes still hopeful and whispers still begging for a better alternative.

"I know this is terrifying, but we have to be receptive to some ideas. Karine is already closing in on Harlem. Many of our own have died at her hands, and she will continue if we do not stop her." Layla gestured across the crowd. "Every reaper needs to find a human to pair with."

There was hesitation at first, but eventually, everyone complied. Layla sensed Elise's nerves while she pulled her sleeve back to allow

Dr. Gray to insert the needle in her arm. They had shared a moment beforehand, where Layla had taken the smallest amount of blood from her. She'd kissed her neck afterward, smiling as Elise blushed at the red still staining her lips.

Layla nodded to Dr. Gray, who brought the poison over in a small glass bottle. Elise cleared her throat and turned her attention back to Layla. "Remember when you used to crave my blood?"

Layla eyed Elise, and her face softened after noticing the badly hidden disappointment in her eyes. "Not just your blood. I crave *you*. Don't worry—I can go back to making you my personal blood supply if that's what you want."

"Shut up," Elise scoffed, but a smile found its way onto her face. She swallowed while Dr. Gray drew closer with the needle. "Are you sure about this?"

Layla glanced over at the waiting crowd, stopping on Sterling and Jamie by the front. Jamie hovered over Nicoletta, who stared up at him from her relaxed position in her chair. Sterling stood beside the gangster, his hand brushing down Jamie's arm while Nicoletta smiled at them both. Her crew took up space behind her, all of them looking rather impressed with the level of willingness in everyone.

"It's a smaller dose, so she should have no side effects," Dr. Gray assured them.

Layla shoved down all her doubts—each measure of conflict untangling in her eyes. She settled her gaze back on Elise and nodded.

One by one, every reaper bonded to a human by blood made the transition. And just as Dr. Gray and Layla had theorized, they survived the poison. For a long, heart-stopping seven minutes, reapers turned into evolved monsters. But they remained more sentient than the evolved reapers Layla had fought before. Under Stephen's poison, Layla had wanted nothing but blood. Now she could think more clearly and curb most violent urges that arose with the effects of Dr. Gray's new poison.

Chest tight and brow damp with sweat, Layla settled beside Elise after turning back to her regular reaper state. "Are you okay?" Her eyes lingered on Elise's hand, which had gone still while hovering over her bite wound.

"It's just…strange," Elise said quietly. "Knowing Karine will start a war the moment that sun goes down."

Layla took her hand and kissed her knuckles. "To war then."

43

As the sun set, Elise prepared for death. She gave herself a few hours to settle with the feeling before she pulled some paper and a pen from one of the cathedral rooms and sat beside her sleeping sister. There were a million things that Elise wished she could have said to Josi over the next few years, but tonight, she had to settle for all that she could fit on a few pages. The most imperative message, with important instructions, was left on top of the pile.

When Dr. Gray came in with a vial and a small syringe that would help wake Josi, Elise leaned over to kiss her sister's forehead. She stroked her fingers over her face, watching the gentle flutter of her lashes against the tops of her cheeks. Once done whispering a quiet goodbye, Elise stood and faced Dr. Gray. "Please wait to do it until after I leave."

Dr. Gray nodded. Her eyes filled with warm sympathy, and Elise felt almost compelled to hug her. "I will take good care of her."

Elise turned before her tears could fall. She walked through the haunted halls of the cathedral, searching for the one thing that would bring her peace at the end of the hour.

The day Harlem was meant to be destroyed and Layla was meant to die, she watched the sunset from the roof. Everything the light touched turned gold, the sun's rays brushing over each building and street to make itself known. Down below, delicate piano notes floated up to her. Layla did not listen to much music, but she would recognize Elise's playing anywhere. She hurried back inside, following the sound until she found the Saint in the front of the cathedral, sitting at the grand piano before all the empty pews. It was an eerie sight to behold—Elise wearing the shadows of the room like a shroud, her hands moving gracefully over the piano keys while the instrument rang out with dark notes. Elise's frame was relaxed as she played, and the music helped Layla breathe easier. It was the most either of them could ask for: some peace in the face of approaching gloom.

Once she finished playing, Layla draped her arms over Elise's shoulders and whispered, "I want you to stay here and hold down the lair while I go to the island to face Karine and set off Nicoletta's emergency-detonation system. The dead will come, but you will be safe with plenty of my clan mates and gangsters protecting the territory." She expected pushback. But she knew Elise understood the time for conflict between them had long since passed.

The Saint heiress turned and stood, allowing Layla's arms to wrap around her waist. Elise gripped the edge of Layla's coat and twisted the black fabric between her fingers as she let out a shaky breath. "Are you sure?"

"I cannot live like this," Layla murmured. *Not knowing I did not do everything possible to keep you safe.* The moment tears welled in Elise's eyes, Layla wanted to look away. But she could not. To memorize her face, and all the beauty and love she found within it, was all Layla had left in the face of the inescapable war standing before them.

The tugging at the end of her shirt stopped only for Elise to lift a hand and wipe her tears. Layla caught her hand and, stroking her fingers over her knuckles, leaned in to kiss the wet streak on her cheek. Elise sighed, her shoulders relaxing. "My love," she whispered. "Promise me you'll come back."

"There is no one I'd rather come back to but you." Layla smiled and stretched onto her tiptoes to kiss her. She was grateful when Elise bent to meet her, pulling her closer. Her arms draped over her shoulders and Layla kissed her harder as Elise gripped her waist. They clung to each other like they stood at the end of the world and letting go meant a certain demise. When they finally pulled apart for air, Layla pressed her face into the crook of Elise's neck. She inhaled deeply, pulling every essence of Elise into her. If Layla could have, she would have stopped the world to hold this moment for an eternity.

But eventually her clan mates grew restless, and the imminence of nighttime pulled them apart. Layla held Elise's hand until the distance separated them. After one last look at her, Layla turned away, her fingers flexing as she departed from the cathedral.

Elise rolled a bullet in Josi's venom. The substance coated the steel until it was slippery between her gloved fingers. She slid it into the chamber of her rifle and propped it up to face the gates at the entrance to the cathedral's courtyard. From above, sitting among the cathedral's steeples, the yard looked rather compact and organized. Reapers, both rogue and Harlem clan aligned, spread out with Jamie's gangsters, Nicoletta's Diamantes, and Sterling's Saints.

It had been nearly half an hour since Layla's departure, and Elise still felt the press of Layla's fingers against her wrist and the nape of her neck. Whether it was the weather or the general lack of hope setting the mood for the night, no one could tell. All their other fights had ended in nothing but death and destruction. Who was to say this one would not be the same?

The rush of feet stampeding on the sidewalk outside brought Elise back to the present. She peered through her scope and found a horde of newly risen reapers heading straight for the cathedral. A few of them had funeral shrouds draped over their decaying bodies, along with pins and glass-embedded jewelry. Elise nodded toward Jamie and Nicoletta, who waited outside the gate with their explosives.

The screams started before the bombs even went off. All around New York, the dead terrorized the living. Screams of terror from various blocks filled the air as the final rays of sunlight faded from the sky. Some of them, to Elise's horror, sounded so young. No one was safe tonight.

Anger pinched her face, and she lifted her hand, closing it into a fist as she nodded at the gangsters awaiting her call. Shouts rang out, and Elise braced herself with her gun as the entryway exploded. Several evolved reapers flew back in the blast, but many of them continued forward. Some were on their hands and knees, crawling with missing body parts and their faces half blown off.

Elise's finger hesitated on the rifle trigger. Already, several gangsters and Saints were firing into the settling dust. She had only so many bullets, and she had even less of Josi's venom to coat them with. There would be worse as the night went on. Elise intended to save her most brutal arsenal for those who refused to fall.

More reapers filled the courtyard, but the combined efforts of rogues, Saints, and gangsters held them off. Elise watched as bodies piled up around the territory—most of them being members of Karine's undead army. It was too much. Layla should have found Karine by now and been able to set off the island's detonation system or at least incapacitate her enough to stop the hordes of reapers leading a bloody attack against them.

She stood and hurried down the stairs to ground level. The moment she touched down, a faint rumbling started beneath her feet, just a few yards from the entrance of the cathedral. No one else seemed to sense it, but for Elise, the sound was all-consuming. She stopped in her tracks.

"Elise? What's wrong?" Sterling asked.

Elise was watching the ground. It had begun to shake, finally drawing the attention of her companions. She looked as cracks slithered through the courtyard, finding Jamie standing right at the center of where they met. Elise's eyes widened. "Jamie—"

Disaster came in the form of the earth falling out from beneath them. Elise threw herself into another unsuspecting gangster while Nicoletta pulled Sterling away from the blow. Those who narrowly managed to avoid the destruction got back to their feet, coughing and waving the dust out of their faces.

A hole had torn open in the heart of the holy ground.

Elise approached the edge of the earth, her vision piercing through the mist of blood from those who had fallen. Countless figures moved below, each and every one of them bearing red eyes and talons that dug into the earth to haul themselves up out of the gaping hole.

Gasping, Elise backed away. She faced Sterling and Nicoletta, who were frantically calling for Jamie nearby. "I have to go to the island. Something is wrong. It should not be taking this long—"

Sterling spoke through breathless devastation and tears. "Elise, you can't—"

"We're losing," she cried. "If I don't go, we'll all die."

After a long beat, Nicoletta gave a sad shake of her head. "One of my men can take you. We have a backup plan." She reached into her pocket and pulled out a vial of Dr. Gray's poison. Her eyes softened on Sterling as she lifted his hand to her mouth, sinking her fangs into his wrist for a deep but quick draw of his blood. When she lowered his hand and spoke, scarlet glistened on her lips, "All of us were supposed to make it out. Do not add yourself to the body count."

Sterling's fingers curled over hers as he accepted the vial. "Ditto, Roma. Catch you on the other side." He gave her a soft smile and dumped half of the vial's contents down his throat before hanging it back to Nicoletta so she could do the same. Sterling turned back to the remaining members of their offense before Elise could see the poison work. His commanding voice trailed off as she faced Nicoletta, whose eyes were beginning to darken with the effects of the toxin. She waved for one of her men nearby, calling to him in Italian.

"Ready?" Nicoletta asked, turning back to Elise. Blood swam in her eyes like snakes and when she smiled, her fangs glinted in the moonlight

Elise nodded. "This ends now."

44

THIS ENDS IN BLOOD.

Layla's presence in Hart Island was greeted by a dark laboratory, in which the only sounds were the sea crashing over the salt-slick rocks it sat on and the wind howling over the roof. Every cell that had once held a human or reaper was empty now, save for one in which a sole human crouched beneath shadows in dirtied robes. Though the others' absence could have meant they were off terrorizing Harlem in their new forms, Layla was glad they would at least know liberation before they died. It was more than most reapers could claim to have experienced in their lifetimes.

The essence of the ancient reaper she had come for washed over Layla before her light footsteps graced her ears. Layla turned, finding Karine standing in the small pool of moonlight being decanted through the high windows around the open entryway. "Your girlfriend will be upset with me after this ends," she said in a perfectly neutral voice.

At this, Layla almost smiled. "You have no idea." Elise had come to be so much more than that. From the moment Layla knew she would always be her best friend, to the time when they were both sprawled out on her bedroom floor with blood covering them, to their reunion, to now—their souls were tied together in ways that went beyond just words.

In the quiet of the main room, she closed her eyes and listened for the approaching and receding sounds of the waves outside. It was hard not to imagine Elise's face and the rest of her clan mates' faces when they realized Layla would not reunite with the rest of them later. She could still hear the hope in Dr. Gray's voice now, despite their conversation having taken place the previous night. *The lab is full of good research I left behind. Continuation of my and my daughter's work toward a cure. Preserving it would be wonderful, but the destruction of the evil that shrouds that place would be for the best.*

Layla could not help but wonder, when this place did fall, would the wonders within it bloom like corpse flowers? Would the rare treasures of knowledge sink to the ocean floor, not to be discovered for the next hundred years? Would the unsuspecting life residing in the water adapt to the new toxins that overtook their home?

"I know you think what I am doing is pure evil. But with the help of Dr. Gray and Julius, both curious and inventive scientists in their own rights—I have made my body a vessel for greatness. My blood can wake the dead and give life to those who never got to fully live. What can you say for yourself?" Karine said in a low voice.

Slowly, Layla opened her eyes. An ancient reaper faced her with centuries of anger behind her stormy eyes, and yet Layla had never felt calmer. "No amount of suffering and sacrifice can take from me the great love I have experienced. The difference between you and me is that I am prepared to die for the cause. My cause is her. Your cause is destruction," Layla said.

Karine's face fell, but she let out a low chuckle and smiled. "You might be a reaper, but you are still so young. You have no idea the things that could await you in the future if you allowed yourself to be what you were made to become." Karine leaned forward, clasping her hands behind her back. Her hazel eyes almost glowed in the low light. In them, Layla saw years of ire and pain, something she might never know until she had lived as long as her. "You have not experienced the turmoil and pure humiliation of being owned as a pet. Whenever a human takes a liking to anyone like you or me, it is never with pure intent. I have been forced onto my knees for hours on end, put on the stage as a spectacle while people watched and cheered as my skin burned from my flesh beneath the sun. Even if you have experienced none of that, surely you understand that reapers were never created to be equal with humans. You must never forget that we were *created*, Layla. They made us like this and punish us for it."

Karine tapped a finger along her jaw. "What does it mean that we did not come from hell but they still curse us and call us demons? If man made us into monsters, then why are we the representations of God's worst evil? I did not emerge from hell as much as I clawed my way away from it, desperate to live and desperate to love. Perhaps then hell is empty and we are surrounded by the makers of its fires.

Forged by their flames of suffering. Ruined because they cannot stand to be alone in their desolation. Humans enact cruelty with no reaperhood in their veins to blame."

"I just want the cure to turn those who wish to be human back and for all of this to end," Layla said.

"Since you love humanity so much, then you will face me as a human in a fight," Karine drawled.

Layla remained standing in the middle of the room, her thoughts racing into oblivion in her head. She had never wished for something—someone—to ground her more than in this moment. Her thoughts circled Elise so much, Layla began to smell that beautifully sweet blood of hers along with her perfume. All parts of her that Layla had memorized consumed her now, and she had to bite down on her lip, drawing her own blood to focus on anything else.

Even that stopped helping. Elise's scent emerged again, fresh and windswept like the damp rocks outside. Too real to be just a figment of her imagination—

Layla whirled around to see Elise standing in the entryway, carrying her rifle. Despite intruding on a tense moment, Elise still managed a lovesick smile of relief.

Layla bristled. She choked on her own air and stepped closer to Elise. "What are you doing here?"

"I told you, Layla. Laisse-moi mourir en premier," Elise said firmly.

Layla stopped breathing altogether. "I said no."

"A lover's quarrel?" Karine returned one of her hands to behind her back. "It seems unfair to be outnumbered in this fight." She leaned her head to the side and gave Elise a smile, though it brimmed with cruelty. "Is this what I deserve for destroying your home?"

Elise appeared wounded, the darkness in her eyes increasing in depth, but she said nothing.

"If you love her, you will walk away. Only then will I give her the cure. Allow her to return to the world of the living—to the light. Do not let your emotions ruin such a momentous occasion. Trust that she will survive this fight and emerge after you as a changed woman." Karine spoke carefully. "But the fight must be between me and her only."

Layla saw the conflict in Elise's eyes. Her thoughts fought back and forth against one another, and all Layla could think about was how lucky she was to be loved by someone who stared death in the face with such conviction.

Finally, Elise spoke up again. "And if I don't walk away?"

Karine did not even hesitate. "I will kill you both."

Though Layla had been on the other end of death threats and promises time and time again, the finality in Karine's tone, paired with the true fear shining in Elise's eyes, made a chill shoot down her spine. She swallowed her rising nerves and gave Elise the most assured look she could manage. "Trust me."

Elise's face went blank. It became impossible to tell exactly what she was thinking in the moment, and Layla desperately wished to be able to read her mind if only to know she was not upset with her.

With her jaw tight and her eyes downcast, Elise whispered. "You've lost every fight against her."

Layla's lips parted. "Well, you certainly did not have to bring that up now."

"You came here to die," Elise said flatly.

A painful lump rose in Layla's throat at the sudden emergence of bright anguish in Elise's eyes. "I cannot live like this, Elise. She's promised me a cure. But I will not go without neutralizing her first and stopping the chaos back home." She touched the Saint's cheek, her finger brushing over a new cut in her skin. Layla kissed Elise and smiled as she tasted Elise's blood for the last time. "Do you trust me?"

Elise nodded without hesitation.

Layla dropped her hand, giving her one final smile. "Then go."

The Saint turned and began to walk back out of the room.

Layla watched Elise leave. She took with her all sense of hope and security. Watching her removed every self-preservation instinct Layla had. She had underestimated just how much it would devastate her—Elise Saint turning her back on her.

A thick, bittersweet scent filled the air. When Layla whirled to face Karine, she found the ancient reaper holding a vial of a dark purple substance. Karine bent to roll it across the floor toward Layla, who picked it up once it hit the toe of her boot. She took the full dose in one swallow. Just the taste had Layla hunching over. The ancient reaper smiled through her pain, watching Layla with calculating eyes.

The following sensations took over so quickly, Layla had no time to process having just been poisoned. Its essence was too similar to the bittersweet drug that Stephen had been developing off Thalia Gray's research all those months ago. The same thing Layla had put all her trust into. From the beginning of the investigation with Elise, when she had still been driven by hate and a darkness only the worst knew, to now, when having her priorities shifted by one person had given her a completely new outlook.

Already, the cure worked in a different way from anything else Layla had been infected with. Her body tensed at first before it slowly relaxed, inch by inch. Her nervous system, once on constant high alert, faded into a passive voice in her body. Any thoughts of blood became more repulsive than necessary cravings. When she ran her tongue over her teeth and felt normal human incisors and flat molars, tears sprang into her eyes.

Above all the other changes to her once-damned body, the thing Layla clung to was the levity. She had not felt this light in years.

There had never been anything as beautiful as her newfound humanity. Layla was almost positive she could die happy in this state. Almost. There was still something missing—a piece of her that she had found only in reaperhood, something she had assumed she would never deserve because of her damned soul.

Her heart pounded more intensely than it had in years, but it did not match the rush of devotion she felt whenever she had Elise by her side.

Layla dropped her hands, noticing the warm blood pulsing in her veins. Once Elise popped into her head, the realization of her new humanity became a dull, secondary thing. It was nothing if she could not share it with the one she loved the most.

With her senses dulled and largely inefficient in comparison to her reaper ones, Layla could concentrate only on what was right in front of her. Her heart skipped a beat when she faced the doorway again and prayed to find the pale outline of Elise.

Elise liked to believe she knew better, but her heart always got the best of her. Life-or-death situations had never taught her anything different. Historically, she was not the prime example of self-preservation. So, when she turned away from Layla, Elise could only listen to the voice screaming at her to turn back.

She had never been good at listening to voices compelling her. Especially when they involved Layla. The first one being her father, begging her to forget the girl of her childhood. As if Elise could tear the roots that had grown around the ones that threaded through her life. The second voice being her own when Layla came back into her life in the form of a death-kissed reaper. Elise had wanted to curse herself a few times for falling back into the hopeless depth of feelings stirred up by Layla. Now they were a blessing and something that had kept her going through countless tribulations over the past few weeks. Turning away from Layla had been a choice. The wrong choice.

The only altar Elise promised her devotion to was one that had her facing the other half of her soul.

Some might have called it madness; Elise could only see it as love.

She turned around.

First, Elise locked eyes with Layla, whose expression displayed several breathtaking emotions. There was hope intermingled with relief and pure adoration. All things Elise had found devastatingly beautiful on her, all things Elise knew she deserved.

But then Elise's eyes found Karine and the taloned hand she held poised for Layla. It had been raised for a while now, as if she was hoping Elise would have turned back for her. But she knew the reaper had always planned to end things this way.

As a human, Elise was not fast enough. She never would have been. But she still tried. Elise lifted her gun and fired it at the lone human crouching in the locked cell. The bullet reached her a split second after Karine's talons sank into Layla's back. Blood sprayed between them. It landed on Elise's face and chest first, seeping into her mouth before Layla stumbled. Elise caught her as she fell. Her knees hit the floor, and she cradled Layla against her while numbness overtook every part of her body. The only thing she felt was Layla's blood pooling around them, warm and wrong.

Karine cursed and crumpled on top of them just moments after her human anchor fell. The laced bullet would never have pierced Karine's evolved body, but it had torn through her human anchor's flesh like a blade through thin ice. Any activity tethered to her blood was poisoned now, a dying war that would end with Karine's waning ancient strength. She grabbed for Layla with trembling arms, but Layla spat a mouthful of blood into her face, stopping her. With a taste of Layla's tainted blood in her mouth, the ancient reaper finally reared back and collapsed, all color leaking from her gaze until cloudy white eyes stared, empty, at the ceiling.

Elise tried to turn Layla over in her arms to see the wound on her back, but Layla whimpered, her teeth gritting together. "Don't."

"You're not healing." Elise allowed Layla to settle back against her chest, her own rising and falling rapidly. "Layla—"

"It worked, Lise," Layla said softly. All the strength behind her words had gone, but Elise recognized the tinge of joy. "The cure worked." Layla clasped Elise's hand in hers and stared up at her with tear-filled eyes. "You see me now. I'm back."

Human again.

"I've always seen you, Layla," Elise said, her voice breaking.

Layla did not have to say the words for Elise to know what this all meant. The amount of blood pouring from her wound was impossible for a human to survive. But the relief in Layla's eyes prevented Elise from cursing it immediately. She would have bled for Layla for an eternity if she could have. If Layla had asked her to. This was not how things were supposed to end, with Layla bleeding out on the floor, with only broken possibilities remaining between them.

While the background fell away behind her, Elise heard faint explosions starting in the distance. The building began to shake around them, debris falling from the ceiling.

Layla's eyes widened, and she tried to sit up, but her body tensed with pain again, keeping her in Elise's embrace. She hissed through crimson-coated teeth. "You have to go now."

"No," Elise ground out. Alarms started around them, but she kept her focus on Layla, sharp and unyielding. "We go together."

Layla shook her head. "I will only slow you down…" Realization crossed her face. "Elise. Elise, *no—*"

Elise nodded. Tears filled her eyes, and before she could process the emotion threatening to choke her, words were spilling out. "We share blood now, Layla. I made you a promise. I am not leaving you. So, either you get up and walk out of here with me and we go home and continue our lives together. Or we go. Together."

Though tears streaked Layla's face now, she still managed a watery smile and a gentle nod. "Okay." Her hand tightened on Elise's as the ground beneath them shook. "When we get home, we're going everywhere. I've always wanted to go to France. I want you to take me to every stage you imagined yourself playing the piano on. And I want to see where you used to spend your time when we were apart."

Elise no longer fought her tears. They flowed freely down her cheeks, splashing onto Layla's blood and now the debris from the shaking walls around them. "That's a lot of places, Layla."

"I want to see everything with you, Elise," Layla whispered. Blood covered her teeth. She coughed, and more of it spilled from her mouth. Her grip grew weak around Elise's hand, but she kept her eyes on her, even as the light dimmed from the once-radiant brown.

Elise's breath hitched. She leaned forward to cup Layla's cheek as her head lolled backward. Her vision blurred with tears, but she blinked past them to find Layla's eyes on her again. "Please stay, Layla. I can't do this without you. I don't want to live without you."

Layla's voice came out as a whisper against her cheek. "I'll find you again. I wish we'd had more time. In another lifetime, I would show you my heart sooner. There's so much of you in my heart, Elise…" Her hand fell from Elise's.

Elise pressed her forehead to Layla's as her final breath passed between them.

Even with Layla's body in her arms now, Elise could think only of every moment that had brought them here together. From two smiling little girls to death and death's angel. Life had taken them through tragedy after tragedy, never leaving Elise with any clear explanation for any part of it. There had only ever been one thing she was sure of.

So, as the explosions began around her, Elise pulled Layla closer to her heart and let the fire consume them both.

EPILOGUE

Dear Josephine,

My dove, I am endlessly proud of who you have grown into. Before anything else, I want you to know that I love you and always will. Nothing will change that, even if I am not around.

Love, I have found, does not just vanish. Even if it is overtaken by hate, love still exists. And even in death, when you lose someone, the love you have for them does not leave you.

I'm just ashes in your life now, but I hope to be remembered as something that brings you light and joy. Because it's what you deserve. Please be happy. Things have changed irrevocably, but you will learn to navigate the changes. It will take time, but I promise you, things will get better.

Still, please let yourself feel everything. Allow the rage and the sadness and the pain. And when you start to see the light again, let yourself feel that too.

Here you can find my last words to you, and I write only the most important things for you to remember. Even when I am not with you, I am with you.

Always.
Elise

Josi lowered the letter and glared at the two headstones before her. She felt stupid, leaving flowers on top of empty graves every year, but she did it anyway, knowing the gesture meant more to Sterling than it would have meant to any lingering ghosts.

"It never makes me feel any better," Josi mumbled as she tucked the letter into her coat pocket. It had grown worn over the past few years, with some of the ink smudged from her tears and the wrinkles starting to give way to full rips.

Sterling gave her a gentle look, his hands in his pockets. He had left a few roses scattered across Layla's grave while a neat bouquet rested atop Elise's. Josi knew why he did it; the roses spread out looked like a dancer's paradise after a successful performance. Layla's dancing was the only thing he truly knew about her. It was admittedly a creatively kind gesture, but Josi found that most things no longer impressed her these days. Not much made her feel anymore.

"You have read it probably upward of a thousand times now," Sterling said gently.

There was no real point Josi could argue with him there, but she tried anyway. "I don't think words postmortem mean as much as the people who write them think they will," she muttered. "And every time I read what she left me, I find new ways to believe I made a mistake in helping blow up the island laboratory."

"Will you be a cynic for the rest of your life? Eighty years, a hundred years, a thousand years—it all sounds so exhausting," Sterling said. "She told you to do it because you didn't know she would be there and thus wouldn't hesitate. You saved Harlem that night. That's it."

Josi narrowed her eyes at him. It wasn't true. Josi had *killed* her sister that night. It would never matter that Elise had *told her* to do it. She opened her mouth to respond, but a warm weight settled over her feet. Josi looked down, her heart lifting when she saw Hendricks blinking up at her.

Sterling continued as she picked the cat up, his voice low and intentional. "It's a tale for the ages. One might say it's beautiful. A human dying for a reaper. A reaper dying for a human. It's such a story that no one could have even imagined mere months prior to it."

Josi huffed out a hot breath that stirred Hendricks's fur. "I like to believe they ran off and are now in hiding. Their bodies were never recovered. Karine lived and went into hiding."

"And she'll die there now that she's mortal. Layla and Elise were incinerated. There was nothing to recover. Do you really think Elise would just leave you?" Sterling demanded.

Something sharp hit her chest, and she struggled to breathe. Josi swallowed a lump in her throat, trying to exhale the resurrected feelings. "I don't know. I don't know much of anything anymore." She squinted under the flickering sunlight coming in from the cloudy horizon. "I'm just tired of feeling nothing. I'd rather hurt than feel a void." She sniffed. "It's been nine years, and I still find myself asking every day for a sign that this was meant to be. I'm older than her now, but I still feel years younger, with no lineage or history to prove my legacy."

Sterling pulled her into his chest. Hendricks purred between them, and for the first time all day, a flicker of warm contentment spread through Josi. "Though all you remember is the pain, never forget that you were in fact loved in return," Sterling whispered. "You've done so much for New York." He nodded to a younger reaper seated on a bench by two human women nearby. "This integration would not have been possible without Elise and Layla's sacrifices forcing people to see that such strife is useless. I would not have become a lawyer without you and me having to learn the law to keep you out of trouble—by the way, Celie is still awaiting your response about starting a new lair upstate. She insists it will be good for you. Get your mind off your more illegal hobbies and hunting Karine down. I cannot defend you forever, Josi, you know that."

The world is constantly evolving, and we struggle to keep up with it. Josi remembered Dr. Gray's words in a recent press release about her newest reaperhood cure trials. *But nevertheless, we try anyway.*

Josi sniffled and pressed her face into his chest, hiding her tears. "I'm leaving Harlem for Europe. I need…I don't know…a nice change of scenery."

"The constant threat of another World War hanging around certainly does not sound like a particularly pleasant change of scenery, but if it's what you want, I will support you," Sterling said.

"With all the work we did, there will likely be no bioweapons in this war. No human will publicly advocate for reapers to be used again; I've made sure of it."

Sterling wiped at his brow. "You really should have thought of the name of your law more. It's a bit juvenile."

"I'm nineteen. And I was asked by Arendale to name the bill when I was twelve," Josi said flatly, sighing. "I wonder what Elise thinks of it. If I find her in France, I'll ask her. Among other things."

"Always the dreamer, aren't you?" Sterling rubbed Hendricks's head and smiled when he purred, nuzzling against his hand.

Josi shook her head and hugged the cat tighter to her chest. "We have nothing without our dreams. If mine keep my sister alive just a little while longer, then I will continue to dream."

It was a lie. Josi tried not to do it often; she knew Elise and her mother had hated lying. But the truth was she had done a lot of terrible things when she was younger, and her dreams were not dreams as much as they were nightmares. Most days, Josi felt too small for her emotions and choked on her own bitterness about the way things had shaped up. "Layla didn't deserve this fate. She had everything taken from her—she deserved a happy ending. Elise was so much better than me. It should have been me and not her."

But Sterling was already shaking his head before she could even finish her thought. "Do not feel bad for taking up the space she left for you. Honor it. Whether it's with your dreams or your fury, just honor it. Honor her. You are her legacy now. There is more work to be done. I hope you know that."

Josi pursed her lips. Her fangs prodded the inside of her mouth, drawing blood. She sighed and looked over the cemetery, finding the glittering sea beyond. "It's better than nothing."

Long after Sterling had departed to return to his family, Josi left the cemetery and stood by the water. She wanted to stare into the sun—feel every nerve burn out until she felt nothing at all. But a slow blinking in the horizon kept her gaze locked on the edge of the water. If she allowed her thoughts to slow and settled only on the flickering lights, a message came to her mind, one word at a time with each illumination. Whether an image conjured by her imagination or the venomous threads forever wrapped around her system, Josi chose to believe the spectacle.

In the end, no matter the risk of ruination, she chose to hope.

TO SEE WHERE IT ALL BEGAN, READ ON FOR A PREVIEW OF *THIS RAVENOUS FATE,* THE FIRST BOOK IN THE RAVENOUS FATE DUOLOGY!

It's 1926 in Harlem: At night the dance halls come to life and death waits in the dark.

Elise Saint is the reluctant heir to her family's reaper-hunting empire, home after five years abroad. Layla Quinn is a young reaper haunted by her past, and she's never forgotten how Elise betrayed her.

But when a series of mysterious and brutal killings are linked to shocking rumors of a reaper cure, Elise and Layla must work together. As they explore the city's underworld, they confront their intense feelings for each other and uncover sinister truths that could destroy them all.

This Ravenous Fate

1

AUGUST 1926

ELISE FOUND THE WORLD MORE BEAUTIFUL WHEN she closed her eyes.

Melancholic jazz music rode the soft sea breeze around the pier, each note lingering like a clandestine kiss. Quiet and unseeing, Elise felt the most herself. Her other senses opened up and softened the edges of her anxieties, making her feel grounded.

Then she opened her eyes. Chelsea Piers came into view around her, the massive docking ocean liner just beyond the piers' entrance ablaze with the glow of the setting sun. Her pulse thundered in her ears and the jazz notes grew fuzzy. Trying to purge the clamminess from her earlier panic, she wiped her hands across her skirt, then stepped toward the waiting car.

Once finished loading Elise's luggage into the trunk, Colm, her family's driver, helped her into the automobile. "Your ship docked late. My apologies, Miss Saint, but we're in a race against the sunset. Your father is already in a mood." He glanced at her through the rearview mirror as the engine roared to life. "Welcome home, by the way."

Elise thought facing her father again sounded worse than being out after the sun went down. As far as she was concerned, the house in Harlem was no longer her home. Not in a city full of monsters who craved the taste of her blood. Monsters like the one her best friend had become.

The car turned north, and though the sky over Manhattan darkened, the streets were still full of people, hats held down against the evening breeze and faces twisted with fear.

Colm stepped on the gas. To settle her nerves, Elise peeked into her bag for what she knew was the fifth time that hour. The letter with the lovely golden seal of the Paris Conservatory was still there, staring back up at her. Her fingers plucked at the loose threads on her coat seven times, her chest growing tighter while the residential buildings of Riverside Drive whipped past her window. They quickly neared Sugar Hill. Elise wondered how much had changed in five years. Whether Layla was even still alive—

Colm cursed in the front seat as he hit the brakes. Pedestrians rushed the intersection the car was trying to cross. "Everyone wants to be close to Saint territory at night," he explained.

Elise nodded. When she was younger and word had spread about her family's reaper-hunting services, it seemed like new neighbors introduced themselves to her father every day. Some wanted to bargain with him for more of his steel bullets; only the ones made with the alloy he'd devised could reliably kill the reapers. Others wanted protection. The empire went from just distributing Saint steel to hiring ex-military who needed jobs and training young men around the neighborhood who were brave enough to hunt reapers. Back then, Elise enjoyed the fullness of their home. People who desired to enter the Saint inner circle brought with them some of her lifelong friends. Though none, not even Mrs. Gray, with her scientific advancements and a tentative hope for a better future, were as special as the Quinns, who had been the ones to welcome the Saints to New York. But friendship wasn't enough to keep people safe.

The business grew larger every year, though the number of reapers seemed to keep up. Elise almost couldn't believe her father had gone from a steelworker in Texas to a top steel manufacturer and distributor in New York.

The car crossed Amsterdam Avenue into the Sugar Hill neighborhood, the noisy traffic fading. The Saint mansion stood on what had once been a block of brownstones, which had been leveled on Mr. Saint's order. Now the iron gates of the Saint estate rose before them, guarded by two of the Saint security officers, their silver badges and guns glinting in the dying light as they moved to let the car in.

Elise waited while Colm opened her door. But he suddenly shoved it shut again as one of the guards called out, "Miss, this is private property—"

Elise looked out the passenger window to see a brown-haired young woman standing just inside the gate.

"The monsters are in my neighborhood, and you must do something about them," she told the guard.

For a moment the young woman looked so familiar, a bitter name lodged in Elise's throat, and her heart lurched. But when she turned to get a better look, Elise realized she saw a stranger—not the girl she had left behind years ago, bloody and bruised.

The Saint guard tried to lead her away from the gate. "Tomorrow we'll send a patrol over—"

"No. They must be dealt with now," the woman snarled. She stepped toward the car and her sharp eyes met Elise's, her lips pulling back to reveal fangs. Elise scrambled back in her seat, though the car door separated them. Bloodlust swirled in the woman's dark irises, her veins bulging and ripe with hunger. But other than her shining eyes and fangs, the reaper looked utterly human. "*Murderers*. Layla Quinn will be avenged—"

A gunshot cracked through the air. The reaper's head exploded, and her body collapsed onto the pavement.

"All clear. Someone clean it up," a guard ordered.

Elise let out a shaky breath and shoved the car door open, avoiding the bloody mess at her feet. As she stumbled out, a gentle voice halted her panic.

"Relax, Lise. She's dead."

Elise looked up. "Sterling," she breathed. She could hardly believe she was looking Sterling Walker in the eye after five years of only exchanging letters. Blood covered her friend's shirtfront, and he held his gun arm steady, but he still smiled. He had gone from a young boy seeking refuge in their home to one of the Saint's leading reaper hunters.

His thumb traced a cross over the handle of his gun, then he lowered it. "Welcome home, Lise." Sterling leaned toward Elise, his amber eyes glowing in the dusk, and kissed her cheek. He had always been beautiful with his smooth brown skin and perfectly styled curls. But Elise thought he looked even more beautiful now. She eyed his gun, knowing every day he worked as a reaper hunter, he put his life on the line for the citizens of Harlem. And for her father.

Elise swallowed. Her music studies had kept her father content for this long, but she had no idea how it measured up to the bloody work his people did for him every day.

Elise wanted to hug Sterling, but the blood kept her back. "Are you all right?" she asked.

"I'm perfect. As always. The blood isn't mine; I've been on a patrol. I've still got an hour or two left of work, but I wanted to catch you as soon as you got home." That overly confident grin of his hadn't waned, and Elise was glad. People said distance made the heart grow fonder, but time also changed people. And she wasn't sure she could handle Sterling changing. Not when everything else in her life had changed so abruptly.

Elise glanced over at the body by the gate. "The reapers know I'm back now." She couldn't even bring herself to say Layla's name out loud.

Sterling shook his head. "Just that one. Whichever guard let her onto our street is getting fired. Though I will admit, it's getting harder to tell the reapers from us. Good thing I caught her just now, otherwise the whole Harlem reaper clan might know you're here. We can't have that."

ACKNOWLEDGMENTS

I honestly thought I would never make it to this point. Writing this book was beyond difficult—in a way I did not expect, even with countless people telling me how hard second books are. Not only had I never written a sequel before, but having to do so after releasing the first book into the world and suddenly bearing the weight of new expectations made me question whether I was even cut out to be a writer. It's bittersweet to finally wrap up this story that I first dreamt up when I was still in college. I'm three years postgrad now, but Layla and Elise are still close to my heart and have been made even more special because of all the lovely people I've met along the way of bringing them into the world. I am so happy to be here (shout-out to my therapist and psychiatrist for literally keeping me sane—OCD is a nightmare I'm still fighting to survive) and beyond thrilled that you all have made this journey with me.

I feel so privileged to get to write about the things I love and know that people love them as well. A huge thank-you to my wonderful agent, Emily Forney, for championing not just this book but all of my books. *TRF* wouldn't exist without you. Thank you to my publishing teams at Sourcebooks and Hodderscape for supporting this book, its world, and its characters from the very beginning. Thank you to my editors, Wendy McClure, Jake Carr, and Natasha Qureshi. Thank you also to the rest of the Sourcebooks Fire team for working so hard to bring this book into the world: Thea Voutiritsas, Jessica Thelander, Jenny Lopez, Delaney Heisterkamp, Lia Ferrone, Karen Masnica, and Nicole Hower.

To my friends and family who had to listen to me rant and cry over how hard this book was—thank you for staying and providing the very reassurance that got me to the finish line.

Last, but certainly not the least, thank you, thank you, thank you, dearest reader, for sticking around and loving my stories like no one else.

ABOUT THE AUTHOR

Hayley Dennings is a recent graduate from Loyola Marymount University, where she double majored in English and French with a concentration in diversity and inclusion. She currently lives in the Bay Area, where she was born and raised. When she isn't writing or reading, she's working her editorial plus marketing day job in tech, spending time with her dogs, painting, or baking. You can find her on Instagram and Twitter @pagesofhayley or check out her website

HODDERSCAPE

WANT MORE HODDERSCAPE?
JOIN US!

Sign up to our mailing list to get exclusive early sneak peeks and offers:

Follow us on our social channels:
@hodderscape

Buy our books, find out more, and discover exclusive content:
www.hodderscape.co.uk